Praise for the novels of Elmer Kelton

"Kelton continues to show his contemporaries how to tell a simple story with clear and concise writing that holds the reader to every page." —*San Angelo Standard-Times*

"Readers who love historical detail laced with dynamic characters and exciting action will be more than pleased by these exhilarating two novels. . . . Elmer Kelton understands what shapes peoples' attitudes and beliefs, and his expansive knowledge of Texas history and the rigors of pioneer life is superb." —*Historical Novels Review* on *Texas Sunrise*

"As with all of Kelton's Westerns, characters are colorful and well drawn, the action is fast and bloody, and the plotting carefully thought out, making this another supercharged yarn." —*Publishers Weekly* on *Texas Sunrise*

"Kelton's writing and grasp of the era are impeccable. . . . More Kelton is always welcome for high-end Western fans." —*Booklist* on *Many a River*

"Kelton provides stirring action and gripping suspense. His portrayal of the chaotic and bloody Battle of Glorieta Pass in 1862 is thrilling. . . . This is vintage Kelton, a solid Western story well told." —*Publishers Weekly* on *Many a River*

"The author, a seven-time Spur Award winner, has created a story rich in historical context, character development, and action." —*Tulsa World* on *Sons of Texas*

FORGE BOOKS BY ELMER KELTON

Badger Boy
Bitter Trail
The Buckskin Line
Buffalo Wagons
Cloudy in the West
Hard Trail to Follow
Hot Iron
Jericho's Road
Many a River
Other Men's Horses
The Pumpkin Rollers
The Raiders: Sons of Texas
Ranger's Trail
Six Bits a Day
The Smiling Country
Sons of Texas
Texas Rifles
Texas Vendetta
The Way of the Coyote

Lone Star Rising
(comprising *The Buckskin Line*, *Badger Boy*, and *The Way of the Coyote*)

Brush County
(comprising *Barbed Wire* and *Llano River*)

Texas Showdown
(comprising *Pecos Crossing* and *Shotgun*)

TEXAS SUNRISE

TWO NOVELS OF
THE TEXAS REPUBLIC

Elmer Kelton

A TOM DOHERTY ASSOCIATES BOOK

NEW YORK

TEXAS SUNRISE: TWO NOVELS OF THE TEXAS REPUBLIC

Copyright © 2008 by The Estate of Elmer Kelton

Massacre at Goliad copyright © 1965; renewal
copyright © 1993 by Elmer Kelton
After the Bugles copyright © 1967; renewal
copyright © 1995 by Elmer Kelton

A Forge Book
Published by Tom Doherty Associates, LLC
175 Fifth Avenue
New York, NY 10010

www.tor-forge.com

Forge® is a registered trademark of Tom Doherty Associates, LLC.

The Library of Congress has catalogued the hardcover as follows:

Kelton, Elmer.
   [Massacre at Goliad]
   Tesax sunrise : two novels of the Texas Republic / Elmer
  Kelton.—1st ed.
    p. cm.
   "A Tom Doherty Associates book."
   ISBN 978-0-7653-2064-3
   1. Brothers—Fiction. 2. Texas—History—Revolution,
1835–1836—Fiction. 3. Goliad Massacre, Goliad, Tex., 1836—
Fiction. 4. San Jacinto, Battle of, Tex., 1836—Fiction.
I. Kelton, Elmer. After the bugles. II. Title.
PS3561.E3975M37   2008
813'.54—dc22

2008034735

ISBN 978-0-7653-2191-6

First Hardcover Edition: November 2008
First Trade Paperback Edition: February 2010

Printed in the United States of America

0 9 8 7 6 5 4 3 2 1

CONTENTS

MASSACRE
AT
GOLIAD

AUTHOR'S NOTE

In the Texas revolution against Mexico, Mexican troops won all the important battles except two: the first one and the last. Between those, the Texians (the early settlers prior to statehood) lost one after another to the numerically superior forces of General Antonio López de Santa Anna.

Everyone knows about the Alamo. Fewer, outside of Texas, know about the massacre at Goliad, where more than twice as many Texians died. The difference was that in the Alamo they fought to the death. At Goliad they were made prisoners, led out, and murdered.

A root cause of the revolution—but by no means the only one—was a vast racial and cultural difference between the native Mexican people and the Americans who had come to settle among them in various colonizations since about 1823. Mexico encouraged these settlers at first, seeing them as a potential buffer against the Comanches and other hostile Indians. Men of good will worked hard for understanding between Americans and Mexicans, none more diligently than Stephen F. Austin, the Father of Texas.

But even the gentle and trusting Austin finally had to concede that President Santa Anna was a vain and hopeless tyrant. Like many others before and since, he began as a liberator but grasped for power until he became a ruthless dictator, capriciously holding life and death in his hands. Not only the Texas Americans but many Texas Mexicans and citizens of northern Mexican states rebelled against him. Most of the true old Texian settlers continued to regard themselves as loyal citizens of Mexico, in revolt against Santa Anna, not against the country. Indeed, the defenders of the Alamo—Mexican

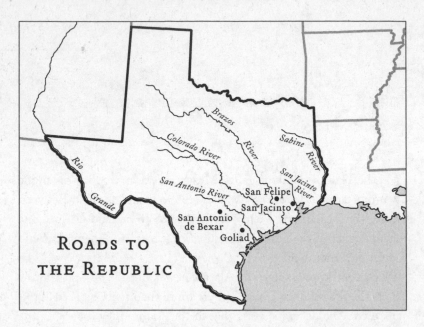

ROADS TO
THE REPUBLIC

as well as American—fought and died beneath the Mexican flag of 1824.

Texians under spirited old Ben Milam drove federal troops out of San Antonio in the fall of 1835 and dogged them to the Rio Grande. In response, Santa Anna butchered his way across northern Mexico, putting insurgents to the sword wherever he found them, then crossed into Texas.

The determined resistance at the Alamo surprised and slowed him, giving Sam Houston time to strengthen his defensive force. At Goliad, indecisive commander James W. Fannin delayed an ordered retreat until too late and was surrounded by Mexican troops under General José Urrea. After a costly battle, Fannin surrendered his command on Urrea's good-faith pledge of fair treatment. The dictator countermanded that promise. On Palm Sunday some three hundred and forty prisoners were marched out of the old mission in groups and shot.

Because the firing squads were smaller than the number of victims assigned to them, some men were able to break and run between volleys. A few more than twenty are known to have escaped. Some joined Sam Houston in time for his crushing defeat of Santa Anna at San Jacinto.

By then the overconfident self-styled Napoleon of the West had divided his forces and force-marched ahead of the larger body in the hope of catching Houston's little army before it could escape into Louisiana. Santa Anna was contemptuous of his own men, declaring that it was their great privilege to be allowed to die for his honor. He disregarded the suffering they endured by being ill-clothed and poorly equipped for Texas' cold, wet winter. His troops had already been decimated by sickness before Houston's embittered men suddenly turned with a vengeance and drove them reeling into the mud of Buffalo Bayou, where the carnage wrought upon them was horrendous.

In an attempt to escape, Santa Anna donned the nondescript uniform of a common soldier but was captured and brought trembling before the wounded Sam Houston. Most of the Texians wanted to hang him then and there, but Houston counseled peace. Dead, Santa Anna could sign no treaties. Alive, he could—and did—acknowledge that Texas was free.

1

*I*N HIS *later years Joshua Buckalew seldom spoke of Goliad and the terrible thing which happened there. Even in his old age there were nights when the memory returned in a dream and he would wake up suddenly with the cold sweat breaking, the horror as vivid as it had been in his youth.*

Yet there was fierce pride in the memory too, for Joshua Buckalew ever afterward considered himself one of the original Texans. He had been a witness to the birth of Texas at Bexar and Goliad and on the marshbound prairie of San Jacinto. So, as each of his sons came of age to understand—and later his grandsons—he would tell them the story that they might share his pride in their heritage, and that they might realize and value the awful sacrifice other men had made for Texas.

Always, he began the story long before Goliad. He began it where it had begun for him, one early spring day in Tennessee. . . .

I COULD have whipped the Keefer brothers without even breaking a sweat, provided I took them one at a time. But the two together were a mite of excess. They had me staggering in the dust of the crossroads where Gailey's Grocery dispensed everything from harness leather and red calico to raw corn spirits in a jug. Dogs barked. Men and boys cheered and whooped and stood back to give us room. Entertainment was scarce in those parts—a horserace occasionally, a shooting match, a barn-raising or a dance. A good fist fight was usually certain to stir the betting blood. But nobody was betting this time. They could tell that I was fixing to get my plow cleaned good and proper.

I was twenty-one then, five feet eleven and tough as mule-hide. But that wasn't enough. I kept lashing out with my fists at Smiley Keefer and trying with my elbows to knock loose from Snag Keefer's heavy weight on my back. Snag clung like a burr under a pantsleg.

I puffed, the breath coming hard. "This ain't noways a fair fight . . . I didn't go . . . to fight the both of you."

"You got us anyhow." Snag tried to sink his teeth into my ear.

I shifted my weight and threw Snag off balance, sliding him onto his back in the dust. I landed with both knees in Snag's belly. I turned to see where Smiley was and caught a faceful of his fist. These were plowmen, the Keefers, and a plowman's fists are as hard as a hickory knot.

I saw my brother Thomas edge through the crowd.

"Thomas!" I yelled. "Come and help me!"

Thomas was tall and strong, and he had a face that could be as grim as a hangman. He was grim now. He sat himself down in an open spot on the porch and eased the butt of his Kentucky longrifle to the ground.

I never was one to beg for help. Both Keefers were rushing me again. Their weight brought me down and crushed the breath from me. All I had left was a bruised and angry spirit.

"Now, Josh," gritted Smiley, "let's hear you holler quit."

They twisted my arms. The shame of defeat was as bad as the pain. I threshed and pitched. Cloudiness came over my eyes. I heard a firm voice say, "Give up, Josh. You're makin' a fool of yourself." Thomas hovered over me.

I clamped my teeth together tightly to keep from hollering out. Smiley Keefer put more pressure on my arm.

Thomas Buckalew said, "All right, boys, the fun's over. Let him up."

The Keefers waited too long. Thomas grabbed a fistful of hair in each hand, then cracked their heads together. "I said it's over now!"

The Keefers let go and jumped back the way men will jump away from an angry bull that might come up fighting. I arose, eyes blazing, but my knees betrayed me. I knelt, unable to stay up.

Thomas said flatly, "Git your rifle and let's be a-movin'. Pa wants to talk to us."

It was a minute before I had enough breath to speak. "What for?"

"That colonel what's-his-name from Texas has been by the place again. Pa's got that glow in his eyes."

Thomas let me struggle to my feet without help. He stood back, making it plain that he disapproved of my foolishness. The crowd was scattering. I swung around to glare at the Keefers, who leaned against the porch, still breathing hard. Snag was tipping a jug over his arm.

Thomas caught my sleeve and said roughly, "The mail has done left. You lost the fight; now let it go."

"You didn't even ask me how come I was fightin' them."

"I don't reckon as how I care. A man ought to have more pride than to git hisself stomped with half the settlement watchin', and laughin' at him."

"They were pickin' on poor old Muley Dodd."

"*Everybody* picks on Muley Dodd. Besides, I didn't see him."

"He was scared. Minute I hit Snag, Muley lit out arunnin'."

"Josh, you can't spend your life pickin' up after Muley. The Lord chose to short Muley on brains, and it's too bad. But it ain't up to you to be his everlastin' keeper."

"Somebody's got to help him. He can't help hisself."

I limped at first as we walked down the dusty wagon road, each of us carrying a Kentucky rifle. The late-afternoon sun slanted into our faces, for the Buckalew home lay west of the settlement. That was the way it had always been with the Buckalews: always west of the settlement.

Muley Dodd waited for us down the road, his hat in his hand, his eyes afraid. Short, stooped a little, Muley had the first whisker of manhood soft on his face. Ragged hair touched his frayed collar. He started talking when we were still fifty feet away. "Josh, I didn't go to leave you there. I didn't noways mean to run. The Devil got in me, and I was afeared. It was the Devil made me run."

Impatient, Thomas said, "It wasn't the Devil caused you to light out, Muley. It was the Keefers."

I cut a sharp glance at my brother. "Hush, Thomas." I walked up to Muley Dodd and put my hand on his shoulder. "Don't fret now, Muley. It's done over with. They ain't fixin' to bother you again."

"You sure, Josh?" Muley brightened up. "Did you whup 'em good? You're a real friend, Josh. And next time there's a fight, I won't run away. I'll stay right there and help you."

It wasn't so, but I nodded like I believed it. "Sure you will, Muley."

We walked on down the road, us Buckalews, Muley standing and watching us with his hat still in his hand. Thomas said, "Josh, you know he'll always run. He'll be runnin' the last day he lives. You can't protect him forever."

We came to a field where a mule stood waiting in endless patience, tied to a stump. At the turnrow lay my wooden plow. I had hired out to old man Higgins for a spell of work the year before, and Pa had made me take my pay in this plow instead of cash. Pa had declared: "Every man needs a plow of his own, time he comes of age. Money is soon spent. But give you a plow and you got somethin' that'll serve you for years."

It was true, I would have to admit. But I'd always said I'd rather stand back and admire Mother Nature than scratch her face with the point of a plow. A man got almighty tired sometimes of working up and down the rows all day, staring an old mule in the rear.

Thomas said, "Better fetch the mule."

Thomas was only a couple of years older than me, but times he acted as if the difference was ten. With Thomas, day was day and night was night; wrong was wrong and right was right. You drew a line and you stayed on one side of it. You didn't step over it, ever. I wondered sometimes where Thomas had inherited that stiff-backed way. It hadn't come from Pa.

The Buckalew home was of a mixed architecture. It had begun long ago as a log cabin but had been extended and enlarged with rough-sawed lumber through the years, as the lumber became available and the family fortunes had allowed us to buy or barter for it. At one time a lot of Buckalews had lived there. But gradually each came of age to go on his own. The boys went west, and the girls married off. Now there were only Pa and the oldest son, Lott, who was to inherit the place according to family custom. And there were Thomas and me.

Pa sat hunched on the hewn-log steps, puffing his pipe and taking his rest. He still worked hard, Titus Buckalew did. But it seemed like he couldn't take as much of it as he used to. He had worn out too many plows, outlived too many mules. He had cleared this land from virgin timber, by himself at first, then with sons to help him as each came along in his own due time. Lott had a large family of his own now.

Pa's old pipe stood black against the white of his beard as he stared at me. I couldn't see any surprise in the pale blue of his eyes. "Mule drag you, Joshua?"

I never did lie to Pa. "No, sir."

"And you didn't fall out of no tree. So I take it you been fightin'."

"Yes, sir."

"Win?"

"No, sir."

The old man frowned and knocked the pipe against the hard heel of his hand to jar the burned tobacco out. "If you got to fight, at least you ought to win."

"Next time, Pa."

His brow twisted into deep furrows, which came easy to him. "That Colonel Ames, he's been by again, talkin' to me about Texas."

Thomas said, "Pa, ain't it a little late in life for you to be thinkin' about faraway places any more?"

"Not for myself. It's you two that I been frettin' about. It's high time you had a chance to take and do somethin' for yourselves, like your brothers have done."

"You wantin' us to leave, Pa?" I asked.

"No, son, it ain't that I *want* you to. A man don't like sayin' good-bye to his young. But it's the way of life. You can see for yourself, there ain't nothin' left here for a growed man. If you ain't already got your land, you never will get it. What we got here will be just about enough for Lott, once I'm gone. Ever since the first Buckalew come across the big water, they've kept a-lookin' west. I done it, in my day. Your brothers have done it. Now I reckon it's your time."

My skin prickled with excitement. "You think we ought to go to Texas?"

"That's for you to say, not me. But Colonel Ames, he talks like it's a powerful good country for a young man to go and build him a life."

The weariness was suddenly gone from me. "Texas! I been hearin' a right smart about it. The Fancher boy went there last year, him and that Whipple girl he married. And the Smith family. And the year before that, old Henry Leech, only he died along the way."

Thomas nodded. The excitement was touching him too, which was a seldom thing. "The Fanchers got a letter from their boy awhile back. He's right taken with the country, Pa."

Pa drew silently on his pipe, enjoying the tobacco. "The colonel, he says this Stephen F. Austin has got him a colony there, and he'll let a man take up more land than he could accumulate here in a lifetime. All that land, just for the askin'. Of course, you'd have to build her from scratch, but us Buckalews, we always done that."

Thomas frowned. "One thing, Pa, you might not've thought about. Texas ain't in the United States. It's part of Mexico. Us Buckalews have been Americans ever since Grandpa froze his feet that winter with George Washington."

"Governments never did mean no awful lot to us Buckalews, son. We always been so far out front that they never was any bother to us. Anyhow, there's been a-plenty of Americans gone there already. I doubt as you'll see much difference." He was silent awhile, studying first one son, then the other. "Something else: you're both of a mar-ryin' age, and neither one has got you a woman."

Thomas shrugged. I didn't say anything.

Pa said, "Colonel Ames tells me a married man gets twice as much land in Texas as a single man. That's somethin' to consider. I don't expect you're apt to find many unattached females down there. Best play the game safe and take one with you. A bird in the hand, as they say." He looked at me. "How about that Merribelle Keefer, Joshua? She's been chasin' around you like a bear after honey."

I shook my head. "She'd be a burden."

"They all are. But think of that extra land."

"She's not the prettiest I ever saw. And I don't love her."

"Love wears off, and looks change. Main thing is that she can cook. You'd be surprised, too, how she can help keep your bed warm in the wintertime."

"Pa, I've tried her." All of a sudden I felt my face turning red. "Her cookin', I mean. She's not for me."

Humor flickered in Pa's eyes. He turned to Thomas. "How about you?"

"I've never seen a woman I'd marry."

"You always expect too much, Thomas, that's your weakness. You got to learn to bend a little. Women are human. There never was but one perfect man, and I doubt there ever *was* a perfect woman."

Thomas shook his head. "There's still none here I'd want to marry."

Pa shrugged. "Well, that's up to you. Down yonder, you ain't apt to find anything except Mexican girls."

Thomas said flatly, "I know we won't be marryin' one of *them*."

WE STARTED when the warm spring sun brought the green rise of new grass. We said our good-byes and pointed the wagon-tongue southwestward, angling to cut across a corner of Mississippi.

There had been a brief sadness at the time of parting, and there would be sad moments again when the awful finality of those long miles of separation at last came home to me. Thomas's jaw was set square and sober, for he was thinking on these things. But for me, riding ahead on a sorrel horse, there was too much new to see, a sudden freedom to glory in. There was no time to waste in looking back.

I had come prepared, or thought I had. A gunsmith had reworked my longrifle, making it like new. On my left hip I wore a big cast-steel knife the gunsmith had fashioned, a heavy thing with a hickory handle, a blade two inches wide and fourteen inches long. It was better than a hatchet or a tomahawk for a man in the wilds, the smith had said. I also had a small skinning knife, worn on a belt slung over my shoulder, with a sack of flints and newly-cast lead bullets.

The wagon lumbered along slowly, for its bed sagged with the weight of things we would use in the new land. If left to my own choice, I would have preferred to travel light, perhaps taking a steamboat down the Mississippi to New Orleans, then going by ship to the coast of Texas. Many emigrants were doing it that way. But Pa had argued that this would land us in Texas with only such goods as we could pack. Wagons, plows, and other implements would be hard to come by in Texas, and the price would be high.

To be sure, the wagon would slow our trip. It would mean back-straining labor and galling delay in time of rain, or in passing through the pine forests and the dense cane-brakes which lay ahead.

"But," Pa had reasoned, "it'll be all yours when you get there. You'll have the wagon and the horses. You'll have a plow apiece, and an anvil and tools. You'll have saddles and harness and plantin' seed. Two cows, a heifer, and a bull. Costs money, Josh, to ride a boat. This way you can live off the country, and so can your stock. What money you've got will still belong to you when you get to Texas."

Two strong gray workhorses pulled the wagon, horses that would be worth a-plenty when they got to where they were going. The cows plodded along with infinite bovine patience at the end of their ropes behind the wagon, udders swinging like the pendulum of a clock. Alongside them walked the heifer, and a big bull calf that we were counting on to sire us a herd in Texas.

We would suffer for this burden on the trip, but we would be better equipped than most folks when we finally crossed the Sabine River into Stephen F. Austin's promised land.

We hadn't gone two miles before we saw a man walking down the road in front of us, an old rifle in one hand and an old canvas bag slung over his shoulder. A spotted hound trailed behind him. It stopped and barked at the wagon. The man turned and smiled broadly. He set the bag down and waved, standing in the road until the wagon drew up almost to him. Then he stepped aside.

"Howdy, Josh. Howdy, Thomas. You-all on your way to Texas?" Muley Dodd waited until we answered yes. Then he said, "I'm on my way to Texas, too."

Feeling pity, I swung down from my horse. "Muley, it's a far piece to Texas. You can't go there thataway."

"I got lots of time, Josh. I got grub in the sack, and powder and lead."

The hound came up and licked my hand. It startled me, and I jerked my hand away. "Muley, you don't have enough supplies in that sack to get you to the Notchy country even, much less to Texas."

"I won't go hungry. I can follow bees. Besides, I got money, too. I got three dollars and fifty-two cents." Eagerly Muley reached into his pocket. "Here, I'll show you."

I shook my head and glanced at Thomas as if to ask him what to do. "Muley, you got to go on back home."

"I already left home. Ain't got no folks there no more, and the roof's about to fall in on that old shack anyhow. I'll built me a real pretty house when I git to Texas."

I motioned for Thomas to get down off the wagon and walk with me out to the side of the road. "Thomas, what we goin' to do about Muley?"

"Nothin'. He's not our responsibility."

"He's not *nobody's* responsibility. He's got no folks."

"You've taken care of him for years, Josh. Now let somebody else do it."

"When Muley gets a notion in his head, he don't turn away from it. If he's got it in his mind to go to Texas, he'll keep walkin' till he dies!"

"You fixin' to tell me we ought to take him with us? If you are, you'll just be wastin' your breath."

Thomas climbed back onto the wagon seat. "Goodbye, Muley," he said, and set the team to moving again.

Muley waved good-naturedly. "Good-bye, Thomas. I'll see you in Texas."

I stared at Muley, worried and a little impatient. Thomas was right: I shouldn't have to be saddled with Muley all my life. Something came to me out of the Bible, something about the faith of the mustard seed. Muley had no conception of what lay ahead of him. But he had plenty of faith.

Muley said, "Thomas is fixin' to go off and leave you, Josh. You better catch up. I'll see you-all again when I get to Texas."

I rode on ahead, catching up to the wagon. But I couldn't keep from looking back. And Muley Dodd kept coming. Sometimes I could hear him whistling at the dog. Finally I said, "Thomas, you'd just as well stop. I'm not goin' without Muley."

ALL MY life I had heard tell of the Mississippi River, but I wasn't prepared. There it stretched in front of us, its lazy brown waters so wide that the river was almost scary to look at. The first money we had spent since leaving home, we spent for passage across on a ferry. It was a long, slow crossing. The ferry heaved, and so did Muley Dodd.

Finally, when we pulled the wagon down onto the west bank and paused to look back across the Big Muddy, I caught for the first time the full sense of parting. It touched me deeper than I expected. Crossing this river was like turning a page in a book. Distance was a relative thing, but a barrier like this was something real, something we could see. It was like shutting a door behind us, knowing we might never cross this river again. It was a sobering thought, as long as it lasted. But it didn't last long. There was a camp to be made, and fresh meat to be hunted.

Crossing Louisiana, we were held up for days by hard spring rains which bogged the wagon to the hubs in black mud that gave way so easily to the iron-rimmed wheels but yielded them up so grudgingly. This was a place where even Thomas was glad to have Muley along. Being as little as he was, Muley had a strong back. He thrived on hard work, as long as somebody told him what to do.

Hunting was poor. Camp meat ran low. We went deeper than we had intended into our supply of ground corn. Muley's own sack had long since run out of grub, so there was a third mouth to feed. But even if we went hungry we would not touch the sack that carried the seed corn, a tough strain that had served the Buckalew family well in Tennessee and would see us through in Texas.

I whiled away the idle hours by studying a map of Texas until I had it memorized in every detail. Muley spent time with his spotted hound, which he had named Hickory, after Andrew Jackson. Muley tried to rename him Texas, but the hound wouldn't answer to it, so finally it was Hickory again.

A friendly sun came out at last to harden the soaked earth. We greased the axles afresh and started the wheels turning once more. Much of the country we crossed now was wild, and we traveled long distances without seeing much sign of people. Some movers would have been tempted to stop here and settle, for it appeared there was plenty of room. But not the Buckalews. We were men of tradition. We always went the whole way.

At length we came out of the thick pine timber to the Louisiana Creole town of Natchitoches, on the right bank of the Red River. This was the jumping-off place for Texas-bound overland travelers. About 120 miles west, across the Sabine River, waited the ancient Spanish settlement of Nacogdoches, the easternmost town in Mexican Texas. It was here in Natchitoches that Stephen F. Austin had disembarked from a steamboat in June of 1821 to make his first trip into that vast expanse of alien country where his father, the late Moses Austin, had dreamed of a rich American colony and a recovery of lost family fortunes.

The Creoles by now were used to travelers, finding them a profitable source of trade. They got little from the Buckalews. Thomas held the purse strings with a tight-clamped hand. What we didn't really need, we would do without. What we did really need, we had brought with us.

"Just a final little jolly, Thomas," I cajoled. "This is our last chance in the United States. Be a sport."

Thomas was resolute. "I've never *been* a sport. You want to dance? Dance around that there wagon and grease the hubs."

I didn't argue with him much. Even if Thomas had been open handed with me—an unlikely development—I wouldn't have spent more than the price of a jug. The weeks of hard, slow travel on dim trails and the painful care we gave our cargo had sobered me considerably. I could understand and respect the responsibility my brother carried.

"Then I reckon me and Muley will go look around some. See what these here French folks have got to offer."

"You watch out," Thomas said sternly. "Don't be gettin' in no fights over Muley. Somebody acts like they're goin' to pick on him, you just bring him on back to the wagon. No arguments."

"No arguments," I promised.

We had hardly left the wagon when we saw the four horsemen. They rode toward the camp in a slow walk, stopping to peer curiously at the wagon from thirty or forty yards.

Muley caught my arm. "Josh, what kind of men you reckon them fellers are?"

"I don't rightly know." Two of them were a lot like the type I had known in the Tennessee settlements all my life—outdoorsmen with sun-browned, tangle-bearded faces. The floppy hats, the homespun shirts, the woolen breeches were familiar enough.

The other two were different, and I guess my mouth was open as I stared at them. They were both small and wiry, hungry-looking. Their faces were dark, but not the same as those of the Negroes back in Tennessee. They wore peculiar hats with tall, pointed crowns and the widest brims I had ever seen. One had an embroidered black vest that must have been something special once, though now it was dirty and threadbare. Both men wore leather breeches and boots, and spurs with huge, wicked rowels. One of them spoke to the other, and the words were foreign. They made no sense to me.

Mexicans, I realized. Yonder, to the west, sprawled the huge Republic of Mexico. It was natural that we might encounter Mexicans here, the first we had ever seen. The strangeness of the men made us hold still in wonder and keep our silence.

At length the four rode closer. One man nodded with some show of friendliness. "Howdy, friends." His teeth were stained from tobacco. "Be you-all headin' for Texas?"

I found myself picking up his manner of speaking. "Yes, sir, we be."

"Where do you-all come from?"

"Tennessee."

The man glanced at his companions. "Hear that, Foley? They be homefolks."

I couldn't keep my eyes from the Mexicans. "*They* ain't from Tennessee."

The man said, "Foley and me, we left Tennessee a mighty long time ago. Miguel and Alfredo, of course, they don't know Tennessee from Massachusetts. They be Meskin."

Excitement stirred in me. I asked the nearest Mexican, "You come from Texas?"

The Mexican glanced at the Tennessean who had done the talking. The Tennessean said, "You got to pardon Miguel. He don't know much English, 'cept a few words like *eat* and *sleep* and *women*."

I felt an awe of these strange men. "You mean you know how to talk *their* language?"

"Sure. You learn it easy when you git to Texas. All you need is a good teacher—a good-*lookin'* teacher."

I grinned at Muley. "It's real lucky, us runnin' into these fellers. They can tell us a right smart that we ought to be a-knowin'." I looked back at the men. "My name's Joshua Buckalew. Just Josh, is all I use. This here is Muley Dodd."

The big man leaned forward in the saddle and took my hand. "I answer to 'Lige'. For Elijah, you know, like in the Book. He was one of them prophets, or maybe it was a disciple—I forgit which. That there is Foley. The Meskins, they got names longer than a hoe handle, but all you need to remember is Miguel and Alfredo. How many with you, Josh?"

"Just us and my brother Thomas. Us three is all."

The man frowned, looking toward the wagon. "Sure got a load of plunder, just for three of you."

"We figured to be prepared. Come meet my brother." I turned and walked ahead. I shouted, "Thomas, come see what's here."

Thomas came around the wagon, halted and stared, a sharp question in his eyes.

I said, "These fellers come from Texas."

Thomas's eyes seemed to harden as his gaze drifted from one to the other. "How do."

His unfriendly manner caught me by surprise. "Thomas, I said they come from Texas. There's a lot they can tell us."

"I already been told a right smart."

For a moment Lige seemed to stiffen. Then he eased again. "How long before you figger on leavin', Thomas?"

Thomas shook his head. "Can't say for certain. Might stay a spell."

That was a lie, for we had planned to leave the next morning. But I held my silence.

Lige rubbed his beard. "Your brother's a cautious man, Josh. And he's right. It don't pay to trust strangers in these parts. Man can't be too careful in a new country." He took a long last look at the wagon and the livestock. "Fine outfit you got. You ought to git off to a good start in Texas." He pulled his horse around. Foley and the two Mexicans followed his example.

I called, "Maybe we'll see you again. There's a heap of questions I'd like to ask."

Lige replied over his shoulder, "Any time, Josh."

When they were gone, I turned angrily on Thomas. "If you'd been civil we could of talked with them. You wasn't like this at home!"

"We ain't at home, Josh."

"But they was homefolks, and they been in Texas."

"Just because a man's from Tennessee don't mean he's gospel-honest." Thomas frowned. "You're in a strange country, Josh. You don't trust nobody till you have time to size them up. And you don't go tellin' anybody what your plans are. Remember that!"

"They been on the trail. You condemned them because of what they looked like."

"Some things, Josh, you learn to take by instinct. Out in the woods, did you ever sense a varmint before you seen it? It was like that with them four. It was like I had come across a pack of wolves. Nothin' you can put a finger on, but the feelin's there. And when it's there, I pay heed to it."

"I didn't get that feelin'."

"It'll come to you. And till it does, we'll go by my instincts."

That should have been the end of it, for Pa had pledged me to follow Thomas in all important things. But I still burned to find out about the country we were heading for. I wouldn't exactly go looking for Lige. But if we should happen to come across him by accident. . . .

Muley and I started to resume our walk down to the town. Thomas said, "Don't you be late. We want to get started by daylight."

Trailed by Muley's spotted hound, we walked up and down the length of the town, pausing to stare at the river, looking at the small boats, listening with a keen ear to the strange Creole talk.

I shook my head. "I expect it means as much to them as English means to us."

Muley said in all innocence, "I don't understand English neither. I just talk American."

"That's not what I mean, Muley. It's just that . . ." I broke off, for there was no explaining to Muley. I wasn't even sure I understood it all myself. Take for instance the name of the town: *Natchitoches*. Anybody could look at the word and see how it was supposed to sound. But these people called it something like NAK-i-tosh. I figured either the people who had named the town hadn't been able to spell, or the people who lived here now just didn't know how to read.

Muley wasn't satisfied. "Those little kids yonder, how are they supposed to know what they're talkin' about?"

I just shrugged.

Muley said, "Looks to me like it would be simpler if everybody in the world just got together and decided to talk like *we* do. It must be the best language anyhow, or they wouldn't of wrote the Bible in it. Ain't that so?"

"I expect."

"Looks like it sure would save everybody a heap of bother."

After a couple of hours of looking around, we hadn't seen anything of the four men. We figured they had left town. Then on our way back to Thomas, we stumbled right into their camp. We found ourselves facing them over the flicker of a dying fire. I sensed a vague hostility. "Let's move in closer, Muley. They probably can't tell who we are."

Lige took a couple of steps forward, hand on a pistol stuck in his waistband. Then he smiled. "Well, I'll swear it's the lads from Tennessee. Set down here, Josh, you and Muley. Share some poor vittles with us. We got a little left."

I looked around for their wagon and saw that they had none. There were only four saddle horses and a couple of pack animals, staked out on the grass. "Thanks, but we wouldn't want to put you out none. We'd drink a little coffee, though, if you got any." We'd been using ours sparingly because we knew it would be expensive in Texas.

"Sure," said Lige, all friendship and smiles. He spoke in Spanish. Miguel fetched a jug. Lige said, "Before the coffee, a little drop of kindness. For Tennessee, and fond recollections."

Muley drank first and went into a coughing fit. Then I tipped the jug over my arm. Whatever it was, it felt as if it would burn a hole plumb through me.

Lige said, "That's Meskin stuff, pretty hot doin's. Not as good as old Tennessee makin's, but it don't lack for authority."

I gasped, "That's for certain sure."

The burn was a while in wearing off. I didn't care for another. Lige laughed as I blinked the tears from my eyes. Muley still coughed a little, trying to clear his throat. It came to me that Foley and the Mexicans were staring at us, their eyes hard. All of a sudden I didn't like these men. Lige was probably all right, but the others. . . .

Even disliking them, I kept glancing at the Mexicans. And Muley stared at them in honest curiosity.

"Lige," I said, "I want you to tell us about Texas."

Lige shook his head. "It's a mighty big subject."

"Just the important things, what we ought to know before we get there."

Lige shrugged. "Well, if I was givin' advice, I'd say the thing most emigrants do wrong is to come unprepared. But from the looks of your wagon, you-all come loaded for bear. So the next thing is to decide where you want to settle."

"We talked to a Colonel Ames back home. He said we could get land in Austin's colony. You know Colonel Ames?"

Lige frowned. "Can't say as I recollect the gentleman. I know Austin, though."

Foley hadn't spoken before. Now he put in bitterly: "Everybody knows abut the good Colonel Austin. Him and his damned whip."

That surprised me. "I thought everybody liked Austin."

Lige replied quickly, "Most folks do. Foley there, he's got a personal grudge is all, and he talks too much." He frowned at Foley. "Austin is pretty much the whole law in his colony. A man who strays off of the straight and narrow has got to answer to Austin. He's a little feller, and he looks gentle, but now and again he rears up and shows his teeth. Now, Foley had a friend who done a transgression, and Austin ordered the man whipped and throwed out of the colony. Foley ain't forgave that."

My flesh crawled. "Whippin' *is* an awful salty punishment."

"It beats hangin'. They can't hang a man in Texas lessen they git permission first out of Saltillo, and that's way to hell south. Takes a long time. So usually they just whip a man out of the settlement and hope somebody else'll hang him. They don't appreciate the rough element in Austin's colony."

Lige paused as if a sudden thought had come to him. "By the bye, you'll be needin' to be able to show you're of good character. *I* can tell by lookin', but Austin sets a heap of store in seein' it wrote down."

"Thomas and me, we got letters from Colonel Ames and some of the quality folks around home. And *we'll* vouch for Muley."

"It takes a little money, too, to pay down on the land. I hope you got money."

A warning tingle of suspicion touched me. I had never traveled before, but it seemed unlikely to me that quality folks would ask a man if he was carrying money. Muley spoke up with enthusiasm. "Sure, they got money. *I* got money, too." He reached in his pocket for it. "I got three dollars and fifty-two cents."

I said, "Muley!"

Lige grinned. "That's good, Muley. That much money'll take you a long ways in Texas." Lige reached into the fire for a burning stick and used it to light his pipe. His eyes fastened onto me, and I began feeling uncomfortable. "You know somethin', lad? I like you two. Yes, sir, I like you. And I'm fixin' to give you a mite of advice. Between here and Texas there's a heap of unpleasant things layin' in wait for the unwary. You got to cross the Redlands. Lots of hard characters in there. Some been run out of the colony and don't dare go back to the States. Others been run out of the States and can't go to Austin's. So they just squat in the Redland and turn their hands to mischief. Dangerous for three young fellers alone with one wagon."

I sipped his coffee and hoped my eyes did not betray the suspicion that was boiling up in me. "We'll do all right."

"Been others felt that way and never got to Texas alive."

I made no reply.

Lige said, "You need to join up with others a headin' for Texas. We'll be goin' that direction ourselves pretty quick. We'd be right tickled to have you with us."

My gaze drifted from one man to another. The eyes of Foley and the Mexicans were cold. And so was my back.

Foley was twisted sideways, his right arm bent awkwardly as he tried to scratch along his spine. The truth came to me like the flash of a pineknot exploding in a campfire: Foley's back was sore. It wasn't a friend of Foley's who got whipped out of the colony. It was Foley himself!

Suddenly cold all over, I spilled what coffee was left in the cup and pushed to my feet. "We'll see about it." I handed Lige the cup.

"Thomas and me, we decided to camp close by here for a week or so and rest up the stock. We'll think on what you said."

It was a lie, but I hoped they wouldn't sense that.

Lige said, "We'll come around and see you in a few days."

As we walked back to our own camp, Muley protested, "I thought Thomas said we was goin' to leave early in the mornin'. It's a sin to lie. How come you lied, Josh?"

I didn't answer him. At the wagon Thomas sat back from the fire, a plate in his hand. He was impatient. "You been gone a long time."

"We ran into those men who stopped at our wagon today, the ones who said they were from Tennessee."

Thomas's eyes narrowed, but he didn't say anything. "Remember· what you told me about bein' able to smell a varmint?"

"I remember."

"Well, I think I smelled *four* of them."

Thomas went back to eating. It was several minutes before he said anything, though I thought I saw satisfaction in his eyes as I told him all there was to tell. At length Thomas remarked, "Four men like that wouldn't have much trouble killin' two, would they?" He glanced at Muley. "Or *three*?"

I shook my head. "Not when the three thought the four were friends."

Thomas nodded. "You're smartenin' up, Josh. Tonight we'll get the wagon ready. Come sunup, we'll be three hours down the trail."

WE HAD a map drawn by Colonel Ames, but we found it more useful to follow wagon tracks and tree blazes than to depend upon the map for more than the most general type of guidance. Looking back over our shoulders every so often for sign of Lige and his three partners, we traveled three days through country that looked as if it would take only a little spit to turn it into a quagmire.

The third night the rain started. It was still raining at daybreak when we hitched the team. The wagon moved ten feet and sank halfway to the hubs.

Thomas accepted it philosophically with no more than a shrug of his shoulders and a frowning glance at the heavy timber just behind us. "If we got to bog down, let's do it out in the open where we can see what's comin' around us."

We hadn't spoken to Muley of our suspicions. Muley was like a little boy—easily made happy and easily frightened. No use frightening him now, for he was having a good time.

"You reckon they'll still come?" I asked Thomas.

"They might, if they don't find better pickin's in Natchitoches. I got a feelin' this bunch of cutthroats wouldn't be choosy."

So we fought the wagon out into the open. I tied the sorrel on with the team and used him to help pull while Thomas and Muley threw their shoulders against the mired wheels and pushed. The spotted dog now and again would bark at the straining team as if trying to do his bit. By midmorning we were two hundred yards out into the clear.

"We'll stop now," Thomas said, his chest heaving from exhaustion, rain spilling from the flattened brim of his mud-streaked hat.

We staked the livestock on grass close by and stretched an extra wagonsheet out from one side of the wagon to give us a place where we could stay out of the rain. This precaution came late, for we were already soaked. We huddled over a small fire which was kept alive with dry wood saved inside the wagon.

No one came that day. In the night Thomas and I took turns sitting up on watch. We couldn't trust Muley to stay awake. Next morning the rain stopped. The sun came out from behind the breaking clouds to raise steam from the black, sodden ground. The second day of sunshine we hitched up and made a try. We moved a hundred feet and quit.

"If they come," said Thomas, "at least we're in a position to see them before they get here."

AND THEY came. The four horsemen emerged from the timber in late afternoon. Lige rode in the lead. They halted, seeing the mired wagon in the open. Lige came riding on cautiously, Foley and the two Mexicans trailing by a length or so. They left two pack horses behind.

Thomas was dozing. I touched him gently. "Thomas, they've come."

He was awake instantly, reaching for his rifle. I saw Muley off in the grass, running with the hound.

"Muley," I yelled, "come here, quick! Run!"

Muley caught the urgency in my voice. He saw the four men and came sprinting. "They Indians, Josh? They Indians?"

"No, Muley, not Indians. But help me bring the stock in and tie them to the wagon. We don't want them run off."

Muley did as he was told. He asked no questions, though his frightened eyes showed a-plenty of them. We tied the team and the milk cows securely. Picking up my rifle, I said, "Muley, you stay right here, tight by the wagon. Don't say nothin' and don't do nothin'."

Thomas stood ten feet out from the wagon, his rifle cradled over his left arm. I joined him.

Lige reined up. He eyed us critically. Finally he said, "I wouldn't noways call this friendly."

Thomas's voice was cold. "Neither would I."

Foley reined up on one side of Lige. The Mexicans stopped on the other. Their eyes were hostile.

Lige made a show of disappointment. "A man would have to take this as a sign of distrust. You must think we're robbers or somethin'."

I replied, "The thought did occur to us."

"Here I been tellin' Foley and the boys that you-all just changed your minds and left Natchitoches a little earlier than you intended to. If I was of a suspicious nature, I might think you just plain lied to us."

Thomas said, "We don't want trouble. You-all just ride on by us and don't be a stoppin'."

Lige's eyes began to harden. "If we *was* robbers, you boys would be in a tough spot now. I judge that you still can't move that wagon. That boy yonder . . ." he pointed at Muley, "ain't goin' to be of no use to you, so it'd be just you two against us four. And you got just one shot apiece."

Thomas's voice was flat. "We'd make those two shots count. You don't know which two we'd kill."

Lige glanced at his companions. "We come to do these boys a favor and see how it turns out! The milk of human kindness has done clabbered."

Foley scowled. "It's a long way to Texas. They got to sleep some-time."

Thus was all pretense stripped away. Lige shed his false friendli-ness like a shabby old coat. He looked at the wagon with unmasked greed, plainly calculating what it and its contents would sell for in Texas.

"Boys," he said, "there ain't no use you-all dyin' for this. You can always git you another wagon someday. But once you're dead, no-body can bring you back to life till the Angel Gabriel hisself blows on that horn."

I said, "We ain't dead yet."

"And you needn't be, boy, you needn't be. Think it over. We'll be back in the mornin'. You just ride out in the nighttime and forgit you ever seen us, or that you ever had a wagon."

Lige pulled his horse around and started back to the timber. Foley and the Mexicans held a moment, their hostile eyes fixed on us and our rifles. They had expected to ride directly into camp and have the whole thing over within a moment of complete surprise.

One of the Mexicans spat something in Spanish that I didn't un-derstand. But the other was clear enough when he drew his forefin-ger across his throat. The three men reined around and went off after Lige.

I just stood there, my hands frozen on the rifle. Muley began whimpering, "Josh, what do them fellers want? Josh, I don't think I like them fellers."

I licked my dry lips. "Thomas, what comes next?"

Thomas shook his head. He lowered his rifle. "Depends on *them*. Like as not they'll lay up yonder in the timber and snipe at us. Let's don't be makin' them a target."

"Like Foley said, it's a long trail to Texas. We can't dodge bullets the whole way."

Thomas shook his head again. "No, we can't. So we'll just lay low and see what kind of move they make."

"What if they don't make one?"

"Then we will."

Muley trembled, and it took all the persuasion I could muster to get him settled down.

Every time one of us stepped out into the clear, a rifle ball would buzz like an angry hornet. The first one bothered me considerably. The second one made me mad. "What do they want to do that for? They can't hit us at this range."

"They might," Thomas said, "if they're lucky. Mostly they want to keep us stuck here till they can pick their own time to come and get us. And maybe they think they can scare us into runnin' away and leavin' it all. That's what they want."

"Well, they're scarin' poor Muley to death, and me too, a little bit. All that friendly talk, sweet as sorghum molasses, and then they want to rob us."

The sun went down. I wasn't too hungry, and Muley was so frightened he never even thought of supper. But Thomas was calm. He built up the fire a little and went about heating some leftover rabbit stew. I got the idea somehow that Thomas might even be looking forward to the inevitable conflict with a certain enjoyment.

I made Muley eat, hoping some hot food in his stomach might make him feel better. I forced myself to eat a little, too, though I had no taste for it. As darkness came, the glow of a campfire showed in the timber.

"Eatin' theirselves a good supper," I said with some bitterness.

Thomas only nodded.

"They could stretch this for days if they wanted to," I complained. "And all we can do is sit here."

Thomas's jaw jutted. "Wrong, Josh. That's *not* all we can do." He stared intently at me. "So far, Josh, what fightin' you've done has been of a piddlin' variety. You've fought at the wrong time and in the wrong places for the wrong things. But a bloody nose or a split lip was the worst you could get. Are you ready to fight now when you *could* get a bullet in your gut?"

"Just try me!"

"Way I see it, they either plan on lettin' us sit here and worry all night, or they'll wait till late and try to catch us asleep. Either way, they'll figure *they're* the hunters. I doubt they'll look for us to come huntin'."

"You mean we're goin' after *them*?"

"It sure beats waitin', and our chances are better. Once it turns pure dark, we got a little time before the moon comes up. We can be on them before they know it."

"I'm willin' to try it. But what about Muley? He'll be hindrance to us, not a help."

"*That,*" Thomas said sharply, "I tried to tell you in Tennessee. But anyhow, he stays here."

"He'll be scared."

"He'll stay if we have to tie him. You tell him that!"

We checked our rifles. Each of us loaded a cap-and-ball pistol. Two weapons apiece meant a total of only four shots, with four targets. That was drawing it mighty fine. If four shots failed to do the job, each of us still wore a wicked Arkansas toothpick strapped to our belts, a heavy hunting knife with razor-sharp blade of cast steel.

Muley watched our preparations wide-eyed. "What you fellers fixin' to do, Josh?"

"We're goin' huntin' in a little while. Don't fret, Muley."

We smothered the fire, then sat awhile in the darkness, listening. In the timber we could still see the glow of the robbers' camp. Worriedly I whispered, "How do we know they won't be comin' after *us*, and we won't run into them in the dark someplace?"

"We don't. We just have to go on faith and hope, and depend on them not bein' in no hurry. You scared?"

I started to say I wasn't, but it would have been a poor lie. "If I was any scareder I'd have to change breeches."

Thomas said, "Well, it's about as dark as it's goin' to get. We want to be in the timber before the moon comes up. You talk to Muley, and be sure that dog of his is tied to the wagon."

Muley trembled. "You leavin' me here by myself, Josh?"

"Just for a little while, Muley. You got to stay and look after the stock. Don't you leave this wagon for nothin', you hear me? Don't leave it at all."

Muley was dubious. "I ain't goin' to like it here, Josh."

"You stay, though. Don't leave it for a minute, or I'll be real mad at you."

"I don't want you bein' mad at me, Josh."

"Then you mind what I tell you."

We moved out, our soft-leather moccasins noiseless on the wet earth. I stayed close to Thomas, for I could hardly see even the outline of him in the darkness. If we ever strayed twenty feet apart, we would lose each other.

We crouched low and moved softly, pausing often to drop to our knees and listen. Hearing nothing but the night birds and the crickets, we would move on a way, then stop again. Back at our wagon, we heard the dog set in to barking. For an awful minute or two I thought the robbers might be stalking Muley. But the barking stopped. Presently we were in the edge of the timber. Ahead, brighter now, glowed the campfire. We paused again to listen. This time we heard voices.

We nodded at each other, satisfied that the four men were still in camp. Thomas signaled for me to follow him. Cautiously, testing the ground each time we put a foot forward, we moved toward the fire.

Thomas's outline showed against the dim glow, bent low and edging in close. Soon we were in the fringe timber around the clearing where the outlaws had made their camp. Without looking back, Thomas hand-signaled me to come up beside him. We knelt to watch, and to consider.

Nearest us, at perhaps twenty feet, Foley sat with a jug, scowling. "I say we ought to've took them, Lige. How do we know they ain't packin' up right now and movin' out?"

Lige stood beyond the fire, thumbs hooked in the waistband of his woolen breeches. "They'd just bog that wagon. I say let them sweat a little. They'll be easier handled when they git good and scared. A scared man don't generally shoot good."

One of the Mexicans sat silently with a long dirk in one hand and a whetstone in the other. The steel blade made a whispering sound each time it passed over the stone. At length the Mexican pulled up a runner of winter-dried grass, left from the previous fall. He slashed at it. The runner floated back to earth in two pieces. The Mexican nodded his satisfaction and said something in Spanish.

The other Mexican lay stretched out on a blanket, evidently asleep. A small jug sat beside him.

I looked for their weapons. Foley's rifle lay on the ground within easy reach. The Mexican Miguel held the dirk. I couldn't see how the sleeping Mexican was armed. So far as I could tell, Lige had no weapon on him. He was twelve or fifteen feet from any rifle in view.

Thomas whispered in my ear, "Rifles first. I'll take Foley. You take the Mexican that's got the knife. We'll have to get Lige and the other Mexican with our pistols."

"Just shoot them? From ambush?"

"That's what they would've done to us!"

The rifle hammers clicked loud and metallic in the night air. Foley and Miguel jumped to their feet. Foley moved so rapidly I hardly saw him bring the rifle up. In the split second between the flash in the pan and the roar of my rifle, the Mexican sent the dirk spinning toward me. I saw him stagger. Then the blade slashed into my arm.

Thomas made his shot good. Foley's rifle dropped harmlessly to the ground.

The other Mexican was awake instantly, groping desperately for a weapon and tipping over his jug. Thomas dropped his rifle and drew the pistol out of his waistband. The pistol flashed, and the Mexican fell.

Across the fire, Lige stood stunned. He made no move toward a weapon. The nearest was too far for him to reach. He turned and ran into the night.

Thomas shouted, "Shoot him, Josh, quick!"

But I was swaying, the warm blood running down my arm. Instinctively I reached up and pulled the dirk out. I stood with it in my hand and stared in blind shock at the dead Miguel.

Thomas leaped forward, grabbed up Foley's rifle and fired it into the darkness. But he missed, for we could hear Lige's footsteps and the man's heavy body, crashing through the timber.

Thomas stepped back into the firelight and methodically began to reload his pistol. Pursuit would be useless. "Why didn't you shoot him, Josh?" Then he noticed for the first time that I was wounded. "Josh, I didn't know. How bad did he get you?"

I shook my head. "It's bleedin'. That's all I can tell."

Thomas led me closer to the fire for a better look. "It's risky, us bein' close to the fire this way. But I don't expect Lige got away with a gun. He'd of used it already."

My stomach turned over. "Look out, Thomas. It's all coming up."

And it did. But afterward I felt better. Thomas bound the wound tightly, and the bleeding stopped.

We heard footsteps again, a man running. Thomas pulled me away from the fire and into the darkness. He held the reloaded pistol ready.

"Josh!" a voice called excitedly. "Josh! Where you at, Josh?"

"It's Muley," Thomas said. "I knew he wouldn't stay at the wagon."

"He stayed till it was over with. That was the main thing."

Thomas called, "Over here, Muley."

Muley came into the firelight, his eyes wide. He shrank back when he saw the bodies.

"It's all right, Muley." I said. "We got them before they could get us."

Shakily Muley asked, "They all dead?"

"I reckon."

Getting braver, Muley moved close to look. He pointed to the Mexican who had been caught asleep. "This one ain't dead, Josh. He's movin'."

The wounded Mexican had inched himself along on the ground

until he had reached a knife. His fingers were closing around it when Thomas leveled the pistol. A faint smile came to my brother's face. The pistol flashed. The Mexican's fingers spread and dug into the mud. Then they went stiff.

A chill ran all the way down to my boots. I stared hard at Thomas, for this was something I had never seen in him before.

Thomas caught the look. "It had to be done."

"You didn't have to enjoy it."

"Was that how it looked?"

I nodded. Thomas said, "I didn't. But on the other hand, I can't say as it bothered me none, either."

From far off we heard a horse running. I knew without having to see. "It's Lige! He's stolen one of our horses."

Thomas swore.

Thinking about it, I shrugged. "Well, maybe it was a fair trade. He couldn't get to his own. We lost one horse but got six."

Thomas shook his head. "No, Josh. We'll pick the best one from theirs to replace the one we lost. We'll turn the rest of them loose."

My mouth dropped open. "Turn them loose? Thomas, we can use those horses. And it's a cinch *these* men will never need them again."

Thomas shook his head again. "*They're* the thieves, not us. We don't steal, even from dead men."

He had a strange sense of values, my brother did. He could smile while he killed a man. But he wouldn't take that man's horses.

He said, "We'll go back to our own camp now. Come mornin', Muley and me will come over here and give these men a plantin'. I doubt your arm will be in shape for diggin'."

He studied the two dead Mexicans, first one and then the other. "A real pair of cutthroats, weren't they? The first Mexicans we ever saw, and they tried to kill us. Gives us a lot to look forward to when we have to live amongst them in Texas."

"Maybe the others won't be like these, Thomas. These were outlaws."

He didn't even seem to hear me. And if he had, it wouldn't have made any difference. Thomas made his mind up in a hurry. And once made up, it never changed. He grunted. "They're a sorry class of people."

"The other two weren't Mexicans," I argued. "They was from Tennessee."

I had as well have kept my silence. Thomas said, "I told you I could smell them just like wolves. I've already decided one thing, Josh."

"What's that?"

"I'll never trust a Mexican!"

Among the towering pines at the far eastern edge of Mexican Texas, hardly a horse-lathering ride from the international boundary of the Sabine River, Nacogdoches was the gateway. Once it had been a sleepy Spanish village, site of the Mission Nuestra Señora de Guadalupe, trying to bring the *padres'* message of God to the heathen of the woods. Now it was awake and bustling, the gathering place for hopeful immigrants bound for Texas, and for the wishful ones who had gotten that far on nerve and could go no further. It had also become a gathering place for a lawless element that had been run out of the colonies or never had been able to get in. It was a lonely garrison for Colonel José de las Piedras and a comparative handful of homesick soldiers serving hundreds of miles from the villages of their birth. This ancient Spanish town was legally Mexican now, since Mexico had broken away from Spain. But in truth it was actually much more American.

Not long before, General Manuel de Mier y Terán had taken a long, painful look and had found Mexican influence all but gone, except that a lax and corrupt municipal government still functioned on old Mexican customs of bribery and self-interest. "The whole population here is a mixture of strange and incoherent parts without parallel in our federation," he had written worriedly. He was right, for criminals from the old Neutral Ground squatted here, along with a scattering of Indians from many tribes, and French and Spanish creoles, genteel American planters, and raw frontiersmen.

Terán wanted to shut off the immigration of Americans before the situation became worse.

True, through here had passed filibusters and freebooters beyond counting. Here in 1812 had come the Gutierrez-Magee Expedition to invade Texas when it was still a part of Spain. In 1819 Dr. James Long had marched down from Natchez with 300 men and had held Nacogdoches temporarily. In 1826 one Haden Edwards had received permission from Mexico to settle 800 families in Eastern Texas but found himself unable to evict Mexican and American squatters and Cherokee Indians from the land which had been given him. He and his brother Benjamin established themselves in Nacogdoches' old stone fort and proclaimed the Republic of Fredonia. This republic crumbled quickly in the face of Mexican troops, bolstered by militia which Stephen F. Austin raised. Austin was for law and order. The law happened to be Mexican, and he respected it.

Terán had gotten his law. Except for the Austin and Green DeWitt colonies, legal immigration of these blue-eyed foreigners had all but stopped.

Illegal immigration was another matter.

WE BUCKALEWS knew little of this as our wagon groaned into Nacogdoches. Colonel Ames back in Tennessee had mentioned that there had been a mite of trouble once or twice, but he had reckoned it was past history. He had written a letter for us which Thomas in turn had given to an Austin representative in Natchitoches. We had been handed an immigration document with Austin's signature on it to guarantee us clear passage.

Lige had stolen my sorrel to get away that night in the timber west of Natchitoches. Now I rode a young bay gelding which had been Lige's. I had talked Thomas into letting us keep one more horse for Muley. I still felt he had made a mistake in turning the other outlaws' horses loose, but I had to respect his version of what was honest.

Though he sat on the wagon seat beside Thomas, leaning forward eagerly for a view of Nacogdoches, Muley usually did his talking with me. "Looky yonder what a town we're comin' to, Josh. Looks like folks is thicker'n jaybirds at acorn time."

I rode close beside the wagon and nodded, excitement building in me too. At the Sabine River crossing we had officially entered Texas, but somehow the feeling wasn't strong. I couldn't tell that one side of the river looked much different than the other. I knew it was a foolish notion, but somehow I had expected the difference to show right off.

I had expected Nacogdoches to have a Mexican look, though I had no clear idea what a Mexican look was. Again I was disappointed, for I saw few people who appeared to be Mexican. Most were light-skinned, like us. The signs were mostly painted in English.

I had no way of knowing these were the same thoughts which had bothered General Terán, for at that time I hadn't even heard of the man. But we were about to be introduced to the results of Terán's observations.

Thomas's voice was sharp. "Get close to the wagon, Josh. We got company comin'."

Half a dozen horsemen approached, wearing uniforms that had been bright when new but now were faded and wrinkled and browned with grime.

"Didn't expect we'd rate a reception like this," I said.

Thomas frowned. "Raggy-lookin' lot. Mexicans."

He pulled the team to a stop as the soldiers came up. One man circled around and halted beside Thomas, touching his hand to the bill of his cap. His face was a deep brown, his eyes almost black. His uniform had been fancier, once, than the others. He was plainly an officer. His moustache was thick and black, but he was still a young man.

"How do," Thomas said stiffly.

"Buenos días." The Mexican took his time, studying the wagon and the animals trailing it. He spoke, but the words were Spanish and made no sense to us. The Mexican turned in the saddle and called. *"Señor* Charters!"

An American was trailing the soldiers. Astride a fine black horse, he pulled around beside the officer. He gave a courteous nod, exchanged a few words with the Mexican, then turned to us.

"Lieutenant Obregón has not yet mastered the English language. Occasionally I help him. My name is Benjamin D. Charters. I hope I can be of service to you gentlemen."

Thomas was not impressed. "What's he need?" he asked bluntly.

"You gentlemen surely know about the law of 1830, which restricts immigration into Mexico? The lieutenant says he trusts you have some documentary evidence of your right to enter this country."

I studied Charters, trying to discover the reason for Thomas's quick and adverse judgment. Charters spoke with the ease and eloquence of a lawyer. His suit was cut of good cloth and well-tailored, though it had seen better days. Thin at the knees and elbows, frayed at the cuffs and collar, it told of a genteel poverty.

Thomas reached back into the wagon and got the document with Austin's signature. Charters passed it on to the lieutenant. Obregón read it critically and handed it back, shaking his head.

Charters listened to the officer, then explained, "He says this is not enough. You must have another permit to go beyond Nacogdoches."

Thomas reddened. "They told us in Natchitoches this was all we'd need to get us to San Felipe de Austin."

Charters smiled thinly. "This is a long way from Natchitoches. Some of these garrisons make their own laws."

Thomas's eyes hardened. "What else we goin' to need?"

"You need a new order signed by a local military officer to pass you through the guard at the road to San Felipe."

"How do we get this order?"

"It is difficult, usually. The wait is often very long; you know how slow the military can be about these things. However, the lieutenant says he likes your looks and has decided to do you a favor. He has ways of cutting through regulations when the reason is good enough."

Thomas clinched his fist. "He wants money?"

Charters winked. "A bit of coin is like grease on the wheels of progress. All men have their price. I think you'll find that the lieutenant's price is reasonable."

Thomas was speaking quietly now. I could feel the anger rising in his voice. "What he wants is a bribe."

Charters made a pretense of surprise. "I didn't say that. Nobody ever bribes anybody in Mexico. This is simply a sort of hidden tax. Everybody pays it when the occasion arises. They call it *mordida*, the little bite. It is one of the facts of life in Mexico, like ground corn and chili pepper."

"What part do *you* get out of it, Charters?"

Charters began to anger. "You are insulting me, sir. Now, if you don't *want* to go to San Felipe . . ."

"We *are* goin' to San Felipe. And we'll do it without givin' you or this leather-colored parasite a penny."

"I don't see that you have much choice."

"Tell those Mexicans to get theirselves out of our way if they don't want to get run over!"

Charters was livid. "This is Mexico. You're a foreigner here. You'll live up to Mexican laws or suffer the consequences."

"This isn't law, this is a try at robbery. We've been tried once already, on the way down here. It didn't work for *them*; it won't work for you."

"Try to move past these men and you'll be stopped."

"You're not gettin' any money out of *us!*"

Charters regained some control. "Look friend, you could afford to put a little silver across the lieutenant's palm. The Mexican government doesn't pay these men much way out here, and what it *does* pay is often slow in coming. You can't blame these soldiers for taking a little extra."

"It's wrong. I'll rot here before I'll pay."

Charters spoke to the lieutenant. From his looks I thought Obregón might order his men to shoot us down like dogs. I didn't know a word of Spanish then, but I knew pretty well what kind of language he was spitting at us. He hadn't learned it in church. He reined his horse around, savage as an Indian, and signaled his troops to follow him.

Charters spoke crisply. "You'll get tired of sitting here, and you'll come begging to pay. Obregón will take a very *big* bite then; you can count on that." He rode off, following the troopers.

I thought we had been whipped, but Thomas had a stubborn look of victory all over him.

I said, "Thomas, we're in trouble now. Wouldn't it of been easier to've just paid the man a little somethin'?"

"That would have been a compromise."

"What would that hurt? We always got to compromise!"

"Not when it's right against wrong. If you come to a fork in the road, you got to turn either to the left or the right. You can't compromise. You do what's right, or you do what's wrong. Bribery is wrong, whether it's a dollar or a hundred dollars."

I shrugged. "A man can get awful hungry, tryin' to be right all the time." The soldiers were about out of sight. But they weren't out of mind. "How do we get out of here *without* payin'?"

"There aren't many soldiers. Ever try to stop a creek flowin' by stickin' your hand in it? The water just goes right on, between your fingers. I'll ask around, find out where they guard the trails. Then we'll go the long way around. We don't have to follow *their* route. We'll just make our own!"

CHAPTER

5

I DIDN'T REALIZE it then, but our encounter with Lige, Foley, and the two Mexican bandits, followed by our experience with the hungry Lieutenant Obregón in Nacogdoches had been enough to start hatred to gnawing at Thomas. He had always been one to make up his mind in a hurry. From this time on he had a cold contempt for all things Mexican. Strange, how some people so easily form a hate, and how hard it is for them to find a liking for the new and different.

We did what Thomas said—took the long way around and got clear of Nacogdoches. It was so easy I felt sure there must be a catch to it somehow, but there wasn't. We didn't know that many others had done the same thing before us. We found out later there was a trail which had been used by so many contraband immigrants that it had even won its own name, the Tennesseans' Road. There just weren't enough Mexican soldiers to patrol the whole country.

As I said, we didn't know this at the time. We thought the idea was original, and we gloried in getting away with it. Not that what we did was illegal in the strict sense. We had the paper from Austin. We had simply avoided having to pay a bribe. But Mexican views of jurisprudence were different than ours. It could have gone hard with us if we had been caught. That's how it was in Mexico in those days. It wasn't the laws written on paper which really counted; it was the men who administered them. In the end, the law was always what they *said* it was.

IF WRITTEN laws were deceptive, so were maps. A mile doesn't look like much on a piece of paper. But on the ground it is something else. The long, long miles passed endlessly beneath the iron-rimmed wheels, and it seemed San Felipe was still a thousand miles away. I had no clear idea of the vast variety of lands we would pass through on the trip—the rolling prairies abounding in wild horses and many swamps and marshes that bogged the wagons and exhausted kinds of game; thickets and canebrakes so dense that once when we strayed off the trail Muley and I had to walk ahead of the wagon and clear a path with axes so Thomas could pick his way through.

As we crossed the map-marked boundary into Austin's colony, we began to come across small settlements and scattered farms. At once we could tell the difference between the legal colony and the squatter element which had prevailed around Nacogdoches. Plainly, Austin had picked these people with a degree of care. Spring-planted crops were coming up in cleared fields which had been virgin grasslands a few months earlier. Log cabins stood along creek banks where Indians had stalked deer or had gathered the native pecans. Wherever we stopped, we found a welcome, for there was a fraternal element in the pioneering experience which made people draw together instinctively. Most of these early colonists were dirt-poor. Their hospitality was almost embarrassing to us, for they would bake us bread from their scant supplies of corn. They would wrap their precious coffee beans in buckskin and beat them with a rock to brew up a drink for us. They were almost pathetic in their eagerness for news of "the States," and we had so little to tell them.

At last we came through a sandy canebrake river bottom to the edge of the broad and lazy Brazos River. Across the river, atop a high bluff on the west side, perched San Felipe de Austin. Situated at the head of navigation, it was the seat of government for most of colonial Texas.

I was disappointed. "That's it? That's *all* of it?"

Thomas shrugged. "Likely there's more that you can't see on account of the bluff. But I doubt there's really very much. Maybe you been buildin' up too much in your mind."

"I thought it would look Mexican. Log cabins is all I see, the same kind I've seen my whole life long."

Thomas shook his head. "I'd as soon not ever see another Mexican. But they're there, waitin' yonder for us across the river."

I could see them idling at the ferry landing on the other side of the Brazos. An uneasiness started, because I thought this might be where we were going to get caught up with for what we had done at Nacogdoches. But Thomas didn't look worried.

A ferryboat slowly made its way across the river and tied up. Thomas pulled the wagon onto the boat, and we all pitched in to secure it so it wouldn't roll with the motion of the ferry.

The ferryman was one of the swivel-jawed kind. "Sure proud to see young fellers like you-all comin' in. Men of the land. Seems to me like this place has gotten overrun of late with lawyers and the like—soft-handed men. We need more with dirt under their fingernails, the way it was when we first come here with Austin. Yes, sir, I been here pretty near from the first. I was one of Austin's Old Three Hundred. Been a right smart of changes, I can tell you."

I got caught up in his enthusiasm. "It sure is a rich-*lookin'* country, all right. Fish and game like I never saw before. Crops show a heap of promise. And trees—I never knew there was so many different kinds of trees in the whole world. Sure, we miss the comforts we used to have at home, and we may be a long time ever gettin' most of them. But it's a great country for growin' things. You just drop a seed in the ground and stand back out of the way."

Muley took it for gospel and whistled softly to himself. "I sure do want to see *that*!"

The ferryman pointed his chin toward the Mexican soldiers waiting on the west shore. "You-all got to stand inspection yonder."

"We have the papers," Thomas said, frowning. "The Mexicans give you much bother?"

The ferryman spat. "It ain't that they *do* anything, really; it's just that they're *here*, that's all. Used to, when we first come, we had a right-smart of Indian trouble, and we could've used some soldiers to help us. They wouldn't send any. Now that we're strong enough to take care of our own selves, Mexico sends soldiers in. Maybe they're afraid we've gotten too strong. I get the feelin' sometimes that they're watchin' *us*, not the Indians."

I asked, "If the Mexicans are so worried about us Americans, how come they ever let any of us settle here in the first place?"

"To protect Mexican people from the Indians. Americans always did have a reputation as Indian fighters. Mexico figured to put Americans in between the Indians and their own people. Worked pretty good, too. Many a red devil has died of indigestion on a Texian rifle-ball."

That was the first time I had heard the word *Texian*. I sensed it was a way the Anglo settlers here spoke of themselves.

The ferryman moved forward as the ferry neared the shore. "Go see Sam Williams over in Austin's land office. He'll introduce you to Austin."

The Mexican soldiers waited as the wagon pulled out onto the riverbank. The dislike was plain and open in Thomas's face while a Mexican sergeant came forward to look at the paper. It was easy to see that the black-moustached man couldn't read the words. He was going by the official look of it. But he read the dark look in Thomas's eyes. Rapid Spanish passed back and forth among the ill-clad troops. Not understanding a word of it, I realized for a moment just how helpless and alone an outsider would be. It occurred to me that this was one major barrier between the average Mexican and the average Anglo settler, this difference of language.

"Thomas," I said, "one thing I'm goin' to do as soon as I can is to learn to speak Mexican."

Thomas shook his head. "English is good enough for me."

Muley watched the soldiers with lively interest. "You mean a man can *learn* to talk like they do, Josh? I figured you had to be born with it."

Without friendliness, the sergeant waved us on.

IT WAS more of a town than I had supposed, once we passed through the tall-tree fringe—pecan, oak, ash, cottonwood—and came out over the top of the bluff. There we found a growing settlement situated neatly around an open plaza. It was still a young town, for most of the log buildings had not yet grayed with weathering. The axe-hewn timbers of many houses remained bright and unstained. A few buildings were of rough-sawed lumber, which indicated that somewhere in the region—downriver, we learned later—someone had set up a sawmill.

Thomas pulled the team onto a street that bordered the eastern edge of the plaza. We began to discover that the town was better in appearance than in reality. Like a funeral procession, perhaps, great on length but somewhat thin.

A townsman directed us to Austin's office in one end of a double log cabin, which sat near the bank of a small creek. A moss-strewn oak stood in front of it. A roofed-over open section divided the office from the sleeping quarters. A chimney stood at each end of the cabin.

I was a little let down. "This don't look much like the head office of the whole colony of Texas."

Thomas shrugged. "Handsome is as handsome does. I bet the roof don't leak."

Sam Williams met us at the door. We introduced ourselves. Thomas was of a notion to get right down to business, but he had to hold off until Williams heard all the news we had picked up along the trail. In time, however, Thomas was able to hand him the document with Austin's signature. Williams nodded. "To be sure, you'll be wanting a grant of land. Do you have an idea where you'd like to settle?"

I put in, "We've studied the map till we know it backwards. We'd like to go somewheres west."

Williams' eyebrows arched. "Why west?"

"Why not?" asked Thomas. "You still got land to the west, haven't you?"

"Yes, but it's wilder, farther removed from the more settled portions. It puts you in more danger of contact with Indians. In short, it's a long way to civilization."

Thomas said, "We'll just take civilization with us."

Williams glanced from Thomas to me and back again.

He had sized up Muley in the beginning and paid little attention to him now. "If that's your wish, then, we'll go forward on that basis. You understand about the Mexican colonization laws?"

Thomas replied. "Some. Colonel Ames told us."

"What it amounts to is that a family man can receive a *labor* of farming land and a *sitio* of grazing land if he wants to raise stock. A *labor* is 177 acres. A *sitio* is 4,428."

I whistled. We couldn't get that much land together in two lifetimes back home. Here it was almost handed to us.

Williams went on. "There will be some nominal fees, of course, for surveying and other costs. I hope you brought enough cash to cover those."

Thomas nodded. "I hope so, too."

"By law, you two brothers as single men won't quality for a full grant each. We can list you as a family, and you can receive that amount together." Williams pointed his chin at Muley Dodd. "How about *him?*"

Muley spoke up eagerly, "I got money for land, too." He dug into his pockets. "I got three dollars and fifty-two cents."

I shook my head. "Muley, that won't be enough. But don't you fret. You can go with us. Whatever we got, you'll have a share of it."

Muley smiled. "Thanks, Josh. You're a good feller, but there's no need. I got my own money. I want to put in my part."

I glanced at Thomas, but he had nothing to say. I shrugged. "If it'll make you happy, Muley. This way, at least, you got a claim on us." My eyes met Thomas's. "Both of us."

As we poured over Williams' maps, we heard a horse trot up to the front of the cabin. A saddle squeaked in thin protest as a man dismounted. Williams glanced through the glassless window. "It's Colonel Austin."

For weeks now, I had been hearing Austin's name. I guess I expected the man to stand eight feet tall. So, for a moment or two as Austin stood in the doorway, I felt the quick sag of disappointment. In reality, Stephen F. Austin was a rather spare man, and he had to lift his face to look at us, even Muley Dodd. He appeared as if he ate irregularly, and not very well. But strength showed in the care-drawn features, and determination in his dark eyes. Only a strong man would ever have dared start the project Austin had fostered here in Texas, much less carry it through this far against all the adversities of nature, human frailty, and Mexican law.

Williams made the introductions. I shook hands with a certain amount of awe, for Austin was the only famous man I had ever met. I was surprised at the strength of Austin's grip. Those small hands hadn't looked capable of taking hold so tightly. Williams told about the grant we sought, and Thomas had to explain again—somewhat laconically—why he wanted to settle in the west. Austin read the letter of recommendation from Colonel Ames and several other letters from various people back home in Tennessee. He glanced questioningly at Muley.

"Muley's with us," I said quickly. "We'll vouch for him."

Austin seemed to sense Muley's problem without being told. "This can be a fine country for those willing and able to work. It can be death for the incapable."

"Muley's with us," I repeated.

Austin nodded, dismissing the question as having been answered. "You'll not regret that you've come. Texas is wealthy in natural resources—fertile lands, timber, pasturage. I've seen much of the United States, but I've seen nothing as fine as Texas. Nature has supplied us everything we need except population. You, and others like you, are slowly supplying that." He paused, studying us with those dark, keen eyes. "You are unmarried, I see. Later on, as you marry, you can each obtain enough land to fill out your individual allotment to full size. And, of course, as the children come, we get our population. I might add that if you marry a Mexican woman, the law entitles you to even more land."

Thomas said firmly, "No chance of that."

Austin smiled faintly. "I would wager you've seen no Mexican women yet."

Thomas replied, "We've seen some of the men."

Austin's smile broadened. "You would be surprised how many American men have found Mexican women to marry. Some of them are quite pretty. And they have one sterling qualification: they are *here!*" He let that matter drop and frowned as another thought crossed his mind. "Have you men any strong leanings toward politics?"

Thomas shook his head. "We never been noways connected with politics. The Buckalews have always voted for Andrew Jackson. Past that, we just never was interested."

"I had a good reason for asking. Mexico is still unstable. Governments change like the wind. Politics can be a perilous thing here. I've endeavored from the beginning to keep these colonies free of the political pressures that have been the bane of Mexico. But more and more new men are coming in who will not let matters be. More and more, our people are being caught up in the tides of change. It is a dangerous involvement.

"Out where you're going, you'll have some Mexican neighbors. In many ways you'll find them different from yourselves. In some ways, they are much the same. All humans come from the same mold. Be friendly; get to know them. Accept the differences and be grateful for the things in which you are alike.

"But above all, remain aloof from their politics. They are the natives here, and we are the strangers. Mexico still has turbulent times ahead. It will require a steady hand and a careful silence to see us safely through."

6

THE SURVEYOR who tied his horse and pack mule behind our wagon and went along with us was a lean, likeable man named Jared Pounce. He had come with the Old Three Hundred, had a farm of his own, and did outside work ranging from gunsmithing to surveys. There wasn't much loose money around the colonies, except some counterfeit which floated in periodically from the Redlands. A man did whatever honest work he could that would let him clasp his fingers over a bit of coin.

Pounce liked his tobacco. Wadding a home-grown leaf into one corner of his mouth, he studied the wagon with open admiration. "You lads come prepared. I'll sure grant you that. I been here since almost the first, and I still ain't got me a wagon. There's three classes of settlers in Texas these days. The upper class are them that owns a wagon. The next class down uses a sled. And the lower class, they just have to walk and tote their own load. You lads are startin' off in the upper class."

Now that we were getting near it, I began to itch with impatience for a view of our own land. I begrudged every stop we made. But Pounce wouldn't be hurried along the trail.

"Just take it as it comes, boys. Life's too short to spend it in a lope. There's too much to see and learn and enjoy."

Pounce was a born talker, and we were good listeners, especially when the subject was Texas.

"It's hell on women," Pounce said, "but it's God's own country for a man. You wake up every mornin' to a brand new world, especially when you go west where the people ain't thick yet. There it stands, all around you, as fresh and new as if God had just finished makin' it. Big sky, a whole world of room. Air so fresh that it makes you grow younger instead of older. You never saw such a country for huntin', either. You just step out of your door with a rifle in your hand and there's dinner standin' there waitin' for you. You don't even have to drag it far to the cabin.

"They plan these grants so that they front on the water. You'll want to locate on a clear creek so's to have clear water all the time. The Colorado is a mighty river, but she runs muddy. That's what the name comes from, Mexican for *red*. Man has got to let it settle before he drinks it, or he'll have to lay over to let his stomach settle instead."

Thomas asked, "What about Indians, Jared?"

Pounce squeezed one eye shut and peered off to the north thoughtfully. "They'll bear watchin'. They don't bother folks much anymore in the settlements. But now and again they'll skulk around the fringes and do mischief. You boys'll sure be on the fringe."

Thomas nodded. "Austin said we'd have some Mexicans for neighbors. We apt to have trouble with them?"

Pounce shrugged. "Mexicans have got their own ways. You'll find good ones and bad ones and indifferent, like there is amongst the rest of us. There's saints, and there's sinners. I'd say if you don't bother them, they ain't apt to bother you."

I said, "I reckon a man could even make friends with them."

Pounce replied, "Sure, *I* got some Mexican friends, and I got a few Mexican enemies. It's like anyplace else: you got to judge each man separate. Trust them all and you'll get your fingers burnt. Condemn them all and you'll miss some people that would've been good friends. Out here, you'll need all the friends you can get."

We didn't have to do all our own cooking. Pounce had traveled these trails many times and was acquainted with most of the people. He knew where the good cooks lived. Once he pointed to a low-built log cabin with a half a dozen loose hogs rooting in the front yard. "Always pass up this place here. See the black smoke risin' out of the chimney? That old woman burns everything she cooks. And she ain't none too clean, neither."

He was more likely to refer to people by their cooking than by their names. One place was "the corn-dodger woman's." Another belonged to "the deer-meat and honey man."

Deer and wild turkey were so many it seemed the Lord was being wasteful. We always had something to take to a settler's house along with our appetites. Thomas said he didn't like to receive more than he gave, and I reckoned that was an honest way for a man to be. We noted that, particularly among the newer settlers, meat was the main thing on the dinner table, and wild meat at that. A few of the older colonists usually had bread, made of rough-ground corn. We hadn't seen an egg since Louisiana.

I was careful to study the settlers and their ways of living, for their ways would be our ways. Most—but not all—of the men wore buckskins, the women homespun. The houses were mostly of a kind, built of logs. Some, where the family was large, were big double cabins with an open dog-run in the center. Most of the floors were of earth, though here and there we found a cabin with puncheon flooring. That was a mark of comparative wealth. The windows lacked glass but had shutters that could be opened for air or pulled shut to keep out wind, rain, and Indians.

Not everybody had a cabin. At one place we came across a new arrival who hadn't taken time yet to put up any kind of building. He and his wife were still living out of their wagon while they broke the land and got a crop started. There would be a cabin later, when the crop was up.

"That's how it'll be with us, Josh," Thomas said. "We'll likely spend most of this summer sleepin' under the wagon."

"That's what we've done since the day we left home," I said indifferently.

"I like it," Muley put in.

Jared Pounce commented, "Most young men just naturally take to the outdoors. Used to, I could've gone for a year without a roof over my head, and I'd never given it a thought. Now, though, when night comes around I like to look up at the rafters instead of the stars. Sign of age, I reckon."

Time and again we came across grazing bands of wild horses. The best Pounce knew from talking with old-time Mexicans was that these bands had been here for generations. Some said they were descended from horses which had gotten loose or been stolen from Spaniards long ago. Whatever their origin, their reproduction had been remarkable.

"Time or two," said Pounce, "I been reduced to eatin' horsemeat. It ain't so bad, when you got nothin' better to compare by. Some people say it's the heart that rules a man, but they're wrong. It's his stomach."

IN DUE time we hauled up to the Colorado River. As Jared had said, it was red with mud carried in upriver.

"On across," said Jared, "and down to the southwest, is Gonzales. That's the headquarters of the Green DeWitt colony. Above you there's not a lot—a few scattered Americans, some Mexicans. And Indian country."

Standing there, looking out across that muddy river, I felt a deep emotion rolling over me like a flood. I felt a strange joy that I'd never known before, and have never felt again in quite the same way. I sensed that somewhere yonder, not far away now, lay the ground we had been looking for. I knew that soon I would set my boots down on our promised land.

It had been three hours since we had passed the last settler's cabin. We had this all to ourselves. "Thomas," I said, "I got a feelin' about this country. I'm goin' to like it here."

Thomas replied, "We've come too far *not* to like it."

Jared pointed his chin northwards. "Boys, let me make a suggestion to you. One time I was through this neck of the woods on an Indian-chasin' party. Not far from here I came across a place on a creek, as pretty a place as ever I seen. For a long time I kept thinkin' someday I'd come back and take it up. Now I know I never will. It's yours if you want it."

"Show us," Thomas said.

We crossed the river, and we traveled awhile. I knew the place instinctively, even before Jared spoke. I touched spurs to horse and rode ahead across a flat stretch of open ground that one day soon would be a field. Beyond lay an uneven stand of timber along a creek—huge old pecan trees heavy with foliage, rugged live oaks with leaves that would stay green the year around, willow, ash. . . . A buck jerked its antlered head toward me, the startled eyes wide and brown. It bounded away into the timber. Three wild turkeys, disturbed by the deer, moved into a trot, then soared at a low level into the shelter of tangled underbrush.

I rode on without slowing until I came to the bank of the creek. Below me was a deep flow of clear water. Looking around carefully for sign of human life and seeing none, I dismounted and tied the horse to a bush. Then, rifle in my hand, I moved down the bank to the water's edge. I tasted it and found it as good as any in Tennessee.

I returned to the flat and waited there, looking around, until the wagon came up. My spirit soared as it had never done before.

"Thomas," I said, "the trip is over. We're home!"

THE SURVEYING job took a while. Jared knew his business, but he didn't rush. "This is for ever," he said. "We can't afford mistakes."

Jared would carry his compass. Muley and I took turns carrying the chain, while Thomas stood watch nearby on horseback, the rifle across his lap. Not once was there sign of a human being. It couldn't have been lonesomer if we had staked out a claim on the moon. We had wanted the "far back," and this was certainly it.

When Jared's job was finished and the new claim plainly marked on his map, Muley and I ground some of our scant supply of corn into meal as a gift to him.

"Jared," I asked, "do they ever have elections here in Texas?"

He frowned, not sure of the reason for the question.

"Sure, we elect what we call an *ayuntamiento*, a local government."

I said, "If you ever take a notion to run, let me know. I'll vote for you twice."

He wished us good luck on this land he had wanted so long for himself, as he set out a-horseback, his pack mule trailing. Jared would eat his way back to San Felipe.

We hated to see him go, but there was no time to worry about the isolation, for too much work was long overdue. First thing we did after Jared left was to begin breaking ground on the big flat. It was hot, back-breaking work. Thomas and I took turns standing guard while the other one and Muley strained, sweated, and swore behind the heavy wooden plows. We couldn't trust Muley to stand guard. We had tried it, only to see him forget his task and go chasing off with his dog after a rabbit or a deer, or hunting a bee tree.

Weather was hot, and a little on the dry side. With summer on the way, we had to get our seed planted and up to a good stand before the full heat came on, or the corn would wither before it ever made a head. So we kept chopping trees, pulling stumps, breaking ground, and putting in seed. It was years and years ago, but I can still remember the rich smell of that fresh-turned earth, opened to the sun after untold ages of darkness.

We didn't allow ourselves to let up from daylight until dark, except for what little time was necessary to hunt game and prepare meals. Thomas was not content with the field. He broke a garden plot near the spot on the creek where we would put up our cabin.

The day finally came when we had caught up, at least temporarily. The corn was rising, and enough rain had fallen so that it would not parch. Now we could begin thinking about a cabin, to get ourselves in from under the wagon. I wanted it closer to the creek, but Jared Pounce had warned us that wherever the wild pecan trees stood, we could expect flooding every so often. Better to tote water an extra distance than to wake up some morning being toted by it.

We built corrals first, for the livestock, and a low-roofed shed open on the south. Then we began felling trees and squaring them up so they would stack and make a neat fit with a minimum of chinking. Because there had been no sign of intrusion, we loosened our reins on Muley, letting him go out after the game it took to keep us fed. Muley was a fair-to-middling shot, though we had to keep warning him about shooting too near the cabin and scaring the game away.

It was Muley who saw the first Indians.

We had begun snaking the finished logs up to the cabin site. Back home we would have made a community celebration out of a cabin-raising, but here there was no community. It was a job we would have to do for ourselves. We had laid the foundation logs and were saddle-notching the first logs for the cabin sides when Muley came running across the flat, shouting all the way. The spotted dog loped along ahead of him. Muley fell once, sprawling face down in the grass. But he was up again in a second, hardly missing a step.

"It's Injuns, Josh! It's Injuns!"

I ran for my rifle. Thomas stood soberly scanning the scattered timber beyond the flat. "I don't see nothin' chasin' him, Josh. You got to remember, Muley ain't bright."

Muley reached us and fell to his knees, shoulders heaving. Gasping for breath, he half turned to point behind him. The words wouldn't come. He dragged himself on his knees to the wooden water bucket and drank thirstily from the dipper.

"I saw them, Josh!" The words were still difficult to get out.

Thomas kept squinting into the distance. "I don't see anything, Muley. Maybe it was just deer, or some wild horses."

Muley shook his head violently. "No, sir! They were there, a whole bunch of them. On horseback."

Anxiously I asked, "Did they shoot at you, Muley?"

"No, Josh. They just sat there and looked at me. They didn't move. Didn't even say howdy." He paused. "I didn't say howdy, neither. I just lit out a-runnin'."

Thomas moved toward his rifle now. "It was likely his imagination, but we better go see."

I slung powder horn and shot pouch over my shoulder and saddled my horse. Muley and Thomas did the same, Muley still trembling from his scare. He pointed the way for us to go, but he was careful not to ride out in front. We skirted the newly-broken field and moved through scattered oak trees. We keep clear of underbrush where a red man might hide, though we scouted it for tracks. For a time Muley was positive where he had seen the Indians. But after a while he began to fidget uncertainly. I knew the signs well enough: Muley was lost.

Thomas had doubted from the first, and now I began doubting too. Muley sensed it, for he started pleading: "They was there, Josh. They was as real as you and me and that spotted dog. He barked at them. He wouldn't bark if they wasn't real, would he?"

I shook my head. "No, Muley, he wouldn't." But the dog would bark at almost anything that moved. And it could have been anything.

We scouted and circled and saw nothing. At length Thomas pulled up. "We're wastin' our time, Josh."

Muley kept pleading, but I agreed with Thomas. "Sure, Muley," I said, trying to pacify him. "You saw them, but they've gone now."

We started back. I kept my gaze on the ground, looking for tracks. I didn't expect to see them. But suddenly, there they were. "Thomas, here's Muley's tracks when he was runnin' for home. You can see for yourself, he was travelin' pretty fast."

Thomas nodded. I said, "Let's backtrack them a ways. Can't hurt nothin' to do that. We can spare a little time."

Thomas didn't want to, but he gave in. "Let's hurry. We need to be gettin' that cabin up."

Taking the lead, I followed the sign of Muley's head-long rush. Presently Muley shouted, "Yonder's the place, Josh! Yonder's where I seen them at!"

A chill ran down my back, and for some reason the doubt left me. My grip tightened on the rifle. "Hang back a little, Thomas. Keep me covered."

I touched my heels to the horse's ribs and started ahead, nerves tightening.

Muley shouted. "That tree yonder, Josh. That's where they was."

Slowly I rode to a huge old live oak. I found the sign there, plain and fresh. There *had* been horses here—two of them. I called for Thomas and Muley to come up. Thomas studied the sign. "Wild horses, maybe."

I shook my head. "Not wild horses. I can feel it, Thomas."

Thomas nodded, after a moment. "So can I. It was Indians."

I pointed out, "They didn't shoot at Muley. Maybe they were friendly."

Thomas said grimly, "There were friendly Indians in Tennessee too, in Papa's time. But there was a heap of unfriendly ones. You couldn't hardly tell them apart till it was too late. Got so folks quit takin' any chances. The dead ones you could trust."

I glanced back at Muley. "Thomas, you're always too hard on Muley. You'll have to admit, he was right about this."

Thomas shook his head. "You don't have to have any sense to see Indians."

I fingered the rifle a long time. My hands had trembled awhile, but now they were steady again. The excitement had gone. "Well, we oughtn't to be surprised none. Folks told us there would likely be Indians. We won't leave here just because they showed up."

Thomas frowned. "No, Josh. Indians go with new land and westering, just like snakebite and the fever. We come to stay!"

CHAPTER

7

AFTER THAT we built the corral fence a little higher, and we rushed our construction work. To clear the view and help reduce the chance of surprise attack, we cut down most of the trees that stood near the rising cabin. When we weren't using the horses in the daytime, we staked them on fresh grass at the end of a long rope. At night we never failed to bring them into the corral and tie the gate shut with rawhide.

Several nights the spotted dog's barking woke us up, afraid Indian horse thieves were trying to open the corral. But always it turned out to be no more than a skunk or a coon, or at most a grazing deer.

One night the dog did not bark at all. Next morning Thomas went out to milk the cows and found fresh moccasin tracks near the corral.

Why the Indians hadn't taken the horses, we didn't know. "If they come stealin'," he said, frowning at Muley, "the first thing they'll take will be the watchdog. That hound of yours is cowardly and no-account."

Muley threw his arms protectively around the dog's neck. "He's a good dog. Sure enough, he is. You ain't fixin' to do somethin' to him, are you?"

Thomas left it to me to reassure Muley. "No, don't fret over that.

But someday when we get time to visit the neighbors we'll see if we can't get him some company. We need a dog around here we can depend on."

The time finally came when the cabin was up, the chimney finished, logs rived for clapboard shingles, and the roof covered over so that it wouldn't leak badly in the rain. They always leaked a little, those days. The field had been hoed and the garden work caught up with. The corn was coming along nicely.

"Thomas," I said, "don't you think we ought to go now and get acquainted with the neighbors we haven't met yet? When the crops start to ripenin', we'll be busy again."

Thomas replied, "We've got along pretty good so far without worryin' about neighbors."

"But we might need them someday, and maybe they'll need us. We ought to get acquainted."

We had met the neighbors on the colony side as we came up here, unless of course some more had come in behind us. According to the map we had copied from Pounce's, the nearest neighbors upriver bore the name of Hernandez. I could tell that wasn't Irish.

Thomas grumbled, "I'd as soon not have any truck with Mexicans. I don't see how any good could come of it."

"They're there," I argued. "I don't expect they'll move away just because we've come. And like Jared said, we'll need all the friends we can get." The truth was, I was curious.

"Chances are we couldn't understand them noway. We'd have to make sign talk, like a bunch of Indians."

"Our rifles speak the same language. Mexicans or not, we'd want them with us if we ever have Indian trouble."

That kind of talk reached Thomas when nothing else would.

"We'll go," he said reluctantly.

We took Muley along, afraid to leave him by himself. We also took the extra horse, leading him for a pack animal. It wasn't so much that he was actually needed, but it didn't seem wise to leave him at home unattended if somebody with feathers in his hair should drop by to call. Anyway, before we reached the Hernandez place we might shoot a deer or two, as a courtesy. The extra horse would be handy to pack in the meat.

We found the country west of us to be much the same as our own—rolling hills with scattered oak and other timber, wide valleys with the grass so tall the seedheads brushed the soles of our shoes as we rode through it on horseback. The grass was still green at the base but maturing now in the summer sun. It was not as lush as in Tennessee, but the look and feel of it showed it was strong.

The cattle along the way confirmed that. They were in good flesh. These were wild-natured cattle of every color in the rainbow, with long horns and long legs that carried them with almost the swiftness of deer.

"Notice somethin' about these cattle, Thomas? They every one got a fire-brand on their hip. And it's always the same brand. Short of an H, done up stylish. H for Hernandez, I reckon."

Thomas was not impressed. "This far out, what difference would it make who they belonged to?"

"I'll bet they can drive these cattle down to the settlements and sell them for beef."

Interest sparked in Thomas's eyes. "You may have an idea, Josh. I'd put up my horse against Muley's spotted dog that these are plain wild cattle that was runnin' free. These Mexicans just gathered them and put their brand on them and made them theirs. We could do that too."

"Take them away from the Mexicans?"

"No, I don't mean that. But we could hunt down wild cattle and burn our brand on them and bring them down to our place. With our three cows and a bull, it's goin' to take us a long time to get a herd together. This way, we could rush things a right smart."

One of our cows had dropped a calf just after we had gotten here. Another had calved just a couple of days back. Thomas was right. Nature's way would be slow.

I said, "Maybe the Mexicans will teach us how they do it."

Thomas shook his head. "We can learn by ourselves."

I nodded, but the thought ran through my mind that I was going to ask anyway, if these Mexicans were friendly, and if we could find some way to talk to them.

Muley and I fell to talking. That is, Muley talked and I listened, about the deer and the wild turkeys and a coon that had gotten into the cabin. Gradually we dropped back somewhat behind Thomas. He rode up over a rise and pulled his horse to a sudden stop. He motioned excitedly for us to stay back. Slowly, carefully, Thomas slipped off of his horse. He motioned again for us to stay back, but I wouldn't have done it for a sackful of silver. I dismounted and moved up, leading my horse. Muley's eyes were wide with wonder as he came along behind me.

"What is it, Thomas?" Muley called innocently.

If Thomas could have found a quiet way to kill him, he might have done it then and there. He put his finger to his lips, then drew it slowly and pointedly across his throat. He turned angrily on me. "Why didn't you do what I told you?"

"Because I want to see."

What I saw made the hair bristle around my collar. Down in a flat, two men rode along horseback, side by side, rifles in their hands, ready to fire in an instant. Flanking them rode six Indians, three on each side. Two of the Indians carried lances. One had a gun of some sort. The other three held bows, with arrows strung and ready to loose. They moved in silent, patient menace.

"Cat and mouse," said Thomas. "They know they got those men in a trap, so now they're playin' it like a game."

"Six against two." A chill ran through me. "They could finish it in a second."

"They're wonderin' a little, though. Those two fellers have each got one shot to fire. When they die, they'll likely take a couple of Indians with them. That's what's holdin' the redskins off." He said it with calm detachment, as if what we watched were nothing more than a good checker game.

"Thomas, there's three of us. That would narrow the odds."

"It would if those were white men. But they're just a couple of Mexicans."

"That doesn't make any difference."

"It does to me. When my time comes to die, I want it to be for somethin' important. I say let the Mexicans take care of their own."

I put my foot into the stirrup. "Then you just sit here!"

Thomas caught my arm. "You're not goin' down there. It's not our put-in."

Muley's face paled. "Josh, don't you go and leave me."

I said, "You stay with Thomas."

Muley protested, "I want to stay with you, Josh."

Thomas didn't often swear, but he swore now at me. "You're as simple-minded as Muley is. But if you're bound and determined, I won't let you go by yourself and get killed." He swung onto his horse, his face twisted. "Just remember if these Mexicans slit our throats someday, this was your idea."

We put Muley in the middle, where he might be less of a hazard to himself and to us. Then, riding abreast, we walked our horses over the crest and started down the other side.

One of the lance-carrying Indians spotted us before we got down to the flat. He shouted and waved the lance. The Indians halted. The two Mexicans immediately turned their horses so that the men were back to back, facing out and ready to fire instantly in any direction. An Indian loosed an arrow. It missed us by a long way. I held my breath as we kept riding, the rifles cradled in our arms. I could see Muley's face whitening.

"Don't show them you're scared, Muley."

"I *am* scared."

"So am I, but we don't want them to know it."

"I'll try to grin at them, Josh."

The Indians stood their ground but loosed no more arrows at us. Thirty feet from them, Thomas said, "We better stop here."

We stopped, our rifles pointed at the Indians.

For a minute or two it was a contest of wills. They tried to stare us down. We stared back. At last one of the Indians spoke in a sharp voice. The six pulled their horses around and started away in a long trot.

One of the Mexicans shouted something I couldn't understand. They quickly stepped down from their saddles. "Down!" Thomas barked. Fifty yards away the Indians suddenly stopped and whirled around. The one who had a gun fired it. The ball fell short. The others loosed their arrows. One of the Mexican horses fell kicking and screaming.

Again the Indians wheeled and moved into a lope, away from us.

The horse threshed, an arrow in its flank. The Mexican waited until the horse laid its head upon the ground, then lowered his rifle and fired point blank. He turned gravely toward us and removed his big-brimmed hat. *"Grácias, señores."*

Thomas made no reply, so I did it. "Mister, I don't know what you're sayin', and I'm sorry about that."

The Mexican was in his early twenties, his face a light brown, his eyes black. The other was much younger, about sixteen. Their resemblance indicated that they were brothers. The older one made a weak attempt at a smile and gave it up. He was beginning to tremble now, the after-shock starting to reach him. "Too much excitement. I forgot, you do not understand."

I glanced at Thomas. "He speaks American."

The Mexican shook my hand, and I could feel the cold sweat on his palm. "I am called Ramón Hernandez. I speak a little, only, of the English."

"I'm Josh Buckalew, and I don't speak Mexican atall. That yonder is my brother Thomas. The other feller is Muley Dodd."

Muley shook hands. Thomas only nodded, staying where he was, aloof and vaguely disapproving. Hernandez turned to his brother. "And this is Felix."

Felix was quivering. The full weight of the experience had come crashing down on him. He settled to the ground and knelt with his shoulders shaking uncontrollably. He crossed himself. The older brother moved up beside him and spoke to him in a gentle voice.

"For Felix," he said apologetically, "this is the first time death is come so close. He can smell its breath."

I remembered how I had felt that night we fought the outlaws near Natchitoches. I could sympathize.

The Indians had disappeared. "You have much trouble with them?" I asked.

Ramón Hernandez shook his head. "Not many times. Most time they just want to steal horses. Today these young Indians, they find two Mexicans and think *Ay*, why not get two scalps to take home, show women. Very easy, he thinks. Comanche, he does not fight much when he is not sure he wins. You come, he goes."

"They might come back."

Ramón shrugged. "Maybe not for months again." He watched his brother as the boy regained his composure. "Where you come from?" he asked me.

I said, "We're neighbors. We got land, yonderways."

Ramón nodded, pleased. "Good to have people here. When some day we have enough people, Indians come no more."

He helped Felix to his feet. Felix gave us a shy, half-ashamed grin. He said something we didn't understand, and Ramón told us he was apologizing for acting like a woman. It would never happen again, he promised.

Ramón said, "Felix and me, we take you home with us. We want family to see you."

I could tell Thomas didn't like it, but I said, "We'd be right tickled."

Ramón smiled. "We will be friends. Maybe you teach me better the English."

I said, "Ain't no doubt about that. Time I get through ateachin' you, there won't be no college professor that talks better. Now, whichaway's the house?"

THE HERNANDEZ house blended into the land, and I didn't even see it at first. It was long and squat, almost flat-roofed, its walls of rock and its roof held up by timbers dragged from the banks of a creek nearby. Smaller houses and sheds clustered around the main house, all within easy running distance in case of attack. We rode through a scattering of cattle and passed a band of small native horses and little Mexican mules, these loose-herded on grass by a boy of ten or so. Half a dozen milk goats followed along, eyeing us with curiosity.

In a flat stretch of open ground beyond the house, a man and a boy with wooden plows and a mule apiece worked a field where young corn was up to a good stand. Nearer the house, women and small girls hoed a garden. They all stopped work to stare at us.

Ramón pointed toward an opening in the heavy corral, which was built of live-oak limbs stacked and wedged between pairs of stout posts. We rode in. A pair of boys came running at Ramón's call. He spoke to them in a fast-clipped Spanish that I could only marvel over. That language, I thought, was going to be a booger to learn.

We followed Ramón's lead and unsaddled. As we started toward the house, Felix and Muley somehow seemed to fall in with each other. Thomas followed along behind, making it plain he was not keen on any part of this.

Near the front door were two homemade crates, each containing a game rooster. The Mexican people all loved a cockfight.

"*Mamá,*" Ramón called. "*Tenemos huéspedes.*"

An elderly woman appeared in the open door of the long rock house, her brown hand up over her eyes. She peered out beyond the broad brush arbor that served in lieu of a porch. She greeted us cordially, even before Ramón began to tell her what had happened. I heard her gasp the word, "*Indios,*" and knew it meant Indians.

She came first to me, then to Muley, and finally to the flustered Thomas, kissing each of us in turn.

Hat off, I had to crouch a little to follow her into the house. Mexicans were inclined toward smallness, and so were their houses. Ramón pointed to several hand-made wooden chairs that had rawhide seats. "Please, it is not much. But sit. Be to home. This house is your house." When we were seated he said, "*Mamá* will bring you to drink. I bring the family."

As the gray-haired mother bustled about excitedly, I took a long look at the room. The house was stoutly built but Spartanly furnished. Almost everything appeared hand-built, probably right here. The rock walls were mostly bare, except for a few clothes pegs and a crude carved crucifix prominently displayed. Heavy shutters were hung inside each windowsill, with a bar which could be dropped to secure them. In each shutter was a small leather-hinged porthole, rifle-size.

"This is more than just a house, Thomas. This is a fort."

Thomas shook his head. "It don't look like much to me." Señora Hernandez brought black coffee. Coffee was very scarce out here. I knew she was cutting into a long-saved supply for us.

Ramón came back, trailed by half a dozen youngsters. "I want you to meet my brothers and sisters." He lined them up by ages, ranging from a boy of six or seven up to a pretty, black-eyed girl I guessed to be fourteen, or maybe fifteen. She was still lank and a little awkward, but in a year or two the woman would begin showing through. *Then* there would be visitors a-plenty to the Hernandez' door.

Ramón counted them off. "Here we have Enrique, Consuelo, José, Margarita, Alfredo, and María." He looked back over his shoulder. "Teresa! *Dónde-estás*, Teresa?"

My heart leaped as a girl walked in. Girl? She was a woman, the most beautiful woman I had ever seen.

Ramón said proudly, "Teresa is the oldest of the sisters."

Teresa bowed. I started to put out my hand but didn't know whether I was supposed to shake hands with her or not. I pulled it back, the color rising in my face. "Howdy, Miss Teresa."

Her answer was in Spanish. Disappointment touched me, for we wouldn't be able to talk to each other. Not, at least, until I learned Spanish. And suddenly I knew I was going to learn in a hurry.

A shadow fell across the open doorway. Another brother stood there, one I judged to be nearly as old as Ramón. He scowled, his gaze touching first Thomas, then Muley, then me. He said something in a sharp voice.

Ramón's smile dimmed, but he managed to hold part of it. He said, "This is my brother Antonio. Next to me, he is the oldest. Next to me, he runs the family since our father is gone. *Next to me.*" He said something sharp to Antonio, and Antonio quit scowling.

Ramón retold for the brothers and sisters what had happened to him and Felix. I found Teresa watching me, and my gaze dropped away from her. It was the younger girl, María, who stepped forward and stood almost toe-to-toe with me. She spoke words I could not understand, but I could read the gratitude in her eyes.

Ramón explained. "María, she says she wish to speak English, so she can say to you how much thanks she has in her heart."

I said, "Tell her, Ramón, that I'll come over here as often as I can. I'll teach her to talk American." I glanced shyly toward Teresa. "I'll teach all of those who want to learn."

Ramón translated. María clapped her hands. I found Teresa smiling. This time I kept my nerve and returned the smile.

Antonio did not miss the look that passed between Teresa and me. He spoke in anger. Ramón answered him in words that cut like a whip. Antonio's eyes pierced me with hostility. He pointed first at me, then at Teresa, and said something more. Then he turned on his heel and strode out of the house.

I saw Teresa drop her gaze, hurt.

"What was that all about?" I asked.

Ramón's face was darker than it had been. "Antonio has a strong mind. He does not like Americans."

Thomas spoke for the first time, belligerently. "What's wrong with Americans?"

Ramón shrugged. "For me, nothing. I have *Americano* friends.
They teach me this little English I speak. I learn much from them,
and I hope teach them a little. But Antonio is like some others of my
people—he hates those who are not the same as he is."

I offered, "Maybe some American did him dirty."

Ramón shook his head. "No, but he thinks they will, someday. So
he hates *now*."

Thomas snorted. "That's a hell of a thing, hatin' us for no cause."

The thought ran through my mind that Antonio was no different
in that respect than Thomas. My brother must have read the
thought in my eyes. "It's not the same thing," he said defensively.

"Ain't it?"

I glanced again at Teresa and found she had turned her face away.
"Ramón," I said, "Antonio said somethin' about Teresa and me."

"It is not important."

"He must have thought so."

Ramón shrugged. "He says I should tell you Teresa is—how you
say?—promised. She has a man who will be her husband."

That came like a dash of cold water in my face. But I tried to keep
it from showing.

Ramón said, "Many years ago it is decided, by our father and by
the father of Diego Esquivel."

My mouth dropped open. "They decided? Didn't she have any
say-so?"

"She was only a child. This is a matter for the fathers."

"It don't hardly seem fair to her . . ."

"Diego is a good man. Good friend of mine."

"Does she love him?"

Ramón shrugged again. "One learns to love, as one learns to
speak English, or Spanish. It is the way of our fathers."

Thomas muttered, "I don't see why it should make any difference
to you, Josh."

But I looked into the beautiful eyes of Teresa Hernandez, and I
knew it was going to matter to me. It was going to matter a lot.

CHAPTER

8

THE PEOPLE kept coming, some with proper papers and some without. Legal or contraband, they trekked across Texas in a hungry search for a fresh start, for land of their own. It was a restless time, a reaching time. Men prowled and hunted until they found what they liked, and then they planted their boots there and claimed it. Sometimes Mexican soldiers came and moved them on, but more often no one came, no one challenged, for the land was still broad and open, and there was room for so many more. What did it matter to a man what was written on paper five hundred miles away when he could reach down right here and scoop up a handful of black earth and almost feel the life throbbing in it? Who cared whether government spoke Spanish or English when the sky was big and blue and the land called out to a man in a voice that touched the soul?

They were all kinds, these early Texians. Most of them came to farm and raise their families and mind their own business. They came seeking peace and opportunity, not a fight.

But there were some who seemed to be looking for trouble from the time they dropped their saddles to the grass and claimed their ground. Four miles to the south of us, three men made camp and started clearing the land. Two were young brothers, Jacob and

Ezekiel Phipps, late of Kentucky. They had come to Texas for the same reasons we had—their father had sent them in search of a virgin land, just as he himself had searched a generation before. They were a decent pair—loud but basically honest—with one bad weakness: they were easily led.

And leading them was a shouting, cursing, irascible old reprobate named Alfred Noonan. Stocky, red-faced, he had been in Texas several times, off and on, through the last ten years. He told us something he evidently had not chosen to tell any of the authorities who granted him his land: once he had smuggled forbidden trade goods down into Mexico. During this enterprise he had been hounded and hunted and shot at by Mexican soldiers, so he nursed a virulent hatred of Mexicans in general and officials in particular. He had managed to rub off this feeling onto the Phipps brothers, though neither of them had ever seen enough Mexicans to count on their fingers—if, in fact, they could count at all.

Thomas, of course, had already developed a strong dislike for Mexicans. So he fell in with Noonan and the Phipps brothers like a thirsty duck that has found a water hole.

We all went down to help them raise their cabin. By the time that job was done I'd had enough of Noonan to last me for twenty years. I never went back. But Thomas went often, and sometimes they came to our cabin.

I could always predict what Noonan would say. "She's too good of a country to be run by a bunch of ignorant Mexicans. I say the United States ought to wade in here with an army and just naturally take over the whole shebang."

When Thomas and Noonan got started talking, it was always a marathon of sedition, with the Phipps brothers eagerly joining in like a pair of young coon dogs following the older hounds. Seemed Noonan always knew of a revolution brewing somewhere down in Mexico—there had been a lot of them—and he was full of ideas about how he and Thomas and the Phipps boys could smuggle guns in there and get rich.

I tried to tell Thomas he ought to steer clear of the old man. Thomas would simply shake his head. "It's all just talk—you ought to be able to tell that. Ain't none of it ever goin' to come to pass."

"This is dangerous talk. You know what Colonel Austin said about us gettin' mixed up in Mexican politics."

"I'd rather be mixed up in their politics than mixed up in their families. The kind of friends *you* got, you have no call to be talkin' about mine."

The argument always came down to that, sooner or later. I'd been going over to the Hernandez *rancho* often. I always tried to explain to Thomas that I was only going so I could learn to talk Mexican, and to teach the Hernandez family how to speak American. But Thomas figured all along that my main interest was in Teresa Hernandez.

And he was right.

María, fifteen, was the best learner. She picked up English faster than any of the others excepting Ramón, of course, who already had a fair knowledge of it. María showed so much interest in learning that Ramón helped her when I wasn't there. That way, she had a long head start on the others.

Teresa was learning English, too. But English was only her secondary interest in the lessons, as Spanish was mine.

Muley always went with me. He never did really get the hang of Spanish; his mind just wasn't bent toward learning. Yet, it always amazed me how he got along with the smaller members of the Hernandez family. They communicated through act and expression, rather than through the words they said. In the years since, I've seen Mexican and American kids get along like cousins without either really knowing a word the other spoke. There's an understanding between children that has nothing to do with words. And Muley, in many ways, was a child. He always would be.

Language wasn't important to Teresa and me, either. We understood each other without stumbling over the problems of translation. A glance, a quick touching of the fingertips when nobody was looking . . . we didn't really need to talk.

The trouble was, though, that we were never alone. Always, someone managed to be nearby, letting us know we were watched. Often it was her mother, sometimes one of the brothers or sisters. Occasionally it was the smoldering Antonio, hating me because my eyes were blue and my skin was light, making it plain that he never intended either of us to forget Teresa was already promised.

Neither did Thomas. He pointed it out every time I started toward the Hernandez place, and he would repeat it when I got back.

Back in Tennessee I had usually taken whatever advice appealed to me, and let the rest alone. I didn't change my ways much in Texas. I let Thomas advise me about planting and plowing and such, but when it came to Teresa I just didn't figure he knew much.

Through the long summer I kept going, and I kept learning. I got so I understood Spanish tolerably well.

I learned more than language. Ramón and Felix taught me a lot about their way of handling the wild native cattle. They taught me the fundamentals of using the rawhide *reata* to catch animals, and I practiced it until I was a fair-to-middling hand. I learned how the Mexicans captured wild cattle and took the vinegar out of them, fire-branding them with a hot iron that stamped a permanent claim of ownership on them.

The Hernandez brothers hated working in the fields and did as little of it as they could get by with. They enjoyed breaking wild horses to ride, or gathering wild cattle and putting their brand on them. That was hard work, but it had an excitement to it that a man never found behind a plow.

Even there, I found there were basic differences between my outlook and that of Ramón Hernandez. Sometimes it would be only the middle of the afternoon and there would still be plenty of cattle nearby for the taking. But he would hold up his hand and say:

"Enough. It has been a good day. One does not want to be greedy."

"Ramón," I would argue, "it's a long time till dark. Why quit now?" Usually I would talk to him in English and he would answer me in Spanish, for that way each of us would express himself best and still be understood.

"Work was made for the convenience of man, and not man for the work. Besides, over that hill lies the home of the most beautiful Gloria Vasquez, and I would like to go and pay my respects. After all, she might one day be the mother of my sons."

Other times it might be Catarina Torres, or Silvia Martinez y Flores, or Margarita Sanchez. No matter. He was always watching for the woman who would be his wife. He said he did not know yet what she looked like, but he thought he would know her when she crossed his path.

Felix would smile and shrug as if to say he and I might as well go home.

Thomas never would admit that anything good came from my being around the Mexicans. But he was quick to pick up the use of the *reata* and the cattle-handling skill I had learned from the Hernandez men—Ramón, Felix, and Antonio. Yes, even Antonio. For, to give the devil his due, I guess Antonio was the best cowman of them all, and horseman too. If he hated hard, he also worked hard . . . harder than Ramón.

It was as if his hatred gave him a special drive. Thomas had that drive too. It crossed my mind often that Thomas and Antonio had a lot in common, but of course they would not ever stop and compare.

In time, Thomas and Muley and I had a fair-sized bunch of cattle with our own brand on them, cattle whose ancestors had strayed from the pastures of the Spanish missions and had gone the way of the wild herds. Come fall, we would pick out the fattest and drive them down to the settlements to trade for supplies, and maybe even a little coin.

I mentioned Felix. He was a year older than María, just at the age when he was looking for somebody to follow. One time it would be the grinning Ramón. Another, it would be the brooding Antonio, who had a way of making a sunny day dark. If Felix was dark and morose, he was following Antonio. If he was joking and enjoying himself, it was Ramón day.

A constant rivalry existed between the older brothers, each trying to bring Felix into his own camp to stay. I sensed that there probably had been a rivalry of one kind or another between Ramón and Antonio from the time Antonio had first grown big enough to hurl a rock in anger.

It pleased me to see that Felix followed Ramón more than he followed Antonio. Felix had the makings of a good man, if he didn't choose wrong.

FROM WHAT Ramón told me about Diego Esquivel, the man Teresa was pledged to marry, he sounded all right. Under different circumstances I wouldn't have hated him. But I lay awake nights, tortured by the thought of his taking Teresa in forced marriage, closing the door behind them and shutting her out of my life. It didn't help much that Ramón said Diego was none too ready for marriage himself. Esquivel was enjoying all the pleasures and privileges of bachelorhood and, among the gay young maidens of Bexar, these were considerable. He had seen Teresa but few times in recent years and had no more romantic interest in her than he might have had in any pretty girl.

Yet I knew that her beauty would quickly develop that interest, once she was his wife. Worse—she might even learn to enjoy his love, eventually. He would have what I had not even dared hope for. Though the sight of Teresa fired my blood, I had had nothing more from her than her smiles and fleeting touches of her hand. Not once had I ever been able to kiss her.

Except for Antonio Hernandez, I might have had a chance. The rest of the family liked me. There was, of course, the old family tradition of the arranged marriage. Even this we might have worked out in some honorable way, had I been allowed the opportunity to reason with Diego Esquivel.

Always there was Antonio and that implacable hatred, standing like a barred door between Teresa and me. I should have expected the thing he did, but it came as a surprise.

One day when Muley and I rode in to the Hernandez place, we found the family strangely silent. María, who usually met me at the door, smiling, only glanced in sadness, then turned away. Teresa was in the front room. I saw tears as her eyes met mine.

"Teresa, what's wrong?"

She ran, crying.

Ramón took my arm. "Josh . . . friend . . . let us go out into the cool of the arbor. We have something to talk about."

I sent Muley to play with the kids, because that was why he came.

Ramón was grave. "First of all, let us be honest. For a long time we have known of your feeling for Teresa. And we have known she felt strongly about you. But you were told from the first that she was promised, in the manner of our people. Perhaps we should have done something to stop this at the beginning, when there would have been little pain. But you were our friend, and we did not know how. Now there is no choice. The pain has to come.

"Do not ask me why Antonio hates you. Do not even ask him, for he does not know, except that you are of one people and we are of another. He has not liked what has happened between you and Teresa. He has taken it upon himself to stop it. He went to Bexar. He talked with Diego Esquivel, and together they planned the wedding. Diego is on his way here now, with his family and the priest. The wedding will be tomorrow."

It was as if he had slashed me with a knife.

"Ramón, she doesn't love him. She doesn't even know him."

Ramón shrugged. "What can be done? It is the tradition. Love comes, and love goes. But tradition lasts forever."

"To hell with tradition. I love her, and she loves me!"

"She will learn to love Diego. It is our people's way."

"I'll take her away from here. I'll make her one of *my* people."

Ramón shook his head. "You cannot do that. She has too much honor to go against the wishes of her father, rest his soul."

I pushed to my feet and strode into the house, Ramón following. I found Mrs. Hernandez in the front room with Teresa and Antonio, watching me worriedly. I spoke in the best Spanish I knew.

"Teresa, this is not going to happen. I'm not going to allow it. You're going to marry *me*!"

Her mother stood silent, shocked beyond speaking. But Antonio's voice lashed at me. "Away from here, American! Teresa is not yours, and she will never be yours! She stays among her own."

I grabbed Teresa's hand. "Come on, I'm taking you away."

I didn't even see the knife until Teresa screamed. There was a blur of a hand, the flash of the blade. He held the point against my throat. It burned like fire. Antonio's voice was as sharp as the steel. "I would see both of you dead first. Turn loose her hand, American, or you die right now!"

His black eyes seethed. He meant exactly what he said. Teresa jerked her hand away and screamed, "Antonio, no!"

Ramón stopped it. "Put the knife away, Antonio!" His voice was quiet, but it carried an authority that penetrated even the fury of Antonio Hernandez. Antonio lowered the knife. I could see a small spot of red on the point, and I could feel a burning where he had brought the blood.

Ramón turned to me. "Josh, we have enjoyed your company here many times. We had hoped nothing would ever come between us to spoil it. But now we must ask you to leave. We must keep the door shut against you until the wedding is over and Teresa is gone. Please go now, and go quietly."

That was it, courteous but to the point. The Mexican people had a courtly way of telling you to go to hell.

There seemed little choice at the moment. I would have to hurt someone—maybe even kill—to get Teresa out of here now. I backed toward the door.

"Wait for me, Teresa. I'll come for you."

Antonio gritted, "Come back and you will be buried here!"

Ramón said, "Please go, Josh. Lose gracefully, so we may still be friends."

I said, "I haven't lost yet."

ALL THE way home I tried to decide what I was going to do. I couldn't develop any definite plan. All I knew was that after dark I was going back, and somehow I was going to break Teresa out of there. Maybe I could get Thomas to help me. And if he wouldn't, I had friends downriver who would.

It was nearly dark when Muley and I reached the cabin. Thomas had the cow milked and the horses penned. I saw three extra horses in the corral.

Muley saw them too. "The Phipps boys are here. And that old man Noonan. He sure does talk a right smart, don't he, Josh? Half the time I don't know what he's talkin' about."

"Neither does he."

The dog set in to barking and brought Thomas to the door, rifle in his hand. It was always like that with Muley's dog: bark when there wasn't any need for it, and hide when he should be making a racket. Thomas said, "Wasn't lookin' for you back. Thought you'd spend the night with them Mexicans again."

I could tell by the sound of his voice that he and Noonan had been talking, and he was in a mood to argue with me about the Hernandez family. I was in no temper for it.

"Thomas, I got to talk to you, and I got to do it right now." I saw the visitors come to the door, their curiosity aroused. "Out in the corral. By ourselves."

Thomas glanced at his company and said he'd be back directly. He followed Muley and me to the corral. I unsaddled and waited until Muley had done the same. "Go on to the house, Muley."

He protested. "I don't want to have to listen to old man Noonan."

"Go listen to him anyway."

Muley grumbled and walked off. I told Thomas that Diego Esquivel was on his way to marry Teresa. Thomas nodded in satisfaction. "Well, maybe now you can set your mind on your plowin'."

"But he's not goin' to marry her. I am."

"How you figure that? I don't expect them Mexicans are goin' to throw roses in your path and tell you to come take her."

"I'm takin' fresh horses, and I'm goin' back to get her tonight. I'm goin' to break her out of there. I want you to help me, Thomas."

"Me? Are you crazy?"

"You're my brother, Thomas. I've never asked you for much. I know you don't agree with me about Teresa, but I hope you'll be a big enough man to put that aside now and help me."

A deep frown creased his face. "Josh, goin' over there and lovin' her up is one thing. Actually marryin' her is somethin' else."

"I'm goin' to do it, with your help or without it. I just hoped it would be with your help."

Thomas stared at me a long moment, then turned away. I didn't realize what he was going to do until he opened the gate. Then he turned and waved his hat, shouting at the horses.

Before I could move, they were on their way out of the corral.

"Damn you, Thomas!"

I ran to my saddle and grabbed a rawhide *reata*. I yelled, "Muley, come help me."

Thomas stood in the gate. As I started around him, his fist came at me. It slammed me back against the fence. Thomas called for his friends, and they came running. The four of them moved in on me. I tried to lunge at Thomas, but strong hands grabbed and held me. Thomas's fist drove into my stomach. All my breath left me.

"Now, Josh," Thomas gritted, "just quit it. What we're doin' we're doin' for your own good."

I heard Muley yelp and saw him come running to help me. I tried to yell at him to stay where he was, but no sound would come. He plowed in with fists swinging. One of the Phipps boys backhanded him, then slashed at him with a rock-like set of knuckles that bent Muley back like a small boy. He dropped.

Thomas told them what was happening. "Looks like we'll just have to tie Josh up and keep him awhile. Never thought I'd see the day I'd have to do this to my own flesh and blood."

I struggled against them, but they had me so tight there wasn't a chance to break loose.

Noonan said, "Thomas, what do you say we take them over to our cabin a spell? There's more of us to keep an eye on them there. And if drastic measures is called for, we might come nearer takin' them than you would, bein' his brother and all."

Thomas frowned. "I don't want him hurt none."

"We'll just kind of salt them down, both of them. You won't have to fret none or feel the least bit uneasy. Come tomorrow, Josh'll still be a happy bachelor. And you won't have no Mexican kinfolks."

My breath was coming back. "I'll get you! I'll get all of you!"

Noonan didn't seem impressed. "Sure you will, Josh. But for now you're goin' to come on along like a good boy. Thomas, how about you bringin' them horses back in?"

After a while the horses came. I tried to fight free, and Jacob Phipps fetched me a clout that put me on my knees. He pushed me down onto my stomach and sat on me while the others saddled up. Then he pulled me to my feet. "We'll be a-leavin' now, Josh. It's up to you whether you get on that horse by yourself or if we clout you again and put you up there."

I knew I didn't have the strength for a fight, so I climbed up. I had some notion of being able to pull loose from them down the trail and get away. I wanted to save my strength for that possibility. But I found they weren't going to give me the chance. They tied my hands to the saddle. Then they tied a short rope to the reins. Ezekiel Phipps held the end of the rope in his big hands.

Muley sobbed. "I tried, Josh. I did try."

"Sure, Muley. You did right good. There was just too many of them."

Thomas said, "Josh, don't you do nothin' to make them have to hurt you, do you hear? The time'll come when you'll thank me for this."

In my fury there was nothing I could say that was half enough. So I held my tongue. I'd be back, and there would be a reckoning.

THEY KEPT us tied all that night, and all the next day and night. They untied Muley to let him eat. They tried untying me once but tied me up again when I attempted to fight my way out of the cabin. If I had any satisfaction at all, it was that I had left my mark on all of them. The afternoon of the wedding, Noonan rode to the Hernandez place and spied on it from a distance. He came riding in next morning, satisfied.

"It was quite a sight, Josh. You ought to've seen it. When them Mexicans throw a celebration, they sure do it up right."

I knew without asking, but I had to ask anyway, the dread coming up in me heavy and cold. "They're married?"

"Sure enough. Handsome-lookin' couple, best I could tell. You got to understand I was too far away to see real clear. I doubt as she'll miss you much, Josh. Mexican gals have got a talent for lovin', and I expect that boy will keep her too busy to be frettin' herself about some calf-eyed *Americano*." He glanced at Jacob and Ezekiel. "Reckon you'd just as well untie him and let him go."

Jacob went to work on the knots that bound me. "Josh, I hope you'll take this in the spirit we meant it. We was just doin' you a favor."

When my hands were free, I rubbed my raw wrists to get the circulation going. I would need it for what I wanted to do.

Jacob grinned at me. "No hard feelin's, Josh."

I don't know where the strength came from, but my fist caught his nose dead-center. His head snapped back and cracked against the log siding. I whirled and caught Ezekiel in the ribs. He grunted and doubled over.

Noonan hobbled toward the door, his eyes wide. "Now, Josh, you wouldn't go and hurt an old man."

I stopped, for dizziness came over me. Noonan said. "You're sure an ungrateful kind, Josh. No wonder you're such a burden to your brother."

I reached for him but missed. He ran out of the cabin, shouting and cursing at me. I untied Muley. We walked out into the daylight. It hurt my eyes at first, but that was only a small addition to the agony I felt in body and in spirit. The whole world had fallen in on me.

I caught up our horses, trying to choke down the rage which fought for release. I think if I had had a gun I would have gone back into the cabin and killed all three men, or tried to.

"Muley, you ride on home."

"What you fixin' to do, Josh?"

"I'm goin' to the Hernandez place."

"Seems like it's a little late now, don't it? I mean, they said there had done been a weddin' and all that. There ain't nobody but God can undo a weddin', is there?"

"Just go on home, Muley."

"When you figure on bein' back?"

"I don't know. Just look for me when you see me comin'."

EIGHT DAYS came and went before the night I finally rode up to our cabin. I swung down woodenly and unsaddled, turning the horse into the corral and tying the gate. Muley's dog barked at me. I trudged to the cabin, my head down, my throat in a knot.

Thomas opened the door and stood there against the candlelight, rifle in his hand. "Josh? That you, Josh?"

I walked in past him without being able to look into his face.

"Josh, it's been over a week. Where you been?"

I couldn't answer him at first.

He stared at me. "You're sure makin' it hard on yourself. You've been blinded by somethin' you take to be love. Hell, you don't even know what love is. You never felt it before, and the first time you get a real itch toward a woman you think you're in love with her. This'll all blow over, and you'll thank me. You'll look at her and tell me how glad you are that you're not tied to her."

Voice came to me. "I'll never see her again, Thomas, nobody will."

His mouth dropped open.

I said, "She's dead, Thomas."

I think that was the first time he ever really saw how deeply and honestly I had been in love with Teresa. "Dead? But how?"

"The mornin' after they were married, the two of them set out alone toward Bexar, ahead of the others. When the Esquivel family came along later they found them . . . what the Indians had left of them."

Thomas looked at the floor, his face frozen. "My God, Josh. . . ."

I said, "If I'd gone back that night, she'd still be alive. I'd have gotten her away from there, and I'd have taken her back toward the settlements, where there wouldn't have been any Indians. That's how it would have been, Thomas, if you hadn't stopped me."

"I was thinkin' of you, Josh."

"Or maybe you were just thinkin' of yourself, and how bad you'd hate to have a Mexican woman for your sister-in-law."

Thomas shook his head. "What can I say?"

"It'd be better if you didn't say anything."

He brought himself to look at me. "Josh, that was over a week ago. Where have you been all this time?"

"Been lookin' for some Indians to kill."

He stared. "Find any?"

I shook my head. "They disappeared like smoke."

"But a week, Josh. How come you to stay so long?"

"Afraid to come back any sooner. Afraid I might kill you." I could see the hurt in his eyes. "I won't do it, though. I got over that much of it. But from now on I'm through lettin' you think for me. I'm through listenin' to you. I don't even want to see you."

Thomas put his hand on my shoulder. "Josh . . ."

I couldn't hold it any longer. I hit him. And when I saw him stagger back, all the anger and all the grief that had banked up in me seemed to explode at once. I tied into him, slashing, jabbing.

IT WAS years before I could think back on it without my emotions getting in the way. Long afterward, remembering, I knew Thomas didn't do much to defend himself. He took all I had to give him, and what I gave him would have killed a lesser man. I fought him until all the strength had ebbed out of me and I lay on the earthen floor of the cabin, sobbing like a little boy.

For a long time I lay there, letting the hurt have its way with me. But finally I pushed to my feet and saw Thomas sitting on a rawhide chair, regarding me gravely. His face was bruised and swollen, his clothing torn. But in his eyes was only sadness.

"Well, Thomas," I said, "which one of us is it goin' to be?"

"What do you mean?"

"I mean one of us has got to go. Will it be you, or me?"

Thomas's voice was hollow. "It's that bad, is it?"

"It's that bad."

He dug into his pocket. "I wish it wasn't this way, Josh." He brought forth a coin. "This is gold. Come all the way with us from Tennessee. You call it."

"Heads I go, tails you do."

The coin caught the candlelight for an instant as it flipped out of Thomas's hand, went up, then fell. It made a faint thump on the floor. Thomas leaned over and picked it up. "Tails."

"I didn't see it," I said.

"That's what it was, though. Tails. The place is yours."

I nodded, too numb really to care which one of us went. "I want you to go tonight, Thomas!"

That shook him, but he shrugged. "All right."

He gathered up a few of his belongings, rolled his bedding, and stepped out into the night to fetch his horse.

Muley said, "Josh, it's awful dark out there. It ain't good to turn a man out into the night thisaway."

"I'd have gone, if it had come up heads."

Muley said with an innocent wisdom that would come back to haunt me in the years ahead: "Maybe it did, Josh."

H ARD WORK has never been popular, but it is a merciful healer. Since Thomas had left, it was up to Muley and me to bring in the crops that fall. If I hadn't been up moving before daylight and laboring like a gray mule until dark, then flopping on my cot too tired to move, I might not have brought myself through those first dark weeks. Even with the work, I would glance up every so often and see Teresa's face in the autumn-red fringe of timber.

If it had been the beautiful face of those fleeting days we had together, I could have stood it. But always I saw her as I had seen her in death, the eyes and mouth open in horror, the blood dried to a sickening blackish crimson. The heart would drop out of me.

At such times, some men drown themselves in liquor. I had no liquor, so I tried to drown myself in work. There was more than enough of it. Muley suffered, because he tried with all that was in him to keep up with me. It's a wonder I didn't kill him.

Thomas stayed out of my sight. Muley tried to hide it from me, but in his guileless way he let me find out that Thomas would come around now and again, when I was somewhere else. Thomas would look things over, question Muley a little, then fade away before I got back. Much of the time he was staying with Noonan and the Phipps boys, helping them bring in wild cattle the way he and I had done, or helping them harvest their crops. At that time of year there was always work for a man like Thomas who wanted to hire out and didn't balk at hard labor. Usually he was paid in kind, for coin was scarce.

Once, I learned, Thomas went off on a long trip with Noonan somewhere to the south. Not for the world would I have admitted it, but I worried about him. I knew Noonan had him mixed up in a smuggling venture or something of that kind. Trouble and contention were like food and drink to Noonan's breed.

Muley got lonesome sometimes, with just the two of us there on the place. "When we goin' back to see the Hernandez family again?" he would ask.

"I don't know if I can ever go back," I told him. "Teresa's gone."

"The rest of them ain't gone. The kids are still there. I like them kids, Josh."

I could sympathize with Muley's loneliness, for I had my own. But I couldn't bring myself to visit again the place where I had known Teresa. Most of all, I knew I could not bear the sight of Antonio Hernandez. Always turning in my mind was the grim certainty that it had been his hatred—and Thomas's—which had killed her. Their blind, selfish, senseless hatred. . . .

The long months went by and Ramón came to see us finally, he and Felix. Muley and I were working in the field where our small crop of cotton had matured into a blanket of white fluff. Ramón sat on his horse and watched me.

"You do not look good, friend Josh. You have carried grief badly."

I laid down my cotton sack. I felt resentment at first, for he could have called a halt to the wedding if he had not been so hide-bound to tradition. He could have spoken one word and stopped it.

"How is a man supposed to carry grief, Ramón? It's a heavy burden, no matter how you try to pick it up."

"Ours is the grief, too. We could help you carry it, if you would but ask."

I shook my head. "I'll tote my own load."

"We have not seen you in a long time."

I turned away and picked up my cotton sack. Ramón and Felix got off their horses. Muley ran forward to pump Felix's hand, his face shining with pleasure. Ramón fell in beside me and silently began to help, putting cotton into my sack. He had probably never picked any before, because the Mexicans themselves rarely grew it. Cotton had come in with the Americans. Sometimes I wondered why we tried it, living so far from the market: we couldn't eat it, and we didn't spin it, but we could trade it for coffee and flour and other necessities down in the settlements. The necessities were so hard to come by that they were almost considered luxuries. As for luxuries, there just weren't any.

Ramón and Felix soon had their fingers torn and sore from the hard, dry burs. Ramón said disapprovingly, "I had rather break my neck with the wild cattle and horses than to break my back in the cotton."

I had softened a little, working beside him. "There's not much fun in a cotton field," I admitted. "But cotton sells, and there's precious little else that does."

"What is money, that one must do so many unpleasant things to get it?"

"Why, Ramón, money is . . . Well, I mean, a man's just got to have money."

He shook his head. "Among our people there are some who live a lifetime and never feel a piece of silver cross their palm. A man can live from the land, if he will be content with what the land chooses to give him. This growing of cotton is not a natural thing, like hunting. Do you see the deer or the wolf or the buffalo planting cotton? No, they live as God intended them to, from what the land itself provides. If He had intended that we have cotton, He could have planted it Himself. This kind of work does no honor to a man."

"Work *is* honor. The Book says that by the sweat of the brow shalt thou earn thy bread."

"I had rather sweat my brow running the wild cattle. What could a man want that would make him do dishonoring work to get money? He cannot eat money. He cannot wear it. All he can do is trade it for something he wants. A few beans, a little corn, enough beef—what more could a man want?"

I knew Ramón was purposely working up an argument with me to take my mind away from Teresa. I also knew he was dead serious in what he said.

He went on, "In the Book you learn of the lilies of the field. They do not toil, neither do they spin. And of a certainty you find no lilies in a field of cotton."

I let go my cotton sack while I wiped the sweat from my brow. It gave me a righteous feeling to know I was earning my bread like the Book said to. But it never had occurred to me that there might be conflict between that part of the Word and the passage Ramón had quoted.

I said, "It's all in the way a man looks at it, I reckon. You and me, we just naturally look at it different."

"I think, my friend, this is the big problem between your people and mine. There is little understanding. Perhaps there never will be. Your people say my people are lazy—that they work no more than they have to. My people say your people are greedy—that you work too long and too hard to get money for things you do not need and that you do not take time to taste life for the good flavor that is in it.

"In too many ways we are different. We shall never be alike."

RAMÓN WAS wise enough to see it, though it took me a long time to admit he was right. Even then, so long before the final and complete break came to Texas, the long shadows of the future were beginning to stretch out across the bold new land. No one ever really left the old country when he came to the new. Wherever the settler ventured, he took with him his customs and beliefs, the individual ways of the land he had come from. That applied to both American and

Mexican. There was no such thing as a fresh, clean start. He resisted whatever was alien to the things he had known before.

True, the American and the Mexican found some points they could agree on. They might join to face the common enemy—the Indian. They could and did get together when it was to their advantage to trade. Individually, they made friends, as I had done with the Hernandez family. Some intermarried, as Jim Bowie had done in Bexar.

But basically, they remained two different kinds of people in outlook. There had been a time, in the beginning, when they might have stressed the points in which they were alike. Instead, they dwelt upon the differences. It is a human trait—not one of the better ones, but one which usually crops out. Where Mexicans and Americans lived in the same areas, the tendency was to group with their own kind. The dividing boundary might be a river or creek; it might be only an imaginary line. But real or imaginary, it was always there.

Often, in looking back, I have tried to decide for myself who was really to blame for it, who had started it. And always the answer comes up the same: nobody, and everybody. The tendency was there in the beginning, and it was on both sides.

That is the great irony of it all: the fact that we pulled apart and made so much of our difference only proved how much alike we were.

It was a big and open country, but bad news had a way of traveling fast. A foretaste of trouble came when a Texian force attacked the guardhouse at Anahuac, on the coast, to release prisoners who had been wrongfully taken. Excitement rippled through the colonies, and it left its mark even after the Mexican government moved to correct the situation that had brought on the trouble. Shortly afterward came a battle at Velasco, when a Mexican garrison tried to stop the sailing of a Texian ship that carried two cannon. The Mexicans ran out of ammunition, and the Texians persuaded them it would be wise to head south without undue delay.

I didn't see him, but I learned that Thomas had joined Noonan and the Phipps brothers for a fast ride to the coast as soon as they heard. By the time they got there, the smoke had cleared. Diplomatically-minded Texians and Mexicans were working to mend the breach that had been torn by their more warlike friends.

If the battles had any good result, it was that Mexico pulled most of her garrison out of Texas. They had been manned mostly by convict soldiers and others of poor repute. They had been a festering sore—a constant reminder that Mexico didn't really trust her new citizens from the north. Santa Anna was a revolutionary leader in Mexico in those days. He took the Texians' side after Anahuac and Velasco. A fresh wave of enthusiasm swept through the old settlers. Here, it seemed, was a new Mexican leader who understood and liked these blue-eyed foreigners—a Mexican who was going to give us all a fair deal.

There was a time—a short time—when it seemed we were about to get the world by the tail with a downhill pull. Mexico let up some on its immigration laws. More people crowded in. It got so that on an early fall morning when the air was crisp, I could hear a neighbor's ax ringing from across the hill.

But not all the newcomers were farmers and stockmen.

Once in a great while there was reason for Muley and me to go to San Felipe. It had grown, stretching out far along the Brazos. It was crowded with lawyers and land men, promoters of every kind. They worked little—some of them. But they never ceased talking, never stopped agitating. Wherever they found muddy water, they stirred it.

One spring day of 1833, Muley and I were nearing San Felipe in our wagon when we came across a familiar figure astride a bay horse. He rode toward us with head down, lost in his meditation. He didn't seem to see us until we were almost upon him.

Muley called, "Howdy, Colonel Austin."

Austin stopped and brought up his hand in greeting. He studied us, trying for recognition. "I'm sorry," he said. "I was absorbed with some worries of my own."

There had been plenty of them. His face was haggard, his eye bleak.

"I should know you," he said. "The faces are familiar."

"Joshua Buckalew, Colonel. And Muley Dodd. We live up yonder on the Colorado. You granted us the land."

He frowned. "Buckalew? Would you be the one who has been making so much talk of war?"

I shook my head and looked down. "I expect that'd be my brother, sir. His name is Thomas. Him and me, we sort of come to a fork in the road. He seems to've took the left hand."

"That's too bad. But he has a lot of company, these days."

I said regretfully, "I'm sorry, Colonel, that things don't seem to be workin' out the way they ought to for you. Anything Muley and me can do, we'd be tickled to try."

Austin shrugged. "There is a need for so many things, I would hardly know where to start."

"Well, sir, like what, for instance?"

He took a long, frowning look at the countryside around him. It was coming alive with the green of new grass and the bright splash of blue and yellow from bluebonnets and buttercups. "It's a beautiful land. I always thought Texas had the greatest potential of any land I ever set my eyes upon. And it does yet, I suppose, if only these war-makers would cease their everlasting talk of disunity and unrest."

"We live way off yonder in the far settlements. We don't hear much of what's goin' on."

"I imagine you hear enough. We have bad trouble ahead of us if we don't curb these restless spirits. For years I've preached that we should go our own peaceful way. And for years, the people would listen to me. But somehow I've lost control now. Other voices speak louder than mine."

"We've always listened to you, Colonel."

"I wish there were more like you." He studied us keenly. "How go things up on the Colorado?"

"Fair enough, sir. Moisture's good for the spring plantin'. Grass is risin' fine."

"I mean politically. Are they talking as restlessly there as in other parts of Texas?"

Uneasy now, I quit looking into his face. "Well, sir, you'll always find people like my brother. They're dissatisfied no matter what. We have Mexican neighbors, and we get along. The government don't bother us much out there. Too far for office-bred people to ride, I expect." I felt my face coloring. "Not meanin' any personal offense to you, sir. I mean, it's different with you."

Austin smiled faintly. "My friend, I had ridden horseback so many thousands of miles in colonizing Texas that a ride up the Colorado River would be like a Sunday picnic. Even now, I'm preparing for another trip to Mexico City."

"It's a mighty long way down there," I admitted. "Farther, even, than to Tennessee."

"Far in miles and in mind. I never look forward to that journey. It's like going to another world. But I have to. I want to reassure the authorities that we are loyal here. With luck, I may be able to persuade them to take action against some of the conditions which have caused grievances here. There are grounds for grievances; I would be the first to admit that. But we must have patience. The Mexicans move slower than we. Change cannot be rushed upon them."

I thought of the Hernandez family. "No, sir, it sure can't."

Austin gazed intently at me. "You're one of the older settlers here now. It's the old settlers I must depend upon to keep things from getting out of hand. Counsel with the new ones when you can— help them realize how precarious our situation is."

"I'll do all I can," I promised. But even as I said it, I thought of Thomas. I thought how useless it would be to talk to my brother, or to anyone like him. I thought of Antonio Hernandez, too. He and his kind wouldn't listen any more than Thomas would.

"Mexico City," Austin repeated. "It's a long, long way. I hope I can be back again before the summer is out."

HE WASN'T. It was two years before we were to see Austin. He would come home a shaken and disillusioned man, no longer inclined to soothe the restless ones. He would come home from a long and unjustified imprisonment, certain at last that Texas had no future tied to Mexico, where all life depended upon the whims of whatever one man happened to have his fist gripped tightly around the whip of government.

CHAPTER

10

Looking back afterward, we could see that war was as certain as the rising and setting of the hot Texas sun. It didn't explode suddenly like a shell. It built gradually step by step, block by block, as methodically as you'd build a church. But the comparison is a bad one, for this war was something out of hell.

Most of us "old settlers" denied its coming as long as we could. We wanted to plow our fields and work our stock and live our lives by our own pattern, and be left alone. But it inched up like a slow-building thunderhead, and we watched it the way we'd watch a storm cloud, hoping it would go around us instead of coming head-on. It came anyway.

On the one hand was the "war party" of Texians who wanted complete separation from Mexico. Some were honest in their fever for freedom; others were only looking for a way to grab new land, or hoping independence would allow them to gain title to the land on which they already squatted.

On the other hand were venal Mexican officials, greedy for personal riches and hungry for power, despotic not only with the Texians but also with their own people. Such men had a strong tendency to regard other people as little more than cattle, to be used for their own gain and driven and cast aside. Zacatecas and Monclova were only words to us then, but we were dimly aware that places of those names existed, deep down in Mexico, and that angry revolts had leaped to flame there. Clear up in Texas, we could smell the smoke. Santa Anna crushed those people with a red-smeared fist. Then his ruthless eyes turned northward. He had taken off his smiling mask. The sense of absolute power had gone to his brain like the fire of bad *tequila*. Now he was a stalking wolf that had gotten a taste of blood and liked it.

Mañana was an old Mexican word which translated into "tomorrow" but usually meant some dimly distant time that would never come. It was a lazy answer for the things that had not been done and might never be done.

But for Texas, *mañana* was almost here.

RAMÓN HERNANDEZ had been on a trip to San Antonio de Bexar with his wife to show their baby to her parents there. She was already with child again, and soon she would not have been able to make the journey. It was no longer the dangerous trip it had once been, for Indians rarely showed themselves any more. Too many settlers had built their log cabins or their stone *casas* along the road. Still, there was always a nagging uneasiness about any traveler until he was home and safe. So I was relieved to see Ramón riding up to our field.

It had been three years since I had set foot on the Hernandez place. The *Señora* Hernandez—Ramón's mother—had gone to join the saints. I had not attended the funeral because it would have meant I would have to visit that house. I knew that just beyond the new wooden cross stood one that by now would be darkened by time and rain, a cross bearing the name *Teresa*.

On a trip to Bexar, Ramón had finally found a long-sought woman who would be the mother of his sons. Miranda was her name. She was tiny, like so many Mexican women, but she could move about like some kind of a spirit, and do work that would break the back of some larger women. What she may have lacked in being a beauty, she made up by being a good cook. Ramón had proudly brought her to our place several times before she became *preñada* and could no longer make the trip. Her meals were a feast after the bachelor cooking Muley and I had endured so long.

What mattered most, of course, was that she was good for Ramón. She could wrinkle her nose or wink her eye and melt him like a slice of butter.

Ramón's Spanish ancestors had spent their lives vainly hunting for treasure. Ramón was luckier. He had found his.

Because she was so tiny, child-bearing was difficult. There was a time when it appeared she might not live through it. But she had, and the trip to Bexar was Ramón's reward to her for delivering him a son, and for promising him another.

"What's the news in Bexar?" I asked after Ramón had slaked his thirst out of my water jug.

Ramón didn't answer me right off. He was too busy explaining to Muley why he hadn't brought Felix along, or some of the younger brothers. Muley hungered after company; he had had so little of it.

Ramón said finally, "Austin is back. It is said in Bexar that he arrived in Velasco aboard the *San Felipe*." His face creased. "It is also said that there was a battle in Velasco harbor, and the *San Felipe* captured a Mexican warship."

I felt a sudden angry impatience. "Why do they have to do it, Ramón? They play with firebrands in a powderhouse!"

Ramón waved the question away. "God made the animals to fight. It is their nature. I am afraid He made the man a little too much like He made the animals." There was acceptance in his eyes, but mixed with regret. "It is born in them. It is beyond them to be able to change the will of God."

"It's not the will of God that we go to war."

"He made men different from each other. He made them to talk different tongues and wear different-colored skins. A great many men have died for that, and that alone." He shrugged with a patience inborn in his people. "It is said that even the Colonel Austin talks now of war. It is said that even he—who always talked of peace—is saying that Texas and Mexico must free themselves of Santa Anna."

"He spent a long time in prison. A gentle man, caged up like an animal and for no good reason. It's enough to make him bitter."

"Or to make him realistic." Ramón's eyes were steady. "He is right, I think. There is far more Americans in Texas than Mexicans. Mexico has always had her Santa Annas. They run in the blood, like some disease passed down from father to son. We Mexicans expect it; we accept it. But you Americans will fight. I think you will cut free from it or die."

"If it comes to that, Ramón, what will you do?"

He gazed out across our fields of ripening cotton, our grain. He looked beyond to the cabin on the timber-lined creek. I could see the love of this land in his eyes.

Sadly he said: "Texas is my home. Yet, I am Mexican. I do not know what I will do."

MULEY SAW the two horsemen first. "Ramón," he called out, grinning broadly, "I thought you said Felix wasn't home. That's him comin' yonder, with Antonio."

They were riding fast. Antonio usually did; he had little regard for his horses. But somehow I could tell this time it wasn't just thoughtlessness. They rode with a purpose.

Anxiety leaped in Ramón's eyes. "Something may have happened to Miranda."

Antonio cut directly across our field, spurring his horse through our unpicked cotton and breaking down the stalks. Felix held up, starting to go around, then thought better of it and cut through after his brother. I thought, *There had better be a good reason.* I was angrier at Felix than at Antonio, for I would have expected this from Antonio any time.

Antonio pulled up. He had passed Muley without a glance. He flashed me a hostile look, then turned to Ramón. "Come, brother, it is time to fight."

Relief washed over Ramón. "Miranda is all right?"

"There is nothing wrong with your woman. But there is much wrong for your country while you stand here and talk with your *Americano* friend. It is time now for shooting, not for talking."

Ramón's eyes narrowed. "Antonio, you have been drinking."

"I do not drink when my country needs me. Fighting has begun, brother, *por allá*, in Gonzales. There has been a call for men."

Ramón's voice dropped to a whisper. "I had not heard . . ."

"You spent too much time on the road home from Bexar with your woman. You missed the news. The *Americanos* have a cannon at Gonzales, and they refuse to give it up. Against the command of Colonel Ugartechea, they have killed to keep it."

Ramón glanced at me, helplessness in his eyes.

Antonio said, "It is time to decide. Shall we bow down to this plague of locusts, or shall we offer ourselves as patriots? Felix and I have made our choice. What is yours?"

Ramón's face was stricken. "Felix? You would take Felix? He is still a boy."

"He will fight like a man!"

Ramón stepped up beside his younger brother's horse and put his hand on the boy's knee. "Felix, this is not for you."

Swallowing, Felix held his chin high.

I shouldn't have interfered, but I liked this lad too much to stand still. "Felix, you'd better listen to Ramón."

Felix would not look at me. Tightly he said, "Yesterday we were friends, Josh. Today we are enemies. I am a Mexican."

Antonio's eyes were like two black flints. "What are *you*, Ramón? The time has come to choose, and choose quickly."

Ramón shook his head. "Antonio, you are crazy."

Antonio spat in front of him. "I expected as much. Stay at home, then. Stay at home with your woman and your American friends.

And when they have you in chains, remember that your brothers had the spine to fight!"

He wheeled his horse around and spurred back through our cotton. Felix paused a moment, eyes fixed on his older brother. He was wavering.

Ramón cried, "Felix, stay here."

But Felix touched spurs to the horse and went off in a lope.

And thus war reached us, even here in the far settlements on the Colorado.

I HAD a strong feeling now that Thomas would return. And I knew what he would be wanting.

That night Muley's dog set up a racket. Rifle in my hand, I eased the door open. On the front step stood a familiar figure, tall and angular. "Howdy there, Josh," spoke the surveyor Jared Pounce. "Might I be a-comin' in?"

Muley grinned broadly at the sight of an old friend. I said. "Sure, Jared. Come in and we'll fix you somethin' to eat."

Jared hesitated. "Josh, I got somebody with me."

His look made me uneasy. "Bring him on in."

Thomas Buckalew halted in the open doorway. He said nothing at first. We stared at each other in silence. Three years had passed since we had stood face to face. He appeared to have aged much more than that, for his eyes were grave, his cheeks brown and lean. I could see the beginnings of a silver glint in the long hair that touched his collar. He was too young for gray, but there it was.

Muley's grin had faded to fright. "Josh," he begged, "you fellers ain't a-goin' to fight each other again, are you?"

I said, "No, Muley, we won't fight." I stared at Thomas. "You've changed."

He nodded. "So have you, Josh. Been a heap of water flowed under the bridge."

We didn't shake hands. Neither of us was ready to make the first move, so it was not made at all. Too much stood between us—the bitterness of the parting, and the long empty years since. We had moved apart like the opposite branches of a tree, still bound by the common trunk but each grown in his own direction, away from the other.

Thomas said, "You been well?"

I nodded. "You?"

"Tolerable, I reckon."

The silence was long and awakened again. At length Thomas said, "I expect you wonder why I've come, after all this time."

"I think I know. It's the war, isn't it?"

Thomas nodded, his mouth drawn into a thin, taut line. "Santa Anna's sendin' up troops from Mexico under General Cos. They'll join Ugartechea in Bexar. If they come for us, and find us scattered, it'll be the death of us all. You've heard about the fight at Gonzales?"

"I heard this afternoon."

"The call has gone out for help. We got to band together and whip them before they pick us off one by one. I'm goin', Josh. I'd like you to go with me."

"Thomas, are you sure . . ."

"I know there's been a lot come between us, Josh. I know how you feel about what I done. But we got to quit fightin' each other now and fight together. Else it's all over for the Americans in Texas."

I already knew what my answer had to be, but I dreaded giving it. "Have you seen Colonel Austin?"

He shook his head. "I've talked to people who have. Jared can tell you."

Grimly Jared Pounce said, "They treated him real bad down in Mexico. He says we got no choice any more but to fight. He's goin' to Gonzales himself."

I clinched my fist. "I've got friends who'll be on the Mexican side."

Thomas said, "In war, a man's got no friends except those who are with him."

I glanced at Muley. "I couldn't take Muley. He's got no business goin' into somethin' like this."

"Muley can stay here. There's neighbors enough now to help watch out for him. Been no Indians in a long time."

"I guess you've got other men ready to go?"

Thomas nodded. "We'll all be gatherin' over at Noonan's. We'll ride for Gonzales in the mornin'."

I turned toward the wall pegs where my old flintlock rested. With it, I had brought down more deer than I could count. Now I would use it to bring down men.

"I'll go. Give me time to gather my plunder and talk to Muley. I'll go."

A CARNIVAL spirit prevailed at Noonan's. The old rogue was boasting loud and long, telling how he had foretold this trouble the first time a Mexican soldier had shot at him, years ago. He didn't mention what he had been doing to get shot at, and nobody seemed of a mind to ask him.

"They're a bunch of yellow cowards," he declared. "They slit a man's throat when they get the upper hand on him, but they'll squeal like a pig under a gate if things go agin them. Give us fifty good men and this war'll be nothin' but a horse race—them runnin' and us chasin'. We'll all be home and plowin' our fields inside of two weeks."

Old Noonan had never plowed a field to my recollection. The only thing I'd ever known him to raise was hell.

I took my blanket and walked away from Noonan's cabin. I stretched out on the ground by his corral, where our horses were penned. Presently Thomas came out and joined me. He said nothing for awhile. He sat leaning against a post in the darkness, drawing on his pipe and savoring the home-grown tobacco.

"Josh," he said finally, "it's been a long time since . . . since that girl died. Have you got over it all right?"

I shrugged. "I can think about her now without it painin' me so, if that's what you mean. It's only that now and again I get lonesome. I get to thinkin' how things would be now if . . ." I broke off.

"There's some single girls around. You haven't found yourself one?"

"I haven't been lookin'."

"Maybe you ought to. I think you need a woman, Josh. And likely someplace there's a woman that needs you."

I didn't mean to, but somehow I let a little of the old bitterness creep into my voice. "There was one once, remember?"

Thomas said, "She was a Mexican."

I knew he hadn't changed.

CHAPTER

11

WE REACHED Gonzales too late to help, for the battle was over. The town's "Old Eighteen" had stalled the Mexicans for three days until reinforcements came from neighboring settlements. Then in a fog-shrouded wood on the Guadalupe, the Texians had touched fire to their cannon and watched it belch forth a load of scrap-iron balls and cut-up chain. Again and again the cannon spoke, the noise echoing and re-echoing up the river in the cool of early morning. When it fell silent, the Mexicans had gone, leaving behind them crippled animals and patches of blood.

The whole affair seemed an improbable parody now, on the face of it. I rode over to look at the cannon which had brought on the trouble. It was an ancient six-pounder mounted on oxcart wheels. In Gonzales, its main purpose had been to make noise that would scare off Indians. As a weapon of war, it wasn't much. As a cause of war, it was ridiculous.

But, of course, it hadn't actually been the cause. It had been only the spark which had touched off the powder. The fact that Ugartechea had heavy-handedly demanded its surrender and had sent an armed group to take it had been the final indignity, the last of a long series of insults against men of strong pride. The defiant band at Gonzales had stood their ground and run up a flag with the words *Come and Take It!*

Austin had said, "A gentle breeze shakes off a ripe peach. Can it be supposed that the violent political convulsions of Mexico will not shake off Texas so soon as it is ripe enough to fall?"

WITH THIS battle won, no one was sure just what should be done next. Men and horses and mules and wagons came pouring into Gonzales, ready for war. But no one agreed just how this war was to be fought. Angry talk and fist fights erupted. A dozen men who had been leaders in their own communities wanted to command this volunteer expedition against the Mexicans. Even narrow-gauge men like Noonan saw themselves as the ones to lead the crusade.

"I been fightin' Mexicans longer than half of you have been drinkin' hard likker!" he shouted at a group of us who had declined to acknowledge his leadership. "I'll take on any one of you now. Choose your weapons—knives, guns . . . I'll even fight you with a chunk of firewood."

I'd had a bellyful of his blustering. "Shut up, Noonan, or I'll get the wind out of you and you'll shrink to where a man could stuff you in a saddlebag."

Noonan railed at me, but I knew he wouldn't fight. The Phipps boys took his side. For a while it looked as though I'd have to do battle with both of them.

Thomas stopped it, the way he had stopped scraps of mine back in Tennessee. "You-all hush up now. We're here to fight Mexicans."

Austin arrived, and just in time. The fury died quickly. Austin was the man who had put these colonies on their feet, the man who had undergone bitter personal hardship and even imprisonment for our sake. Some of the fire-eaters had long preached against him because of his peaceable ways. But now we all gathered to listen. Always in the past we had turned to Austin for counsel. We turned to him now.

Seeing him came as a shock to me. He looked much older than when I had last encountered him, that day on the road near San Felipe. His hair was graying. His face was thinner than ever before, his shoulders stooped. Those strong eyes which used to look a hole through a man were melancholy now, and tired.

"Gentlemen," he said in a voice so quiet we strained to hear it, "we have come upon a bitter time. The tyrant has torn up the good constitution of 1824 which first established us here and started us toward prosperity. He has declared that from now on we have only those rights which he chooses to confer. We have striven for peace but have been given war.

"I know there are some among you who have differed strongly with me in the past. But let us put that aside and bind ourselves together. The salvation of Texas is in our hands. And, perhaps, the salvation of all Mexico. Let us fight for the constitution of 1824."

I heard Thomas speak out. "To hell with the constitution of 1824. Let's cut ourselves loose from Mexico. We'll write our own constitution."

There were some who agreed with Thomas, but the "old settlers" dominated the crowd. Their aim was not so much independence from Mexico as simply to rid themselves of Santa Anna.

Austin was not a well man. The mark of imprisonment lay like a shadow upon him. But hardship had been his constant companion these long years in Texas. He was used to it, and he granted it no concessions.

"We can no longer retreat," he said. "The die has been cast. We must fight and win, or Santa Anna will kill us as traitors."

A council of war was set up. Though Austin protested that he knew little of military matters, he was unanimously elected the general-in-chief.

"Very well, then," he said, and regret was plain in his gentle voice, "I shall accept. And my first order is this: we march at daybreak. We march against Cos and Ugartechea. We shall go to San Antonio de Bexar."

AND SO we marched, our little "Volunteer Army of Texas." There were less than 400 of us at the beginning. And what an army! Our only uniform was a grim look of determination. Each man wore whatever he had, and most of us had only buckskins, darkened by long wear and smelling strongly of sweat and tobacco and smoke and rancid grease. The richer men—and they were few—wore boots or shoes. For most of us there were only moccasins. There were coonskin caps and Mexican sombreros, Kentucky longrifles and short-barreled muskets. Some men rode big, well-bred horses they had brought from the States. Most of us straddled raw Mexican ponies or mustangs, and a few rode mules.

Along the line we picked up volunteers—a pair of mustang runners here, a beehunter there. From Goliad trooped a group of dark-skinned Mexicans, stirred by reports of the bloodshed in Zacatecas and eager to join us against Santa Anna. Their arrival caused a ripple of uneasiness.

"Spies," Thomas gritted. "I never could trust a Mexican."

But they were accepted, for every gun would count.

With the group from Goliad—long called Bahía by the old settlers—came word that Texians had stormed the fortress there and had captured the Mexican troops, along with a large store of arms and ammunition left by General Cos on his march toward San Antonio. That was welcome news—as welcome as the arrival of Big Ben Milam.

I had never seen Milam before, but his name was heard often in the colonies. He was one of the "strong men" of the war party. He had agitated against Mexico for years. Only recently he had escaped from a Monterrey prison and brought news to Texas of Santa Anna's invasion preparations. A tall man, he had picked up Mexican clothing somewhere along the way to replace the filthy prison garb. And because Mexican people were usually small, the clothes he wore were short in sleeve and leg. His scarecrow looks made it hard to realize the caliber of man he really was.

Travis rode in—another name I had heard often but whose face I had never seen. Six foot tall, blond, still in his twenties, William Barret Travis was a lawyer by profession and a fighter by inclination. His name was at the top of Santa Anna's proscription list, for he had been bitterly opposed to the Mexican government almost from the minute he had set foot on Texas soil four years before.

Then came another whose name had conjured up many a legend. Jim Bowie rode into camp, leaving staring, whispering men in his wake. Fresh from Nacogdoches, he had pushed hard to get here before the fighting started. He swung down from a lithe gray mare, a big man in buckskins, that famous Bowie knife sheathed in leather scabbard, two pistols in his belt.

I knew him on sight. There could be only one.

Bowie looked older than I had expected, older than he really was. But I knew that if even half the stories told about him were true, he had lived a fuller life than a dozen ordinary men combined. The deep lines in his face, the dark pouches under his eyes, had been gained the hard way. Bowie had tried to drown himself in whisky after cholera had swept away his Mexican wife and family. *Borrachón*, they called him. The Big Drunk.

But now here he was, a strong man still, sober and ready to fight, ready to seek redemption at the cannon's mouth.

And Austin, still an *empresario* rather than a general, and despite his past disagreements with the sentiments of Milam and Travis and Bowie, was glad to see them in camp. He was a quiet man, a builder, and here he was out of his element. But these were fighting men. Austin badly needed their help to control his volunteers. They were eating up all their corn, drinking up all their whisky, killing for beef the work oxen that had pulled the Gonzales cannon all the way to Sandy Creek, then left it there, stuck.

Austin needed the peculiar talents of these three fighting leaders, and they were glad to oblige him. This was their line of work.

Probably none of the four suspected what was to come. Shortly, every one of them would be dead.

WE CAME to Salado Creek, about five miles from San Antonio. Scouting parties went out to reconnoiter, but Austin made no move for an immediate attack on the Mexican force. We had visits by several delegates of the Texas Consultation, which had been called so that the leaders of the various communities could decide what course the settlers would follow in their stand against Santa Anna. It seemed that with all the excitement the Consultation was having a hard time keeping a quorum.

Even Sam Houston, that towering giant of a man, vastly able and gloriously vain, came to make us a speech. He said that right now he thought we would do better to drill and prepare ourselves than to get tied up in a death battle with the Mexicans. After all, he pointed out, we were citizen farmers, not soldiers, while San Antonio de Bexar was fortified and manned by professionals. That was largely true, though most of us knew that a big percentage of the Mexican soldiers were actually convicts, serving their prison time in uniform instead of within stone walls. Their hearts would not be in it if they came against us.

This was pretty well proven true in the battle of Concepción. Austin called for Bowie and Captain J. W. Fannin, Jr., to take a detail of 92 men and find a good camp site as near the city as possible. I missed out getting into this bunch, but Thomas was with them. He had been restless as a caged cat, lying around camp. A chance to ride—anywhere—was as welcome to him as rain on new-planted corn.

He got more than he bargained for. Bowie and Fannin selected a place near the old Concepción Mission. It being late, they camped their men there for the night. Next morning they found they had been surrounded and were outnumbered by at least four to one.

When the smoke cleared, the Mexican troops were in wild retreat for town, leaving their artillery and twenty to thirty of their men behind them dead. The Texian loss: one.

Thomas came back flushed with excitement. The battle had fired his blood like raw wine. "It was beautiful!" he declared, his eyes flashing. "If we'd just been able to get word back here and have the rest of you brought up we could have finished the whole thing. Bowie said we'd have tied Cos's tail in a knot."

The way it was, the situation degenerated into a kind of Mexican standoff. We had Cos and his troops bottled up in Bexar. He couldn't get out, and no help could get in. But our leaders were skeptical about taking us into that town against the Cos cannon, against those soldiers waiting behind the heavy stone and adobe walls. We sat . . . and we sat . . . and we sat.

Sitting, I think, was worse than fighting. Time got to be more cruel an enemy than the Mexican troops who watched us from the flat roofs and the church towers.

Of course, some men always find ways to occupy themselves. There were certain of the Mexican women in town who found the fair-skinned Texians not really so terrible. Sometimes at night they would come strolling out to assure the men that they weren't really that kind of women. And some among the men were always willing to prove that they really were.

Jacob Phipps had found himself one. "I don't care if we never go in there and fight them soldiers," he told us, grinning. "I'd rather just wrestle with Guadalupe." He gripped Thomas's shoulder. "Thomas, she's got a sister. Real little *tamale*, that one. All pepper. Come with me tonight. See for yourself."

Thomas gravely shook his head. With the same hardshell pride he had always shown, he said, "I wouldn't dishonor myself. I would never pollute myself with a woman I wouldn't marry. And I wouldn't marry a Mexican."

I flinched, and he saw it. "Meanin' no offense, Josh. But it's the way I see it."

"None taken."

How could you take offense? He meant every word he said. You could get angry enough at a man like Jacob Phipps to pound his head against a wagon wheel, for he talked one way and acted another. But right or wrong, Thomas always did as he talked.

A few scattered skirmishes were fought, and finally one battle which got to be known as the Grass Fight. Bowie and a patrol of forty or so men jumped a Mexican pack train which they thought was bringing in silver to pay the soldiers. When the fight was over and the blood spilled, the packs were slashed open. There wasn't any silver. There was only grass, gathered to feed the horses.

That wasn't enough action to keep free men happy. Thomas paced restlessly in camp, a war fever burning in his eyes.

Every day the number of men became smaller and smaller. They were pulling out by ones and twos and threes, going home to see about the crops, going to comfort the wife and kids. The word we got in camp was that Austin wanted to march into the town and take it, but others were counseling against him. The longer he waited, the more desertions he suffered, the lower sagged the troops' morale.

I'll admit that if it hadn't been for Thomas I'd probably have pulled out like so many others did. I thought often about Muley all by himself out on the place, probably scared half to death. But Thomas was duty-bound to stay. All hell couldn't have pried him loose.

Word came from the Consultation. Austin was being sent to the United States to try for money and men. We didn't know it then, but he would work so hard on this mission that he would wreck his already frail health, and he would die without seeing the full fruit of his labor.

It looked as though we were going to lose the siege of San Antonio de Bexar by deterioration, rather than by battle.

On the fourth of December—two months after the cannon had spoken at Gonzales—Ben Milam walked among the discouraged men who still remained. A grim determination was in his eyes, and in the hard set of his jaw. Danger was an old acquaintance of his. They had never been far apart since the first time he had set foot in Texas nearly twenty years before.

His strong voice challenged us: "Who'll go in with Old Ben Milam into San Antonio?"

By twos and threes, by tens and twelves, men rose to their feet and reached for their rifles. Thomas spoke not a word, but he tucked the old Kentucky flintlock under his arm and felt for his shot pouch and powder horn. He glanced at me, his eyes asking the question.

"I'll come along," I said.

Commander Burleson had taken over after Austin left. He didn't like Milam's move, but he gave us the support of his artillery, dropping cannon balls into an ancient, half-ruined mission which the Mexicans had long ago turned into a fort. Cottonwoods stood around this once holy place, and around the high stone walls which surrounded it on all but a part of one side. Because of this, the mission had long since lost its church name and had become known by the Spanish word for cottonwood: *Alamo*.

There were some three hundred of us, divided into two companies. Ours was under Milam, the other under Colonel F. W. Johnson. We were outnumbered by three to one.

Six long, hard days we fought. It was toe-to-toe battle, and we moved by inches. Again and again the din of gunfire became so loud that I thought my head would explode from the pain of it. The sharp smell of gunpowder was always there, and the smoke kept my lungs afire. Now and again my hair would bristle at the death scream of a mortally wounded man on their side or ours.

The Mexican soldiers were tired and hungry and scared, but give them this: they fought like men. Surrounded, they could not run. So they stood and fought, and every inch of ground we gained was soaked by someone's blood. Crossing open streets was suicide. Rather than suffer terrible casualties by frontal assault, we bludgeoned our way toward the enemy's strongpoints by taking battering rams and plowing through the stone and adobe walls.

We moved on room by room, house by house, for most of these Mexican houses were built one against another. We would grasp the heavy poles used for rams, swing them a few times for momentum, then drive them into a wall. Sometimes women and children would scream in terror as the wall crumbled away and they stared at us through the swirling dust. Sometimes there would be Mexican soldiers in these rooms. Rifles would roar, knives would flash, clubs would swing viciously, and men would go down never to rise again.

But slowly we made our gains.

The cost was high. The third day, Ben Milam stepped out into the street, and a bullet struck him in the head. He never knew what hit him.

At last we had the crumbling old Alamo itself under our guns. Rifleshots crackled, cannons roared, and dust and gunsmoke hung heavily in the air. Our battering ram smashed through the adobe wall of a small Mexican house. For a second I glimpsed brown faces and excited black eyes before the guns flashed red and bullets went whining. For a minute it was as if we had torn open a hornet's nest. Then, all lay quiet. In the room only the dust and the smoke still moved, suction drawing them out through the gaping hole. Half a dozen of us stumbled into the room, our rifles ready to fire again. Crumpled on the floor lay five Mexican soldiers, all of them dead but one, and he mortally wounded. He cried out weakly to Holy Mary, the Mother of God. I don't know what drew my gaze to the slight figure slumped in a corner. Even before I saw the face, I felt my heart skip.

I dropped to one knee and gently turned the body over. I could tell at a touch that life was gone. A mass of blood had welled out of two holes in the front of the dirty shirt.

I knew that begrimed, crimson-smeared face.

Felix Hernandez.

I knelt there a long moment, my throat tightening as if a huge fist had clamped over it.

I heard Jared Pounce's quiet voice behind me. "Friend of yours, Josh?"

I nodded. "A kid is all he was. I've known him for years."

"Too bad," the old Texian said sympathetically. "He ought to've been on our side."

"At his age," I replied, "he oughtn't to've been on anybody's side."

I pulled at a small chain and found the crucifix Felix had been wearing around his neck. It would be the only thing of value he had on him. The family would want it for remembrance. Carefully I removed it and put it in my pocket.

"Looky yonder," I heard Jared shout. "Look at the Alamo. There's a white flag goin' up!"

I stared in disbelief, but there it was, rising to the top of a pole, the breeze catching it and flapping it wildly. The gunfire slowly died away. And in its place came the wild, jubilant shouting of the Texians.

"We've won! We've won! They're givin' up!"

Six days of hell had ended. I slumped to the dirt floor of the little house and leaned back against the adobe wall, exhausted, numb. Within reach of me lay the body of Felix Hernandez, but I couldn't bring myself to look at him again.

Why couldn't they have raised the flag an hour earlier?

I had thought I knew what it meant to be weary, but until now I never really had. I was sick of San Antonio, sick of fighting, sick of the sight and smell of blood.

A SHARP chill had come. The light clothes, the single blanket were no longer enough, for this was mid-December. I stood beside Thomas as we watched Cos march out of San Antonio on the road that led south to the interior of Mexico.

With him went the remnant of his troops. In two weeks there wouldn't be a hostile Mexican soldier left in Texas.

I had looked up Antonio Hernandez among the prisoners after the battle. I had tried to tell him about Felix. He heard me—he had to—but he gave no sign of it. He refused to look at me, to answer me. His face was like something carved out of stone. He was with the troops as they moved south.

"Thomas," I said, "it's over. I'm goin' home."

Thomas shook his head. "It ain't over, Josh. It ain't hardly even begun. They'll be back, and next time there'll be more of them than there was before."

"What do you figure on doin'?"

"There's some of us that want to go down into Mexico and carry the fight to *them*. Burn their towns, spoil their land."

"Thomas, weren't the last few days enough for you? Haven't you seen enough blood spilled to last you for a lifetime?"

Again he shook his head. "It's them or us, Josh. We're not half done fightin'."

I wrapped my blanket around my shoulders and looked off toward the Colorado. "I've had enough. I'm goin' home."

I had almost rather have taken a whipping at the hands of Santa Anna himself than to have to go to the Hernandez house with the message I carried. I took Muley with me, for he had stuck to me like a bur. Like a pup whose master has been a long time gone, he would not let me out of his sight.

We rode the familiar trail, and I dreaded the first sight of that stone house. When it came in view, I could see that very little had changed in the three years since I had been there. I reined my horse to a stop and looked at the place a long time, trying to get my courage up. Old memories came racing through my mind, memories I had forcibly buried long ago.

Muley looked at me worriedly. "How come we stopped, Josh? I thought we was goin' in."

"We're goin' in, Muley. It's the hardest thing I've ever had to do, but we're goin' in."

The dogs greeted us a hundred yards from the house and gave us a noisy escort. The younger Hernandez kids came running out, shouting joyously. I stepped down and handed the reins to Muley.

"You stay out here with the little ones, Muley. I'll go on in and do what I've got to do."

I gripped the crucifix nervously in my fist. I look a deep breath, then walked up under the brush arbor to the front door. The door swung inward. The breath all left me.

"Teresa!"

The girl at the door stared in surprise, then slowly shook her head. "Not Teresa. It's been a long time since we've seen each other, Josh Buckalew. Don't you know me?"

It was a minute before the shock left me so that I could answer. "María?"

"Yes, I am María. I've changed since you saw me last. You've changed too, Josh."

I could tell that in some ways she looked like her sister, and in other ways she didn't. The swift first impression had brought the image of Teresa back to me. María was not quite so tall. She was pretty, but she didn't have quite the fragile beauty of Teresa. María looked stronger, surer of herself. I doubted there was anything fragile about her.

"The wind is sharp outside, Josh. Come into the house."

I found myself trembling a little. "I'm sorry if I look like a fool. It's just that, for a second or two, you gave me an awful start."

"I would never take you for a fool, Josh. Please, come on in."

I followed her. Now Miranda came out of the kitchen, drying her hands. On her tiny frame her pregnancy was showing strongly now. It wouldn't be many months before Ramón would have another son—or a daughter.

"Josh Buckalew," Miranda smiled, "this is a surprise. After all these years, you've finally come to see us. I thought you were off to war."

"I was. Fighting is over now. I'm home again."

The two women looked quietly at each other. "It is over?" María said. "Then perhaps Antonio and Felix will be coming home."

My fist tightened on the crucifix. "Miranda, where's Ramón?"

"He rode out to find a horse. He should be home in a little while."

María pulled out a leather-bottomed chair. "Please, Josh, sit down. Tell us about the fighting. Was it terrible? Were you wounded?"

Gratefully I took the chair. I looked at the dirt floor. "Yes, it was terrible. No, I was not even scratched."

"And it is over now? All the men will be home?"

I shook my head. "Not all the men."

It seemed an eternity before Ramón finally came. I had to keep answering the women's questions while trying not to let them see in my eyes or sense in my voice the message I had come to give them. When I could, I stole glances at María. She was a woman now, not a girl.

At last Ramón came. I gathered all my courage and told them about Felix, and Antonio. I held out my hand with the crucifix in it. I saw María's eyes flood with tears before she turned away and buried her face against a white-plastered wall. Miranda clutched Ramón's arm as he took the crucifix from my hand and tenderly ran his fingers over the raised figure.

"I wish there was something I could say, Ramón, besides that I'm sorry."

Ramón's voice was brittle. He did not look into my face. "Thank you, Josh, for coming and telling us. Now, please, I would like you to go."

CHAPTER

12

Muley and I finished the scrapping that was left on the little bit of cotton he had not already picked. Later we planted a crop of wheat for spring harvest. It seemed there was always too much work to do.

We saw nothing of Ramón Hernandez. I dreaded any return to his place, and he evidently felt no wish to visit us. I could imagine his heavy sense of loss and knew it was not unreasonable to assume that he attached blame to me. I had been part of the attacking force.

The war news we received was scant and mostly contradictory but strong rumors kept drifting in that Santa Anna was gathering an army in Saltillo. How large it would be was something we could only guess at. Many Texians were not prone to worry, for they felt sure one American could whip ten Mexicans. After San Antonio, I didn't believe this—if I ever had.

In any case, no one thought Santa Anna would start north before spring. We all figured it would be late March or even April at the earliest before his troops would wet their feet in the Rio Grande.

In the meantime, precious little was being done to get Texas ready. Wrangling in the privisional government left it impotent. Personal feuds and jealousies kept it going in futile circles. Our Texas army was small and badly scattered, ill-disciplined and ill-equipped. Worse, its officers were quarreling among themselves just as the officials of the government were doing in San Felipe. Sam Houston had the command—on paper—but not many of the subordinate officers paid much attention to him. The command was splintered.

It was at this time that Travis, sharing a command with Bowie in San Antonio, wrote to Governor Smith that the people were "cold and indifferent . . . and in consequence of the dissensions between contending and rival chieftains they have lost confidence in their own government and officers." He added with disgust: "The thunder of the enemy's cannon and the pollution of their wives and daughters—the cries of their famished children and the smoke of their burning dwellings only will arouse them."

And that was the way things stood when Santa Anna's advance guard crossed the Rio Grande on the twelfth of February, six weeks to two months earlier than anyone really expected.

He caught us scattered, quarreling, and totally unprepared.

The first word of Santa Anna's advance was much worse than I had any idea it would be.

It was brought by red-faced old Alfred Noonan. Though any Mexican pursuit had been left days behind him, he spurred into our yard as if Santa Anna were reaching for his shirttail.

"Josh Buckalew!" he shouted. "You better go see about your brother!"

I never had felt any respect for the old man, and after the battle of San Antonio I had only contempt. I couldn't remember ever seeing him at any time when the action was heavy. Only when the conflict was over did he present himself, and then he was blustering and posturing as if he had won the battle by himself.

I walked out into the yard to meet him now. I didn't want to offer him any favors, but I could tell that his mount had been badly used. I pointed down toward the creek.

"Muley, go water Noonan's horse for him, will you?"

Noonan stepped down and handed the reins to Muley. "Much

obliged." Noonan's face was flushed even more than usual, his eyes bloodshot.

"Now," I said, "what's this about Thomas?"

Noonan swung his arms in a wide gesture. "Old Santy Anna's done crossed into Texas with the biggest bunch of Mexicans that you ever saw in your whole life. He's acomin', Josh. There ain't nothin' goin' to stop him but the good Lord Hisself, and the way things are goin' He must be busy someplace else."

"What about Thomas?"

"Boy, I'm afeered your brother is wounded. Maybe dead. There was a scrap down on the Rio Grande. A little bunch of our boys got caught by them Mexicans. It was like a panther pouncin' on a mouse. Most of our boys got theirselves kilt. Thomas was with that bunch."

Ice touched the pit of my stomach.

"You sure, Noonan? You're not just scared and excited?"

"They was down there, him and the Phipps boys and some others. Was all fixin' to go and raid Matamoros, but the orders never did come through. So they stayed down there and watched along the river. I was supposed to've been with them, only somethin' else come up."

Bet your life it did, I thought darkly. You hid.

"Jacob Phipps come back, shot in the arm. He said he seen his brother Ezekiel get his head blowed off. The last he seen of Thomas, he was ridin' off into the dust and the smoke to where the big shootin' was. There was an awful scatteration after that. A few of the boys like Jacob come a-limpin' back. Most of the others never did. Far as I know, Thomas didn't."

"As far as you *know*?" I grabbed him by the shirtfront. "Didn't you try to find out?"

"Boy, them Mexicans was acomin'! I'm tellin' you, they wasn't like any Mexicans I ever saw. They was thousands of them, and they was lookin' for blood!"

The terror of it was still naked in his eyes. I realized the old fraud couldn't help himself. Like many a big talker, he had feet of clay. I let go of him and stepped back, my heart sinking.

"If Thomas did come back, Noonan, where would he most likely be?"

Noonan shrugged. "Hard to say. Maybe Bexar, where Travis and Bowie are at. Maybe Goliad, because Fannin is there, and we was sort of under Fannin's command there towards the last."

I clinched my fists. For a moment hopelessness swept over me. Surely Thomas was dead.

And yet again, he might have gotten out.

I knew what Noonan's answer would be before I ever asked him. "You want to go back and help me look for him?"

Noonan shook his head violently. "No, sir, thank you. I had enough Mexicans to do me for the rest of my life. I'm takin' the Sabine chute!" That was a way of saying he was heading for the Sabine River and the safety of the United States.

"You got a farm here," I pointed.

"Old Santy Anna can just have it back."

I was too numb to offer him anything to eat, and he was in too much of a hurry to have accepted it. Soon as Muley brought his horse back, Noonan spurred away. I leaned my shoulder against the log cabin and stood there weakly, watching him disappear over the hill.

"Muley," I said, "I got to leave you again."

Muley cried and begged me like a little boy. But I had no choice except to leave him here. I couldn't take him with me into God knew what.

"Muley, you listen to me, and listen tight. There's no tellin' when I may get back. If the Mexicans come—and they may—don't let yourself get caught by them. You run. Take the best horse we got and run just as fast as you can. If you have to cross the Sabine, you do it, and don't stop to look back. When this is all over, I'll come find you."

"Josh," he cried, "I don't know what I'd do if you was not to come back."

A lump came in my throat. I wasn't sure either what would ever become of Muley. Alone, he would be as helpless as a child.

"I'll come back."

"You promise, Josh? You promise you'll come back?" His eyes brimmed with tears.

"I promise, Muley. Now you take good care of things while I'm gone. And remember what I said. Watch sharp. Don't let the Mexicans find you here."

IT WAS now past the middle of February. Riding for San Antonio de Bexar, I found people still not certain what to do. Some were packing their belongings and getting ready to head east. A few were already on the road. But most were waiting, still hopeful that the Texian forces could turn back the assault.

I rode into Bexar a little less than three months after I had left it. The city still showed all the scars of the awful battle, many of the stone and adobe houses caved in, gaping holes knocked in their sides by cannon balls or battering rams. I rode along the main street and found to my amazement that despite the dozens of rumors that Santa Anna's column was not far from the city, business still went on more or less as usual. Most of the stores were open, peddling whatever stocks they still had after the December disaster.

I rode up to the high old stone walls of the Alamo and found them fortified. If it came to the point of making a stand, I thought, Travis would probably pull his men into the mission. Its enclosure was big and rambling, containing more than two whole acres. In that respect it would be hard to defend with a small force. There was an alternative: the Concepción Mission, where Bowie's men had first come into conflict with the Cos troops back in November. But Concepción was outside of the city. The Alamo was the more likely choice.

A familiar voice called my name, and I looked up at the wall. There stood the tall, stooped figure of Jared Pounce.

"Howdy, Josh!" the old surveyor shouted. "You come to help us fight Santy Anna?"

I waved back at him and pointed to the open front gate. Jared climbed down and met me there as I rode in. We clasped hands. "Jared, you're lookin' good. To me, you always look good."

He smiled. Somehow I could tell he hadn't been smiling much. "Then I look better than I feel." His smile gradually left him. "I reckon you know what's comin', Josh."

"I've heard rumors. All of them bad." I grasped his arm. "Jared, is Thomas here?"

He shook his head. "No, is he supposed to be?"

I knew I shouldn't feel disappointed. I hadn't really expected to find Thomas in Bexar. But the disappointment was there, just the same. I told Jared what Noonan had told me. Jared listened solemnly.

"Josh, I think you better make up your mind to accept it. Thomas is likely dead."

"There's still the shadow of a doubt, Jared. I can't stop lookin' till I know for sure."

"I was hopin' you'd stay here with us. We'll be needin' all the men we can get."

A short way along the wall I watched Travis supervising the building of an embankment for emplacement of a cannon. The strain of command had left its mark. He was impatient and snappish with the men doing the work.

Jared said dryly, "He's tryin'. But he's fussin' with the wrong men. The ones he needs to crack the whip over are out in town, enjoyin' theirselves. Seems like the men are ready to fight and die with him, but they ain't willin' to follow his orders."

Across the courtyard came big Jim Bowie, walking unsteadily.

"Drunk?" I asked Jared.

"He's been drinkin' a little. Mostly he's just sick. Needs to be in bed. He and Travis don't get along, but they have to put up with each other. Half the men here won't listen to anybody except Bowie."

Travis and Bowie fell to arguing almost as soon as Bowie reached the embankment. They were too different to be able to get along. Travis was a gentleman born. Bowie had acquired the manner of a gentleman, but he had come up in a rough-and-tumble world of brawling and dueling and wild adventuring. Beneath the polish he was still a backwoods-man.

Their quarreling would soon end, for the enemy was almost at the gates. Then they would stand together, shoulder to shoulder, and leave the world a legend that would never die.

JARED POUNCE shook hands with me again at the open gate of the old mission. He said again, "I wish you was stayin'."

"I can't. I expect I'll go next to Goliad. Thomas could be there."

"If you don't find him, come back. The Alamo walls are high and stout."

None of us had a premonition then of what would so shortly come to pass. I did remember, though, that one reason General Cos had surrendered his Mexican troops to us in December was that he considered the Alamo indefensible.

Even now, most of the old Texians were not thinking in terms of independence. They were thinking only of defeating the despot Santa Anna and getting a fair shake from the Mexican government.

Jared said, "Josh, I been doin' a lot of thinkin' lately about what I'm goin' to do when the fightin' is over. You remember, it was me that showed you the place that you boys settled."

"I remember."

"There's still some land close by open for settlement. I think when we get the shootin' finished and square ourselves with Mexico, I'll take up some land out there and be neighbors with you. I always did like that country along the Colorado."

"We'll look forward to it, Jared."

I glanced back once as I rode away and caught a last look at the lean old man there by the front of the Alamo. I would never forget it.

THE ROAD from San Antonio to Goliad roughly paralleled the San Antonio River. I set out from the city without delay, for I had a strong feeling there wasn't much time. And there wasn't. Not far from San Antonio my horse suddenly pricked up its ears. It turned its head a little to the right, and I glanced in that direction. I saw horsemen, ten or fifteen of them. Texians, I thought, on their way to join Travis's garrison. Then I caught a glimpse of blue, and I knew. These were Mexican cavalrymen.

They saw me about the same time I saw them. There was no point in trying to do battle with that many men, even if I had had the inclination, which I didn't. It was a horserace for awhile. But eventually I lost them somewhere in the timber.

So they were here. I had been lucky in running into this bunch, then getting away. I was still alive, and free. At least now I knew I had to be alert.

I knew I would have to do a lot of hard riding and very little resting until I reached Goliad.

I learned something else, too. The lesson was abrupt and unexpected. I rode up to a Mexican house, expecting to ask for a fresh drink of water, for this was a place where the trail had dropped back away from the river. What I got was a blast from an old *escopeta* in the hands of a Mexican farmer. He missed me, but he taught me that from now on I had to avoid habitations.

A good percentage of the Mexican people in Texas disliked Santa Anna. But he had proclaimed this a holy war, Mexican against American. It was, he said, a racial war, dark skins against the light. Other matters of politics were put aside for the duration of this crusade. A great many of the Mexican people who otherwise opposed him accepted this at face value because they basically disliked Americans even more than they disliked the little Napoleon of the West. Now that Mexican troops were in the country again, I could not afford to trust any Mexican—civilian or soldier.

From this point on, I moved carefully, leaving the road and skirting any houses I came to.

———

THE OLD presidio at Bahia, generally known as Goliad by the time of the Texas revolution, had changed hands often, usually with violence. It had been a pawn in the Mexican war of independence against Spain. Its grounds had been tramped by the boots of filibusters. Last October it had been wrested from the Mexicans by Collinsworth and Milam. Now it was probably the chief Texian stronghold, for James W. Fannin had between four and five hundred volunteers quartered there.

The town had once held a thousand or so inhabitants, but now most of its brush *jacales* and its mud and stone houses stood empty. The Mexican people had withdrawn from this place of contention to the comparative safety of the *ranchos* down the river. A scattering of abandoned mongrel dogs roamed its deserted streets, hunting for enough food to keep themselves alive. Cattle blundered in and out of the doorless dwellings, some of which had already caved in.

Built on solid rock atop a hill stood the presidio itself, its thick stone-and-lime walls weathered to an oppressive gray by the long years. A chapel stood in the northwest corner, fronted by an artillery emplacement. The parade grounds were all enclosed by high stone walls which ran south and east from the chapel. This was the finest fort the Spaniards had ever built in Texas, for it straddled an important road from Nacogdoches to the interior of Mexico, and it was also near the sea. If there was a fort which could hold out against Santa Anna, I thought, this would be it.

Soldiers stood along the walls and out in front. One patrol stopped me briefly but quickly let me go.

Riding into the fort, I was struck by the fact that most of these men were not actually Texians. A majority were volunteers fresh in from various Southern states. Something else struck me, too—the strong faith in these men that they could whip anything that came along.

"Bring any Mexicans with you?" somebody shouted at me. "We're ready for a fight."

I explained my mission and was taken directly to Colonel Fannin.

He didn't give me time at first to ask about Thomas. He insisted on hearing how things stood in San Antonio, and back in the settlements. I told him San Antonio had still been open when I had left there. Then I told him about running into Mexican cavalry. His face creased. He paced, his hands behind him.

"How many did you see?"

"Just a patrol, ten or fifteen."

"You saw no others? You saw no columns?"

"Nothin' but that patrol. Other than that, all I can tell you is the rumors I've heard. You've likely heard those already."

He frowned. "A hundred of them, and no two alike. We are in darkness here. We don't know what's going on to the south. For that matter, we know very little that's going on to the north and east. We're isolated. Sometimes I think they've all forgotten us."

"I doubt that's so, sir. One story I've heard is that a lot of men are gatherin' in Gonzales. Buildin' up an army. I expect General Houston will take command of them if it's true. And they'll most likely be marchin' in this direction."

Fannin still paced. "I hope so. Meanwhile I wish they'd let me know what's going on. I wish I could tell just what to do."

I told him it looked to me like this fort was situated to stand off a big siege.

Fannin nodded briskly. "You know how Mexicans fight. It'll take a lot of them to dislodge us. We'll never give up the ship while there is a pea left in the dish."

I nodded agreement, but it occurred to me he was overconfident, like his men appeared to be. The Mexican troops he had seen so far had seemed amateurish and even comical to his West Point-trained eyes. He was downgrading them too much. That could be a costly mistake.

"Colonel," I said, "I've come looking for my brother. I wondered if he might be here."

I explained to him what Noonan had told me. Fannin went to his duty rosters and slowly ran his fingers down the pages, shaking his head as he came to the bottom of each one.

A chill passed through me. I knew before he had finished what his answer had to be. "I'm sorry, there doesn't seem to be a Buckalew listed here anywhere."

I swallowed. "Colonel, does what Noonan said sound like anything you've heard of? Do you know of any scrap that fits the description?"

Fannin rubbed the back of his neck.

"Our reports from down that way have been very sketchy, Buckalew. There could have been a dozen engagements and we wouldn't have heard of them." He turned to a big Texas map which had been pegged to his wall. His finger sought out Goliad. "Now, it's possible your brother could be attached to Johnson's force at San Patricio." His finger dropped south on the map. "It is highly probable that Johnson would be keeping patrols out south of San Patricio, possibly all the way to the Rio Grande. And, if the Mexicans have crossed in force, it is likely that some of these patrols have made contact with them. Violent contact." He turned and faced me. "If you're going that way, I hope you find him alive. And, Buckalew," he paused, "if you find out what the Mexicans are up to, find a way to get the information to me."

"I'll do what I can, sir." I left him then and started for San Patricio.

CHAPTER

13

I T WAS all strange country to me, for I had never been in this part of Texas before. This was the coastal region. When the wind was out of the east I could smell the Gulf, or fooled myself into thinking I did.

I wasn't interested in seeing the country, though. My immediate concern was to get to San Patricio without falling into Mexican hands. I followed the trail, for without it I wouldn't know the way. But as on the road to Goliad, I took pains to skirt around any Mexican dwellings.

I came at last to a house that was plainly American-built. Here, at least, I would be welcome. I rode up to it boldly.

That turned out to be a grievous mistake. A Mexican civilian stepped into the yard, a blunderbuss in his hand, and fired at me without so much as a howdy-do. I wheeled the horse around and spurred away, thankful for fast horses and poor Mexican marksmanship.

That was my second such experience. Santa Anna's race war idea had taken hold. I knew now I would have to live by Thomas's old credo: never trust a Mexican.

There were creeks along the way: Blanco, Medio, and some that weren't named on the map one of the Goliad officers had sketched for me. The rations I'd carried with me from Goliad gave out and I ate dry bread until I came across a fat cow, caught, and butchered her. Taking some of a hind quarter, I rode a long way before daring to stop and cook the meat.

I had lost count of time, but I knew it was the last of February or first of March when I ran into the three stragglers.

They could have been Mexicans, for all I knew. I drew off the trail and into a clump of timber, covering my horse's nose with my hand, hoping they hadn't seen me. My rifle was cradled in my arm, ready. The horsemen came directly toward me, one slumped forward, another helping hold him in the saddle.

Their horses sensed mine. One of them nickered. Instantly two of the men slid off onto the ground, thrusting their rifle barrels up over their saddles. They could have been either Mexican or American. I held my breath and brought my rifle to rest across the branch of a tree. My hand tightened on the stock.

One of the men shouted, "Grab Bill. He's fallin' off."

The man who had been slumped was sliding out of the saddle.

The voice had been enough. They were American. I shouted, "It's all right. I'm a Texian." They still didn't trust me. I led my horse out of the timber and dropped the rifle down to arm's length to show I wasn't hostile. The two men on their feet still kept their rifles pointed at me. I saw that one—a man with red hair and a tangled red beard—was holding his leg out stiffly. A dried crimson spot showed on the dirty cloth wrapped around the leg. The wounded man in the saddle had a gray coat bundled around him, one sleeve dangling empty. Bloodstains showed he had been shot deep in the shoulder.

"It's all right," I repeated. "I come from Goliad."

They lowered their rifles. One said, "Lord, it's sure good to see a friendly face. I hope to God you got somethin' with you a man could eat. And maybe a little water? Bill here is burnin' up with fever."

I helped them lower the wounded man to the grass and brought my canteen. While I carefully doled out water to the one named Bill, the other two hungrily tore into what was left of the beef.

"It's been much hidin', little water, and no rations for us since them Mexicans hit us at San Patricio," one man said, his jaw bulging.

I looked up sharply. "San Patricio?"

"They came on us unexpectedly. Killed nearly every man. I never thought there was so many Mexicans."

"I was on my way to San Patricio. Lookin' for my brother."

"Mister, if he was there, I expect he's dead."

"His name is Thomas Bucaklew. Do you know him?"

The man frowned, thinking. "Buckalew? I don't believe I recollect such a name as that. There wasn't no Buckalew at San Patricio, was there, Red?"

The red-bearded one stopped chewing. His lips moved as he formed the name quietly to himself. Then he said, "I seem to remember there *was* a Buckalew, but not at San Patricio. He was south, with a patrol that worked down all the way to the Rio Grande."

Excitement began to build in me. "Where would he be now?"

Red shook his head. "In heaven, I expect, or in hell. Most of the boys down on the river were killed by the first Mexicans that crossed over."

"Did you see anybody who said they saw him die?"

"No, but there was only a handful came out alive."

I looked south, my eyes narrowed. "He could be down there someplace hidin' out, maybe wounded. I might be able to find him."

The bigger of the two men said. "You'd be throwin' your life away to try. You know that country down there? Ever been there before?"

I told him I hadn't.

"Well, there's nothin' down there now but Mexicans, thousands of them. They caught even the boys that knew the country. You would go down like a rabbit in a wolf's den."

It took me a long time to decide to turn back north with these three battle survivors. I could think of a dozen reasons why I should go on south, but these man had an answer for every one of them. They stressed that it was unlikely Thomas could still be alive. That I could find him was even more unlikely. And to fall into a Mexican trap was almost certain death, for Santa Anna's orders were to kill.

"I seen one boy that lost his horse throw his hands up and try to surrender," said Red. "They shot him to pieces."

"That's why you got to go back with us," argued the other, named Jimson. "You got no chance atall. And besides, we need help with Bill."

My jaw went tight when I looked down at the worst wounded of the three. He wouldn't live to reach Goliad. That bullet had been in him too deep, and too long.

So when all the talking was done I had to turn my back on Thomas and San Patricio. I had to accept the probability that Thomas had fallen with the others, and that even if he hadn't, there was nothing I could do for him.

ONLY THREE of us lasted to reach Goliad. We scratched out a shallow grave for Bill and left him near Blanco Creek. We led his horse on in. At a time like this, horses would be worth more than gold.

Nobody paid much attention to me, for hardly anyone in the fort at Goliad knew me anyway. Most of them hadn't been in Texas more than a few weeks. They were volunteers from the States, for the most part, come to whip the breeches off a bunch of dirty Mexicans. Besides, I hadn't been in any of the recent fighting. But the men thronged around Red and Jimson, eager for details of the battle.

"Battle, hell," Red snorted, favoring his leg. "It wasn't no battle. It was slaughter."

Colonel Fannin sent for us as soon as he heard. We found him in his quarters, worriedly studying a map. He frowned at me. "Aren't you the man who was here looking for his brother?" I said I was, and that I hadn't found him. Fannin nodded sympathetically, as if he had known all along that I wouldn't. He turned gravely to Red and

Jimson. "I've already had the bad news from San Patricio. But I'd like to hear it from your viewpoint."

They gave it to him briefly and simply. They didn't have to embellish it any, for the truth was bad enough. Fannin questioned them closely about the Mexican strength. They could only guess, for like the field soldier anywhere, their knowledge of the war was limited to what went on in front of them. The war, to them, was whatever their own part of the battle had been. And for Red and Jimson, it had been bitter.

Fannin said, "There weren't enough of you, and you had no position of strength. So, the Mexicans took you. Here we have one of the best fortifications in Texas, and adequate men to defend it. When they get here, we'll stop them cold. I can use you men—all three of you—if you'd care to stay."

Red gingerly touched his leg. "I'm tired of ridin' with this. I'd sure admire to rest. And I doubt there's a safer place anywhere than Goliad." Jimson agreed. Fannin looked at me.

I nodded, grimly accepting what had to be the truth. "I'll take up where my brother left off. And here is as good a place as any to turn and fight."

So, without ceremony, we were marched into Fannin's command of volunteers inside that gray, grim stone fortress on the hill.

Fannin believed in drill, and he tried to carry it out in West Point style. It honed the discipline of a military command to a fine edge, he said. We were well honed, for we had several hours of it every day. Some of the volunteers complained that they had come all the way from Georgia and Kentucky and Tennessee to fight, not to drill. They drilled anyway. And when we weren't drilling, we were busy strengthening the rock walls, building new emplacements for artillery.

I was at the gate the day a courier came downriver from the direction of San Antonio and spurred up the hill on a worn-out horse. Stiff and weary, he almost fell from his mount as he reined to a stop. I helped grab him. On his feet, he leaned back on the sweat-lathered animal.

"Colonel Fannin," he gasped. "Message for Colonel Fannin."

I said, "We'll take you to him. Where did you come from?"

"From San Antonio de Bexar. The Mexicans have gotten there."

"How bad is it?" somebody asked.

"Bad. Travis, Bowie, and the others, they're forted up in the old Alamo. Travis sent me to fetch help."

We took him to Fannin's quarters. The courier braced himself with a strong shot of whisky while Fannin read the message from Travis, his brow furrowed. At length he said.

"My last orders were to hold Goliad. If I split my force to go to Bexar, I would jeopardize our position here."

The courier argued, "They're goin' to need help if they hold the Alamo."

Fannin's sense of futility showed plainly as he turned and looked at his map. He ran his finger along the road from Goliad to San Antonio de Bexar. "Ninety miles to San Antonio. Even with a forced march it would take us time to get there if we took the equipment we need." He rubbed his hand across his face. "I wish to God I knew what to do."

I thought he was going to make a decision, but he didn't. He said he needed time to think. He ordered us to leave while he continued to talk with the courier.

Later, Fannin made his decision. Against his better judgment he ordered us to prepare for a forced march to the relief of the Bexar garrison. We hadn't gotten far before we had a breakdown. Still not certain he had done right, Fannin was discouraged. Somewhere to the south—and probably not far—was a strong Mexican force. If it caught us on the road, we might have a hard time fighting through. The officers counseled.

Fannin reversed his decision. The order came to retreat to Goliad. It was a foregone conclusion now that the Alamo would not stand. Better to stay together and hold Goliad, Fannin declared, than to risk the loss of all.

So James Bonham, the courier, disregarded the admonitions of all around him and spurred once again toward San Antonio to carry the bad news to Travis: Fannin wasn't coming. He could have stayed. To return was death, and he knew it. But he went.

It was a cold grim, gray day when the expected news came from San Antonio. The Alamo had been overwhelmed. The garrison had been slaughtered to the last man.

Even expected, it was a staggering thing. Travis, Bowie, Crockett, Bonham, and all those others . . . men we had fought beside, men we had eaten with and drunk with.

And for me there had been someone special, old Jared Pounce.

A pall of gloom descended upon the garrison at Goliad.

Yet the strange thing was that few really thought it could happen to *us*. Not here at Goliad. When the Mexicans came we'd show them how Americans could fight. We'd repay them for the Alamo.

WHAT BEGAN to break our back was the division of our forces. Word came from the village of Refugio, some thirty miles east toward the Gulf, that families there wanted to leave and needed an escort. Fannin sent Captain King of the Georgia Battalion and a company of twenty-three men. Reaching Refugio, they found themselves hard pressed by Mexican cavalry. They took cover in an old mission. A messenger managed to break through the Mexican lines and reach Goliad. This time Fannin sent out Colonel Ward with the Georgia Battalion of about a hundred and fifty men to relieve King.

We didn't know it then, but these men would never come back. We expected their return at almost any time. But a day passed, two days, and still no word.

Then came a courier from Sam Houston, bearing orders to Fannin that we abandon Goliad and retreat to Victoria, to the area of heavier American settlement.

Had we followed the orders when they arrived, things might have turned out differently. But Ward and King were still out. We couldn't just abandon them. We were told that Fannin was restlessly pacing the floor of his quarters, trying to decide what to do. He was between a rock and a hard place, between military obligation to his commanding officer and the moral obligation he felt toward the men he had sent out and had not heard from.

So again we waited . . . one day, two days, three days.

The Mexicans weren't waiting.

At last Fannin found out for certain what we had all begun to feel in our bones: Ward and King and their commands had been taken.

Fannin gave the order to prepare for evacuation. We worked through the night packing up and getting ready to be on the move. We mounted the artillery that we could transport. The heavy artillery, we spiked. The rest we dumped into the trenches we had sweated so hard to dig, and we covered them up. We set fire to everything that would burn.

With daylight we set forth into heavy fog on the road to Victoria, two hundred and fifty or so men afoot, about twenty-five a-horseback, a company of artillery, nine small pieces of ordnance, and a mortar, all drawn by oxen. Because I had a horse, I was attached to Colonel Horton's scouts. We rode ahead to the ford on the San Antonio River, half expecting attack there, for we had seen Mexicans and had even had a scrap with a Mexican patrol. The attack didn't come, but the largest cannon stuck in the river. We lost an hour pulling it out of the mud.

In all the bustle, nobody had thought to feed the oxen. They were hungry and contrary. All in all, it started out to be a hard day.

We were well across the prairie about ten miles from Goliad, and the oxen were still giving trouble. Ahead of us lay Coleto Creek and a heavy stand of timber. But we came across a patch of new grass in an area that had been burned over by the prairie fire. Fannin decided we had better rest and graze the oxen, or they might never get us to the timber. So another order went down the line: stop and unyoke.

I didn't like it, but nobody asked me. Somewhere—not far away—there had to be a large force of Mexicans. We had seen enough of their patrols to have no doubt about it. Even so, few of the men seemed overly worried. There was still that powerful conviction of our own superiority. Most of them agreed we couldn't be beaten by a ragtag bunch of greasy Mexicans.

Our scouting group went out to look around while the command rested. We didn't go far, and we didn't see anything. When we returned, the oxen were yoked again and the march resumed.

We could camp when we reached the timber, the officers agreed.

We never made it. A vague dark line began moving up in timber to the south of us. As it detached itself from the timber, we saw that the line was made of horsemen, and many of them. We looked back. Behind us came another line. Both lines approached rapidly and began spreading out.

"My God," Jimson shouted, "there are thousands of them!"

There weren't, but there were enough to take a man's breath away. We began crowding the oxen, struggling to make the timber.

Colonel Horton shouted an order. One of the six-pounders was quickly unlimbered. A shot was fired at the horsemen, and another, and another.

"That'll scare them off," the colonel said hopefully.

But all three rounds fell short. The Mexicans kept coming.

Our rear guard came galloping up. We pushed on a little farther. The ammunition cart broke down. We lost time while men transferred the load. By then the Mexican cavalrymen had circled around to the front of us. They had cut us off from the timber.

"Circle up, men!" Fannin shouted. "Circle up!"

Some of the volunteers began firing their rifles, but the range was still much too long. Fannin ordered the shooting to stop. No use wasting powder and lead. We formed a hollow square, facing our artillery outward to fire on the enemy from whatever direction they might come.

Now we could make out the horsemen distinctly. We could see the flying pennants. We could hear bugles in the chill of the March air.

They sounded what must have been the charge. The Mexican

cavalry spurred toward us from three directions. Our artillery opened up with grape and cannister shot. We could see horses and men go down. The Mexicans kept coming, right into the range of our rifles and muskets. We began to fire, timing ourselves by ranks so that one group was in position to shoot while another was loading. Great gaps were blasted through the Mexican ranks. Still, on they came.

Their forward riders were upon the square itself when the rapid and deadly fire of our volunteers stopped them. The Mexicans reeled back, loose horses running wild, stirrups flapping . . . wounded horses threshing and screaming. Mexicans afoot looked around desperately for comrades to pick them up. Some were abandoned and fell under the Texian fire.

While the Mexicans pulled back, we reloaded and surveyed our own damage. It was heavy. We had already lost most of our horses and oxen. We had several men killed and a number wounded.

To my dismay I found that the man named Red lay lifeless behind one of the cannons, a gaping hole in his chest. He had taken a bullet through the leg at San Patricio but had survived to rejoice that Goliad would be safe for him. Now he was dead. The irony of it was bitter.

Before this was over, he would turn out to be the lucky one.

Overconfidence appeared to curse both sides. The Mexicans evidently had expected to sweep over us with ease. The steel-coated resistance of these volunteers had come as a deadly surprise. They feinted at us several times, but they kept falling back as soon as they reached rifle range. They quit trying to charge and set up a constant fire of muskets and *escopetas*. We answered their fire. Some of the Mexicans began crawling toward us, hiding in the tall dry grass. But a lot of our volunteers were crack riflemen. Any time they saw enough of a man to draw a bead on, they usually hit their mark. The Mexican losses were heavy.

The fire continued until nightfall. Then the enemy withdrew to the timber. That gave us time to look around and consider our situation. The longer we looked, the less we liked it.

Ahead of us, so near and yet so far away, stood the timber we had been trying for. Once in it, we could take advantage of its cover and stand off a force several times our size. Out here in this open prairie, we were paralyzed.

But how could we ever reach the timber now? In the growing darkness we could see the wink of Mexican campfires around us. Our teams were gone, either stampeded by the gunfire or killed by it. The officers took tally and found that we had seven men dead, sixty wounded. A majority of these wounded would be unable to walk.

Among the wounded was Fannin himself. He had taken a rifle ball in the thigh.

What water we had with us was gone. Most of the ammunition for our cannons was used up. Food supplies were scanty, for the officers had felt confident we would reach Victoria and had not wanted to overload the wagons.

Now night fell upon us, cold and terribly dark. I still had my blanket, but I found that many of the men had dropped theirs when the fighting started. Now they were without. I tucked my blanket around a wounded man who lay shivering from the cold. He cried for water, but I had none.

Fannin called the men around him. Calmly he outlined the seriousness of our situation, something most of the men had become painfully aware of already.

"We still have a chance," he said, "to reach Coleto Creek and the timber. The darkness will help cover us. And I think that if we run into Mexican troops we can fight our way through. But we'll have to go afoot and there are many among our wounded who cannot walk. We can go, and we can reach safety. But if we go, we'll have to leave those who cannot make the journey afoot."

Someone said, "Colonel, what will the Mexicans do to the men we leave?"

Fannin minced no words. "You all heard the report that came to us about the few of Captain King's men who surrendered at Refugio. They were taken out and shot."

"That means," the soldier declared, "they'll probably shoot any-body we leave behind."

Fannin said, "That is the way it appears to me. We can save our-selves by leaving the badly wounded behind to die. Or, we can stay with them and all take our chance together. I won't command you to do either. I'll leave it up to you men to take a vote."

There was a minute or so of hushed conversation among the men. Almost every one of them had a close friend or relative among the wounded. The decision was unanimous.

"Very well," said Fannin, and I could tell that he approved the de-cision. "We'll stay. We'll build whatever fortifications we can during the night. And then we'll see what the morning will bring."

T HE NIGHT was long and black and cold. The groans of the
wounded raised the hair on the back of my neck. Not even in
the battle of San Antonio last fall had we been involved in a situation as desperate as this. In their fever, wounded men begged for
water that no one had. The little bit of water had long since been
used up. All of us thirsted, but for the injured the night was torture.
A light mist hung in the air, though not enough to afford relief. On
the contrary, it made the cold bite deeper.

Hungry, cold, sleepless, those of us who were able worked through
the night digging trenches, fortifying ourselves the best we could. It
was too cold to rest long at a time. Instead, we worked.

When we had the ditches two or three feet deep, we dragged up
the oxcarts and the carcasses of horses and oxen, and placed them
for breastworks. Through the long night we listened to the Mexicans
blowing their bugles, far out in the darkness. If it was an attempt to
keep us awake, they needn't have bothered. We were too cold and
hungry and thirsty to sleep. Once in a while a Mexican sentry would
cry out, "*Sentinela alerta*," a sign that all was well. For them, it might
have been.

Daylight finally came. It was Sunday, March 20. As the darkness began to fade, we could see the Mexicans moving. Three or four hundred men were coming up as replacements, bringing with them a hundred or so pack mules. They had two new brass nine-pounders and would certainly have a fresh supply of ammunition.

The cannons roared. We threw ourselves face down into the tramped-out grass and dirt. The shots were too high. They were over our heads. Fannin, wounded and in pain, gave the order to hold our fire. "The range is too great, and our ammunition is too low. Let's wait until we can hit what we shoot at."

The Mexicans fired their cannons several times, not a single shot hitting inside our tight square. Again movement started among the ranks of the Mexican cavalry. We brought up our rifles and muskets, sure the charge was about to commence. Instead, an officer rode out, carrying a white flag.

"Maybe they want to give up," somebody said dryly.

One of our majors and some other officers walked out to meet the Mexican about halfway between our position and the enemy lines. They talked a little, then came back. The major went straight to Fannin.

"That's General Urrea's command out there. The general sends word that he wants to avoid shedding blood without reason. He guarantees that we'll be dealt with leniently if we surrender at discretion."

Fannin exploded. "At discretion? That means unconditional. That means we retain no rights. We turn ourselves over to them to be treated in any way they see fit."

The major nodded solemnly. "I reckon that's what it means."

Fannin looked at us then, his gaze slowly sweeping the whole miserable little band huddled behind the embankment of earth and the upset carts and dead animals. He shook his head. "Go back and tell him we shall *not* surrender at discretion. We had rather die to the last man in these trenches!"

The major delivered his message. The Mexican officer wheeled his horse around and carried the report to General Urrea. Shortly the whole Mexican line began to move again. It looked once more as if the charge would start at any moment.

Instead, a handful of men rode out toward the truce area. Jimson whistled. "Look at the uniform on that Mexican. That must be Urrea."

Fannin, propped against a pack, his injured leg extended in front of him, lifted a spyglass to his eye. "It is Urrea indeed. He wants to parley. Major, I guess this time I had better go. I'll need your help." The major and half a dozen of us moved quickly to aid him.

Fannin, on his feet but favoring the wounded leg, turned and looked again at those of us gathered around him. "Men, I suspect that this time he has a better offer, or he wouldn't have come. I know that as commander I am supposed to make the decisions. But this may mean your lives, and I'll not make the decision alone. If you choose, we'll stay here and fight until we die. But if you vote to surrender, and we are offered acceptable terms, I shall abide by your vote. What say you?"

The officers huddled first. Then they divided us into our own companies for a quick discussion.

When the question came around to me, I said, "Either way, we lose. We're trapped here. If we stay we'll either starve or be killed. We can't break out without leaving the wounded, and the longer we stay the more wounded there'll be."

Jimson took it up. "We couldn't leave the wounded. So it comes to this: we stay here and die for certain, or surrender and hope."

I pointed out, "You know what happened to King's and Ward's men who surrendered. They were shot."

Jimson shrugged. "A chance of war. If it was an easy decision, we wouldn't be standin' here arguin' over it."

In the end, the decision was made. We would surrender if Fannin could get us good terms. Otherwise, we would stay here and die like the men of the Alamo had died.

Fannin went out, the major and some of the other officers with him. Every step he took was agony.

After a long time, Fannin and the major came back. And with them came the resplendent General Urrea himself, bringing several aides. They wrote down the agreement, a copy in Spanish and one in English. All signed it. Fannin folded the English copy and put it inside his coat.

So we gave up our arms and marched out of the trenches, carrying our wounded with us.

It was a slow, painful, pride-killing return to the fortress we had left. Nobody talked much, for the shock and hurt went too deep. Most of these men had come to Texas lightheartedly looking for the grand adventure, the great crusade, to strike a blow for liberty and show a contemptible enemy how Americans could fight.

It was all for nothing. They could fight, these volunteers, but they had been wasted by poor planning and indecision and a fatal contempt for the enemy. The cause was good, the spirit strong; but it had all been thrown away.

The officer who had superintended the surrender of weapons was a German mercenary. Many of Santa Anna's officers were Europeans. In good English he said, "Well, gentlemen, in ten days it will be liberty and home!"

It sounded good at the time. But it would come back bitter as gall.

THEY PUT us in what had once been the chapel, and we began to wish we hadn't worked so hard to destroy everything in the fortress before we left it. That first night was torture. We were crowded so tightly that not all had room to lie down. The trapped air was hot and stifling. We gasped for breath.

Our wounded needed attention and fresh bandages, but the Mexicans had few or none for themselves. Contrary to the terms of the surrender agreement, which had guaranteed to respect private property, the Mexican soldiers methodically robbed us of whatever individual possessions we had. In my case, it wasn't much. I had already lost my horse, my saddle, and my blanket.

The wounded suffered severely for want of attention. The Mexicans had taken our few doctors away to treat their own men. Gangrene developed in some of the wounds. The stench and the moaning of the men made cold sweat break out on the rest of us. We had water now, for details were permitted to go down under guard and fetch it from the river. But there was little food, and no chance to make broth for the men who so badly needed it.

Some of our wounded passed away, and death came to them as a friend.

It was the following Friday that a call went up.

"More prisoners!"

The gates opened. More than a hundred men dragged in—I couldn't say they marched—and the gates closed behind them.

"It's Major Ward," one of the officers declared, and hurried forth to meet the new prisoners. With Ward was the tiny remnant of his men who had survived the battle at Refugio. In addition there were a hundred or so fresh volunteers, taken at Copano the minute they stepped down from their ship. They never had a chance to take a rifle in hand, much less to fire it.

Their faces were sad, angry, frustrated. They had tried, and they had failed. Now they were at this dreary hell with us. I couldn't bring myself to look at them. I dropped my gaze, staring at my dirt-crusted moccasins, my ragged breeches.

I thought I heard someone call my name.

"Josh?" It was more a question than anything. I raised my eyes, and my heart leaped.

"Thomas!"

I jumped to my feet and grabbed him. We hugged each other, blubbering like children. At last he groaned, and I saw what I had overlooked in my haste and my joy. He was wounded. His tattered coat was buttoned with his left arm inside, the sleeve hanging empty.

"Thomas," I cried in relief, "I thought you were dead."

He looked as if he wanted to smile but couldn't. "I thought for a while that I was too. Damn it, Josh, I hate to be a-findin' you here."

"I'm glad to find you here, or anyplace. I'd given you up."

Thomas's eyes showed pain. "You shouldn't have gotten yourself into this. You ought to've stayed home."

"Old Noonan came by the place. Said he thought you'd been wounded, or killed. I set out to find you."

Thomas gritted, "Noonan, that old scoundrel! Big talk, but a yellow streak as wide as your hat. Time for fightin' come around, he wasn't to be seen." He looked at me again with those sad eyes. "I'm sure sorry to find you here."

I said, "Where were you? How bad is that wound?"

He shrugged, and the effort hurt him. "I was south of San Patricio. On patrol. The Mexicans caught me by surprise. Killed most of the boys. They shot me in the shoulder, then killed my horse. He fell on top of me. They left me there for dead. I finally got out from under the horse and started walkin' north. It was mighty slow going." He looked around. "Josh, I sure hope you got somethin' here to eat. I'm starved."

I shook my head. "There's not much. We've all been hungry for days. A few of the boys managed to hide away a little coin when the soldiers looted us. They been buyin' a small bit of bread and coffee from the camp followers. Outside of that, the Mexicans have been bringin' us a little beef . . . nothin' more."

Thomas found an open spot by the stone wall and dropped down to stretch his legs out in front of him. He flinched as pain from the bad shoulder grabbed him.

"Thomas, you better let me look at that shoulder."

He waved me off. "The bullet's out. Time will take care of the rest of it. If we've got any time."

"What do you mean?"

"These Mexicans haven't been takin' prisoners."

I told him we had a guarantee from Urrea. Colonel Fannin still kept a copy of the agreement in his pocket, as far as I knew.

Thomas asked, "Where is Urrea now?"

"He left. Went on to wherever the fightin' is. A colonel by the name of Portilla is in charge now."

"Urrea signed the paper, and now he's gone?"

I nodded. Thomas grunted, then dismissed the subject. He started asking me how things had been at home when I left. I told him all I could.

It was strange how all our past differences faded away under these cruel gray walls. Whatever bitterness might have lingered in me had disappeared in my relief at seeing him. The trouble we shared now, the oppression of captivity, made us brothers again.

Thomas told me how he had wandered afoot after the battle, the wound causing a fever that set him to staggering, half out of his head. An old Mexican found him, took pity on him, and carried him to his *jacal*. There the old man and his wife dug the bullet out of him. They hid him for days while Mexican patrols scouted for stragglers.

"Josh, I always said I'd never take a favor off of a Mexican, but that pair saved my life. I owe them more than I could ever say. If I get out of this alive, I'll find some way to pay them. If I don't get out and you do, I want you to pay them for me."

"Thomas, you'll get out. The war is over for us. They say they're goin' to send us home."

He grimaced. "Maybe." He told me the old couple's name and how I could find them. "You remember now, I want you to see that those old folks don't ever need for nothin'."

I agreed, to get him to quit fretting. "Sure, Thomas, if it comes to that. But we're both goin' to live. If the Mexicans take Texas away from us, we can always go home to Tennessee. And we'll go together."

CHAPTER

15

PALM SUNDAY, March 27. It was a beautiful morning, bright and shining with the hope of freedom. Some of the friendlier guards had brought us the rumor that a ship was being sent to Copano to take us on board and carry us to the United States. A feeling of vast relief had swept gloom from the prisoners' compound. Now there was rising jubilation.

"Home," the man said. "They're sendin' us home!"

Last night we had all sung, "Home, Sweet Home," and the words brought tears that burned many an eye.

We didn't know that as we sang, a courier arrived from Santa Anna. The general had flown into a black rage when he learned about Urrea's prisoners. So the courier had brought Colonel Portilla a written order that the officer crumpled in horror. We didn't know the colonel had paced in his quarters all night, racked by conscience, praying for forgiveness for what he had to do.

THE GATES opened. We stood up—those who could—hoping the guards had brought beef. Instead, a Mexican officer stepped into the yard and signaled for us to gather around him.

Thomas was stiff and sore from his wound. I helped him to his feet. He leaned on me for support a moment, until he had the strength to walk alone.

"Good news, my friends," the officer said. His mouth was smiling, though it struck me that his eyes were not. "You are starting home today. The ship is arriving in Copano. You have but to walk there."

More than three hundred voices lifted in a lusty cheer. I shouted with them, then glanced at Thomas. I saw hope flicker in his eyes, but I saw doubt there, too.

The officer said, "Those who are able to walk will do so. The badly wounded will stay. They will be taken later in carts. It will be necessary for guard purposes to divide you into groups."

He picked out our officers and told them to gather us into their own commands. Because Thomas had been captured alone and belonged to no group here, I kept him with me. The men who had been captured as they got off the ship at Copano had been given white armbands to wear while they were in the fortress. Now this group was all gathered in one section.

I saw Fannin lying on the ground, unable to walk except with the greatest pain and difficulty. He was smiling as he watched us. The Mexicans up to now had not honored all the terms of the capitulation. They had allowed their soldiers to rob us. They had not fed us as they had agreed. But now they were sending us home. Fannin, I thought, must have felt gratified about this. It meant that after all his defeats, at least he had made a decent bargain for us.

"Thomas," I said, "you'd better stay here. Let them bring you in a cart."

He shook his head violently. "I'll make it. I want to get out into the clear air."

I had some serious doubts, but I figured if he gave out they would let him ride.

I got to thinking then about Muley, back there at our place. Not much telling what would happen to him now. It seemed a certainty that the Mexican army would overrun everything in its path. If he didn't run, they would catch him. If he did run, where would he go?

We were marched out the gate, one group at a time. Ours was the third to leave. The last—the men with the white armbands—were still inside. As we moved out into the open, it struck me that spring was coming now. The brush was leafing, the grass turning green. The sky was a light, clear blue. I didn't remember when I had ever seen it so beautiful.

They started us down toward the old ford on the river. Thomas kept looking back over his shoulder.

"Funny thing, Josh. They didn't bring the other two bunches this way."

"What do you mean?"

"They took them off in other directions. This is the road to Copano."

I didn't have an answer. I looked at the armed Mexican guards who marched on both sides of our strung-out line, an uneasiness stirring in me. About a hundred volunteers were in our group. The other groups which had gone out before us had been much the same. There weren't as many of the guards as there were of us. That didn't look like treachery. And yet, Thomas's contagious suspicion began to work on me.

Several Mexican cavalrymen leisurely worked their way down on horseback from their encampment, carrying lances under their arms.

Jimson was in fine spirits. "They must be figurin' on proddin' up the slow ones. But goin' home, there ain't nobody apt to be very slow."

We walked along in silence. I kept watching Thomas now, and I saw his suspicion gradually change into alarm. He turned now and again, counting the guards over and over, seeing where they were. His restless eyes followed the lancers.

"Josh," he said quietly, "if worst comes to worst, the lancers are the ones you got to watch. Half of these guards probably can't shoot. But those lancers will sure run you through."

"Thomas, you're just borrowin' trouble."

"I'm talkin', that's all. But you listen, and listen good. There's lots of brush along the river. A man could hide himself in there, if he ever made it that far. With luck he could hold out till dark. Then he could head out across country. He'd have a chance to get back to our own lines and maybe strike another blow at Santa Anna."

He walked along hunched a little, for the shoulder was hurting him. I said, "You ought to've stayed and ridden in the cart, like I told you."

He shook his head. "If we're really goin' to Copano, I'll make it. If we're goin' to die, I'll die out here where the air is clean."

"Thomas, you quit talkin' about dyin'."

"You remember what I said about that old Mexican couple. See after them, you hear?"

I wondered how he figured—if something was going to happen—that I would live through it and he wouldn't. I guess he knew that with his bad shoulder he couldn't run far.

We had walked about half a mile from the fortress when a Mexican up front raised his hand and shouted. *"Alto!"* We all stopped.

Jimson called in high good humor, "Tell him we're not tired yet. Tell them we want to keep on a-walkin'."

Several commands were given in Spanish. The squad of guards on the upriver side of us began to move. They split, half going around in front of us, half in back of us. In a moment they filed up to join the guards who were stationed between us and the river.

Thomas stiffened. I saw his face turn a leaden gray.

Then, from far off in the distance, came the ragged sound of musketry.

Jimson gave voice to the sudden horrible realization that swept over us all. "My God, boys, they're goin' to kill us!"

I heard someone cry out. Men began to pray. One man dropped to his knees, his head bowed. Someone shouted, "Rush them, boys! It's our only chance!"

Thomas clutched my arm. "The river, Josh! The river!"

Some of the men began to run toward the Mexicans, hoping to overwhelm them. At a command the soldiers raised rifles to their shoulders. I stood paralyzed, my mouth dry, the cold hand of death holding me there in horror. I looked down the barrel of the rifle that was going to kill me.

Thomas moved suddenly. He stepped directly in front of me. The rifles roared. The impact slammed Thomas's body back against me, men fell like wheat beneath a scythe. I could hear the thud of bullets driving into flesh and bone. Some men died without a sound. Some cried out in mortal pain. I clutched Thomas, but my hand was sticky and warm. I knew instinctively that he was already dead.

For a moment I lay there—half pinned down by his weight—numb, unable to move, to think, to speak. Around me men still prayed and cursed and moaned and died.

Then the realization came to me that I was still alive. I had not even been hit. Thomas had taken the bullet that would have been mine.

And it came to me that men who had been missed by the volley were beginning to run. There had not been enough rifles to kill us all with the first shots. More by instinct than by conscious will, I lay still. I lay there and looked into Jimson's open, dead eyes.

The Mexicans were reloading their rifles as rapidly as they could, many of them moving awkwardly forward as they rammed powder and ball down the barrels. In pursuit of those men who ran up the hill, they moved over us and away.

This was my chance, if I had one at all. Stealthily I eased out from under Thomas's weight. I gripped his hand, saying a silent good-bye, my heart pounding. Then I jumped to my feet and sprinted toward the river.

A ball whizzed over my head. I cut sharply to the left and ran even faster. I glanced back over my shoulder, half expecting to see a mounted lancer bearing down on me. I was lucky, for they were all busy elsewhere. But I saw a rifleman drawing a bead. I cut to the right. Again a ball missed me.

Then there was the brush. I plunged into a thicket, the branches and the thorns clutching at my ragged clothes, ripping into my skin. I could hear a horseman loping toward me. I glanced back and saw him coming, the lance tipped forward.

I would make it tough for him, catching me in this brush.

Something struck my left arm. It felt like a red-hot poker. I reached up with my right hand and touched the arm and felt the thin flow of blood. I had been nicked by a rifle ball. But I kept on running.

I pushed through the brush until I reached the steep river bank. They were still coming behind me. I dived. The icy-cold water paralyzed me a moment. Then I started to swim. My first thought was to try to make the opposite bank, climb out, and keep running. But the current was swift. I let it carry me along and only treaded to keep my head above water. I kept trying to look back, to see if I was being followed. So far as I could tell, I wasn't.

In a few minutes the current carried me to a spot where the opposite bank was not steep, and where a growth of old grass would hide whatever marks I might make as I climbed out. I clambered over the bank as quickly as I could and tried to lose myself in the timber. I dropped down on hands and knees in a heavy growth of underbrush, clutching my arm, feeling the warm trickle of blood. My heart was still in my throat. I could hear firing across the river as the Mexicans found and murdered one after another of the unfortunate volunteers.

The terror of it swept over me in a spasm of shuddering. Unable to control myself, I lay flat on the ground, clenched my fists, and let the bitter tears flow.

When I was able to collect my wits, I realized I was alive but a long way from being free. It was still less than a mile back to the fortress, with many open stretches of prairie to cross whenever I tried to move farther away. Riders splashed across the river. I could hear the horses grunt as they labored up the bank. They were coming toward me. I huddled in the thicket and prayed softly.

I heard the sound of running feet. Thirty yards away a young volunteer was pounding through the brush as hard as he could. The lancers came yelping eagerly behind him, like hunters after a fox. The youth screamed, "No! God, no!"

The first lance impaled him. A second caught him and drove his body to the ground. The lad gave one horrible cry. One of the soldiers got down, put his foot on the body and pulled the lances free. Another soldier dismounted. Together they stripped the dead man of his clothes, laughing as if this were a sporting event, and they had just killed a deer.

Now I could hear firing in the fortress itself. The wounded! They were killing the wounded—Fannin and the rest.

More than three hundred helpless men—slaughtered like cattle!

I had not had time to feel anger. There had been only fear, and horror. Now came the anger, a bitter, driving, helpless rage. I pounded my fists against the ground.

I knew now that I *had* to get out of there.

Thomas, I swore, *someday, somewhere, somehow, there'll come a day of reckoning for this. And I vow to you and Almighty God, I'll be there!*

Soaking wet, hungry, bitterly cold, I huddled in the brush all that day. Now and again patrols passed through the timber, hunting for stragglers. I stayed low. My arm stiffened and burned, but at least it was no more than a deep scratch. The ball had taken a bite of flesh and passed on. I would live. Or at least, it wouldn't be this wound that killed me.

I tried to decide what I should do. Even with the best of luck, it would be difficult to escape from here. With any bad luck at all . . .

I had no hat, no coat, only these ragged clothes between me and total nakedness, with the chill of winter's breath still lingering into spring. My moccasins were thin. They probably wouldn't survive a long walk home, or even farther if the Texian line had retreated beyond it. And if there even was a Texian line. For all I knew, the Mexicans could already have swept to the Sabine River.

I knew that without food I would never get far. I'd nearly starved for a week now on the meager ration they gave us in the compound, and today there had been nothing at all. I wondered about the deserted Mexican *jacales* in the town of Goliad. I might find something there, if I had the nerve to go and look. A coat, a blanket—something. Probably no food, for the people had been gone too long. They had fled downriver last fall to the scattered *ranchos*, where they thought they would be safe from the war. Maybe if I could get to one of the *ranchos* I could steal some food and some clothing.

I had never stolen anything in my life, but now I was going to try without the slightest twinge of conscience. What did it matter? They were just Mexicans, I told myself. I realized I was thinking the way Thomas had always thought.

Well, he was dead now, and Mexicans had killed him. Maybe he had been right all the time, and I had been wrong.

I KNEW from description where the *ranchos* lay. My clothes had fairly well dried out through the day. Still, I was chilled to the bone. Even walking, I couldn't get warm. So most of the time I kept going, for the cold hurt me worse than being tired.

I had no firm plan, other than to try to sneak into a house and get some clothes to wear, some food to take along. Ahead lay a small rock house, very much like the one the Hernandez family lived in. Around it were scattered several brush *jacales*. A lingering smell of woodsmoke touched my nostrils. My stomach growled, for woodsmoke meant food.

Dogs were one thing I hadn't counted on. It never occurred to me they would pick me up so quickly. They set in to barking and raced out to meet me with a noisy clamor.

"Hush up," I hissed at them. They didn't savvy English. I crouched behind a bush and tossed rocks at them, trying to scare them away. They didn't scare. Presently a man appeared in the doorway, an ancient musket in his hand. I backed away in the darkness without his seeing me. I couldn't go up against that musket. Maybe there would be another house, one without dogs.

A mile farther on, I saw it. I moved in slowly, expecting the same reception. But this house was quiet. No dogs. I approached stealthily, flattening myself against the rock wall. I eased myself up to the open window and listened. Inside, a man was snoring.

It was somewhere past midnight. I didn't know where I had heard it, but a dim recollection came to me that someone had said people sleep soundest in the hours just after midnight. If that was true, I had a chance here.

Something moved beside me. My heart flipped. I jumped a couple of feet, whirling to face whatever it was.

In a square crate made of green willow branches I saw a rooster, one of the fighting breed so beloved by the Mexicans. I had disturbed his rest. I swallowed hard, regaining control of myself.

The door was closed, but it moved easily on its leather hinges when I lifted it slightly and pushed. I opened it only enough to give me entrance. But I didn't rush anything. I stood outside and listened carefully. The snoring continued. On the ground I saw a long chunk of firewood and picked it up. Flattening myself against the doorjamb, I slid through the open door and raised the club, ready to strike against anything that moved. Nothing did.

Slowly I lowered the club, though I kept a tight grip on it. I looked around the tiny one-room *casa* a full minute, getting my bearings. I could see two people sleeping on a cowhide bed, a slightly-built man and a rather stout woman. They had a couple of blankets wrapped around themselves. How I wanted one of those blankets! But any kind of clothes would be an improvement. I saw the Mexican's shirt and trousers and a ragged old coat hanging from a peg. Carefully I reached for them, took what I thought was a firm hold, and lifted. Something fell. It hit the floor with a light thump. Instinctively I reached down and grabbed. It was a knife in a leather scabbard.

The sound stirred the man. He raised up, blinking uneasily.

"Qué es? Qué es?" His movement awakened the woman. She opened her eyes and saw me. She screamed.

The Mexican jumped out of bed and rushed me. I had no choice but to use that chunk of firewood. It flattened him.

The woman screamed again, her hands against her cheeks. *"Americano!"* Before I could move, she had yanked the door open and was running out into the night crying, *"Americano! Americano!"*

On the floor the man swayed to his hands and knees. I looked around desperately for a gun, any kind of gun. There wasn't any. The man was pushing himself to his feet. Out in the darkness the woman was running, screaming. In a minute or two the neighbors would be on their way. They wouldn't be friendly.

I wanted to ransack the house for food, but there wasn't time now. I clutched their clothes under my arm, determined to get away with at least that much, and hurried out the door. I stumbled over the rooster's crate and sprawled on the ground.

By George, *there* was food. I gathered the stolen clothes under my left arm and yanked the rooster out of his crate with the right. Then I took off in a hard run. I didn't stop running until my lungs arched and my legs seemed ready to buckle. Then I stopped and fell to the ground to rest. The rooster struggled. My first inclination was to eat him raw, for I was hungry enough. I knew I had to kill him right away, or he would more than likely get loose from me. I wrung his neck and waited for him to quit flopping. At least he had died for a better cause than someone's sport.

I put the Mexican's clothes on over my own. They fitted me better than I had any right to expect. And inside the pocket of the trousers I found a flint and steel.

My situation was still bad, but it was improving.

After gutting the rooster and resting for a little, I set out walking, moving in what I judged to be a northeasterly direction. I carried the dead rooster under my arm, for I couldn't afford to build a fire and cook him until daylight came to mask the flames.

When it was light I picked a good thicket and went into the heart of it. Using the flint and steel, and strips of cloth, I eventually got a small fire underway. The rooster was much too thin and stringy to be good eating, but this was no time or place to be choosy. Little as he was, he would be the best meal I had had in a long time. I impaled him on a spit, scorched him a little, and ate him.

Exhausted, I slept most of the day. Terrible dreams of that awful massacre finally brought me wide awake, trembling. I lay there awhile, my eyes wide open. I had a horrible feeling that if I turned over and looked behind me I would find the Mexicans there with their muskets and lances, waiting to kill me. I managed after a bit to roll over. There was no one. I was alone.

My heart pounded from the terror of the dreams. My eyes burned with tears as the awful memories rushed back unbidden like floodwaters breaking through a dam.

My arms were swollen and sore, but that wouldn't slow my walking. Though still hungry, I had at least had a good rest. With the dark to shield me, I would set out walking. I could walk a long way before morning came again.

CHAPTER

16

IT WAS well that I had obtained the coat, for a norther blew in, bringing a cold, drizzling rain. With the bite of cold, hunger came back stronger than ever. That rooster had only whetted my appetite. It was a bad time of the year to find berries, wild fruit, or pecans, for the first were out of season and the others had fallen to the ground to be picked up by the wild hogs, deer, and other animals.

That was the ironic thing. All around me flocked an abundance of game—deer, wild turkeys. But without a gun I was unable to bring any of them to hand. The best I could find was some wild onions.

The third night my luck took a brief turn. I came across a tree where some of the turkeys roosted and managed to get one.

Not having seen a Mexican all day, I decided to risk building a fire to cook the turkey. Rain had left the wood wet. It took half the night to cut wet bark away from enough dead timber to have dry wood to burn. I got the turkey partially cooked, then ate it all except the feathers and bones. But much of my safe walking time had been wasted. And there was no telling how far I was from home. There hadn't been any familiar landmarks.

Hunger appeased, I decided to do some daylight traveling. The arm was still stiff but no longer painful except when I put pressure on it. With the new strength that came from a good meal, I was able to put some miles behind me. Instead of looking for a motte of timber when daylight came, I kept on walking.

In due time I came to a river and judged it to be the Guadalupe. It was running high and muddy from the heavy rains. My heart sagged. With this stiff arm, I probably could not swim it.

I gritted my teeth in disappointment. It would be a grim joke if I had escaped the firing squad at Goliad, only to drown here unseen, a hundred miles from home.

Upriver somewhere would be Gonzales, but it would do me no good to go there. Undoubtedly the Mexicans had it by now.

Somehow I had to find a way across that river but I had not the faintest notion what to do. I thought of trying to make a raft of some kind but had never done it before and didn't know just how to go about it. Besides, that current probably would be more than I could handle. It would likely carry me downriver a way and then dump me to drown.

Well, maybe something would turn up. I started walking upriver.

I had walked a long time when I heard the sound of moving horses. Mexicans, I figured. I flattened myself in undergrowth near the riverbank and strained to see. When the horses came in sight, a chill ran down my back. It wasn't Mexicans, it was *Indians*.

Somehow, in my anxiety, I had considered only the danger of Mexicans. Now I realized I had an equally dangerous foe to watch for, because these appeared to be Comanches. Nothing would please a Comanche more than to come across a straggling Texian and lift his hair. I lay flat until they were well past me, moving downriver. Then I arose and left in a hurry.

In one way the Indians were even a greater threat than the Mexicans. They saw more. They were hunters born and bred. Their eyes could read meaning into a boottrack or a broken limb that might be overlooked by a Mexican or a Texian.

I came at length to a log cabin, or rather, the ruins of one. Only a blackened hull remained, with the charred roof caved in. Cautiously, crouching and taking my time, I picked my way through it, alert for sign of life. There was no evidence of battle. The owners probably had fled ahead of the enemy advance. More than likely Mexican soldiers had burned the cabin, or Indians had come along and done it. If there had been anything of value inside—clothes, for instance—it was gone now. I hoped to find something to eat—chickens or a hog or a milk cow's calf—that had been left behind. If there had been such, someone had beaten me to it. For me, the cabin was a total loss.

No, not quite. At the river bank, partially hidden by undergrowth, a small boat lay mostly submerged in the water. A short length of rawhide rope held it to a tree.

My one bad arm made it heavy pulling against the current. A determined effort finally brought the boat up out of the river. I turned it over to empty the water out and examined it carefully for sign of a hole. A few minutes' search produced the oars.

Now, at least, I was able to cross the river. On the far side I hid the boat and struck out walking again.

During the day I saw four Mexican horsemen. I was crossing an open prairie where last year's dry grass still stood tall and coarse. Dropping down in it, I lay unseen while they passed two hundred yards away. Later I saw a small band of Indians, though they were at a greater distance and were more of a scare than a threat.

I considered going back to my original plan—traveling at night and hiding by day. It was safer. But I was still a long way from home. I found myself worrying more and more about Muley, waiting there for me. With that boy's mind of his, he was probably frightened half to death. He might stay instead of running as I had told him to. He couldn't defend himself when the Mexicans came—if they had not already come. Because of Muley I decided to take my chances and keep traveling during at least part of the day.

My worst scare came the second day past the Guadalupe. Moving across the prairie, I spied a small cloud of dust. It was coming my way. Presently I heard hoofs. A troop of Mexican cavalry, or a band of Indians, I was certain. I tried to flatten and hide myself in the grass, but it was too short. It wouldn't hide me unless they were all blind. And they wouldn't be. The hoofbeats came closer.

I had my chin on the ground, but gradually I gathered my courage and raised my head to look. It was horses, all right, and they were coming upon me fast. But there wasn't a rider on them. They were wild mustangs, running free. I waited until I was sure no one was chasing them.

Then, afraid they might run over me, I stood up and waved my arms, shouting. The horses slid to a stop. They stood a moment watching me, their ears all cocked forward. They probably had never seen a man afoot. But they didn't care for what they saw. They wheeled around and galloped off, getting well in the clear. Then they stopped and turned to watch me some more, from a safer distance.

That night, just at dusk, I came upon the Mexican camp.

I would have done like the mustangs and gone way around, had I known. But I almost stumbled onto the camp before I saw it. They were cavalry, nearly twenty men. They had their horses tied on two picket lines, feeding them corn which they probably had found at some abandoned settler cabin. The soldiers were building up a campfire and preparing to cook supper.

I lay on my stomach and watched them. The wise thing, I knew, would be to ease myself well around them in the darkness and be long gone before morning. But the horses had caught my eye.

I had been walking for days. I knew I wasn't far from home now, but it might take me several more days to get there at the rate I was moving. With a horse, I could reduce the time.

The temptation was almost overwhelming. With my knife I could run in there, cut a horse loose, and be gone before the single Mexican guard would have time to lift his rifle. But it would be like punching at a hornet's nest with a stick. They would be after me in minutes. Whether I could get away or not would simply depend upon whether my luck was better than theirs.

I had seen enough of Mexican luck lately not to want to take the risk.

But I wouldn't leave until I had made a try of some kind. I lay and watched the soldiers cook and eat. My stomach growled. I had eaten only at irregular intervals, and the last interval had been a long one. I watched the dirty-uniformed men move about, and my mind inevitably turned back to that awful morning on the road to Copano. There was no way for me to know whether these men had personally had a hand in it. But they wore the same uniform, and that was enough. Hatred stirred in me. I thought of a dozen ways to kill them all, like finding their gunpowder and throwing it into the fire. But they were all crazy notions, too wild to work.

At length, their hunger satisfied, the Mexicans began wrapping themselves in their blankets and stretching out. They left one guard with the horses. The men quickly dropped off to sleep. From that, I guessed they had had a long, hard day. And so, probably, had the guard.

I crawled closer to the lone Mexican awake, who sat with his back to a live oak tree, his musket across his lap. The dry leaves rustled under me. The Mexican looked around, startled. I froze. For a moment it appeared he might get up and investigate, and I tensed, ready to run. But when he heard nothing more, he gradually relaxed. He probably thought it was some night-prowling animal.

The campfire burned low. Out in the darkness wolves began to howl. They had howled every night since I had escaped from Goliad. Once they had come so close that I had finally climbed a tree. The wolves made the horses restless. The Mexican spoke softly to them but didn't get up. After a long while I saw his head begin to tilt forward. It jerked as he came awake, then sagged again. He was too tired to hold out. I knew I had only to wait.

The longer I watched him, the more I thought about the Mexican officer who had come to us on Palm Sunday morning with the report that we were leaving for Copano. He had known what was about to happen, but he had lied to us with a smile on his lips. I fancied I could see a resemblance between this guard and that officer. I found my hand straying down to the handle of the knife. It would be easy to rise up and steal over to him and slit his throat. Hell, he deserved it. They *all* deserved it, I thought. I ground my teeth, struggling against the temptation.

Even dying, he might cry out and arouse the camp.

No, it was more important to get myself a horse. Vengeance could wait.

It seemed an hour before I heard his gentle snoring. His head was tilted forward onto his arms, his arms across his knees. I arose quietly and moved toward the picket line, the knife in my hand. For a long time I had studied the horses, making my choice.

I wanted very badly to cut all the horses loose and run them off. But I knew I could get shot doing it. I might get away with one horse, but not all of them.

The knife was dull. I had to saw on the rawhide. The horses stirred restlessly. I kept glancing back at the Mexican, thinking he would wake up at any moment. The leather finally parted. Carefully I backed my horse out of his place on the line. I led him in a slow walk, pausing only to pick up a bridle, blanket, and saddle which lay there handy to my reach. I held onto them—and onto my breath— until I had the horse well away from the camp. Then I paused long enough to bridle and saddle him, swung up, and was on my way.

The camp never stirred.

CHAPTER

17

ONCE I struck the Colorado River, I had no trouble finding our place. I passed many others first. Without exception, they had been burned. My hopes sagged. The Mexicans had been here. No telling what had happened to Muley.

Though I nursed some faint hopes, I knew pretty well what to expect when I rode across the field. The winter wheat was growing fine. The corn had been planted—Muley's work. I slanted down the trail to our cabin. The cabin was gone, all but its blackened skeleton. I swallowed, anger rising momentarily. I eased the horse toward the cold ruins, looking for signs of Muley. Actually, though I wouldn't have admitted it, I was watching for his body.

I found no trace of him. When I felt safe in doing so, I began to call: "Muley! Muley! It's me, Josh!"

I had some thought that he might have hidden in the timber. It would be like him. He might be there yet, waiting for somebody to come and get him. Waiting for me.

There wasn't a sign of Muley. But on a closer examination I found familiar dog tracks.

"Hickory!" I whistled a few times, then called again. "Here, Hickory!"

The old spotted hound slunk out of the timber, tail between his legs. He crouched uncertainly, knowing my voice but still not trusting.

I called him again and rode slowly toward him. Recognition came finally, and he fell to barking joyously, running at me, his tail wagging so hard he almost fell over. Always a chaser but never a hunter, he was thin and hungry-looking. That settled it: Muley was either dead or gone. He wouldn't have let the dog do without.

Hickory jumped all over me in his joy. He whimpered and cried while I petted him and tried to get him quieted down.

Now the worry I had carried for days turned to genuine fear. I knew from bitter experience what Santa Anna's soldiers were doing to prisoners. They might not have killed Muley here. They might have taken him to be killed somewhere else, on somebody's cruel whim.

Still, there was a chance Muley was all right. He might have run like I told him. From appearances, all the American settlers in this part of the country had pulled out hastily. Lots of people around here knew about Muley. Maybe somebody had taken enough time to come by and get him.

There was one place I might be able to find out. I found my eyes lifting to the trail I used to ride toward the Hernandez *rancho*. I couldn't be sure, of course, that the family was still there. They might have pulled out too. But I had noticed that by and large the Mexican families were tending to stay put as the American families fled. They didn't seem to feel they had much to fear from the Mexican soldiers. After all, they were of the same blood. A goodly percentage of them, as I had found to my sorrow, sided with the soldiers against us.

I couldn't know what reception to expect at the Hernandez place. I'd thought many times of the way Ramón Hernandez had hedged on an answer when I asked him which way he would go if it came to war. I'd remembered often the look in his eyes when I took him the news that his younger brother had been killed in the battle of San Antonio de Bexar.

Ramón might have gone over to Santa Anna's side by now. Friendship is one thing, but blood is another.

I sat on the hill a long while and surveyed the stone house before I touched my heels to the horse's ribs and started him down in an easy walk. Muley's hound tagged along close. He was sticking to me like a mesquite thorn.

The kids—Ramón's youngest brothers and sisters—played outside. A couple of horses stood droop-headed in a corral. Grazing cattle were scattered in the grassy draw and across the field.

The youngsters raised a frightened shout when they saw me. My beard had grown untouched for weeks and now was ragged and tangled and black. My clothes hung on me like they would on a scarecrow. I must have looked like some devilish apparition. There was, in those days, a strong tendency toward superstition in the Mexican people. Whatever or whoever they thought I was, they ran screaming into the house. The door slammed behind them. I heard the bar drop.

In a moment a shuttered window swung open. The barrel of an old musket poked out. A woman's voice cried, *Ándele! Ándele!* It was a way of saying to move along.

I raised my hands. In Spanish I called, "I am Josh Buckalew."

The musket was pulled back out of sight. The door opened cautiously. A young woman stood there, the musket still in her hands but no longer pointed directly at me.

"Josh, is it you? Is it really you?"

Weak, desperately hungry, I almost fell as I slid off the horse. I caught hold of the stirrup and pulled myself up. "Yes, María, it's me."

Hesitant, she came out under the brush arbor. Finally certain, she ran and threw her arms around me, musket and all.

"Josh, Josh, we thought you were dead!"

She hurt my arm, and I flinched. It never had healed completely. She stepped back, eyes wide in concern. "You are wounded."

"Not bad, still just a little raw. It'll be all right."

She hugged me again but went easy on the left arm. Then she studied my face. "You look terrible. Where have you been?" She didn't give me a chance to answer. "You shouldn't be here, Josh. Patrols come by every day or two. If they find you, they will kill you."

"I had to come. I need to talk to Ramón."

She shook her head. "Ramón has gone to the army."

My breath stopped for a moment. "The Mexican army?"

"No, Sam Houston's army. He went to fight Santa Anna."

The relief that came to me was only momentary. "María, I can't find Muley. I hoped Ramón could tell me what happened to him."

"Muley is all right, or was. Ramón was afraid to leave him by himself with Santa Anna's army on the way. He made Muley go with him to join Sam Houston."

I sighed. A terrible weight slipped from my shoulders.

"Thanks to God, María." For a minute all I could think about was that Muley was all right. Then I glanced toward the door and saw Ramón's wife. Miranda stared, still not sure who I was.

"María," I demanded, "why did Ramón leave the rest of you here? Why didn't he take you and run?"

"It was too near Miranda's time. She could not travel. We decided we would be safe here. We are Mexicans. We thought the soldiers would not hurt us. And it has been true. Many have been here, but none have done us any harm."

I frowned, remembering the trouble Miranda had had with her first baby. "You will need help with her, María."

"When Ramón left, it was all arranged. Señora Ramirez is a midwife, and she was going to stay. But her husband became frightened and took her east with the rest of the runaways. So I will have to do the job myself."

"Can you?"

"I have been told what to do. I will do the best I can." She took my good arm. "Come, Miranda and the children are frightened. They still don't know who you are."

Miranda hugged me and cried a little. The children cautiously shook my hand, but the smaller ones were still unconvinced that I was not some kind of devil. María set about cooking beef for me. I took a pair of scissors and clipped away most of my beard. I then borrowed an old razor that had belonged to María's father and shaved my face clean.

As I ate, I told them briefly what had happened to me. I skipped most of the details, for the thought of them still made my blood go cold. I trembled as I told how Thomas had been butchered. The women wept silently.

I intended to leave after I had eaten and ride through the night. But I was so weary I thought I would lie down on one of the cowhide cots and rest an hour or so. When I awoke, it was morning. I sat bolt upright, staring in confusion and alarm. The women were preparing breakfast.

"María," I demanded, "why did you let me sleep?"

"You needed the rest. See, you look better already."

"I've got to move on. I want to catch up with Houston's army."

"You will eat first."

Impatience was like needles prickling my skin, but she was right. I had needed the rest. And I needed another good meal, for it might be a long time before the next one. So I sat on the cot and watched the women. Miranda moved slowly because of her size. María tried to get her to sit down, but she would not. I watched María particularly. It struck me that she had changed a lot since the first time I had seen her. She was a woman now, moving with purpose and sureness. And, she was a pretty woman.

I was eating when one of the boys ran into the house. *"Soldados!"* Soldiers were coming.

I jumped to my feet. "I'd better run. It'll go hard on you if they find me here."

Muley's dog was barking wildly. María glanced out the window. "Too late, they are too close. We'll have to hide you."

I thought of the horse and the Mexican saddle I had stolen. They would be a dead giveaway.

María shook her head. "I had Pepe turn the horse loose. We hid your saddle under the hay. Come!"

She let me out the back door. We glanced around for some place I could get out of sight. I saw nothing but the woodpile. I sprinted around that and dropped flat on my belly. I lay there with the knife in my hand, the only weapon I had. If found, I intended to sell out at a high price.

I heard the horses at the front of the house, and Hickory's barking. One of the soldiers must have hurled something at the dog, for he yelped in terror and ran around behind the house. He caught my scent and came crying to me.

"Get away, Hickory! Git!"

He wouldn't leave me. He tried to crowd in with me behind the woodpile. My mouth went dry, for I was afraid one of the soldiers might follow Hickory around the house to chunk at him again. None did.

"Damn you, Hickory, I ought to cut your cowardly throat."

But he stayed. It was a long time before I heard the patrol start moving away. Hickory ventured forth to bark at the soldiers from a respectful distance. Cautiously I peeked out to watch the horsemen moving eastward, singing. One of them paused to throw a rock back at Hickory.

I stayed put until finally María came.

"They are well gone," she said, as I got to my feet.

"They sure stayed a while."

"They made us cook for them."

"They didn't hurt you?"

"We told them our men had gone to help Santa Anna. They didn't hurt us."

"María, I've got to leave here. The longer I stay the more dangerous it is for you and for me."

She nodded gravely. "I'll have the boys bring you a fresh horse. We had to hide the good horses from the runaways. They took all they could find."

We returned to the house, María gave orders to the older boys, and they hit the door in a run. Turning to Miranda, I found her trembling. "Please, Josh," she said, "do not think I always am this foolish. It is my time and my condition, I suppose. I was frightened to death."

Taking her hand, I tried to give her reassurance. "I'll be gone in a few minutes. Then you won't have to worry."

A twinge of pain creased Miranda's olive face. "I think I have much to worry about. I think the time has come."

María's eyes widened. She glanced at me, then at Miranda. "You could be wrong, Miranda. Remember, there was that other alarm two days ago."

Miranda paled, flinching again. "This time, I think, it is real. The excitement has been too much." She cried out as a sharp pain hit her. It looked as if she would fall. I grabbed her.

"María, what do we do now?"

María's lips tightened. "I suppose we will deliver the baby."

The boys brought my horse up outside, saddled and ready to go. But there was no leaving now.

"María, I've never been around where a woman was having a baby."

"Then we shall both learn together."

Mostly I stood by and did whatever María said to do, while Miranda bit her lips and gripped the wooden edge of the bedframe, fighting against the pain.

The children were kept outside, watching for another patrol. María and I bustled about, making the preparations she thought were necessary. When the time came for delivery, I turned my face away and left that part up to María. I held Miranda's hands. Or rather, she held mine, digging her fingernails in, gritting her teeth to keep from crying out.

"Cry if you want to, Miranda," I said. "Sometimes it's better."

But she shook her head. She had no intention of giving in to the pain.

Then, suddenly, the baby was there. María clutched it in her hands, a tiny reddish-brown thing.

"Josh," she cried, "Josh, do something! It's not breathing, Josh!"

The breath had not started. I saw the fear in Miranda's eyes, and in María's. I remembered something I had heard about spanking a new baby's bottom. I took the infant in my left hand and tapped its backside smartly with the palm of my right.

I felt a quiver of life, then heard the whimper that lifted into a cry. I looked at María. Relief flooded her face. She smiled, then laughed thinly. Her laugh grew louder, and I was laughing with her, the baby still dangling from my hand. María threw her arms around me. We stood there holding each other and laughed like a pair of fools.

Later I watched María tuck the blanket around Miranda and the baby. "María," I said, "you're a wonder."

I found myself studying her again as I had at breakfast, admiring the quick and easy way she moved, the slimness of her, the pleasant eyes and face. She was conscious of the way I appraised her, for color rose in her cheeks.

I said, "It's amazing to me, the way you resemble Teresa."

"I am not Teresa," she said pointedly. "I am María. I shall always be María. I would never be a substitute for someone else."

"I didn't mean it that way," I said hastily, realizing I had hurt her. "I would always want you to be yourself. I would always want you to be the way you have been today. With all respect to Teresa, I doubt she would ever have been able to do what you've done."

María said, "Teresa was my sister, and I shall always love her memory. But she was weak, Josh. Had *I* loved a man, I would have turned my back on family and all. I would have spit in the devil's eye to have him. I would never have married someone else because it was expected of me and I had not the courage to say no."

"No," I said with admiration, "I don't suppose you would."

The children came in to look at the new baby. One of the smaller ones marveled that he hadn't seen anybody come and bring it.

Smiling wisely, an older boy said, "Your horse is here, Josh, and we see no soldiers."

"Thanks, *muchacho*. I guess I'd better leave."

Miranda called me to her bedside. "Josh, if you see Ramón, tell him I will be waiting for him. Tell him I have given him another son."

I squeezed her hand. "I'll tell him. He'll be proud of you."

María walked out with me, carrying a sack of food she had prepared. She also had the old musket.

"We do not need the gun, Josh. You might."

I took her arm and pulled her up close. I didn't want to leave. "María, if this war ends in our favor, I'll be back. I'd like to come and visit you, if you'll let me."

Her eyes glistened. "Will you be coming to see me, or will you really be seeing Teresa?' "

"Teresa was a long time ago. That is over. I'll be coming to see you, María."

"Then come back, Josh. Come back soon."

She clutched my arm and leaned forward and kissed me.

I swung into the saddle and rode away, looking back over my shoulder.

Tʜɪs ᴡᴀꜱ a time that would ever after be known in Texas as the "runaway scrape." American settlers packed what possessions they could carry and left the rest behind them as they fled in their wagons or on horseback or afoot—often in panic—before the onslaught of Mexican troops. The news of the Alamo and Goliad had put an icy chill in Texian veins. A cold, hard fury set in, and a desperate desire for revenge. But there were practical matters to be attended to. Family men left Sam Houston's ranks to hurry home and see that their loved ones were evacuated to the sanctuary that waited for them across the Sabine.

It was a cold, rainy time, with mud that mired wagons to the hubs. Open prairies became vast lakes that sometimes had to be forded. Indians and Mexican guerrillas harassed the stragglers, striking and lashing and running away. Sickness swept the struggling caravans of wagons and carts and sleds.

How many died and were left behind in this awful backwash of war, no one ever really knew. The toll was heavy among women and children.

And all this time Sam Houston's dwindling army retreated,

seething for revenge, falling back to first one river, then another— avoiding any full-scale clash. Houston was buying time, giving the runaways an opportunity to reach safety, waiting for the chance to strike the Mexicans when the odds were in the Texians' favor. Always outnumbered, always held back by Houston's caution, the Texians wondered if they would ever get that chance. Impatience turned to anger, and slowly anger built toward open mutiny.

But, grim as the crowded bear, Houston stood up to the abuse and the criticism. His was the only fighting force Texas had left. Texas could not stand another defeat. When he committed his men to battle, he wanted to know they had a better than even chance of winning. If they lost, the war was over, and Texas was gone.

I finally caught up to Houston's army opposite Harrisburg. That had been the capital of the newly declared Republic of Texas, though by now the officials of the government had fled. Santa Anna had already been to Harrisburg and had left it in ashes.

I had come across many Mexican patrols and details of cavalry since leaving the Colorado River. I always kept out of their sight. I had trailed the retreating army to Groce's plantation. East of the McCurley place I came to the fork in the road. The left-hand fork was the trace leading toward the Sabine and safety. The right-hand fork led toward Harrisburg, and a certain head-on clash with Santa Anna. Though it had rained heavily, and two or three days had passed, I could still tell where the army had gone. It had taken the right-hand fork.

I had a feeling I was getting close now. I hadn't seen a Mexican in some time. Sitting in a clump of timber, I watched four horsemen coming my way, rifles across their laps. I took them to be Texians, though I hid myself until they were close enough that I knew for sure. Then I rode out into the open.

They hauled up quickly, their rifles swinging toward me. I raised my right hand and moved on, slower now.

"All right, friend," one of them said, staring at me over the barrel of his rifle, "before you come any closer we want to know who you are."

"I'm a Texian. I was at Goliad."

The man lowered his rifle. I got a look at his face, and a chill touched me. I knew him from somewhere, and it wasn't a pleasant memory. I reached back in my mind to long ago. Natchitoches. That was the face I had seen at Natchitoches so many long years ago. Lige, his name had been.

I knew a bitter moment then. Had I escaped from Goliad, dodged Mexicans and Indians across most of Texas, only to fall into the hands of cutthroats?

Lige squinted. "By George, I do believe I know you from someplace. Where have I seen you at?"

I said, "Try Natchitoches, several years back. You and some friends of yours tried to rob us on the trail to the Sabine."

Recognition came, and with it a moment of astonishment. Then, a broad grin. "Well, if that don't beat all. That was a long time, boy, for the chickens to finally come to roost. Been a lot of changes made."

"I doubt if you've changed much," I said.

He still grinned. "I know what you're thinkin', but I long since give up my sinful ways. You boys kind of give me a push in that direction. We're fightin' on the same side now, boy. A lot of us have had to turn our backs on old feuds and face the Mexicans together. Goliad, you say? And you got away? Rememberin' Natchitoches, I can't say as I'm surprised none. Come on, we'll take you to camp."

My arrival caused a stir, though I found out I wasn't the first Goliad survivor to catch up with the army. Several had made it here before me, individually picking their way across Texas just as I had done.

I was taken directly to Sam Houston's tent. He sat there and stared at me, a huge man with a strong, square face and piercing eyes. He reached into the pocket of his black coat and took out a bottle of salts of hartshorn, which he applied to his nostrils as I told him briefly what had happened to me.

"You've been through hell enough," he said finally. "You should have gone on to the Sabine instead of coming here."

I shook my head. "Not many of us got away from Goliad, General. I figure I owe a debt to all those who didn't."

Houston's jaw ridged. He glanced at his officers. "Has this man been fed?" When they said I hadn't, he ordered, "Then take him and feed him. See if you can find him a decent rifle and something to put in it."

I saluted him and turned to go. Houston called after me, "You can still go across the Sabine if you've a mind to. You've done your share."

"If it's all the same to you, General, I'll stay." In fact, I had made up my mind to stay whether it was all right with him or not.

One of the officers led me to a small company which he commanded. "Here's a man from Goliad. Feed him."

I wolfed the food down. As I was finishing up I said, "Major, I'm lookin' for a friend of mine, a partner. Name is Muley Dodd."

He shook his head. "We have almost eight hundred men in this camp. I couldn't know them all."

"He's supposed to have come with a Mexican friend of mine named Ramón Hernandez. You'd probably remember Muley if you came across him. He's . . . a little slow. He's not real bright."

One of the men said, "Major, I'll bet I know who he's huntin'. There was a little feller came into camp with a Mexican while we was at Groce's. The Mexican joined up with Juan Seguin's company. The little feller stayed with him. A bunch of us tried to talk him into joinin' a white man's outfit, but he wouldn't. Stuck to that Mexican like a pet dog."

I said, "That'd be Muley. Take me to him."

The name Seguin was familiar. The Seguins were a wealthy Mexican family, with large landholdings around San Antonio. General Cos had mistreated old Erasmo Seguin. As a result the Seguin family sided with the Texians with their land, their cattle, their money, and their arms. Juan Seguin, I was told, had been in the Alamo in the early part of the siege, but Travis had sent him out as a courier. There had been no returning.

The officer led me across the camp to where the Seguin company had bivouacked. A shudder ran through me as I looked at the dark faces and listened to the rapid flow of soft-spoken Spanish. Though these men were on our side, and though a few months ago I would have found it easy to call any of them friend, bitter memories stood between us now. I found myself blaming them all for being Mexicans.

"I am looking for Muley Dodd," I said in Spanish.

"The little *Americano?* He is here somewhere with Ramón Hernandez." He called. "*Señor* Dodd! *Dónde está?*"

I saw a slight figure rise up from some muddy blankets and look around wide-eyed. "Muley!" I broke into a run toward him. He jumped to his feet. "Josh! Josh! Josh!" He grabbed me, and we hugged each other. Muley began crying. "Josh, Ramón said you was likely dead. But I told him you wouldn't be. I told him you promised to come and get me, and you didn't never break any promise you ever made. I told him you wouldn't let them old Mexicans kill you if it was goin' to go ag'in your promise."

I clenched his shoulder and stood back to stare at him. He looked about the same as ever, except a little thinner. Rations hadn't come regularly.

Another voice broke in. "Josh, it is good to see you."

I turned to Ramón Hernandez and gave him the *abrazo.* He smiled broadly. "I thought Santa Anna had nailed you up with his trophies."

I said, "He did get Thomas."

Ramón's smile disappeared. He gripped my arm in sympathy. "Now we have each lost a brother. Where did it happen?"

Once again I told it. The Mexicans gathered and listened, those who could understand English.

Ramón said, "And so now you want to fight, to get even."

"It's somethin' I've got to do."

"This is a good company, Juan Seguin's. We would like you to join us."

I looked around me at the dark faces, the black eyes. Again I felt that uncomfortable stirring. I knew it was unfair, but I couldn't help it. Friends or not, when I looked at them I would see those other dark faces at Goliad, peering at us down the barrels of their rifles.

"Thanks, Ramón. But after what I've been through . . ." I tried to find the words to explain and couldn't. "It's nothin' personal, it's just . . . Well, I'd best find a place among my own people. I'll take Muley with me."

Ramón was silent a moment, perhaps hurt a little, though he didn't show it. "In your situation, I would be the same. It took me a long time to decide that my place was here."

I started to go, then turned back. "Ramón, I went by the *rancho*. You have another son."

"She is all right, my Miranda?"

"She came through fine. Said tell you to hurry home."

"We shall soon see if *any* of us go home."

WE WERE waiting to cross Buffalo Bayou when Houston rode into the center of the army on his big white stallion Saracen. Far in the distance we could see smoke. Santa Anna was burning everything as he moved.

Houston sat on that big stud and made us a speech. He said we would win the battle that lay ahead, that we would have vengeance for those who had fallen in the Alamo. For those slaughtered at Goliad.

"Remember the Alamo!" he thundered. "Remember Goliad!"

It became a war cry. It spread through the army like a brushfire. Men raised their rifles over their heads and shouted the words over and over again. "Remember the Alamo! Remember Goliad!"

SAN JACINTO. Moving down Buffalo Bayou, we reached the San Jacinto River on April 20. Houston ordered us into camp in a grove of live oaks. Buffalo Bayou to our backs, the San Jacinto to our left. In front of us lay a pretty stretch of open prairie, rising slightly toward groves of moss-strewn live oak trees.

Later in the afternoon the cry went up. "The Mexicans are coming!"

We already knew that, for scouts had been bringing in reports at regular intervals. They said this was Santa Anna himself. We prepared ourselves for attack. With the river and the bayou at our flank and our back, and with Santa Anna coming up in front of us, we were in no position anymore to retreat. If the Mexicans came, we had to stand our ground and fight.

They didn't come. Santa Anna went into camp on the opposite side of the prairie, a broad lake to one side of him, the marshes behind him. He sounded us out by sending forward a six-pounder with a detachment of cavalry for protection. The cannon opened up. Some said Santa Anna probably hoped we would reply with musket fire and give him a good idea how we were lined up. On orders, we held our fire and answered him only with a few rounds from the Twin Sisters, a matched pair of cannon recently arrived as a gift from the people of Cincinnati.

There was one brief cavalry skirmish that afternoon as a group of volunteers attempted to rush forward and take the Mexican cannon. They failed to get the cannon but came back satisfied they had drawn blood.

The night was cold but quiet. Our scouts brought the report next morning that General Cos had arrived with reinforcements for Santa Anna. They had us outnumbered now by a little less than two to one.

This, then, was the time to fight, if we ever were going to fight. Some of the officers quarreled over it, but the men were of a temper to go ahead, with officers or without them. It was about three o'clock in the afternoon of April 21 that Houston ordered us paraded and announced that we were not going to wait for Santa Anna to come to us. We were going to go to *him.*

With the Twin Sisters in the center of the line, infantry on both sides, and cavalry on the right flank, we stretched out for some nine hundred yards.

There was a popular song in those days, a simple little tune called "Come to the Bower." A love song, not a battle song. But now the drummer and three fifers struck it up.

> *Will you come to the bower I have shaded for you?*
> *Our bed shall be roses all spangled with dew.*
> *There under the bower of roses you lie*
> *With a blush on your cheek but a smile in your eye.*

Astride the big white stallion, Sam Houston rode all the way across the long line, making an inspection. What he found was a motley gathering of buckskins and homespuns and clawhammer coats, of farmers and hunters, lawyers and locksmiths, preachers and teachers and sinners and saints. Done, he returned to the center of the line. He sat there a moment, looking back, then looking forward. He shouted a command that I couldn't hear. He dropped his arm. The ragged line began to move across that stretch of open prairie toward the camp of Santa Anna.

The cavalry rode far around on the left to create a diversion. The rest of us walked through the grass, our rifles ready. In the center, artillerymen pulled the Twin Sisters along on rawhide ropes.

The order was to hold our fire until we crested the hill and were well within range. We all walked silently, each of us going back over his own reasons for being here. I felt a prickling of my skin. My hands clutched the rifle I had been given to replace the old Hernandez musket. I knew fear, for I had learned at San Antonio and at Goliad how terrible a battle can be. But I knew also a fresh sense of anger, for now once again I saw Thomas, and I saw all those tragic men with whom I had spent that miserable time in the fortress at Goliad. In my mind I heard again the rattle of musketry, heard the screams of the helpless dying men as they fell on the Copano road. I found myself walking faster and faster, the sound of remembered gunfire exploding in my ears. I found myself muttering quietly. "Goliad. Goliad. This is going to be for Goliad."

We topped over the rise. Now there came a scattering of rifle fire from the Mexican camp. But we saw comparatively few Mexican soldiers. Most of their rifles were stacked.

Siesta! We had caught them at *siesta!*

A Mexican cannon boomed. Our own artillerymen stopped and fired the Twin Sisters. They reloaded and came again, pulling the two cannons closer.

Now that the firing had opened up, men began running. They were shouting, too.

"Remember the Alamo! Remember Goliad!"

The Mexicans of Seguin's company took up the cry in Spanish. *"Recuerden el Alamo!"* The shouts rose up like thunder.

On the far left, the cavalry tore into the Mexican line with a crushing fury.

The Mexican fire was still weak, but it was starting to count. Houston's white stallion went down. Almost instantly someone brought Houston another horse. He remounted, only to go down again, this time with a bullet in his own leg.

Shouting at the tops of our lungs, we raged into the Mexican line, firing, slashing with our bayonets, swinging our rifle butts. The Mexicans who had tried to return our fire went down in those first moments. The others, caught asleep, tried desperately to reach their stacked arms. Most of them never made it.

Riderless Mexican horses galloped through the camp, running over tents in their panic, trampling *soldados* who did not scramble out of their way in time.

Here and there soldiers stopped in their flight to turn and fire at us, but their aim was erratic. Most of the Mexicans simply ran, leaving their weapons behind them.

It has been said that the battle of San Jacinto lasted only about twenty minutes, but the slaughter of San Jacinto went on for hours.

The fleeing Mexicans found themselves trapped by the bayou. Some dived in and tried to swim, many bogging down hopelessly in the mud. Others cowered at the bank, turning helplessly to face the Texian fire. And it was merciless fire, for these men were primed to fury by Santa Anna's vicious slaughter across the entire face of Texas. The screaming *soldados* raised their hands in supplication, only to be cut down.

I had been firing until my rifle barrel was so hot to the touch that it was hard to reload it. As I pushed to ram powder and ball for another shot, I saw a running Mexican confront a bayonet-wielding Texian. He dropped to his knees and cried out, "Me no Alamo! Me no Goliad!"

The Texian rammed the bayonet through the man's heart, put his foot against the body, and jerked the rifle free.

It was no longer a battle. It was a hell of shouting, shooting, screaming men, of panic-stricken riderless horses dashing back and forth, of thundering cannon—our own now, altogether.

Through the smoke I saw a rider loping toward me. I could tell by the uniform that he was Mexican. I raised the rifle to draw a bead. He came through the smoke. I saw his face and gasped.

Antonio Hernandez!

I couldn't shoot. I lowered the rifle. He had his sword raised to strike me, but he recognized me and hesitated.

Beside me, another Texian's rifle roared. The bullet took Antonio in the chest. He jerked backward and toppled to the ground as the frightened horse surged forward, almost running me down.

I turned to see who had fired. It was the one-time highwayman Lige. "I swear, boy, you was about to let that Meskin git away!"

I dropped to one knee beside Antonio. The life was ebbing out of him.

I don't know just what had happened to me then. A cold fury swept over me, a fury at this whole useless, senseless war, a fury for what had happened to Thomas, to all the men at Goliad.

In front of me stood a Mexican officer, no weapon left to him but a saber. I fired and missed. He charged at me, swinging the blade. I raised my rifle and let it take the force of the blow. The saber slid down the barrel, bounced off, caught my arm, and ripped into my sleeve. I felt the deep bite of the steel. But I had too much momentum built to stop now. I swung the rifle butt around and caught him in the stomach. Much of the breath burst out of him.

But he managed to bring up the blade again. Once more I blocked it with the rifle, and this time I stepped in close and gave him a blow in the groin. He stiffened.

My imagination swept me away. For a second I looked at that face and thought I saw the officer who had spoken to us that morning at Goliad, the one who had smiled and led us like a Judas goat leads sheep to the slaughter.

The fury took over. I brought the rifle butt up and caught him under the chin. I pounded him in the face until he fell. In a black rage I used the rifle as a club to pound him and pound him and pound him, taking out on this man all the pent-up bitterness I had carried with me these long weeks.

Finally someone touched my shoulder. I whirled, the bloody rifle ready to strike again. It was Lige.

"Boy, he's as dead as he'll ever be."

That voice brought me crashing down to reality. I shook my head and blinked. Through the gray smoke I could see a vague swirling of figures. Texians still moving on in pursuit of fleeing soldiers. I could hear the ragged pattern of shooting, of continued slaughter. It would go on until darkness finally came to bring it to an end.

But for me, the battle was over. Santa Anna had been destroyed. The Alamo and Goliad had had their bloody vengeance.

It was over, and the fury I had brought with me was spent.

I raised my arm and found blood flowing slowly where the saber had taken its cut.

Lige said, "Boy, you better go and get somebody to see after that arm."

I nodded. I dropped the rifle and walked back in a daze, gripping the arm, the warm blood trickling out between my fingers. But I felt no pain. I felt only a vast relief. It was over now. It had to be.

I sat under a big live oak tree, wearily leaning back against its rough trunk while the doctor wrapped clean cloth around the cut to stop its bleeding. Across the way I could see Sam Houston lying on his blankets beneath another tree, his wounded leg stretched out in front of him. Whatever the pain he suffered—and it was great—he must have been feeling an intense satisfaction. This battle, this victory, was a vindication of his long weeks of silent retreat, of watchful waiting.

Slowly the various companies began to re-form. Weak from the shock of the wound, I nevertheless had to satisfy myself that Muley and Ramón had come through all right. I had told Muley to stay behind.

I found Muley alive, whole, and jubilant. "Josh," he announced proudly, "I fought in that battle. They gave me a rifle and I used it and fought and didn't even run. You ought to be proud of me, Josh. I didn't run this time."

I gripped his shoulder. "I *am* proud of you, Muley."

Muley went with me as I hunted for Juan Seguin's company. It was still badly scattered, but after a long search I found Ramón. His face was begrimed, sweat still running down and leaving tiny trails of mud. He was exhausted, but he didn't show a scratch. He looked at me in alarm, but I assured him it was no worse than I had already received once before, at Goliad.

"It's been a hard day, Josh," he said. "But it was a great victory."

I nodded soberly. "A great victory." I tried to find a soft way to tell him, but there wasn't any.

"Ramón. I saw Antonio."

He read the rest of it in my eyes. "Dead?" I nodded. His eyes closed a moment, and his mouth went hard. Then: "He chose his own way. But he was my brother. Do you think you could find him for me?"

"I could try."

We picked our way across that red-soaked battlefield. Mexican soldiers lay all around us, crumpled in a hundred different attitudes of death. Now that the smoke was lifted and most of the noise and excitement were gone, it was a sickening sight. Muley's face was pale, but he found the courage to stick close beside me, and not turn back.

"There he is, Ramón," I said, pointing.

Ramón dropped to his knees beside his brother's body. He lifted the still hand and felt for a pulse. Gently he eased the hand down, removed his hat, and made the sign of the cross. He knelt there a long time, while we stood in patient silence.

"He is of the enemy," Ramón said finally. "But I will ask General Houston to let me take him home and bury him among our own."

THEY BROUGHT in Santa Anna next day. A great hue and cry arose in camp to hang him, but Houston said no. He argued that Santa Anna, for all his bloody deeds, was of more use to Texas alive than dead. Dead men sign no treaties.

Up to the time of the battle, I would have shouted as loudly as anyone else for Santa Anna's death. But somehow San Jacinto had taken the bitterness out of me. Clubbing the life out of that officer had drained me of anger.

Ramón came to me and said, "Josh, I have permission to leave for home, and to take Antonio."

I could tell it was a way of asking me to go without bringing the question straight out.

"Josh," he continued, "I know you have had some bitter times, and you have had terrible things done to you by Mexican people. But I still consider you my friend."

He turned away, leading a packhorse with its sad burden tied securely.

I glanced at Muley. "When did you plant the corn?"

"First of March, just like you told me to."

"It ought to need plowin' about now, wouldn't you think?"

Muley nodded. "I expect it needs it pretty bad."

I called, "Ramón, hold up. Wait, and we'll all go home together."

AFTER
THE
BUGLES

THE BODIES would lie there till they went to dust, for Santa Anna had lost the battle. And with the battle, he had lost the war.

His saber-cut arm resting in a loose sling, Joshua Buckalew silently waited while his horse was being saddled. His sober gaze drifted across the still and somber San Jacinto battlefield, where score upon score of lifeless Mexican soldiers lay crumpled on the ground or bogged in black mud or floating in the reedy marshes of Buffalo Bayou. Two days ago a swaggering Santa Anna had gone into his tent for siesta, confident that he held victory in his hands, for he had a ragged rabble of hungry Texans backed against the bayou. He awakened in panic to find the sodden plain slashed by musket and rifle and cannonfire, his red flag trampled by desperate men whose voices clamored in fury above the thunder of the guns: "Remember the Alamo! Remember Goliad!"

Now it was over. The war was won. A victorious army had repaired to its camp at the edge of the plain, shouting for the blood of the captured Napoleon of the West. Big Sam Houston, nursing a shattered ankle, grimly refused to let them have him. Dead men write no treaties, he declared. And Texas would have her treaty of independence.

Home. The exultation had faded now in the barren stillness of the battlefield, and the Texans thought of home. A bitter taste lay sharp in Joshua Buckalew's mouth, for he knew his home lay in ashes. What the retreating Texans hadn't burned, the Mexican army had. He gazed westward, his mind reaching far beyond what his pain-pinched eyes could see. He knew the desolation that waited there: the gutted homes, the burned-out towns, the unmarked graves scattered from here to the Rio Bravo. The land itself still lay there, neglected but otherwise unchanged by the war, still possessed of the elusive promise that had drawn Americans by the thousands into Mexican-owned Texas to colonize under the laws of Mexico. Yes, the land remained, but everything else would have to be built back again with sweat and blood and determination. After all those hard years of work and privation and gradual accomplishment—years that had drifted away in smoke—Joshua Buckalew wondered if he still had it in him.

Times, winning the war is only the beginning of the battle. After the bugles fall silent, there is always the long road back.

Short, shaggy-haired Muley Dodd finished saddling Buckalew's horse and looked worriedly at the sling. "Josh, you reckon maybe we ain't rushin' a mite? You'd travel better if that arm wasn't so angry-lookin'."

Joshua Buckalew had been standing hunched in unconscious deference to the throbbing arm. Now he drew himself to his full five-feet-eleven. "It'll heal as good on horseback as here in this cursed swamp. I've seen enough of San Jacinto to last me a lifetime."

There was another reason to be moving on. He looked gravely at Ramón Hernandez, who finished lashing a blanket-wrapped bundle across the back of a captured Mexican packhorse. Beneath that blanket lay the body of Antonio Hernandez. "Ramón wants to bury his brother at home. If the weather turns warm, we got no time to waste."

IN THE early 1830s, Joshua Buckalew and his older brother Thomas had come to Texas from Tennessee to try to build a home in Stephen F. Austin's new land. They had drifted west and west and west, until at last they found what they wanted far beyond San Felipe de Austin, beyond even the Colorado River, near the Mexican colony where the Hernandez family squeezed a living out of the raw frontier by plowing their fields and raising cattle and catching wild horses. The Buckalews, copying the pattern, farmed some and branded wild cattle and broke mustangs to trade for supplies and now and again a handful of hard money in the eastern settlements. It had been a primitive life, in the main. But the Buckalews by their nature had been west-moving men, ever since Grandpa had frozen his feet that winter with George Washington.

Then had come Santa Anna, bringing cannon and sword to impose a terrible will upon his own people, finally crossing the Rio Grande to lay the same lash across the shoulders of the *Americano* colonists. He had slaughtered his way up by the Alamo and La Bahia. At Goliad, Thomas had fallen, cut down with more than three hundred other helpless prisoners in the shadow of that grim stone fortress. Joshua Buckalew had been among the fortunate few who escaped in the confusion of smoke and fire and dying men.

Now, suddenly—he still didn't completely comprehend it—the war was over. From Houston's camp the prisoner *presidente* had sent orders by courier for all Mexican troops to retreat beyond the Rio Grande. Texas no longer belonged to Mexico; it was a free and sovereign republic, rich in land and hope, but in all other things as poor as Job's turkey.

This was April. Time to go home now and plow the corn.

Muley Dodd pointed westward across the intermittent stretches of water which dotted the greening plain. Heavy rains all month had made eastern Texas a hell for both armies—Mexican and Texan. It would be slow, traveling home. "It's awful far, Josh," Muley worried. "You reckon we can make it there with Antonio?"

Josh shook his head, for he had his doubts. "We'll try."

Except for a bit of sugar, coffee, and cornmeal scrounged from among the defeated Mexicans—who were poorly fed themselves—they would have to live off the land. But Texas had deer and wild turkey aplenty, and sometimes bear. Farther west, where the settlements thinned, there would be wild cattle descended from the original mission herds. The diet was monotonous sometimes, but nobody ever starved.

Josh swung carefully up onto his horse, favoring the wounded arm, sucking a sharp breath between his teeth as the pain gripped hard.

Ramón Hernandez' brow creased. "Josh," he said in Spanish, "that arm will give you trouble. Perhaps it is better if you wait a few more days. I can get home alone."

Josh doubted that. A lone Mexican rider caught by a roving Texan patrol would probably be shot before he could bring out his army papers and explain that he had fought in Juan Seguin's Mexican company on the side of Sam Houston. The dark brown man's skin would be taken as evidence enough that he belonged to the enemy.

Josh replied in English. They did that most of the time, the two, each talking in the language that came easiest but understanding the other nevertheless. "I'll heal." He glanced at little Muley Dodd, who was off saying his goodbyes to men he had met in Houston's camp. "Besides, I'll be obliged for your help. Muley's intentions are good, but sometimes his results are poor."

"He fought well," Ramón pointed out.

Josh nodded but held his opinion. Muley had always been what people charitably called "slow." Like some lonesome hound dog, he had attached himself to Josh and Thomas and had trailed along with them all the way down from Tennessee. He had no home, so the Buckalews gave him one. Muley was good help if someone told him what to do; he would break his back without a whimper. But he had to be watched like a child whose curiosity outweighs its judgment.

The matter settled, they rode in silence among the huge old oaks, from which the long beards of Spanish moss hung in cheerless disarray like funeral wreaths. Josh never looked back. Most of the time he gazed through the rain at the trail ahead, though now and again he quietly studied the faces of Muley Dodd and Ramón Hernandez.

Ramón. Pity, what the war had done to Ramón. He had always been the jovial one, quick to smile, quick to sing, the best at roping wild cattle, the quickest to throw a raw-treed Mexican saddle on an unbroken mustang and swing up shouting. His brother Antonio had been the grim one, never smiling, never seeing anything but the flat and the gray and the black. Now Antonio lay wrapped in that blanket, dead, and Ramón had taken on the face of Antonio . . . solemn, unsmiling. It was not a face that fit him. But that was the way of war.

They rode hunched against the slow, chilling rain, minds running over the violence they had put behind them. Ramón's and Josh's, anyway. Muley seldom thought back. His mind was always foraging ahead, flushing out one wild notion after another, the way a pup flushes rabbits but seldom catches one.

Muley's stubbled face twisted as he tried to puzzle through an idea. "Josh, them fellers at camp, they was tellin' me Texas don't belong to Mexico no more. They was tellin' me it's a republic. That's really somethin', ain't it?"

"I reckon so, Muley."

"I thought it must be." He frowned. "Josh, what *is* a republic?"

"Well, Muley, it's . . ." Josh didn't know quite what to tell him. "It means we're free, Muley. We're independent."

"You mean we're like a slave that's had his chains took off?"

"Somethin' like that. We belonged to Mexico and had to do what they told us to. Now we do what we want to."

"Like, we don't have to work no more unless it suits us?"

Josh scratched his head. "Look, Muley, a man is free, but still he *ain't* free. I mean, nobody can tell him he's got to work, but if he don't, he goes hungry. It's like that with a republic. It's free from other countries, but it ain't ever free from responsibility. It's got to raise food or starve. It's got to make its clothes or go naked. It's got to keep up an army or its enemies will run over it. In other words, it's got to take care of itself. Nobody else is goin' to."

Muley fretted. "Used to, we could just let Mexico worry about all them things. Maybe we was better off when we wasn't free."

Josh shook his head. Trying to explain politics to Muley was like trying to empty a river with a wooden bucket.

Ramón rode along listening, his black-whiskered face furrowed in thought. "His talk is not all foolish, Josh. It is not easy to be free."

"You wishin' we hadn't fought?"

"I wish we had not had to. We fought because of Santa Anna, not because of Mexico herself. It is as if we had to spit in the face of our mother."

"A mother who beat and chastised us?"

Ramón's face was sad. "But still a mother."

Josh knew no way to reply, and he didn't try to. He knew Ramón's tie to Mexico was one of tradition and blood. Josh had felt a strong tie once, too, but mostly one of gratitude for opportunities offered. That tie had not been strong enough to endure, once the trouble began. Josh thought he could understand Ramón's feelings, even though he was unable to share them. And therein lay one of the main factors that had brought difficulty in the first place. The cultural difference between the new *Americano* settlers and the native Mexicans had been too great for deep understanding. Even when the hand of friendship was extended, there had been reservations and mistrust. The settlers tried hard, many of them, but even between good friends such as Ramón Hernandez and Joshua Buckalew there remained that last tiny distance they could never quite reach across, that final measure of understanding that never quite came.

It's not our fault, and it's not theirs, Josh thought. *The Bible said all men would be imperfect. Take a horse to a strange country and he'll always try to go back home, to stay with what's familiar to him. Men are no different.*

They made a long ride in the rain and at dusk camped in the

ruins of a homestead the Mexicans had put to the torch. Under a caved-in shed they found blackened wood which hadn't been altogether burned away and which was still dry enough to set ablaze. They made coffee and ate cold *tortillas* and huddled around the meager warmth of the little fire, trying to dry out. The damp cold brought a new ache to Josh's arm, and it showed in his face.

"Josh," Muley worried, "you ain't fixin' to get sick on us, are you?"

"Long as we keep travelin' west, I'll make it."

"Don't you worry none, Josh. I'll take care of you."

The thought was pleasant, if not reassuring.

The rain stopped next morning, but they rode across a trackless country, for any sign of recent movement had been washed away. So far as they could tell, they were the first to travel here since the fighting had ended. They came upon mute evidence of the terrible "Runaway Scrape" which had swept across Texas after the fall of the Alamo and the horror of Goliad. They saw burned-out houses. Along the trail they found abandoned sleds and scattered remnants of the loads they had carried. These had been left behind when the livestock broke down and were unable to pull further, or when pressure of the Mexican army forced fleeing settlers to leave their possessions, mount their animals, and make a wild run for the Sabine River and the sanctuary which awaited on the other side.

Twice they came across broken-down wagons, only a fractured wheel and the wagon bed itself remaining, the good wheels having been salvaged. Always they searched the relics for food or useful items, but inevitably someone else had done it first. Whatever one man threw away or abandoned, some other man had need of. Texas had nothing to waste, those days. Nothing but land.

Riding, Joshua Buckalew looked back occasionally in cold regret at the burden which trailed behind on the packhorse.

The day was long. His arm throbbed with fever, and each step the horse took came as a jolt of pain. The cold *tortillas* lay like lead in Josh's stomach. Muley frowned. "Josh, you ain't lookin' good."

Ramón reined up and pointed his chin. "*Mira, hombre,* over there. I see a trace leading off into that canebrake. It is so faint I almost missed it. If we follow it, we might find something."

After all the years of exposure, Muley had picked up only a smattering of Spanish. He understood only enough to scare him. "Like what?" he asked, full of doubt.

"Whatever it is, it will be no worse than what we have. Maybe a house the Mexican soldiers missed. Maybe hot food."

"And maybe Mexicans," Muley worried.

Josh had to blink to keep the haze cleared away, for his fever was rising. The trace could have been an old one, not used in a long time. At any rate, it had not been used since the rains. The horses were making tracks six inches deep in the mud. Anyone else's would have done the same. "Let's try it. If we don't find nothin', we can always come back."

The trail meandered through the dense growth. It had been used fairly recently, for cane had been hacked away to clear a path. The horses floundered through the swales, and the packhorse almost fell. Ramón desperately fought to keep it from crushing the body of his brother.

Josh had a futile thought: *It's too far. We'll never get Antonio home.* But he knew that so long as Ramón wanted to, they would keep trying.

They came at length to a sappy-green clearing. A log cabin stood in the center of it. A pair of muddy dogs bounded out to meet them, barking, but they were not hostile. They were tickled to death to see a human being, for they circled around and around the riders and tried to move right under the horses' feet.

"*Hyaww,*" Muley shouted at them, waving his arms. "*Hyaww!*"

The horses snorted and shied. Muley's let fly with a hind foot, narrowly missing the younger and less observant of the dogs. In the yard, hogs grunted and scattered, a pair of them bumping and squealing, teeth flashing. Chickens flapped their wings and fluttered out of the way, clucking and cackling.

Muley grinned, for chickens meant eggs, unless these two dogs abandoned to hunger had been sucking them all. "I could eat half a dozen of them hens, feathers and all."

Ramón said quietly, "This place belongs to somebody."

Muley replied, "He must've lit out in a right smart of a hurry. Probably figured old Santa Anna was grabbin' at his shirttail, him leavin' all this behind."

"He probably intended to come back to it. If we eat his chickens, he will have no eggs. And if he has no eggs, he will have no more chickens."

Seeing disappointment in Muley's eyes, Josh said, "Don't fret yourself, Muley. If we don't find somethin' else, we can kill one of them fat barrows. Man don't get any pig crop out of a barrow."

Josh eased down from the saddle, cautiously holding the arm tight against his ribs but feeling the pain anyway. Muley took his reins. "Go set, Josh. I'll take care of the horse."

The dogs reared up, licking at Josh's hands. One bumped his arm and caused him to double over from the shock of it. Muley came shouting. "Git, dogs! Git, I say!" The dogs took after Muley then. Seemed natural, somehow. Dogs had always taken a liking to Muley, the way they would to a kid. Perhaps they sensed that in ways he was just a boy.

Rain had caused the rough wooden door to swell tight, but Ramón pushed it open. The cabin smelled musty from the rain, and from the fact that all the shutters had been closed. In those times there probably were not three sheets of glass in a hundred miles. Ramón opened the shutters to let the air circulate and told Josh to sit down. But Josh had been in the saddle all day. He wanted to move a little. The arm would hurt anyway.

Muley poked around and discovered a cribful of corn, part of which he shelled for the horses. He brought some to the cabin for supper. Josh found the smokehouse, cured hams hanging from the rafters, and abundant supplies of bacon. Muley took dry wood from under a shed and kindled a blaze in the stone fireplace while Ramón whittled the outer edges off of a ham and threw them to the half-starved dogs. Ramón started coffee boiling in a can and from somewhere rustled up a pan. Muley ground the corn for bread, and they all ate as they hadn't eaten in weeks.

Afterwards, a momentary smile crossed Ramón's face as he leaned back, his stomach full. Josh took pleasure in the sight, for he hadn't seen Ramón smile since San Jacinto. For a while then, Ramón had forgotten the blanket-wrapped burden that lay yonder in the shed, out of reach of the hogs.

Josh said, "What are you thinkin' about, Ramón?"

Ramón's voice was quiet. "Of home. Of Miranda, and the baby I have not yet seen. What do you think of, Josh?"

"Of home. And of a girl."

"María? My sister?"

Josh nodded.

Ramón smiled and changed the subject. "It is a good house, this one."

Josh shrugged. Actually, it was a crude cabin built hurriedly of logs and later chinked with liberal slivers of wood and heavy dabs of plaster in an effort to seal out the wind and rain. But they had been so long out of doors, a chicken coop would look good. "By rights," he said, "they ought to've destroyed this so it wouldn't fall into Mexican hands."

Ramón said, "But aren't you glad they didn't?"

Next morning they ate their fill again. Perhaps it was the food; perhaps it was sleeping dry and warm in a house; but at any rate, Josh felt better. The fever had gone down. He stood in the open door and stared across the clearing into the orange sunrise. Not a cloud was in sight.

Muley said, "I wish we could stay here a week."

Ramón looked gravely toward the shed. "We can't."

"Just wishin', is all."

When the three men rode away, they carried one of the hams and some bacon from the smokehouse. The rest they left behind, for it belonged to someone else. Maybe he would return, and maybe he wouldn't. In the Runaway Scrape, many hadn't stopped until they had crossed the Sabine River into United States territory. Once there, some would never return to the uncertainties of a land which lay so near to hostile Mexico, no matter how great Sam Houston's victory. But if this one *did* return, he would not find his property looted. At least, not by Josh and Muley and Ramón. They took only what they needed, and in exchange they left behind a Mexican rifle Muley had picked up on the battlefield. A rifle was something a man could always use.

The dogs followed a long way before they gave up and quit, forlorn as lost children. The three riders did not retrace their steps but instead followed a faint old trace that led southwestward. It hadn't been cleared in a long time and was often slow going. The sun had risen halfway to the meridian before they broke out of the canebrakes and into open prairie.

They hadn't gone two hundred yards when suddenly they wished they had stayed longer at the cabin. Half a dozen horsemen appeared unexpectedly in front of them. Josh had seen enough Mexican cavalry the last few weeks that he recognized these at a glance.

The surprise was as great to the Mexicans. They sat staring, not a hundred yards away. Ramón wheeled his mount and pulled the packhorse after him. "Back to the brakes!"

Whatever worry Josh's arm might have been, he forgot all about it. For a wild instant he could hear the guns of Coleto Creek, and the brutal massacre of Goliad. He spurred like a wild man. The horses tried, but their feet dug deep into the wet ground, and their hoofs left a shower of mud behind them. Shots rattled. Ramón shouted, and his horse went down, sliding on its side. The packhorse jerked free and kept running. Ramón crawled away from his horse as it lay threshing. Josh leaned low to pull Ramón up behind his saddle but to no avail. Ramón tried to get up but went down again. Blood spread across the torn leg of his trousers.

Josh shouted, "Muley, you keep a-ridin'!"

But Muley had stopped. And then there was no use in running, for the Mexican soldiers had closed in around them, and there was nowhere to go. The rifle under Josh's leg might just as well have been in Tennessee for all the good it did. The Mexicans would have put half a dozen holes through him before he could have drawn it. He looked into their rifles and slowly raised his good arm.

Muley drew close, his face paling. "What'll we do now, Josh?"

"Pray some. And do what they tell us to. Climb down slow, so they won't get nervous and shoot you. We got to see about Ramón."

The Mexicans grabbed the horses as quickly as Josh and Muley touched the ground. Josh knelt by Ramón. "How bad, *compadre?*"

His face pinched in pain, Ramón pointed his chin toward the officer in charge. "Not good. It will be worse, I think. We will all get a bullet in the head."

The officer dismounted with the flair of a man in triumph. Of all the riders in the patrol, only he seemed to carry a pistol. The others carried cumbersome rifles or the clumsy *escopetas* that had enough recoil to knock a man out of his saddle. The officer waved the pistol and announced sharply that all three men were his prisoners.

Josh pointed at Ramón and said in Spanish, "This man is wounded." The officer seemed to ignore Josh. His eyes were hostile as he stared down at the bleeding Ramón. "You are Mexican. Why do you ride with these *Americanos?*" Ramón replied cautiously that they were friends.

"No *Americano* can be friend to Mexicans while there is a war."

"There is no war. Not anymore. Have you not heard?"

The officer showed surprise, but he remained wary. "I have heard nothing."

Ramón gripped his leg, his face twisting as the fire of it began to break through the numbness of the first moments. "The war is over. *El general* Santa Anna has ordered all troops across the Rio Grande."

The officer stared at Josh in puzzlement. "Then we have won. But why are these *Americanos* here?"

Ramón shook his head. "Santa Anna did not win. He lost. There was a big battle at San Jacinto. Houston and the *Tejanos*, they won it."

"You lie!"

"It is the truth, I swear by the Holy Mother."

The officer's hard gaze shifted from one man to another. "Men are sometimes known to lie, even by that which is holy."

Josh said in Spanish, "What he tells you is truth."

The officer's pistol wavered. Josh thought he was likely to fire it at any minute. "No *Americano* is to be believed. And a Mexican who would ride with an *Americano* is even worse. I think I will shoot all of you and end these lies."

One of the Mexicans had ridden out after the packhorse, which had stopped at the edge of the canebrake. Now he came leading the animal. The officer turned to Ramón. "What is tied on the horse?"

"My brother."

The officer's eyes widened. Ramón went on painfully, "My brother died in the battle I told you about. We were trying to get him home to bury him in holy ground with my mother and my father."

The Mexican who had fetched the horse said with face twisting, "He may be telling the truth, *capitán*. Something is dead beneath that blanket."

"Untie it!"

The Mexicans' horses were shying away, their nostrils keenly aware of the smell of death. A couple of the soldiers eased the bundle to the ground. They unwrapped it gingerly, wanting to get the job over with and move away. Josh didn't look as the blanket was pulled back. He didn't want to see. Ramón turned his head away, too. Muley knew no better than to look, and his face went white.

They would never have gotten home with Antonio.

The officer swore. "That is the uniform of a cavalryman."

Ramón nodded, his face grave. "My brother was in the army of Santa Anna."

Only then did Joshua Buckalew begin to doubt that they were all about to die.

CHAPTER

2

THE OFFICER motioned for the two soldiers to spread the blanket back over the body. They did so hurriedly and moved away. The officer studied Ramón, his disbelief fading. "You say we lost. How badly?"

"Very badly. Many hundreds were killed."

"And *el presidente*? Did he fight gallantly?"

"He fled in the uniform of a common soldier. The *Tejanos* found him anyway. Sam Houston has him as a prisoner. *El presidente* sent messages by courier for all Mexican army units to retreat from Texas."

"We have been on a long patrol. We have heard nothing."

The soldiers showed it. They were ragged and dirty, and some of them looked sick and emaciated. Their threadbare uniforms showed evidence of being rain-soaked many times and drying on their chilled bodies. Santa Anna had brought most of his troops up from deep in Mexico, ill-fed, ill-clothed, poorly prepared for a climate far colder than they were accustomed to.

The officer said to Ramón, "Your brother was in uniform. You are not."

Ramón shrugged. "There were not enough uniforms for all who

volunteered." It was not in Ramón's nature to tell a deliberate lie, Josh knew. But he *could* tell only that part of the truth which would serve to convey a false idea. Josh held his breath, hoping Ramón could get away with it.

The officer still worried. "You say *el presidente* fled. Did he not first lead the charge against the *Americanos*?"

"He did not charge. He was caught asleep."

The officer nodded bitterly. "That, I believe. He has always been a vain fool, Santa Anna. Mexico will be better off without him."

Listening, Josh was surprised. He had not fully understood that many of the Mexican army officers who gave the tyrant their professed loyalty harbored a carefully hidden contempt. They had little genuine regard for the callous bumbler who fancied himself the new Napoleon but sacrificed his soldiers with no more remorse than if they had been pawns in a chess game.

Ramón said, "He has given Texas away."

The officer swore. "After all the blood that has stained this land?" At length he gave the sad Mexican shrug that signified resignation to fate. "Mexico will be better off without Texas. It is too far from the mother country to be of value. It is a back-breaking land, full of trouble and tears. It is not good enough for Mexicans. Let the accursed *Americanos* have it. It will serve them right."

He ordered his men to bind up Ramón's wound. The job done, one of the men motioned toward Josh and Muley. "What of these? Are we to leave Texas and not get to kill even one more *Americano*?"

The officer frowned. "I am tempted, but they are friends of this man. We shall do them no harm. Let them stay and struggle in this hell they call Texas. That is a punishment worse than death." He turned to Ramón and pointed at the blanket. "You said you were taking him home. How far is that?"

Ramón told him. The officer shook his head. "You have carried him too far already. A soldier should be buried where he falls, with honor. We shall bury him here."

"It is not holy ground."

"When it receives the body of a Mexican soldier, it becomes holy."

Ramón made no more protest, for by now he could see his hope had been in vain. Besides, Ramón would be in no shape to ride now, not for several days.

The ground was soft from the rains. Muley and the Mexicans dug with bayonets and their hands and a bucket that Josh carried for boiling coffee. The hole, when they finished, was far from six feet deep, but it was better than the Mexican soldiers were getting at San Jacinto. It was better than the Texans had gotten at the Alamo and Goliad.

The Mexicans crossed themselves and the officer said a short Latin prayer and they covered the hole. They confiscated the ham and bacon, the coffee and corn. They rode south, leaving the three men at the edge of the canebrake.

Ramón sat on the ground, his bandaged leg stretched forward, face pale. "It is not what I had hoped for. But it is better than if we had left him on that slaughtering ground."

Josh said, "He saved us, Ramón. If they hadn't seen Antonio's uniform, they'd have killed us by now."

"God's plan, Josh. This war came between Antonio and me. For a while we were brothers no more, until we found him dead among the enemy at San Jacinto." Ramón made the same shrug of resignation as the officer. "God's plan. Man sees only what lies behind him. God sees what lies ahead."

THE WOUNDED horse lay still now. One of the cavalrymen had cut its throat as an act of mercy. Josh's mouth was still dry with the realization that he and his friends had almost ended the same way, and not through mercy. He told Muley to maneuver Ramón's saddle off of the dead horse and put it on the pack animal. Then, somehow, he and Muley got Ramón astride. They had no provisions left, and a long ride was out of the question for Ramón.

"We'll go back to the cabin," Josh said.

If they had to be stranded, this was a good place for a couple of cripples and a slow-moving Muley Dodd, he thought. Food was plentiful, and if it rained anymore the roof wouldn't leak. The settler who had built the place had done well for himself, considering the times. Nobody bragged much in Texas those days because nobody had much to brag about, except perhaps endurance. But this man had a decently tight cabin. He had a good field, chickens, hogs, some scattered few cattle. And from evidence around the shed Josh was sure there had been a team and a wagon, which the settler no doubt had taken with him on the Scrape. Wagons were exceedingly scarce in pre-revolution Texas. A man who owned a wagon was considered well-to-do. If he owned two wagons, he was rich.

They had had a wagon once, the Buckalews. It had gone up in smoke like almost everything else they owned except the land itself.

Josh's arm healed faster than Ramón's leg, for it had several days' start. Mostly they laid around the cabin sleeping, eating, reading the handful of books they found there. Josh read them, anyway. Ramón could understand spoken English well enough but had to pick his way along slowly with printed words and soon wearied of it. Muley couldn't read at all. Muley spent his time running happily with the dogs, chasing after game but seldom catching any. He hunted bee trees, too, for he always had a knack at that. It didn't worry him that he found none. For Muley the fun was in the chase, not in the catching.

Ramón's leg kept him from pacing the floor, physically. He paced it anyway, in his mind. Josh could read his thoughts almost as well as he could read the books. Up yonder past the Colorado waited Ramón's wife and a new son. Because the time for her delivery was so near, there had been no question of taking her when he went east to join Juan Seguin's Texas-Mexican company. He had counted on the family's Mexican blood to be protection enough from Santa Anna's troops. Though Santa Anna had been ruthless with his own people south of the Rio Grande, up here he considered his war to be with the *Americanos*. His supply lines were stretched a thousand miles or more, so he needed the cooperation of the Texas-Mexican people. In large measure he got it, for he had proclaimed this a racial war, the Mexicans standing shoulder-to-shoulder against the evil blue-eyed *extranjeros* who had come from the other side of the Sabine under a gracious dispensation of the mother country and had then turned against her. But there were those such as the powerful Seguins of Bexar who saw Santa Anna as a blackguard and rallied some of the Mexican people to stand against him. That this made them allies of the *Americanos* could not help but cause them doubt and uneasiness at times. But they rallied just the same.

"We'll get home in due time, Ramón," Josh said.

"There is no due time. I want to be there *now*."

"That baby will wait for you."

"That baby will walk before I ever see him. I want to see them all . . . the baby, Miranda, my sister María . . ."

María . . . Josh went silent then, for he also began thinking of María, a tiny girl with raven hair and dark eyes who laughed and sang. It was a memory to make a man look west, and make him itch to be on the move again.

IN A few days Josh's arm was no longer sore. All that remained was a little stiffness. He had read all the books and impatiently watched Ramón cripple around with a crude crutch he had whittled out of a limb, wishing the leg would hurry and heal so they could be on their way. Muley didn't care. He was having a good time with the dogs.

Then one afternoon Muley raced for the cabin, shouting, his face flushed with excitement. One of the dogs ran at his heels. Josh could hear the other one down in the meadow, setting up a racket. Instinctively Josh grabbed up the rifle he had brought from San Jacinto.

"Josh! There's people comin'! I seen them. There's people and horses and mules and some wagons."

"Not soldiers? Not Mexicans?"

Muley vigorously shook his shaggy head. "I seen a couple women."

Ramón pushed up from a chair and reached for the crutch. Josh motioned with his hand. "Stay put. If they're Texans and see you, they're apt to shoot first and ask about you later." He stepped out into the yard with Muley.

Muley eyed Josh's rifle with apprehension. "You reckon they'll come a-fightin', Josh? I already had enough fightin'. I sure don't want no more."

Josh shook his head. "Chances are it's the man who owns this place, come back to claim his own."

"Reckon he'll be mad because we been stayin' here, eatin' his vittles?"

"He'll understand. Anyway, that Mexican rifle we're leavin' will pay for all the vittles we could eat if we stayed a month. We ain't killed none of his layin' hens, or none of his sows. We've left the breedin' stock alone."

Three wagons moved out of a patch of cane and into the open meadow, in good view. Besides the teams, Josh figured there must be a dozen or so extra horses, some running loose, some being ridden by men and boys and one by a little girl. A small boy rode a gray mule.

A man in the lead raised his hand, and the procession stopped. The man touched heels to his horse and rode forward in a slow trot, leaving the others behind him. At the distance, Josh couldn't see their guns, but he had a feeling they bristled on those wagons like cactus. Fifty yards from the cabin the rider slowed to a walk and came in warily.

Muley whispered: "Looky there, Josh. He's got a rifle acrost his lap."

"I see it. Stand easy. Try to grin at him, why don't you?"

He said that to ease Muley's mind, for the violence of the past months had bewildered Muley. He was of a simple nature and had never raised his hand in anger against any man. Muley managed a grin of sorts, but his worried eyes showed it didn't go beyond his teeth.

The rider was tall and gaunt, in ragged homespun. Josh took him to be middle-aged until he came close enough for a look at his face. He was a young man. War and hard times had put years on his shoulders that the calendar didn't account for, Josh reasoned. Well, it had been hell for everybody. Big hands, sun-bleached eyes. Farmer, Josh figured, by the look of him. Most people were, in this country. The call for lawyers and such was none too strong. A man worked with his hands and his back. The rider held his left hand up as a sign his intentions were peaceful, but his right hand still gripped the rifle. Josh got a cold feeling he knew how to use it, and well.

"Howdy," Josh said. "Git down and rest yourself."

The man's eyes touched Muley a moment, then flicked suspiciously back to Josh. "Who be you, mister?"

"My name's Joshua Buckalew. This here is Muley Dodd."

"Names don't mean nothin'. I mean, how come you here? This your place?"

"Nope. Thought maybe it was yours. We was on our way home from San Jacinto."

The eyes narrowed. "How do I know you was at San Jacinto?"

"I just told you."

"If you was there, maybe you can tell me which wing Lamar's cavalry took."

"The right."

"And what horse was General Sam ridin' when the charge started?"

"A big white stallion. I don't know what they called him."

The man relaxed. "They called him Saracen." The hand went easy on the rifle. "I thought we was about the first to come back thisaway. When we seen your tracks dried in the mud, we figured you might be some kind of stragglers or renegades, foragin' around to see what you could steal. You already been here some days, I take it."

"We left pretty soon after the battle. We got this far and ran into a Mexican patrol."

The man's jaw tightened. "A patrol?"

"That was some days ago. I expect it's clear enough now. Of Mexicans, anyway."

"Folks in them wagons, they need a good night's rest. Horses need a feed."

"They can get it here. Mexicans must've missed this place."

"I don't expect they missed many." The rider swung down stiffly, for he had been on horseback a long time. He held out his hand. "My name's Ocie Quitman." His gaze was steady and not unfriendly, but Josh saw pain deep in the pale eyes. There was no happiness in this man.

When Josh shook hands with him, Quitman noticed the stiff arm. "You get that at San Jacinto?"

"Saber cut. About healed now."

Bitterly Quitman said, "We all lost somethin' to Santa Anna. I wisht they'd of let us hang him. Him and all the rest of them. I wisht there was dead Mexicans strung on every tree limb from here to the Rio Grande!" His eyes hardened, and a cold shudder ran down Josh's back as he sensed the depth of Quitman's hatred.

Man, whatever you lost, it must have been really something.

Quitman waved, and the wagons moved again, the lead wagon's canvas sagging on uneven hoops that seemed to shift with each jolt of the wheels on the rough ground. Towering in the seat, hunched over the leather lines, was a big, square-shouldered, middle-aged farmer. His raw-boned wife sat beside him, her face all but hidden beneath a sagging bonnet. Halting his team, the big farmer handed the reins to the woman and climbed down, walking toward Josh, extending a huge hand that looked as if it could smite a mule to its knees. "Howdy, friend. We're sure glad to see a new face after all these days. My name's Aaron Provost. This here your place?"

Josh told him it wasn't, that they had stopped here to recuperate.

Provost said, "We was a little concerned at first over who you might be, but you got a good face."

Josh felt his bewhiskered cheek and wondered how the farmer

could tell. He couldn't remember when he had shaved. "You got a lot of people here."

"That yonder's my wife Rebecca. Them young'uns you hear whoopin' and hollerin' back there with the stock . . . the missus and I are responsible for all of them but one. The Lord's been more bountiful with children than He has with some of the other blessin's." He didn't say it as if he were complaining, and Josh doubted that Provost regretted sowing the seed. Provost pointed a thick finger. "Fellers on that middle wagon, they're Wiley McAfee and his partner Dent Sessum. That last wagon yonder, it belongs to Ocie Quitman."

Josh saw a woman sitting on the seat, handling the lines. "I suppose that's Mrs. Quitman."

Ocie Quitman turned away. Provost said, "No, it's the Widow Winslow. Heather Winslow. Husband fell to the Mexicans a while back. Ocie let her have the borrow of his wagon. That lad on the gray mule, he belongs to Ocie."

"How far you-all goin'?"

"Long ways yet. Rebecca and me, we had us a place up on the Colorado. The Quitmans, the Winslows, they was all nearby. Sessum and McAfee, they got no land as yet. They're just lookin'."

Josh counted the men who could use guns. "You got four men who can shoot if it comes necessary."

"Five. My eldest, Daniel, ain't but fourteen, but he's a right peart shot when he has to be."

"He might have to be. Last I knew, Comanches was prowlin' the western country, lookin' for easy pickin's. Didn't take them long to find out about the war. Them slow wagons make a good target of you."

Ocie Quitman came back. "Whichaway was *you* headed, Buckalew?"

"West."

"If you was to join up with us, that'd be seven guns."

"Eight. We got one more man in the cabin. Mexican patrol put a bullet in his leg."

Two dusty, lanky men in homespun and buckskins shared a whisky jug, then climbed down from the second wagon and lazily stretched themselves, one of them scratching his ribs. They didn't offer the jug to anyone else. One chunked a rock at the barking dogs. The other hungrily eyed the chickens. Josh featured them as being likely to spend a lot more time in the woods than in the fields.

The woman on the third wagon had her face shaded by a large bonnet similar to Mrs. Provost's, but when she turned toward Josh, he caught a glimpse of her features. He judged she was in her mid-twenties. The little boy reined his gray mule up beside her and stuck close, his large brown eyes abrim with curiosity as he stared at Josh and Muley, and with joy as he looked at the dogs.

Josh said, "She don't look old enough for a widow."

Provost replied, "Wartime, it don't take long."

"She's got no business goin' west again, a woman by herself."

"It's her land, and she's got no place else to go. No people left back in the States."

"She can't work a farm."

"She's stronger than she appears to be. Give her a few years and she'll look like my Rebecca yonder." Josh couldn't see that as a recommendation, but the farmer seemed to think it was. "Anyway, she's got determination. That counts for as much as muscle. And she's a fair handsome woman. I expect there'll be bachelors enough more than willin' to lend a hand." Provost appraised Josh with a wry squint. "You a bachelor, Buckalew?"

The dogs quit barking when the kids started hitting the ground. They made the rounds of first one child, then the next, tails twitching. A smile stretched across Muley's face, for Muley and dogs and kids had always been a happy combination. Before the war, he had gone often to laugh and run with Ramón Hernandez' kid brothers and sisters. Most of them were growing up now, but Muley never would.

Mrs. Provost took charge, shouting orders to the boys and girls from her perch on the wagon seat. The chickens fluttered and cackled in alarm as the youngsters ran around the yard to loosen their tired legs, the dogs yipping merrily after them. The man named Dent Sessum took a few steps in Josh's direction, impatience in his eyes. When Provost strode off to his wagon to speak with his wife, Sessum muttered, "A damned menagerie, that's what it is."

Dryly Ocie Quitman said, "*They* invited *you*."

Provost tramped back in a few minutes, leading his sun-browned wife by one arm. The young widow followed a few paces behind. "Rebecca . . . Heather . . . this here is Joshua Buckalew. I do believe that if we tried right hard we could talk him and his party into throwin' in with us as far as Hopeful Valley. We sure could use their company."

Mrs. Provost smiled pleasantly and proceeded to look Josh up and down as if she were buying a workhorse. She was a weathered but hardy woman who looked as if she could stand up to just about anything chance might decide to throw at her. Most of the early Texas women were that way. Those who weren't either died off or went back to where they had come from. Josh could feature Mrs. Provost skinning game, dressing a baby, quoting Scripture, and cussing the weather all at the same time.

Heather Winslow said, "Mister Buckalew may not know me, but I know him."

Surprised, Josh stared. She slipped the bonnet back from her face. "Your farm was west of ours, a good ways. One time you stopped at our cabin on a trip to San Felipe with the old surveyor, Jared Pounce. Whatever became of Mister Pounce?"

"He was in the Alamo."

Her mouth went into a thin, sad line. "He was a good man. They were all good men." She dropped her chin and turned away. Josh figured she was thinking of her husband. He vaguely recalled now, though he wouldn't have if she hadn't spoken up. Jared Pounce, always fond of good vittles, had called her the "corn-dodger woman." She was smallish but strong. She had large blue eyes that would catch a man's gaze so that he didn't pay much attention to whether the rest of her was handsome or not. Josh would have considered her pleasant to look upon, though he would have hesitated to call her pretty. *María Hernandez* was pretty.

He said, "I remember. You-all had you a nice place started."

"It could've been a real good place. Lord knows my Jim tried. Seemed like bad luck always dogged him one way and another. Finally came the Scrape, and the Mexicans caught up to us while we were trying to reach the Sabine." She paused. "Do you remember my Jim?"

He shook his head. "Met him once, is all. I'm afraid I wouldn't know him if he was to come ridin' up here."

Sadness lay like blue ice in her eyes. "I wish he would. But he never will, not ever again."

Dent Sessum shouted to his partner, "Wiley, we're goin' to have fresh meat on the table tonight. See that fat sow yonder? She'd feed all of us for a month." Sessum walked toward her, rifle in hand, moving as if to haze her away from the wagons and shoot her.

Josh called to him, "There's cured meat in the smoke-house. You leave the man's livestock alone."

Sessum turned defiantly. "They ain't yours."

Josh moved closer to him. "They ain't *yours*, either. You'll eat cured pork, and you'll leave the sow to fetch more pigs."

For a moment he figured he was fixing to get an argument from Sessum. And if he did, he'd probably have Wiley McAfee to contend with too. Sessum muttered, "Some people act like they was meant to rule the whole blessed earth." But he turned on his heel and walked away from the sow.

Quitman said, "For what it's worth, Buckalew, they ain't no partners of mine."

Josh glanced at Aaron Provost, who seemed to feel obliged to explain his own position. "They had their own wagon, and they had guns. I figured we needed both."

Josh said, "I been hopin' when the war was over, we'd have a lot of new folks come in . . . folks of the better sort."

Quitman said: "These ain't the ones you been waitin' for, then. They was on the Sabine when the fightin' was goin' on at San Jacinto. But the Lord makes all kinds."

The big farmer remarked, "The buzzard as well as the eagle. The sparrow as well as the hawk."

They turned toward the cabin. Provost said, "We best see if the place can be made comfortable for the women-folk. They'll enjoy sleepin' under a roof. God knows they probably won't find one when they get home."

Ramón Hernandez had pushed to his feet. He hobbled to the door, leaning on the crutch.

Heather Winslow's hands went flat against her cheeks, and she screamed.

A hissing sound broke from Ocie Quitman. His rifle swung up. "A Mexican! A damned dirty Mexican!"

Josh grabbed the gun barrel, thrusting it aside. "Hold on! He's with us!"

He had expected momentary hostility; after the last few months it was only natural. But he was not prepared for the fury in Quitman's tight-drawn face. He wrestled with the man, who tried to wrench the rifle free of Josh's grasp. Instinctively Josh knew Quitman would kill Ramón if given the chance. Sharp pain lancing through his stiff arm, Josh shoved the weapon forward, jamming it into Quitman's belly. He jerked it to one side, wresting it from the big hands as Quitman coughed for breath. Quitman kept grabbing for the rifle as Josh stepped back. Josh blew the powder out of the pan.

"Quitman, I told you he's with us. He fought at San Jacinto too."

Quitman struggled for breath. "The hell! Which side was he on?"

"He was with the Juan Seguin company."

Quitman stopped trying then, his fists still clenched, his face dark. He stared at Ramón with eyes that wanted to kill.

Josh said: "You're not goin' to hurt him. He's my friend."

Quitman stared a moment longer at Ramón, then the sudden rage began to ebb. "To you, maybe, but not to me. No Mexican will ever be a friend of mine again."

He turned and strode toward the wagons, leaving Josh standing there with the rifle in his hand.

As Quitman neared Sessum and McAfee, Sessum spoke. "Just say the word, Ocie. We'll kill that Mexican for you."

Quitman made no reply.

Josh dropped Quitman's rifle to the ground and brought up his own, backing toward the cabin door, tensed and ready. The children had stopped running and stood watching open-mouthed. Aaron Provost had turned to watch Quitman, to see what he would do. But Quitman did nothing, except keep walking away. He strode past Sessum and McAfee as if they were not there. He didn't stop until he reached his wagon that the widow had been driving. He leaned against a rear wheel, his back turned, one hand gripping a spoke as he wrestled with whatever private devil was tearing at him.

Mrs. Winslow stood where she had been, except that she had turned away from Ramón, her face paled, still twisted with the shock.

Josh thought now was the time to make one thing clear to everybody. He brought his rifle up across his chest, not pointing it at anybody but letting it be seen. What he had to say would be blunt, but it would not be misunderstood. "Get this down and be damned sure you swallow it, all of you. We're willin' to join you, but we don't have to. We got by before you came, and we can get by if you leave. If you want us, you got to take all three . . . me and Muley *and* Ramón. Anybody that moves a hand against Ramón has got me to whip."

Sessum muttered, "We fought a war to get rid of them Mexicans."

"Way I hear it," Josh spat, "*you* didn't fight nobody."

"We stood guard at the river. Somebody had to. Ain't our fault we never got to kill no Mexicans."

"You're not killin' this one. You better get that through your head."

Aaron Provost frowned, studying Ramón. "How long you known him, Buckalew?"

"Since we first come down from Tennessee."

"And you're sure of him?"

"As sure as I am of myself."

"Well, you're a man who's pretty sure of himself. Me, I didn't worry over Mexicans one way or the other before the war. They went their way and I went mine. Live and let live, was the way I seen it. If you stand up for him, he's all right as far as I'm concerned." Provost turned to face the other men. "We agreed when we started out that if there come a disagreement, we'd take a vote. So we'll decide whether we want Buckalew and his bunch to go with us. Whichever way it comes out, we don't bother Buckalew's Mexican. How about it, you boys?"

Sessum grumbled, "Damn Mexican is apt to stab a man in the back when he ain't lookin'. We ought to shoot him and be safe."

Provost's voice was as big as the man himself, when he became aroused. "But you ain't goin' to, is that understood?" Sessum reluctantly nodded, and McAfee followed suit. It seemed to Josh that whatever Sessum did, the other one tried to do the same. The farmer turned and called after Quitman, "Ocie, how about you?"

Quitman didn't answer until he was asked the second time. Slowly he turned his head. "Just keep him out of my sight!" He walked off beyond the wagon and stood looking across the meadow.

The farmer turned dourly to Josh. "We'll wait awhile to take that vote. Let Ocie have time to get hold of himself and think things through."

Josh said, "I reckon I already know how he'll vote."

"Don't be too quick to put a judgment on him. That'd be as unfair to him as he was to your Mexican. Ocie's got cause to hate. At least, he thinks so. And he's a good man to have on your side. I don't think I'd want him agin me."

Josh had already decided that. But Ramón had a prior call. Right now it didn't look as if there was a place for both of them.

Provost walked away with his wife. Heather Winslow said, "Buckalew . . ."

"Yes?"

"I didn't mean to set things off. It isn't like me to scream. But I didn't expect to see him. He just bobbed up there all of a sudden. He's the first Mexican I've seen since . . ." She looked at the ground.

Josh said, "Don't blame yourself."

She turned and looked toward Ramón, and Josh could tell it was an effort for her. Ramón stood in the doorway. He hadn't moved an inch.

"I'm sorry," she told him.

Ramón said in forced English, "It is for nothing. I did not mean for to scare you, *señora.*"

"And I didn't mean to cause you any trouble."

Josh said, "Looks like trouble would've come whether you'd screamed or not."

Mrs. Winslow said, "I want you to know this, Mister Buckalew, if they let the women vote, I'll vote for all of you to go along."

Josh glanced at the wagon where Quitman had disappeared. "What about him?"

"What *about* him?"

"You ridin' on his wagon and all, I thought . . ."

Her blue eyes hardened a little. "Ocie Quitman is a kind man, inside. He saw I needed help, and he gave it. In return, I've been taking care of his little boy. I still think for myself."

"No offense meant, ma'am. I just didn't want to be the cause of trouble between you and him if there *was* anything . . ."

"There is not. Mister Quitman is a gentleman."

"I never thought no other way."

The new arrivals unloaded what they would need out of the wagons and hobbled the teams out on the meadow. When the men had finished the necessary chores, Aaron Provost summoned them all back beside his wagon. He cast one frowning glance at Josh and Ramón, then turned to the others. "Ain't no need us waitin' no longer to take a vote. We'd just as well get the air cleared so this thing don't lie there and simmer between us all night."

Ocie Quitman jerked his head toward Rebecca Provost and Heather Winslow. "How about the women? They get to vote?"

"You got any objection to it, Ocie?"

"Everything we do affects them the same as us. I say give them a vote."

Aaron nodded. "Suits me. Dent . . . Wiley . . . how do you-all feel about takin' Buckalew and his friends?"

Sessum scowled. "The Mexican too?"

Watching silent anger rise in Ramón, Josh said, "It includes him."

Sessum spat on the ground. "Then I say the hell with it." McAfee agreed. "We got on pretty good so far. We can do without them."

Aaron switched his gaze to Quitman. "Ocie?"

Quitman stared at Ramón. "I say no."

Aaron grimaced. "That's three against. Well, I don't agree. I think we're apt to be glad we took them along, even if one of them *is* a Mexican. I don't reckon the good Lord asked him his preference." He glanced at his wife. "Whatever I say, Rebecca will agree to. So I cast our two votes for takin' them with us. Heather, how do you vote?"

Josh was watching Quitman when Heather Winslow half whispered, "They ought to go with us. I vote yes." Surprise flickered in Quitman's eyes, and disappointment.

Aaron said, "Well, that winds us up in a tie. What do we do now?"

The silence hung so hot Josh thought he could light a fuse with it. Finally Quitman shrugged. "If the womenfolk feel better to have them come along, so be it. But keep that Mexican out of my way! I don't even want to look at him!"

Aaron frowned. "Ocie, you have to understand that the war is over. As the Book says, we shall beat our swords into plowshares, and the lion shall lie down with the lamb."

Dryly Quitman replied, "They may lie down together, but the lion will be the only one that gets up."

RAMÓN MOVED out of the cabin when the women moved in. Both were silently apologetic. Ramón hobbled out to the shed on his cane while Muley and Josh carried their few belongings. Muley said, "Josh, how come they got it in for old Ramón the way they do?"

"Temper of the times, Muley. Me and you, if we was to go to Mexico we'd get treated the same way."

"It don't hardly seem fair."

"Nothin' is fair in war. Or in what follows after the war, either. Not here, not in Mexico, not noplace."

"Old Provost was right when he said the Lord didn't give Ramón no preference. Reckon if He had, old Ramón would've chosen to be American like us?"

"That's hard to say, Muley."

Muley's face brightened as he examined other angles of the notion. "The Lord didn't give *me* no preference, neither. You know somethin', Josh? If He *had,* I'd of sure been different than I am. I swear, I'd sure ask for a change."

"You would?"

"Yes, sir! I'd have brown eyes instead of blue ones."

They dropped their gear on the packed ground in the rude shed. Ramón carefully lowered himself to a sitting position, stretching his leg out in front of him. His eyes were averted from Josh, but the quiet anger clung to him like heat around a bad stove.

Josh said, "You oughtn't to blame them too much, Ramón."

Ramón gritted in Spanish, "That is what I keep trying to tell myself, but I can't hear it."

"We don't have to go with them. We'd figured all along on goin' by ourselves. We could get up and strike out in the mornin' and on to the Colorado River. We could even leave tonight."

The Provost children and the Quitman boy had followed at a respectful distance. For a few moments they stared from across the open corral that closed off the south side of the shed. Gradually they edged closer, poised to break and run if anybody raised a hand. Their attention was riveted to Ramón, their curiosity gradually overcoming the fear they had for his darker skin. A couple of the children whispered in the little Quitman boy's ear, and he firmly shook his head. They whispered again, nudging him forward. The boy took a few hesitant steps, glancing back over his shoulder to see if his friends were backing him up.

They had been around Mexicans before, Josh reasoned; they *must* have. But Ramón was probably the first they had seen since the Runaway Scrape.

The boy tried to speak but couldn't bring it out. A larger Provost boy stepped up and whispered in his ear again. Finally the little one blurted to Ramón, "Is it true? Are you really Santa Anna?"

Ramón held his silence a moment, his face unreadable. Finally a faint humor gleamed in his black eyes, and for a second Josh thought he was going to smile. "No," Ramón replied in English. "I am not Santa Anna. I am Sam Houston."

The boy's eyes widened in surprise. The other youngsters began to snicker, and the Quitman boy gradually realized he had been taken. "Awwww, you're not."

The other youngsters tittered and ran. The Quitman boy suddenly realized he stood all alone, and he whirled, racing across the corral and scaling the fence.

Ramón watched them go, and the gleam remained. "The wagons are slow. Do you think they will run into trouble?"

Josh said, "You never can tell about Comanches. They could be out west huntin' buffalo, or they could be up thisaway huntin' hair to braid their leggin's with. Not likely there's any Mexican soldiers left, but you couldn't take an ironclad oath on that either."

"And *renegados*?"

"Renegades, you got any time you have a war. Sneakin' around the brush pickin' up the leavin's, stealin' what they can, killin' if it comes handy."

Ramón said, "This war is not the children's doing. I have a son of my own now. If harm came to these little ones, and I had not done what I could, I would not feel entitled to enjoy my own son."

"Folks may treat you dirty, even when you help them."

"I have been treated dirty before. I have not died from it."

By and by Heather Winslow came with a can of steaming coffee and some fried bacon. "Mister Buckalew, Mister Dodd, supper's ready up at the cabin. I brought this out for your friend. With his bad leg and all, I thought he'd rather not have to walk."

She glanced at Josh with apology in her eyes for the weak lie. Ramón accepted the food and coffee with dignity and quiet "*gracias*," but Josh knew he held no illusions.

Heather Winslow paused, looking back at Ramón with regret. "I am sorry, *señor*, for the way things are. Maybe they won't always be."

Ramón thanked her quietly, then stared at the plate. At length he asked, "Do you think it will get better, Josh?" Then he answered his own question. "No, it will get worse. It may get much worse."

THEY ATE breakfast before daylight. Josh and Muley took theirs to the shed, along with Ramón's. They had decided that if Ramón wasn't welcome in the cabin, they wouldn't go either. After breakfast the men and boys hitched teams to the wagons and brought up the loose stock. Muley and Josh saddled their horses.

Ramón said, "Saddle mine too, will you, Josh?"

"With that leg, you'd better ride in a wagon."

"Which wagon?" Ramón grimaced. "The farmer Provost, he might take me, but his wagon is too loaded. McAfee and Sessum, they would not let me ride on their wagon even if I wanted to. And I do not want to."

"There's still the wagon the widow drives . . ."

"She would say yes, but the wagon belongs to Quitman, *no es verdad?* I have no wish to cause her trouble from him. She is a widow. She will have need of him, I think."

"I'll talk to Quitman."

Ramón shook his head. "The leg is not so bad that I cannot ride. I will not beg or owe a debt to anyone. No one can later say he did a big good for this Mexican!"

Rebecca Provost took charge of loading her wagon, shouting orders to the children, who seemed endless in number, the way they swarmed over, around, and through the wagon, getting the load settled and tied. Before long the Provost and Winslow wagons were ready to go.

"You-all roll out," Sessum told Provost. "Me and Wiley, we got somethin' to fix. We'll catch up to you directly."

Josh rode by their wagon and failed to see anything that appeared to be broken down. It would have suited him just as well if the two didn't catch up at all. Aaron Provost flipped his lines, shouting roughly, and his team strained against the traces. Heather Winslow followed, shouting in a voice that lacked the coarseness of Rebecca Provost's but which carried authority, nevertheless. Quitman's small son rode the gray mule again, dropping back to join the Provost youngsters in herding the loose stock a short way behind the wagons. The children whooped and frisked along. Whatever terror they had been through, they had shrugged it off. Or at least it appeared they had. Josh wondered, though, if sometimes it would not come back to them in the night, in the screaming horror of a nightmare that the mind is helpless to shut out. War had a way of leaving scars that didn't show.

The dogs followed the youngsters. Aaron yelled back for the kids to chase the dogs home, but nothing worked, not even chunking rocks at them. The dogs would tuck their tails between their legs, drop back a little, but continue to follow.

Josh rode up beside the Provost wagon. "Looks like they're bound and determined to go. They been left here too long to want to stay."

Provost frowned. "I hate to git away with a man's dogs."

"He may not come back. You don't mind your kids havin' the dogs, do you?"

Aaron shook his head. "They ain't likely to have much else when we get home." Rebecca Provost nodded in solemn agreement. "War and hard times has robbed these young'uns. A dog or two would be good for them."

"Then," Josh said, "let's don't worry about it. A hog or a cow is property, but a dog is a free agent. He goes where he wants to and does as he pleases. If it pleases him to tag along with your young'uns, who's to blame?"

Presently, looking back, Josh could see the third wagon moving along, making some progress but showing no hurry about catching up. Every little while he would look back and gauge how much distance it had closed. The rate Sessum and McAfee were traveling, they wouldn't be up to the other two wagons till the noonday stop.

Suspicious, Josh turned his horse and started back toward the trailing wagons. Muley shouted, "Josh, where you goin'?"

"You stay here, Muley. I'll be back directly."

He heard a horse loping up behind him and turned to speak sharply to Muley. He saw Ramón instead, the wounded leg thrust out. "Ramón, you just as well stay with the wagons."

"I am curious too."

"It'd tickle them to find an excuse to shoot you."

"I have been shot at by better men."

"You bein' there might cause trouble that I wouldn't otherwise have. I'd rather you stayed here, Ramón."

Reluctantly Ramón reined up. "I will watch from here. If it looks like a fight, I will come."

Josh rode in a slow trot. Approaching the wagon, he could see hostility. Sessum said, "You needn't have fretted none about us, Buckalew. We're gettin' along just fine."

Josh didn't say so, but that was the thought which made him fret. Tied to the rear of their wagon he saw chicken coops, quickly and crudely put together. He said brittlely, "Looks to me like you're doin' a mite *too* well. I told you yesterday, the breedin' stock belongs to somebody. You got no business takin' it."

"He may never come back."

"On the other hand, he might come back today. Ain't no use you robbin' him."

Sessum argued, "Think how good it'll be, havin' fresh eggs every day we're on the trail."

Josh was sure that even if they *did* have eggs, they wouldn't give him any. He judged the distance back to the cabin and decided the chickens would work their way home if he released them here. "You'll open them coops and dump them chickens out."

Sessum said stiffly, "We hadn't figured on it."

"Then figure on it now. Either you dump them out or *I* will."

Sessum's eyes narrowed. "Just because you done a little soldierin', you don't need to think you can run over the rest of us."

McAfee put in with a sneer, "Anybody who runs around with a stinkin' Mexican has got no call to think he's so much."

Josh rode toward the coops. The two men had packed so many chickens that half the birds would smother before the day was out.

Josh heard a metallic click that brought up the hair on his neck. Sessum gritted, "You touch that coop, Buckalew, and that Mexican is goin' to be awful lonesome, just him and that halfwit."

That was what did it, his calling Muley a halfwit. Josh reined around, turning his back on the coop. He took a hard look into Sessum's eyes and decided the man didn't have the guts to pull that trigger. Josh moved straight at the rifle. He grabbed the barrel of it with both hands and thrust the stock back as hard as he could. Caught by surprise, Sessum took the blow in the belly. He doubled over, coughing for breath as Josh jerked the rifle out of his slackened hands. Josh eased the hammer down and pitched the weapon out into the grass. Turning, he slipped a knife out of its sheath at his belt and slashed at the nearest coop. It was almost open when he heard the scuffling of heavy boots. He looked back to see Sessum climbing across the loaded wagon.

Sessum leaped at him. The impact and Sessum's weight dragged Josh out of the saddle and jarred him against the ground. The horse jerked loose and trotted away. Sessum pounded Josh with his fists. Josh tried to fend him off with his stiff arm while he struggled to free the other arm, pinned beneath him. He gripped Sessum's collar and yanked, then shifted his own weight and pulled the good arm out. Wrestling in the grass, the two men rolled into a narrow ditch that runoff waters had cut across the sloping hillside. Somehow Josh landed on top of him. He shoved his knee into Sessum's belly and took most of Sessum's breath. That put both of them on a fairly even basis, for the fall from the horse had taken most of Josh's.

Sessum wheezed, "Wiley, come help me."

But the struggle had excited the team, and McAfee's hands were full with the reins, fighting to keep the horses from running away. Josh picked up the knife from where it had fallen and finished slashing the coop open. The chickens rushed out with a flapping of wings and a sudden burst of squawking. Some landed on Sessum in their first attempt at flight. He threw his arms over his face, cursing. The horses kept dancing, wanting to run.

Josh started on the second coop as Sessum brushed the chickens away and pushed to his feet, feathers clinging to his dusty clothes. He rushed, cursing. Josh dropped the knife and met him halfway. He gave him a couple of underhanded licks he had learned back in Tennessee. They weren't fair, but no fight is fair unless you win it. Josh had no intention of losing this one.

Sessum doubled over. The horses had quit straining, and McAfee jumped down, ready to join the fight. But he stopped as a dark shadow fell across him. Ocie Quitman sat there on his horse. Behind Quitman, Ramón loped up, his leg outthrust.

Quitman said, "You better hold on, McAfee."

McAfee protested, "He don't look like God to me. He's got no call to be a-tellin' us what to do."

Quitman said calmly, "Then forget what he told you, and listen to what *I* tell you. Turn the rest of them chickens out."

McAfee pointed toward the other two wagons, which had halted. "They're takin' the dogs with them. I don't see where there's no difference in takin' the chickens and takin' the dogs."

"Only way them dogs would stay here would be if you tied them, and then they'd starve to death. But the chickens will stay if you don't tote them off. And you're not goin' to." His eyes were sharp as fine-honed steel. "Now do what I said and open them other coops."

Sessum was on his feet now, glaring at Josh but not putting up any resistance to Quitman. There was a look about Quitman which reminded a man of a loaded rifle, pointed straight at him. Sessum picked up Josh's knife from the ground and cut the coops open, releasing the rest of the chickens. Feathers floated in the morning breeze. Done, Sessum hefted the knife, then hurled it sideways at Josh. Josh's instinct was to duck away from it, and he had to go and fetch it after it fell.

By now Ramón had arrived, but there was nothing for him to do except watch. He did that in silence.

Sessum jerked his chin at Josh and said to Quitman, "I don't know what you have to go and take up his fight for. None of us ever even seen him till yesterday."

"It ain't for him. I just believe in doin' what's right, and carryin' off a man's chickens ain't right. You ought to see that for yourselves."

"All I can see is this Buckalew, makin' out like he was the Lord of all Creation."

"Forget about Buckalew, then. You just worry about *me*."

Quitman turned his horse and started back toward the other

wagons. As if he considered the incident over and done with, he never looked behind him.

"That man," Ramón murmured, "is like ice in the river."

Josh said: "I'd sure rather have him for me than against me. Right now I don't think he's either."

Ramón observed, "He is against *me*."

CHAPTER

4

Heather Winslow let the leather lines sag in her hands as the wagon creaked slowly through the greening grass. Now and again her eyes followed the hopping frogs, brought out by the recent long spell of rains. She flinched each time a wagon wheel crushed one, its body making a distinct "pop" as it exploded under the weight of the iron rim. She was glad Quitman's boy Patrick was back yonder on that gray mule, riding with the Provost youngsters, for it upset him to see the frogs die. He had seen too much of death already for a boy of five.

She glanced back over her shoulder when she sensed that the children had grown quiet for the first time all day. They rode sleepily in the pleasant warmth of the mid-afternoon sun, loose-herding the extra stock, keeping it drifting along after the wagons. She sought out Patrick and beckoned until he saw her. He rode up, trying to push the lazy mule into a fast trot but unable to get him out of a walk.

"Sleepy, Patrick? Why don't you crawl up here with me and take a nap?"

He nodded. "All right, Mrs. Winslow." She had tried to get him to call her Heather, but the training was too strong in him. A boy called a grown woman Miss or Mrs. That was Ocie Quitman's teaching. She stopped the wagon to let him tie the mule at the tailgate. Climbing up, he stretched his short frame in the wagonseat, legs hanging over the edge, his head in the woman's lap. She flipped the reins and set the team to moving again.

She stared down at Patrick as he drifted into slumber, trying to find in his features those points that resembled his father.

It had always been a disappointment to her that she had never been able to give Jim a son. She didn't know whether the trouble had been with him or with her, and it didn't matter now. At least Quitman had the boy as a tangible reminder of his wife. Heather Winslow had only a memory of Jim, and a piece of land that might have nothing left on it but ashes.

Ahead yonder, a few days up the trail, waited the farm. She had tried to make plans, tried to decide how she could operate it by herself. There would be the fields to work, the garden to tend, the stock to take care of . . . if she had any left. In all probability there would even be a cabin to build. In all the long miles west from the Sabine she had seen only one left intact.

The farm had been hard enough even when Jim was alive. Lord knew he had tried. He'd always had good intentions, Jim had. He had been given to melancholy periods when things didn't go right, but he never complained aloud or blamed anybody. He always tried again. And often as not, he fell short again. Seemed things had a knack of going only halfway for Jim. Never total failure, but never actual success. Heather had tried to rationalize that they expected too much from this raw land, that they should be content with less. But other men did better. Other men worked no harder but came up with better crops. Other men seemed to go farther on good luck than Jim did by breaking his back.

Heather hadn't realized this when she married him. Orphaned young back in Missouri, she had been brought up by her grandmother and grandfather, who were kindly and well-meaning but hard-pressed to raise her after having finished with their own brood and being well along in years. Jim Winslow had come along, a handsome young man full of promise if short of the world's goods. He talked of going to the new land of Texas to seek his fortune and of wanting a nice girl to share it with him. The old folks pushed her to take advantage of the opportunity before some wiser girl beat her to it. She accepted their judgment and his proposal and headed west with him in a wagon. They were forced to trade the wagon for supplies before they ever got past Louisiana, and they made it into Austin's colony riding two horses and leading a packmule. Their luck had run to the same pattern ever since.

Though their marriage had been arranged more by mutual agreement than by any actual romance, she gradually developed a genuine affection for him, and he for her. If sometimes she looked at other young married couples and sensed a fire which her own marriage lacked, she tried not to let herself dwell upon the thought. Sure, life was hard. The country itself was hard. But surely there would be better times ahead. Surely luck would change. Anyway, she had observed that the fire of young love inevitably died down, and in doing so it often left the couple with a sense of loss and frustration. Better to have an affection that was genuine even if it never blazed. At least, Jim would always be there.

But Jim was not here, and he never would be again. As always, luck had run against him. Heather Winslow looked down upon the peaceful face of the sleeping boy and wished for that kind of peace. The terror still came to her, sometimes, in a nightmare. She could only hope it would fade . . . that she could forget the awful morning Jim Winslow had made his final sacrifice to let Heather go on to safety. Seeing the Mexican patrol catching up, knowing the two of them could never make the timber, he had given his protesting wife the fastest horse, kissed her goodbye, and had ridden back with a rifle to hold up the patrol.

The firing had stopped about the time she reached the timber. Under cover of the trees, Heather had waited, praying desperately. When she saw the patrol come over the hill, she knew the outcome of the fight. She rode on alone, pushing all night, leaving the patrol far behind.

That one time, at least, Jim Winslow accomplished what he set out to do.

Heather Winslow could see Ocie Quitman now, riding the point position far out ahead of the wagons. He rode now as he always rode . . . alone. She remembered the way she had seen him the morning after Jim had died. Near exhaustion, the horse so tired he was barely walking, she had come out of the timber and into a clearing. A bewildered little boy had stood there by a wagon, and a man sat with his head in his hands beside a newly filled grave. Easing down from the saddle, she had reached Ocie Quitman before he even sensed that anyone was near. Looking up and seeing she was a woman, he had cried out, "Oh God, why couldn't you have come sooner?"

She had remembered him as being from the same general part of the colony, out on the Colorado. Brokenly he told her he had just buried his wife and a newborn son. The Runaway Scrape had killed her. It had been too much—the hard trip, the rough flight barely ahead of the Mexican army at the time for her delivery.

"There was no one to help her," Quitman had cried. "No one but me."

After a while, when he had time to think, he decided what to do. "My boy needs a woman's care. I need your horse, and you need my wagon. So you take the wagon, ma'am, and get my boy to the Sabine. I'll take the horse and catch up to Houston's army."

"How'll I get the boy back to you, and the wagon?"

"I'll find you. You stay put, the other side of the river. When the fightin' is over, I'll come and find you."

She had already seen what could happen to a man. "And if you *don't* come?"

"I got folks in the States. You can send the boy to them. And the wagon is yours." He gave her what little money he had and rode off across the valley and out of sight.

She never got across the Sabine. With hundreds of other refugees, she had been stranded on the Texas side by high water, within sound of the cannon at San Jacinto. The day after the cannons stopped, Ocie Quitman came.

All that was behind her now. She could not afford to dwell upon it too much. What mattered was the times that lay ahead. She hated to think of them, but she knew she must. The thought of operating the farm alone was staggering. She didn't know how she could do it all by herself. But what else could she do? Hire a man? With what? How could she pay him? All the cash money she owned in this world probably wouldn't add up to three dollars.

There was one possibility, of course, though even to think about it so early was brazen, and her conscience plagued her. She knew it must be considered shameful, her husband just a few weeks dead.

She could marry again.

Surely she would, in time. She was still a young woman, not yet even twenty-five. And though the years of hard work and frustration had left their mark on her face and on her hands, she knew she was still considered a comely woman. Not as pretty as some who hadn't been through so much toil and care, but still not bad to look upon. She was credited with being a right smart of a cook. And in this land where unattached women were far fewer than the men, she should not have to worry that she would be passed over unnoticed. She would have to wait a while, of course, for it would not be seemly to show interest in men so soon. And in the meantime there was the farm, and the problem of operating it. There was the problem of how she would live and how she would eat, how she would protect herself in this big, lonely, savage land where tranquillity and happiness stood always in jeopardy of being shattered in a few short moments of violence and terror.

If there had been anywhere else to go after the Scrape, she would never have started west again. But the grandparents were dead now. There had been nowhere else, unless she decided to cross over the Sabine and throw herself upon the pity of some unknown community that already had problems enough of its own, some community that did not know her and owed her nothing more than the impersonal charity which all mankind owes to the unfortunate. In the west, at least, she had the farm.

That was it, then. She would follow along and trust the Lord to mark the way. But she would keep her own eyes open, too. She always had.

Joshua Buckalew rode close to the wagons. Heather Winslow found herself looking at him often, wondering. He had told little, and all she could remember of him was once when he and the happy little man, Muley Dodd, had come by her cabin with the surveyor Jared Pounce. She smiled, remembering how Pounce had bragged about her corn dodgers. He'd been a great one for eating, old Pounce. And he had been fond of Buckalew, she remembered. That spoke well of him, for Pounce had been a shrewd judge of character.

Now Muley Dodd spent most of his time back with the youngsters and the stock. He came up once and took a long look at little Patrick, still asleep with his head on Heather's lap. Muley tipped his hat and smiled. "Sure do look peaceful, don't he, ma'am?"

She nodded and gave him back his smile. "He'll be with you again directly, when he gets his nap."

"Just wanted to be sure he was all right, ma'am. Didn't ever want to see him sick or nothin'."

Muley turned to ride back to the other youngsters. Heather Winslow's gaze followed him. Joshua Buckalew dropped back beside her wagon. "Muley's a good hand with kids, Mrs. Winslow. He'll take care of the boy."

"I'm glad you two came along. Little Patrick thinks the sun rises and sets with Muley."

The breeze carried the sound of Muley's tuneless whistling, as if there had never been any trouble in the world. Josh said, "Sometimes

I think maybe it does. Times, I'd swap places with him and never look back."

"You've known him a long time?"

"Since back home in Tennessee. He needed a friend. So did I."

Her gaze found Ramón Hernandez, riding alone on one flank of the wagons. "And *him*?"

"We were neighbors. And we were friends, long before the war was ever thought of. We decided to stay friends, no matter what."

"Hasn't been easy, has it?"

"Been a strain. I lost my brother Thomas at Goliad. For a while it was hard for me to look at Ramón and see anything but his brown skin. But I had to get it through my head that he wasn't noway to blame for whatever Santa Anna did. I had to get it straight that I wasn't just lookin' at a Mexican . . . I was lookin' at an old friend. It wasn't him that had changed . . . it was the times." Josh frowned. "Ramón worries you, don't he?"

Heather nodded, her lips drawn tight as she glanced down at the sleeping boy. "I know better, but I can't help it. The feeling crawls over my skin every time I look at him. I know it wasn't his fault about my Jim, but the feeling is there, just the same."

"You tried to be kind, takin' him his supper, tryin' to save him from the treatment some of them would've given him in the cabin."

"Guilty conscience, I suppose. I knew I was doing him a wrong, and something inside of me was trying to make up for it. I hope he understands. I can't help the way I feel."

"He understands, ma'am."

Joshua Buckalew pulled away and drifted out toward Ramón Hernandez. Heather Winslow watched him from under the shadow of her bonnet, wondering what kind of farmer *he* was.

OCIE QUITMAN was riding point, up ahead of the wagons. In late afternoon he turned back, looking over his shoulder, his worried manner indicating something was wrong. Josh rode forward and met him abreast of the Provost wagon. Quitman spoke to Josh and Aaron Provost together. "Men up yonder a-horseback. Five or six, at least. Maybe more."

"Indians?" Josh asked.

"Not Indian, and from the looks of them I'd say probably not Mexican either. They're movin' in our direction."

Aaron squinted. "Could be settlers like us, on their way home."

"Possible. But if they was, they'd be movin' in a different direction. Unless, of course, they seen us and decided to come down and get acquainted." Quitman's hands moved restlessly on the rifle held across his lap.

Tensing, Josh reached down and brought up his own rifle. In the backwash of every war roam the scavengers feeding on other people's misery. In this one, that breed rode along behind the fleeing settlers during the Runaway Scrape, falsely telling them the Mexicans were about to catch up, then plundering the goods the frightened people dumped in their haste.

Rebecca Provost groaned. "Aaron, look how far the young'uns have dropped back." The children had allowed the loose stock to graze, and now they were at least a quarter mile behind. But Muley had come forward hungry, wanting to know how long it would be before they stopped to camp. He was still with the wagons.

Josh said urgently, "Muley, you go fetch them kids up here and do it in a hurry. Leave the stock. We can pick them up later. Get them kids to the wagons before those riders reach here."

Alarmed, Muley held back to ask questions. Impatiently Josh shouted, "Muley, I said move!" Muley spurred away, but he kept looking back.

Sessum and McAfee had lagged with their wagon, sulking all day since they had lost the chickens. Now they caught the excitement and saw the riders. They brought their team up in a hurry. Sessum's eyes were big with alarm. "What's happenin'?"

Provost said tightly, "We got company comin'."

Rebecca had stood up in the wagonbed, looking back worriedly toward the children. Heather Winslow had stopped her wagon, and Mrs. Provost was telling her about the horsemen. Aaron Provost threw out a question which didn't seem to be pointed at anybody in particular. "What do we do?"

Josh waited to see if anybody else said anything. "First thing is to see that every gun we got is loaded and in hand. Rifles, shotguns, whatever we have."

Wiley McAfee hadn't grasped the situation. "If they ain't Mexicans, and they ain't Indians, what we need to worry about? The war's over."

Quitman clipped, "Not everywhere, it ain't. See after your guns."

Josh quickly took inventory. He and Quitman each had a rifle. Provost had a shotgun, which probably was best because Josh suspected the farmer might have a bad case of buck fever if it came to a shooting. A shotgun was good insurance against bad marksmanship. McAfee and Sessum each had rifles. An extra rifle lay in the Provost wagon. It belonged to the oldest Provost boy, Daniel, but he was back yonder with the youngsters. Josh glanced in that direction, then once more at the approaching horsemen. It was too late. The kids weren't going to reach the wagons before the visitors did.

"Mrs. Provost," Josh said, "you better take charge of your son's rifle. You may have to use it."

"Lord, not me," she protested, fright beginning to show. "I can do lots of things, but I can't shoot a man."

"Have it ready, anyway," Quitman said.

Josh glanced back at Heather Winslow, who was watching the children, her fist balled against her mouth. Josh dug a Mexican pistol out of his blanket roll and loaded it. It was his first intention to hand it to Mrs. Winslow, but on second thought he doubted she would use it. Better he keep it, for he *would* use it.

The riders were close now, and he could tell that Quitman hadn't seen them all. There were nine. Josh totted up the odds and didn't like them. One of the riders peeled away from the rest and spurred out to intercept Muley and the youngsters. Josh felt his heart go down. Muley had a rifle with him, but he wouldn't use it.

Josh found Ramón watching the youngsters. He could read the thought in the Mexican's mind: ride to them.

"Forget it, Ramón. If they got mischief on their minds—and they act like it—they'd never let you live long enough to reach them kids. Sit tight. We'll need all our guns right here in a bunch."

The riders slowed to a trot, then to a walk. They approached in a ragged line, some carrying pistols, some carrying rifles, one toting a Mexican *escopeta*. The man who appeared to be the leader pulled a length ahead and raised his hand to signal a halt. He moved a little closer, but not close enough to reach.

"Howdy." A thin smile flitted briefly across his bearded face. His eyes hungrily surveyed the wagons. "Nice outfit you folks got here. Headin' west, I take it?"

Aaron Provost waited until he saw that neither Josh nor Quitman seemed inclined to answer. "We're goin' back to our homes. We understand the Mexican soldiers have all gone. It's safe now."

The bearded man slouched lazily in his saddle. "Not altogether, it ain't. There's still a chance some stragglin' Mexicans are left. And then there's always the Indians. You-all think about the Indians? Man thinks he's got everything goin' on a nice downhill grade and then some sneakin' Comanche goes and takes his hair. It ain't right, good folks havin' to fret over things like that. So us boys here, we have done gone and formed us a kind of a frontier rifle company. We're here to kill any stray Mexicans and Indians we come across and make this country safe for the good folks." His gaze fell on Ramón. "This one here a prisoner of yours? We'd be right tickled to take care of him."

They were a dirty, unkempt, hungry-looking bunch, all of them. Josh had seen their kind, and he thought he had them pegged already: renegades operating out of the no-man's territory known as the Redlands, that wild and lawless region that lay between the Texas colonies and the settled regions of Louisiana. These people turned their hands to all sorts of mischief: smuggling, counterfeiting, making bad whisky, stealing horses, and waging a bloody brand of banditry, preying on travelers who tried to use the dim traces across western Louisiana and eastern Texas. Stephen F. Austin had organized militia bands against them and had driven them out of the colonies. But now, in the turmoil of Santa Anna's invasion and defeat, they were back again, straggling across Texas like roving, hungry wolves dogging the buffalo herds to pick up the weak and the unwary. They were as bad as the Comanches. Worse even than the Mexicans, for at least the Mexicans had considered that they had a cause.

Provost looked over his shoulder. "One of your men has stopped our children. I'd like to know what he done that for."

"That's Beau," came the smiling reply. "He's partial to young'uns." The smile faded. "Them is good-lookin' wagons. They're loaded too. Looks like you-all have come out of the war pretty good."

"Everything that's in these wagons is rightfully ours."

"I didn't go to make it look like we doubt you none. Anybody can tell, you're quality folks. What I'm gettin' to is, we're poor men, all of us. You can see that for yourselves. They ain't nobody payin' us nothin' or feedin' us nothin' for the protection we're givin' folks and their property. We got to live off of the land or starve. And starvin' ain't much to our likin', I'll guarantee."

Quitman asked, "Anybody authorize you to give all this . . . protection?"

"We're doin' it on our own. Not everybody can fight with old General Sam and git the glory of it. Some has got to do the dirty little jobs that don't rate even a thank-you or a howdy-do. We ain't complainin' none, but we figure you owe us, friends."

"Owe you what?" demanded Aaron Provost.

"Depends. Depends on what-all you got in them wagons."

He made a move toward the wagon which carried the widow Winslow. Ocie Quitman blocked him. "That's as far as you go, *friend*."

The black-bearded one darkened. "I don't believe you-all have quite understood the situation yet."

Josh said, "We understand it. You come to rob us."

"Not rob. *Rob* ain't a good word. *Commandeer* is better. Got a military ring to it, *commandeer* has. Sounds nice and legal too."

"There ain't nothin' legal about you," Josh declared. "You ain't militia. You probably never fired a shot at a Mexican, unless he was some helpless settler or stragglin' soldier you caught out by himself. You got nothin' comin' to you from us. If you're hungry, there's game enough around here. You got no call to starve."

The leader shrugged broad shoulders that stretched a ragged old black coat almost to the ripping point. Evidently the coat hadn't been made for him. Josh guessed he stole it from somebody. Somebody dead, more than likely. The man said, "We'd intended to handle this nice, but looks like you-all are bound and determined not to have it that way. So, we'll have it your way instead. You'll notice there's more of *us* than there is of you. And you'll remember we got one man down yonder close-herdin' that bunch of young'uns. Now, I sent old Beau on purpose, because he don't shrink from nothin',

Beau don't. If I was to tell him to put his pistol up to some young'un's head and blow his brains out, he'd do it and not wink an eye. He's mean, Beau is."

Rebecca Provost cried out, and Heather Winslow's face went white.

The man nodded with satisfaction. "I do believe you-all are gettin' to see things the way I do. Women always seem to understand quicker'n men."

Shaken, Aaron Provost rubbed his whiskered chin. "What do you want from us?"

The dark-clad man slouched a little more, exuding an air of victory. "Well now, we ain't sure till we see what you got. We find we're needin' a little bit of everything."

Josh knew that was what they would take. *Everything.*

Provost looked at Josh and Quitman, his eyes begging for help. He said to the renegade, "You let our young'uns come on up and join us. Then we'll talk to you."

"You'll talk a right smart better the way things is. Beau'll take good care of them."

Provost said, "We got to have a few minutes to talk this over."

"We'll give you a few minutes, then. Here's our proposition: you turn them wagons over to us and walk away from here. You get yourselves good and clear of the wagons and we'll let the kids come on up. Afoot, of course. We find we sure do need us some horses."

"You'll want our guns too," Josh said dryly.

"Naturally. We need more guns. How else we goin' to fight Mexicans and Comanches?" He started to rein the horse around. "We'll give you three minutes to talk it over. If you ain't made up your mind by then, I'll have to send a little message down to Beau. I'd sure hate to do that. Like I told you, Beau is mean."

He rode off a short distance, he and his men. Then they turned to watch. But at least it was too far for them to hear.

Quitman's face had darkened. "You thinkin' the same as me, Buckalew?"

Aaron Provost broke in gravely, "There ain't no thinkin' to be done. They outnumber us, and they got the kids. We can't take no risks with them young'uns."

Quitman's gaze went back to Josh. Josh said, "Years ago, when me and Muley and my brother Thomas were comin' to Texas from Tennessee, we ran into this kind of trouble over in the Redlands."

"What did you do?"

"We killed them before they could kill us. They was sure goin' to. And if we walk away from these wagons, we're all dead. Us *and* the kids. Don't you see, Aaron, they can't steal a bunch of slow wagons and leave us to tell about it. Too much risk of people findin' us before they've had time to get in the clear. Soon's they get us afoot and helpless, they'll kill us all and make out like it was Indians or Mexicans. It's the only thing they *could* do."

Provost repeated, "They got us outnumbered."

"Only by three, and they've sent one man down to the kids. That leaves two more men here than we got. Bad luck that your oldest boy and Muley both got cut off, but we got to make do without them."

Quitman glanced doubtfully at Ramón. "What about him? Can he shoot?"

"He can pick your teeth at fifty yards."

Quitman counted on his fingers. "If every one of us hits a man, that leaves two of them alive here and us with empty rifles. Chances are one or maybe both of them will turn tail and run."

Incredulous, Aaron demanded, "You mean we're just goin' to shoot them down? That don't hardly seem Christian."

"What they're figurin' on doin' to us ain't Christian, either," Josh pointed out. "And remember, they'll do it to the women and the children same as us. You're damned right we'll shoot them down." He remembered that other time, in the Redlands. He'd had the same feeling as Provost then, but Thomas had been older and tougher. Thomas had made him see it through. Looking back afterwards Josh had realized it was the only way. Hard, even brutal. But you don't make deals with a hungry wolf. You may bribe him off so long as you keep feeding him, but when you've nothing else to give him, he'll take you.

Dent Sessum and Wiley McAfee had pulled their wagon in close so they could listen. Cold sweat broke out on their faces. Any enmity between them and Josh was momentarily shoved away in the face of this outside threat. Sessum asked, "What if two or three of us shoot at the same man?"

Quitman replied, "We got to parcel them out. McAfee, you get the one with that Mexican-lookin' sombrero. Aaron can shoot the one with the beaver hat. Hernandez'll take the one sittin' next to him, the one with the crooked neck that looks like he'd been hung and cut down early. Buckalew can take the one on the end, and I'll get the man that done all the talkin'."

RAMÓN HAD kept quiet. Now he motioned back down the trail toward the youngsters. Normally he spoke in Spanish, but now he had to force himself into broken English that came hard for him. "The children. That *hombre* Beau. Somebody got to shoot Beau."

Quitman frowned. "I was figurin' him for Sessum. From where you're at, Sessum, you got the best chance to shoot Beau. You can rest your rifle barrel across that stack of goods and draw a fine bead."

That would leave three men here alive, even if everybody hit his target.

Provost was murmuring, "I sure as sin don't like it."

Josh said, "What they got in mind, you'd like a lot less. Everybody better shoot straight. Kill them the first shot and you won't have anything to do over."

The three minutes passed, and the scavengers closed in, fanning out to form a semi-circle. Every one of them carried a gun of some kind, and every gun was ready. The only thing Josh figured his group could count on was the renegades' conviction that this was to be easy pickings, that the settlers would give up.

That, he thought, *gives us a couple seconds jump on them, because at least we know what we're going to do.*

The leader was coming close to the wagons, so sure was he of surrender. That would make an easy shot for Quitman, anyway. Josh let his attention settle then on the man at the end who was to be his target. He hoped the man wouldn't see it in his eyes.

Josh had shot a few men in the war, and he'd always wondered about it afterwards . . . who they were, where they had come from, how it came that they were destined to be at that particular place at that particular moment and to die by his hand rather than someone else's. It wasn't a pleasant thing to dwell on, after the bloody task was done. It was even less pleasant to dwell on *before* the deed. All he could see in the flesh was a wind-reddened face, a heavy cover of dirty whiskers streaked by tobacco, a set of pale eyes that found Josh's and stayed there. That and a pair of rough hands gripping a rifle that he intended to use for killing. Josh wondered if he had a family back home . . . a wife, maybe, and even some kids who would always wonder what had become of him, kids who would grow up wild and unrestrained and perhaps turn out in his own cruel image, not wholly at fault because they had known no other way. And was it really even *this* man's fault that he was here now, about to die but not knowing it? Had a careless fate pointed him in this direction when he was too young to understand? Josh would always wonder, but there would never be any way for him to know.

The men were so close now that he knew he could not miss. Cold sweat made the rifle slick in his hands. He felt the man must see the tension drawing his face tight, and he hoped it would be taken for fear.

"You made up your minds yet?" the leader asked casually.

"We have," Quitman replied. He waited a moment, then shouted, "NOW!"

Six weapons roared. Horses plunged and squealed. Men shrieked and cursed and fell. Through a cloud of black powdersmoke drifting out from the wagons, Josh watched his man jerk backward, clutching his stomach, then slide off and crumple in an awkward heap. Another man crawled on the ground, screeching, going limp as a terrified horse trampled him. The smoke was heavy, but Josh could see that at least four men had been left untouched. Someone had completely missed his target.

The fusillade had caught the renegades by surprise. Two of the ones not hit wheeled their horses and ran, coattails flapping as they spurred in panic. Josh saw a rifle flash from one of the two men who were left, but he didn't turn to see if one of his party was hit. He kicked his horse and moved quickly through the smoke, drawing the pistol out of his waistband. Ocie Quitman swung his riflebarrel, clubbing one rider out of the saddle. Josh saw the other one holding the *escopeta*, trying to find a target in the gray smoke. Josh brought up the pistol and squeezed the trigger. The man went down.

He heard Wiley McAfee scream, "Help me, somebody. He's got me!"

Josh wheeled. On the wagonseat, Aaron Provost sat frozen, the smoking shotgun in his hands, as he stared in hypnotic dismay at the renegade in the beaver hat, writhing on the ground. This was probably the first man Provost had ever shot.

On the far side of the wagon, Wiley McAfee and one of the Redlanders rolled in the grass. A knifeblade caught the sunshine for an instant. McAfee had failed to kill his man, and now he was fighting for his life.

Josh remembered the extra rifle in the Provost wagon, the one that belonged to the oldest boy. He made a move, but Ramón had thought of it before him. Ramón was closer, and he got to it first.

McAfee saw him, for he was shrieking, "Help me, Mexican! Help before he kills me!" He had never even bothered to learn Ramón's name.

Ramón climbed out of his saddle and onto the Provost wagon, moving awkwardly because of his bad leg. He grabbed the rifle, and for a moment Josh thought he was going to shoot the renegade who had McAfee down. But Ramón brought the rifle to a level and propped it across a box to fire it. Josh saw then what he was aiming at.

Sessum had missed his shot at the man called Beau. Now Beau pursued the little Provost girl, evidently trying to gain a hostage.

McAfee screamed again, "For God's sake, help before he kills me!"

But Ramón ignored him. Beads of sweat broke on the dark forehead as the barrel followed the moving Beau. The rifle roared. Beau slumped, grabbing at his horse's mane. In an instant Provost's oldest boy and Muley together had pounced on him and dragged him to the ground.

Josh ran to help McAfee. He was too late. The renegade plunged the knife into McAfee's throat. Quitman got there first. He leaned down from his saddle and jabbed the butt of his empty rifle savagely against the renegade's head. The man went slack, and Quitman clubbed him again. The skull broke like a melon.

Josh hadn't seen Sessum all this time, but now the man came running, eyes big as a washtub. "Wiley! What's happened, Wiley? Wiley!"

Wiley McAfee lay gasping, struggling as his lifeblood spread a stain in the grass. His hands reached up in fearful supplication, but no one could help him.

Sessum crouched over him a moment in shock, then grabbed up McAfee's fallen rifle and frenziedly began to club the fallen renegade.

Quitman said, "Sessum, that won't help none. He's already dead."

Sessum shouted, "I heard Wiley holler to the Mexican for help. Why didn't he help him?" His gaze fastened on Ramón, and he gripped the rifle barrel as if to use the weapon for a club. "Answer me, Mexican! How come you didn't help him? You wanted him dead!"

"The children," Ramón gritted. "McAfee was a man. First came the children."

Sessum seemed not to hear him. "You had a rifle in your hands, and you stood there and let him die."

Ramón shrugged. He'd made his explanation. Sessum could accept it, or he could go to hell.

Josh put in, "Sessum, it was your job to shoot Beau. You missed him and left them young'uns in his hands. Ramón had to finish your job." Pausing, he saw no sign that his words were taking any effect. "If you'd done what you was supposed to, McAfee would not have had to die."

Sessum gave no indication he had even heard. "That Mexican could've saved him. He let him be killed." Sessum made a move forward with the rifle barrel gripped in his hands. Josh caught him by the shoulder, spun him around, and struck him on the chin. Sessum sprawled. Josh picked up the fallen rifle to keep it out of Sessum's hands.

Over the hill he could see two men riding away, still spurring. The wise thing would be to go after them, to make sure the whole den was killed out. But here with the smoke still thick enough to choke a man, and with the dying men groaning on the ground and women sobbing softly in the wagons, he was glad to let them go.

Muley and the oldest Provost boy rode up with the children, and with the wounded Beau staggering at the end of a rope.

Muley said quickly in self-defense, "There wasn't nothin' I could do, Josh. He taken my rifle before I even knowed what was goin' on."

Josh looked at the captured man. "You did fine, Muley. So did you, Daniel."

The Provost boy sat straight and proud, though he trembled from the excitement. "We wasn't afraid of him, Mister Buckalew. Quick as we got the chance, we grabbed onto him."

Muley shouted, "He was fixin' to kill the children. That's what he told us. Said if anything went wrong he was goin' to kill them off one by one, like he'd wring chicken necks. He was tryin' to catch the girl when somebody shot him."

Quitman's eyes were sharp. He told Beau: "Your friends are dead, most of them. You know any reason we ought to have mercy on you?"

"I'm bleedin' to death," Beau whined. "You can't let a man stand here and bleed to death."

"No," said Quitman, "we can't." He squeezed the trigger. Beau jerked, stared in horror till his eyes went blank, then he pitched forward in a heap.

Quitman said to no one in particular, "That's what he was fixin' to do to the young'uns." He switched his gaze to Josh. "What you waitin' for? Any others still alive, we better do the same to them. No use them healin' up and pullin' this on somebody else."

Josh said, "We're not the law."

"Aren't we? There ain't no law right now except the law we make. Mexican government is gone. We got no Texas government except on paper."

"There's still God's law."

"God ain't come west of the Sabine River."

"You're not goin' to kill anybody else, Quitman."

"You figure on stoppin' me?"

"If I have to."

Quitman's gaze could cut steel. All Josh knew was to stare back. They watched each other like buck deer trying to decide whether to lower their horns and fight. Finally Quitman shrugged. "You could take lessons from that Mexican of yours. He knows when to let his blood run cold."

Provost came out of his daze and climbed shakily down from his wagon. They all scouted around, picking up the guns and looking over the blood-soaked renegades, scattered in a grisly semi-circle where they had fallen. It would have been a sickening sight, had Josh not already seen so many others, most of them worse. The man Josh had shot with the pistol lay breathing raggedly, already unconscious. He would never open his eyes. The rest appeared dead except the one who had worn the beaver hat. The hat lay crushed beneath him. Provost had shot him, but nervousness had spoiled his aim. The blue whistlers had shattered the leg.

Quitman said, "Leave him be and he'll bleed to death."

This one, of all the renegades, showed no whiskers. Bending over for a close look, Josh exclaimed: "He's a young'un, is all. Not much older than Daniel Provost. Seventeen . . . maybe eighteen."

Quitman frowned. "A young'un can kill you as dead as an old one. He's part of that trash."

"He's not old enough to know what he's doin'."

"The hell he ain't. He's old enough to kill a man. That means he's old enough for somebody to kill *him* and not worry over it none."

Searching the lad, Josh found a knife but no other weapon. He slit the shot-torn trouser leg. The youngster choked off a cry. Josh grimaced. "Busted into little bitty pieces. We got to do somethin'."

Quitman growled, "Leave him."

"He's just a kid."

"We was all kids, one time or another. I knew right from wrong by the time I was six. He's growed up with a wolfpack, Buckalew. You can't change a wolf's habits. Save him now and he'll kill again. Leave him die. It's best for everybody."

"We can't."

"While ago you helped me plan how we'd kill them all. It didn't bother you then."

"He had a gun in his hands. Now it's different. He's helpless."

"You think he'd of fixed *you* up? He'd of cut your throat."

Aaron Provost said, "Ocie, it was me that shot him. We got to give him a chance."

Quitman shrugged. "Do it then. But remember, if you save him he'll like as not be at your throat first chance he gets."

Josh looked to Muley for help, but Muley's face was clabber-white at the sight of so much blood. "Muley, you gather the young'uns and take them to the shade of that tree yonder to wait and rest. No use them bein' here at this slaughterhouse."

Still shaken, Aaron Provost said, "I'll help you with the boy, Josh. I feel like it's my responsibility. What you want me to do?"

"Let's take a better look at this wound." Josh ripped away the trouser leg, his brow furrowing. It was even worse than he thought.

A chill crawled up his back. Looking away, he saw that Aaron's boy Daniel had taken it upon himself to round up the renegades' horses. Nobody had had to tell him. And Josh remembered how Daniel had pounced on Beau the moment Ramón's rifleball struck. Good boy, that Daniel. Aaron and Rebecca had pointed him right. Pity there hadn't been somebody to point *this* boy right. "Aaron, why don't you look through them saddlebags and find out if any of them had a bottle of whisky or somethin'? This boy is goin' to need it. He's goin' to need a-plenty of it."

Josh made a tourniquet of the trouserleg, then walked to the widow Winslow's wagon where Ocie Quitman had his arms around his little son Patrick. "Mrs. Winslow, could you get a fire goin' and heat some water, please? We're goin' to need it directly."

Aaron found a couple of bottles. Josh removed the stopper from one and tilted it up to drink. He gasped and wiped his sleeve across his mouth. "Man who'd sell that stuff would club his grandmother. But it'll do the job. Here, boy, drink. Drink it all."

By the time the water was boiling, the boy was floating away in a drunken stupor. Josh had whetted his knife until the blade was keen. He held it in the boiling water, glanced at Aaron, and said, "You hold him."

The boy surged against Aaron, screaming, then fell back in a faint. Cold sweat broke out on Josh's forehead. Once he turned away to be sick. But he came back, and presently the job was done. Heather Winslow fled while Josh and Aaron cauterized the stump. Then she forced herself forward with some homespun cotton cloth. "You'll need bandages."

Quitman and Dent Sessum had placed Wiley McAfee's body in the Sessum wagon. Josh walked up to Quitman. "We got to put that boy in a wagon too. We want to use yours."

Quitman frowned. "What if I said no?"

"You and me would have to fight. And when it was over, we'd put the boy in your wagon anyhow."

Quitman shook his head in resignation. "You got a soft heart,

Buckalew, and a soft head to match. Like as not, it'll get you killed someday. But go ahead. If it's all right with Mrs. Winslow, you can use the wagon."

They put a couple of miles behind them, leaving the battlefield with the bodies lying where they had fallen. They camped on a little creek beneath a canopy of freshly-leafed pecan trees. Josh and Muley and Aaron gathered old leaves into a soft mat, spread blankets, and placed the wounded boy on them. The lad was groaning.

Dent Sessum and Ocie Quitman carried shovels up to a high point and dug a grave for Wiley McAfee. After supper, Aaron read from the Bible, they all bowed their heads, and each man took a turn with the shovel.

Josh watched Sessum carve McAfee's name onto a cross Muley had fashioned. He suspected Sessum had misspelled the name, but he saw no need in making an issue of it. He asked, "Did McAfee have any relatives you know of? Is there somebody we ought to send a letter to?"

Sessum shook his head. "We was partners, him and me. There wasn't nobody else."

"Bound to be somebody . . . a mother, maybe, or a sister or brother . . . somebody who ought to get the stuff that belonged to him."

Sessum put aside the cross and clenched his fists, his face darkening. "We was partners. Whatever belonged to him belongs to me now. Everything in that wagon, it belongs to me. Just me! You ain't goin' to take away or give away what's mine!"

"I had no intention . . ."

"I'm warnin' you, Buckalew. Touch one thing on that wagon and there'll be big trouble. It's all mine now, do you hear?"

Josh turned away, disgust welling in him. He picked up a shovel and started toward the wagon. Aaron Provost trudged out to meet him, his shoulders slumped, his face grim. "Don't put the shovel away, Josh."

"The boy?"

The farmer's voice broke. "He died fightin'."

Somberly Josh pondered the waste and the futility of it all. At length he made a Mexican shrug of resignation. "At least we tried."

Anguished, Aaron cried, "It was me that shot him, Josh. How am I goin' to carry that burden? He was a boy like my Daniel."

"No, Aaron, not like your boy. This one was suckled on wolf's milk, taught to kill like an animal. It wasn't your fault. The blame goes on the people who raised him that way."

THE DAYS were long and the miles passed slowly under the wheels, but gradually the Spanish moss country of the coastal lands fell behind them and the gently rising prairies marked the way into the higher, dryer inland regions of Texas . . . across the Brazos, past the charred ruins of Stephen F. Austin's San Felipe, across the San Bernard, and finally west to the Colorado.

Ocie Quitman had never talked much, and as the wagons rolled farther west he said even less than before. He rode ahead, alone, a morose silence gathered about him like some dark cloud. Now and again Josh spoke to him and received no answer, for Quitman's mind was somewhere far away.

Aaron Provost said, "We're gettin' close to home country now, to the place we all called Hopeful Valley. I'm right uneasy, Josh, how he's goin' to take it when he first sets eyes on his farm. You can tell, lately he's done a lot of thinkin' about *her*."

The farther they moved across the prairies, the more uneasy Josh became about Comanches. The only horse tracks they had encountered crossing their trail had proved to be bands of wild mustangs, grazing free. While Quitman rode his solitary point, Josh and Ramón would each move far out on the flank, watching. They stirred up deer, which would bound away in long, fleet leaps. Sometimes antelope raced across the prairie ahead of them, their white-puff tails bobbing. The riders found wild cattle, a few of which they promptly brought in for beef. But they saw no Indians, and no sign of any.

A day came when Quitman rode forward to the top of a hill and sat his horse there unmoving. After a long time Josh became uneasy and loped up from his flank position. From on the other side, he could see Ramón follow his lead. At the hilltop, Josh stopped and looked down upon a small field, evidently plowed last winter but now growing up in weeds. His searching gaze picked up a small, crooked stream, its green banks lined with massive pecan trees. Finally, just above the stream, he saw the black skeleton of a cabin, the charred logs of its tumbled walls spread out like burned ribs.

He knew with a cold certainty. "Your place?"

Quitman made no answer. Josh thought he had never seen a face so sad. He held his silence, studying the place. He could tell it had been a good farm. It would be again, with some work. "Cabin's easy to build," he offered finally. "Soon's we all get our field work caught up with, we'll help you put it back up."

Quitman shook his head. "Cabin don't mean nothin' to me. Mary is what mattered, and there ain't no way to bring her back."

Josh thought, *A man has to put his dead behind him and go on living.* But he figured it would sound cruel, no matter how he said it.

Quitman pointed at the remains of the cabin. "It wasn't much, but she loved it there. Had her some flowers in front of it, and her garden out back, where you see that square plot with the log fence. I remember how aggravated she'd get when the coons would come slippin' in at night and tear the garden up. She'd take a broom and chase them out—she wouldn't hurt one for the world. Then she'd go out next mornin' and try to fix the damage. She could make anything grow, Mary could. She had the touch of life about her. She could take a sick plant or a sick animal or a sick bird—didn't matter which—and she could make it live." His eyes pinched. "But when her own time come, she couldn't help herself. Whatever touch she had, it wouldn't work for *her*."

"It was a hard go of luck, but I reckon there wasn't anything anybody could do."

Quitman gave a quick, hard glance at Ramón. "There *was* somebody could've done somethin', but they wouldn't." His head turned slowly, and Josh followed his gaze southward. He thought he saw a wisp of light-colored smoke beyond the trees. He glanced at Quitman, but he didn't ask the question.

Quitman's voice was barbed. "Faustino Marquez." His hands balled into fists. He stared toward the thin column of smoke, his face darkening. Finally he said, "Buckalew, you want to do me a favor?"

Josh frowned, dubious. "If I can."

"Come along with me, then. I want you to stand back and keep quiet. I don't want you to interfere or get in the way of whatever I do except for one thing. The last second before I kill him, I want you to stop me. Let me burn him out. Let me beat him to within an inch of his life. But don't let me kill him."

"I don't know . . ." Josh rubbed his jaw. "Before I'm a party to this, I better know how come you hate him so bad."

Quitman turned to Ramón. "I'd rather *you* didn't go with us."

Ramón glanced at Josh, his eyes asking. Josh said, "It's all right, Ramón. I'll go with him. Maybe you better go help watch out for the wagons anyway."

Quitman touched heels to his horse's ribs and started down the hill toward the smoke. Josh hurried to follow.

"Quitman, you didn't answer me."

Without slowing his horse, Quitman painfully spilled out his story. "Time I'm finished, you'll know why I can't stand the sight of a Mexican. Not even that pet of yours. Faustino Marquez as good as killed my wife. He could've saved her, but he wouldn't lift a hand." Quitman spat. "Two years, we was neighbors. Faustino was the hungry kind, never satisfied with what he had, takin' everything else he could get. A grasper. Whatever he needed, he come borrowin' from us, and I'd have hell gettin' it back. But the times him or his wife got sick, Mary would go over and take care of them. The big fever come last year. Mary stayed there most of a week, nursin' Alicia Marquez, pullin' her back after the fever all but took her away. Faustino swore if there was ever anything Mary needed, he'd give up his life to help her.

"Well, the time come. We had another baby on the way when the war commenced. I went off to help fight. After the Alamo and Goliad, when the Scrape started, I got leave to go home and see after Mary. All our *Americano* friends had packed up and left. They'd tried to get Mary to go with them, but she'd waited for me. I got home and found her so close to her time that it was dangerous for her to travel. Santa Anna's Mexicans was almost on top of us by then. I was afraid ridin' in a wagon would kill her.

"Bein' Mexicans themselves, Faustino and his wife didn't see no need in them runnin' from Santa Anna. I decided that if Mary stayed with the Marquez family, the soldiers wouldn't bother her none, so I put her and Patrick in the wagon and took them over there. Faustino met me at the door with a gun in his hand. Said for us damned *Americanos* to get off of his land. I told him he owed Mary protection, but he said if we didn't get away, he'd shoot us all and maybe Santa Anna would give him a medal. Said this land was for the Mexicans anyway, and the only reason they'd ever let any *Americanos* in here in the first place was to help them fight off the Comanches. Said our place was *his* place from now on.

"We rode all that day and through the night and hid in a thicket at daylight. It kept rainin' and washin' our tracks out behind us. While we was in the thicket, a bunch of Mexican soldiers come ridin' by, tryin' to find us. And up front, helpin' them, was Faustino Marquez." Ocie Quitman's eyes closed. "We traveled by night and hid by day. But it turned out like I was afraid it would. Mary's time came, and the trip had been too much for her. She died hard. The baby never drew a breath. I reckon you know the rest of it."

Josh said, "Heather Winslow told me."

"Mrs. Winslow was in a lot the same shape as I was. She'd lost her husband, and I'd lost my wife. I gave her Patrick and the wagon and went on to find Sam Houston. I'd made up my mind to kill as many Mexicans as I could. And I did, Buckalew. I made them pay."

"But it wasn't enough, was it?"

Quitman shook his head. "No, it wasn't enough. All the time I knew Faustino was still here. I laid awake nights, thinkin' about all the slow, hard ways I could use to kill him. None of them was good enough. Once he was dead, he wouldn't feel anything, and I wanted him to feel. Then I got to thinkin' about how greedy he was. I decided the way to punish him most was to run him off of his place with nothin' but the shirt on his back and let him spend the rest of his miserable life rememberin' what he had thrown away. That's a way you can kill a man and still leave him alive."

"That's what you want me to help you do?"

"Not help me. I'll do it all myself. You just be there to make sure I don't forget myself and kill him. Agreed?"

Josh hesitated. "I reckon you got cause enough to hate him. But I'll stop you whenever I think it's time."

The Marquez house lay beyond a recently-tilled field. It was of stone, Mexican style, rather than the log type the *Americano* settlers favored. Smoke curled from the chimney, and Josh thought he saw movement inside. No one came out. Quitman's eyes narrowed.

"Faustino!"

No answer.

"Faustino! You drag yourself out here, and be damned quick!"

A broad-hipped Mexican man showed himself uncertainly in the open doorway. He stared at Quitman with the horrified eyes of a man who has seen the dead spring to life. "Quitman!"

Ocie Quitman carried his rifle across the pommel of his saddle. His voice was quieter now but keen-edged. "Thought they'd got me, didn't you? Thought I'd never come back." Quitman's gaze swept over the yard. It fastened on a plow, and his eyes crackled. "That's *my* plow you got. And that chair under the arbor . . . it's one I made for Mary."

Marquez stammered. "All this I save for you, Quitman. I say to myself, that Santa Anna, he burn everything. I bring it over here, and I save it for my good friend Quitman and his wife." He trembled. "I save it for you, Quitman."

"You stole it. You didn't think I'd be back."

"No, Quitman, I no steal from you. You and me, we friends."

"So friendly you led the Mexican troops to try and find us? You wanted us dead, Faustino. You wanted to steal everything for yourself."

"Long time we are friends," Marquez quailed. "You and me, your wife, my Alicia. Do you forget that?"

"*You're* the one that forgot it." Quitman swung down slowly, the rifle's muzzle pointing in Marquez's general direction. Marquez began shrinking back inside the door.

"Faustino! You stay out here or I'll put a bullet in you!"

The Mexican slumped, stricken with fear. "Please, you don't kill me, Quitman. Please."

"You killed my Mary. Why shouldn't I kill you?"

"I did nothing."

"You did nothin', and that is why she's dead. You owed her a debt, but you let her die. Now I owe *you*, Faustino, and I'm goin' to pay."

The butt of his rifle caught Marquez in the stomach. The man bent forward, arms coming around instinctively for protection. Quitman jabbed the butt straight forward, hitting him again. Marquez stumbled backward into the house. A woman screamed. Josh dismounted, looped the reins through the brush fence and moved quickly through the open door. He saw a plump Mexican woman cowering in a corner, face covered with her hands, but her fingers spread enough that she could see. Each time Quitman hit her husband, she screamed. An old rifle stood in another corner, but neither she nor Marquez made any move toward it. Josh picked it up and took it out of contention.

What Quitman did to Marquez was slow, methodical and brutal. He drove him back against a stone wall and there proceeded to beat him with his fists. Each time Marquez slipped to the packed-earth floor, Quitman hauled him up again. Marquez made only a small attempt to defend himself. He whimpered and pleaded that he did not want to die.

About the time Josh was preparing to step in and stop it, Quitman flung Marquez halfway across the room. "Get up, Faustino. Get up and get out!"

Marquez pushed himself up onto hands and knees, staring without comprehension. *"No entiendo." I do not understand.*

"I said get out. You and your wife, get your oxen and hook up your *carreta* and go. Don't you ever come back."

The woman spoke for the first time. Up to now, all she had done was scream. "This is our home."

"It *was* your home. You're leavin'."

"Where?" she pleaded in Spanish. "We have nowhere to go."

Quitman strode across the room and hauled Marquez to his feet. "You hear me, Faustino?" The man nodded in terror. Quitman said, "If I was you I wouldn't stop till I got plumb the other side of the Rio Grande. Don't stop in Bexar, because I might go there sometime. Don't stop at the Neuces, because I might be *there* sometime too. I promise you this, Faustino: if I ever see you again . . . any time, any place . . . I'll kill you on sight!" He turned loose. The Mexican fell to his hands and knees, scrambling for the door, not pushing to his feet until he was outside. The woman began gathering up clothes and cooking utensils. Quitman raised his hand. "Leave them."

She stared in disbelief.

He repeated, "Leave them. I'm givin' you Faustino. That's all you're leavin' here with."

Josh said: "You're makin' it awful tough. How're they goin' to live?"

"That's their problem. They didn't give a damn what happened to Mary."

Josh watched somberly as the Mexican yoked his oxen to a high-wheeled wooden cart. The couple left without so much as the old rifle.

Josh said, "They might run into Comanches."

"They might."

"They'd have no chance at all."

"They'd have all the chance they gave Mary." Quitman turned back inside the little rock house. The anger still rode high in his face. "Damn near everything in here—the chairs, the table, all of it—came from our house. Faustino cleaned it out. Then he burned it."

"So now you've cleaned him out."

"Clean as a hound's tooth."

Quitman walked toward the homemade wooden bed. Josh guessed by the way he looked at it that it had been his—his and Mary's. Quitman picked up a pillow and let his fingers run over the fine embroidery work, and he turned away, his head down. Josh decided to leave the cabin and give the man his moments of peace . . . if ever he had any.

They rode in silence across the field and over the hill to Quitman's own place. Quitman moved his horse in a slow walk around the rock pens, the burned cabin, the weed-grown garden. He kept his eyes away from Josh's, and Josh tried not to intrude. He held back, willing to listen if it would help but not wanting to put himself in where he wasn't needed.

At length Quitman reined up, shoulders slumped. "I don't think I can do it, Buckalew."

"Do what?"

"Live here again. I could come here and work the land, maybe, but I couldn't live here anymore. There's too much that'd try to take me back, and there's no goin' back. Like as not, I'd go out of my mind."

"What do you think you'll do?"

"Texas owes me free land for my soldierin'. Didn't you say there's good land up your way?"

Josh nodded. "There's a lot that ain't been claimed."

"Then I'll pick me a piece of it by and by and put in my claim. This place I'll keep for my boy Patrick."

"You'll be welcome." Josh frowned. "There's just one thing . . ."

"What's that?"

"You'll have Mexican neighbors again. You'll have Ramón Hernandez. It won't be like it was with Faustino. Push Ramón and he'll fight. What's more, I'll help him."

Quitman stared at him unflinchingly. "I got a notion I'll have to fight you sooner or later anyhow."

CHAPTER

7

HEATHER WINSLOW had thought she would be prepared to face the sight of her burned-out home, for she had seen enough others along the way to know she could expect nothing else. But the tears came anyway as she stared at the cold, blackened chimney which towered as a silent sentinel over a pile of charred logs.

Gaunt Rebecca Provost stood behind her, strong hands gripping Heather's shoulders. "Go ahead, child, cry if it'll help you any. But there's plenty more logs where them come from. The men'll put you up another one. All it takes is time and labor and some good timber. You'll have you a home again."

It will take more to make this a home, Heather thought. *Without Jim, there will be no man in the house. And without a man in the house, it won't be a home.*

She heard a quiet voice which she knew belonged to Joshua Buckalew. "Mrs. Provost is right. First thing we got to do is see after the crops, includin' yours. Then we'll get to work buildin' the cabins back the way they was, or better, even. We'll put a good roof over your head, you don't need to be worryin' about that."

Aaron Provost declared confidently, "Bound to be one of us has a cabin that didn't get burned. We'll all stay together till we know it's safe for us to break off on our own. If Rebecca and me has been lucky, you'll share our house, Heather. You'll share it as long as you need it."

But the Provosts hadn't been lucky either. Their big double cabin lay in black ruins, even one of its two tall chimneys broken off and lying in a heap of rubble.

Heather was not much surprised to see a lone tear roll down Rebecca Provost's tight-stretched cheek, nor was she surprised to see the tall woman square her shoulders and jut her chin forward, shutting off the tears like she would shutter and bar a window.

Aaron Provost's eyes were grim. "Where to from here? Think your cabin might still be standin', Josh?"

Josh shook his head. "It was already burned the last time I came this way. Indians, I figured. No use us goin' by there."

Sitting on his horse, Ocie Quitman shook his head in resignation. "Then there's noplace else. We'd just as well set up camp here."

Josh said, "Wrong. There's still Ramón's. It's a good ways from Hopeful Valley, but I know the place will still be there. His family stayed. Be all right with you, Ramón, if we set up camp there till we get everybody's fields plowed out and the cabins rebuilt?"

Ramón nodded. "We would be happy."

Ocie Quitman's gaze fixed itself on the Mexican. "You don't need to be doin' us no favors."

Ramón shrugged. "Would you not do the same for me?"

Quitman looked away, not answering. Heather thought she knew the answer, and she suspected Ramón knew it too. She wondered if Hernandez might purposely be twisting the knife a little.

Josh said, "They got a good rock house that the Indians have never tried to hit. It'd be a safe place for the women and children till we find out about the Comanches. We can't afford to go scatterin' right now anyway before we know how much of a hazard the Indians will be."

Quitman glared at Ramón. "I've always been careful who I let myself owe favors to."

Heather looked for resentment in Ramón's eyes, but if it was there he kept it well concealed. He said, "You owe me nothing. It is protection for my family if all of you go there. Everything is even."

Ocie did not yield. "I won't be beholden. I'll pay you out of my crops this fall. There ain't goin' to be no debt."

Ramón shrugged. *"No le hace."*

Josh looked at Dent Sessum. "How do you feel about it?"

Sessum glowered, not liking the situation but accepting it sourly. "I'll go along with whatever the majority wants. But I'll tell you this: I think if I help provide protection, that's pay enough. I ain't payin' that Mexican no extry."

Ramón repeated, "Nobody owes me."

Muley Dodd grinned happily. "Does that mean we're goin' to Ramón's now, Josh? Does that mean we're goin' to see all them Hernandez kids?"

Josh smiled. "And your old dog Hickory, too."

Muley rubbed his hands together, laughing. "Lordy, Josh, I'd almost forgot old Hickory. Bet he'll be right tickled to see us come. I can't hardly wait to go huntin' with him again."

Josh placed his hand on Muley's shoulder. Heather watched, admiring Buckalew for the friendship and the sense of duty which held him to the smaller man. Muley Dodd was like a child, she had realized from the first time she saw him. His heart was good and his intentions were honest, but an adolescent helplessness held him dependent upon Joshua Buckalew. She suspected that at times Muley must be burden enough to make a man weep.

If he's gentle like that with Muley, he'd be even gentler with a woman, she thought.

Jim had been gentle. In that respect he had been like Buckalew. Yet in other ways he'd been a bit like Muley Dodd, too. Not slow-thinking, the way Muley was, but somehow dependent, unsure. He had leaned on Heather for strength and she had tried to give it, even when she was stricken with anxiety herself.

Heather stared at Buckalew, then at Ocie Quitman. She doubted that either man ever leaned on anybody. They were strong men, self-confident, able to stand on their own feet and well aware of it. Either one of them would make a woman a good home. *Either one would make me a good home,* she told herself. Again she felt a touch of shame for this errant direction her thoughts were taking. It didn't seem there had been proper time yet for her to begin measuring other men as candidates to take Jim's place. But, then, these were not normal times, and this was not the settled homeland of her girlhood where the old rules could be applied without question. Out here a woman alone was a woman in jeopardy.

Well, she wouldn't be brazen about it. She would observe the amenities of widowhood and show all the proper respect. But she had to be realistic about the facts of the situation. The facts were that she was alone and couldn't afford to remain that way indefinitely. So she would watch and weigh and compare. When time had erased the obligations of propriety, and when Jim's face quit coming back unbidden in her dreams, she would know which man—if either—she wanted. And she would get him.

THE MOST direct way to the Hernandez place did not include Joshua Buckalew's land, but it passed within a few miles of there. Heather could see nervousness building in Buckalew until he could stand it no longer.

"Aaron," he told the big farmer, "I just got to ride over and take a look. I'll catch up to you later."

He rode off over the hill, Muley Dodd spurring desperately to catch up. For hours Heather found herself watching, hoping to see them. At last they came, and she smiled a little, relieved. But she stopped smiling when she saw the sober expression in Buckalew's face. She asked no questions. She sat impatiently on the wagonseat and listened for Aaron Provost to do the asking.

"Burned out, was you, Josh?"

He nodded. "I knew that, of course. I'd seen it before."

"How do your fields look?"

"Muley got the corn planted before he and Ramón took and went to join Houston. Rain's got the field growed up in weeds pretty bad. It sure needs plowin'. And then, there's the garden to plant and all."

"That don't sound so bad, then. By your face, I thought it was goin' to be worse."

Buckalew glanced at Rebecca Provost and then back to Heather Winslow. "Ladies, I don't want to get you-all upset or nothin', but me and Muley, we found horsetracks. They was made in the mud, maybe a week or more ago, but tracks just the same. And they wasn't just wild mustangs wanderin' over the country. They had riders on them."

Provost's mouth curved downward. "Indians?"

"I expect."

"Could've been just a huntin' party, already long gone back west where they come from."

"Could've been."

"Might not see any more Indians around here for months . . . maybe not for a year."

"Might not. But if they *are* here, I damn sure want to see *them* before they see *me*."

Without being told, Heather sensed that they were nearing the Hernandez place. Ramón Hernandez kept drifting farther and farther forward, till he was up even with Ocie Quitman on the point. Rather than ride with him, Quitman stopped his horse and waited for the wagons to catch up, then he drifted out to Ramón's customary place on the flank. Often Heather could see Ramón turn to look back over his shoulder as if to ask why the wagons were moving so slowly.

And finally she saw him take off his hat and wave it in a wide circle over his head. The warm south breeze brought the sound of lusty shouting. Beyond him she saw two horses and made out the figures sitting on them. The riders moved into a lope toward Ramón, and Ramón spurred into a run. When they all reined up together, she could see Ramón throw his arms around first one of the riders, then the other.

She heard Dent Sessum grumble, "Hell of a lot of guardin' he's doin' for us right now. A whole herd of Indians could ride in on us and he'd never even see them."

Heather felt compelled to speak. "He's found some of his family. You can't blame him for that."

"I didn't know Mexicans had families. I figured they just had litters, like dogs."

Heather wished she could have seen Joshua Buckalew beat Dent Sessum instead of simply having to hear about it.

She could see that the two riders with Ramón were boys, wearing plain homemade cotton shirts and trousers, with floppy straw hats perched on their heads. Their feet were bare except for simple leather *huaraches* which covered little but the soles. Joshua Buckalew rode forward and embraced them. Muley Dodd jumped off of his horse, pulled the boys down and whirled around and around with first one of them, then the other. From fifty yards away, Heather could hear his happy laugh.

As the wagons pulled up, Ramón put his hands on the two boys' shoulders and led them to the Provost wagon. "Mrs. Provost, Mr. Provost . . ." He glanced toward Heather. ". . . Mrs. Winslow, I want you all to meet my brothers. Demons, these two. But good demons."

The boys stared at the wagons and the people on them and made their *mucho gustos* with cautious grace and bubbling curiosity. Aaron climbed down and shook hands with them as if they were adults, and Heather could tell that the gesture had made him their friend for life. Aaron asked, "Ramón, did they give you a good report on the rest of your family?"

Ramón grinned. English failed him, and he replied in Spanish, which Heather understood imperfectly. "Everyone is well. My baby son is almost big enough to smoke tobacco, and I have not even seen him yet. Josh, I think I will ride on ahead."

"Go on, Ramón. We wouldn't have it no other way."

"Perhaps you would like to go in with me?"

Muley nodded his enthusiasm, but Josh waved him back. "No, Ramón, you have your reunion first. We'll be in with the wagons directly."

Muley was still eager. "Josh, I'd like to go with him."

"We'll need you here, Muley. With Ramón goin' on ahead, and all, we're a man short."

One of the boys spoke, "We'll tell María you are coming, Josh."

"You do that, Gregorio."

Heather frowned, for she had understood enough Spanish to catch that. She wondered who María was. It suddenly occurred to her that Josh had taken time this morning to shave his face clean. She hadn't given it much thought at the time except to note that he looked strongly handsome with the whiskers off.

Heather, she told herself, *it's none of your business. You've got no claim on the man. Maybe someone else has.*

But she wondered, nevertheless.

IT WAS an hour before the wagons climbed the last hill and Heather looked down on the Hernandez *rancho*. At first glance she almost missed seeing the buildings. They were made of rock that blended with the color of the land around them. Their roofs were almost flat, so that the main house and the little buildings clustered close around it seemed to huddle just barely above the ground, and seemed to be almost a part of it. A scattering of gardens and green little fields lay on the slope and down in the shallow valley below the house. The fields had been freshly worked. They weren't weed-grown like those of the *Americano* settlers who had been forced to flee ahead of Santa Anna's army.

She heard Sessum grumble loudly to Ocie Quitman, "Looky yonder, will you? Everything neat as ever was. House standin', kids playin' in the yard. Couldn't even tell there was a war. A lot different than for all the white folks. All he's got to do is pick up things right where he left off. And him just a black-eyed Mexican. Kind of gorges you a little, don't it?"

Heather could not hear Quitman's reply, if he gave one. For a moment she found herself sharing a little of Sessum's resentment, until she realized that Ramón had fought for Texas, and Sessum hadn't fought for anything. He had been sitting on the Sabine, he and his partner McAfee, waiting for others to shed their blood and make the ground safe for him.

Aaron Provost spoke reprovingly, "Don't be envious, Sessum. Rejoice in another man's good fortune. Next time it may be yours."

"Damn it, Provost, there's that Mexican down yonder got him a good house and a bunch of fresh-plowed fields and it don't even make you a little bit mad. Don't *nothin'* ever provoke you?"

Aaron's eyes narrowed, and his voice went deliberately flat. "*You* provoke me sometimes, Sessum. It'd please me a right smart if you'd just tend your wagon and hold your silence."

Resentment flared in Sessum's face, but he said nothing more. Heather had an idea that one hard blow from the farmer's big fist could knock him off his wagon, and Sessum probably knew it. She had a devilish wish to see it happen but knew it was unlikely she ever would. Aaron Provost used his great strength for labor, not for strife. She had seen him grieve over that renegade boy he had shot. Provost would fight if he had to, but it would be with reluctance.

Josh and Muley rode down the hill a little ahead of the wagons. Muley broke loose and raced on, sliding his horse to a stop, jumping down and scooping up the smaller members of the Hernandez family one at a time, swinging them round and round. The youngsters then would run to Josh and throw their arms around him.

Heather could see Ramón and a tiny woman standing proudly by the door of the stone house, Ramón holding a red-blanketed bundle in his arms. Then she saw another woman who had moved out into the yard, behind the children but well in front of Ramón and his wife. This, Heather knew, would be the María whose name she had heard. María was watching Josh intently, her hands clasped in nervousness as she obviously fought a strong wish to run out and meet him halfway. Josh broke free of the youngsters finally, and he turned toward María. He stood there a moment, looking at her, then moved. She broke into a run and threw her arms around him.

The proper thing, Heather knew, would have been to look the other way and give them their moment of privacy. But she watched. She glanced at Ocie Quitman, finally, and she found he was watching, too. His eyes disapproved.

"You look troubled, Mister Quitman."

"Never did set good with me, seein' American men dally with these Mexican women. Always thought they ought to have more pride."

"Every man needs a woman sometime. There aren't enough American women to go around."

"Then a man ought to do without." Quitman looked at the ground. Face twisting, he swung down and dropped to one knee to examine a wide mark. "*Carreta* track. Been one of them big Mexican carts along here."

"I expect these people have one."

"This one passed not very long ago." Anger welled in his face, anger Heather could not understand. "Faustino!" he said bitterly.

"What is Faustino?"

"Never mind."

Ramón had all of his family line up. He introduced Aaron and Rebecca and Heather. He made no effort to introduce all the Provost children because he simply hadn't had a chance to get them all separated in his own mind. Last of all he named Ocie Quitman and Dent Sessum. Neither man did more than nod.

Heather said quietly to Quitman, "I know I have no right to criticize you . . ."

"No, you don't."

Muley's old hound Hickory made a fuss over him, then he and the Provosts' dogs warily circled, sizing each other up, testing one end and then the other.

Heather somehow thought at first that the Mexican children were sons and daughters of Ramón, but it was made clear to her they were his brothers and sisters. His father and mother had been taken by the fever before the war began. The only child he had of his own was the baby he proudly held in his arms, opening the blanket so everyone could see the tiny brown face, the dark eyes blinking defensively against the brightness of the sun. Ramón's wife Miranda stood beside him, smiling happily, her small hands tightly holding onto his arm as if she never intended ever again to let Ramón out of her grasp.

Heather had seen Mexicans before, but she had never been around them much. The few she saw were transient horse traders and the like, and the handful of resident Mexicans who lived in Austin's capital town of San Felipe. She could not remember that she had ever seen a family group like this one, at their own home and wholly at ease.

"They don't seem so different, do they, Mister Quitman? I mean, they remind me of when I was a girl, back home."

"They're different, Mrs. Winslow."

Ocie Quitman tied his horse to the wagon wheel and walked up to Ramón. Ramón opened the blanket a little to show his child, but Quitman didn't look down. He stared at Ramón. "How long since Faustino left here?"

Ramón's smile faded. "Forget Faustino. He is gone."

"I asked you, how long?"

"When I came. I saw him here, I told him go."

"You gave him stuff?"

"Food, blankets."

"I didn't want nobody helpin' them."

Ramón reverted to Spanish. "This is *my* place, Mister Quitman. *I* say who is helped here, and who is not. You are my guest, and *only* my guest."

Quitman turned toward his horse. "I can fix that. I don't have to stay here."

"Wait." Ramón pointed at the boy Patrick. "Your son has need of this place. Where would you take him?"

Quitman fought for control of his temper. He glanced toward Heather Winslow as if to ask her for help. She had none to give him. She said, "He's right, Mister Quitman."

Quitman stood with his back to Ramón. His fists clenched a moment, but slowly he gave in and turned. "All right, Hernandez. Long as Faustino has left for Mexico—long as he don't ever come back—I reckon that's the last I'll say of it. But I want you to understand one thing: you're not givin' me nothin'. Whatever you do for me or my boy, I'll pay for it. I'll pay you in work or in goods or in money, but I'll pay you. I'll not stand beholden."

Ramón nodded. "Then, I see no argument. We are agreed."

THE FIRST thing they had to do was to place the wagons, for they would have to continue to live out of them until the crops were planted and the cabins rebuilt. The teams were maneuvered so that the Provost wagon and Quitman's sat a few steps apart, not far from the stone house. Aaron Provost motioned for Dent Sessum to pull his into the same line, but Sessum hauled his team around and moved off down toward one of the sheds.

"No use us gettin' our stuff mixed up with each other," Sessum grunted. "Keep 'em apart, I say. Then there ain't no chance of one of us gettin' off with things that belong to somebody else and causin' hard feelin's." He spat, his gaze touching the house, then falling on some of the Hernandez youngsters. "Besides, the further I stay away from *them* people, the better I'll sleep of a night."

Provost made no argument. When Sessum was out of earshot, the big farmer sighed in relief, "I'll sleep a lot better knowin' he's that far away from *me*. He'd bust a gut if he thought somebody would get off with a tin cup or a piece of rope that belonged to him. I believe he's the greediest livin' thing I ever seen, outside of a hog pen."

Quitman turned toward Josh. "Where do you intend to camp?"

Josh grimaced. "I *had* figured on the shed. But with Sessum down there, Muley and me will have to find us some other place. That arbor, I expect."

Quitman frowned toward the door of the rock house, where María Hernandez had gone. "Kind of thought you might choose to camp with her."

Josh's voice sharpened. "You better get one thing straight, Quitman, and get it now. She's as honest as the best you ever met."

"If you say so." Quitman paused. "Mind if I camp with you?"

"Suit yourself. I'm surprised you'd want to."

"It's either you or Sessum. There's some things you do that I don't care for, but at least you're open about them."

Josh stared at him, still surprised. "I'd have to say the same for you, Quitman. Times, I'd like to take a club to you. But I always know where you stand."

As SHE had been doing on the trail each night, Heather Winslow shared camping chores with Rebecca Provost. Cooking together, washing the utensils together, they managed to make the load easier than if each tried to maintain a separate camp. The children helped unload what they would need out of the wagons. Aaron Provost dug a pit for the fire.

Heather noticed that the Hernandez youngsters gathered around, well out of the way, watching the Provost boys and girls and Ocie Quitman's son. The Provost children gawked back.

"Come on, young'uns," Mrs. Provost scolded, "we got work to be done." But it wasn't being done very efficiently. The oldest Provost boy had his eye on the oldest of the Hernandez girls. Suddenly he leaped toward her and shouted, "Boo!" She jumped. The others giggled and laughed. Mrs. Provost shooed them all away. "Go on, all of you. You're no help here anyway. Go on out yonder and get yourselves acquainted."

Heather smiled. "You're not afraid they'll be contaminated?"

"You been listenin' to Ocie Quitman. A lot he knows . . ."

María Hernandez came out again and approached the two women hesitantly. "Pardon. Is there anything I can do to help?"

Mrs. Provost stretched, her hands pressing against her back. "I reckon we got it in order . . . as much order as we're goin' to have."

The Mexican girl said apologetically, "If the house was larger . . ."

Mrs. Provost shrugged, smiling. "Well, it ain't, and there's nothin' you can do about that, child. We'll have our own cabins in due time."

Heather Winslow studied María. She found her slight in build, not weighing much over a hundred pounds. Long black hair, carefully brushed and ribbon-tied at the back of her neck, framed a pretty oval face. It was the skin Heather noticed most—olive skin, clear and smooth, as if it had never known the harshness of the sun and the wind. Heather felt of her own face and knew it must be chapped and rough, for this had been a hard trip, and exposure had been extreme.

The girl's gaze moved to Heather, and Heather looked down, embarrassed to be caught staring. "I like your place here."

María Hernandez smiled. "It is home. Not pretty, like some places in Bexar. Have you ever been to Bexar?"

Heather shook her head. María went on, "It is very pretty in Bexar, or was before the trouble. Big stone houses by the river, tall churches, pretty gardens . . . You would like it."

"I like it here."

"I would be pleased to show you all of it."

"I'd like that. How about you, Rebecca?"

Mrs. Provost shook her head. "I'm a little tired, and anyway I got a meal to start. You young folks go ahead. I'll see it in due time, I expect."

María led Heather first to the house. Heather paused at the arbor in front of the door and looked at a couple of crude willow crates, which stood open and empty.

"For the roosters," María said. "The fighting roosters. My father, my older brothers, they all liked the fighting roosters. But the war came, and there was no more time."

"You mean people raise roosters just to fight?"

"They fight to the death, if you let them."

"How do they provoke them into it?"

"They do not have to. It is bred into the birds to hate and to fight. There does not have to be a reason. You put them together and they fight, that is all." Sadness touched her. "With people, it is the same. They do not need a reason. They just fight. They fight and they die, and they know not why they do it."

The house was as plain inside as outside, Heather found. The furniture was handmade from materials found close to home. The walls were mostly bare, coats hanging from pegs secured by the mortar between the stones. Heather's eye was caught by a huge hand-carved crucifix hanging in a corner, the figure of Christ meticulously done.

María said, "My father made that. He had the priest to bless it because we are so far from the church. We look at it, and we do not forget what is holy."

María started to lead her into another room but stopped. Heather caught a glimpse of Ramón and Miranda sitting on a bed, their hands clasped as they looked down on their sleeping baby. María smiled and whispered, "They have no need of us."

She led Heather outside and up the slope. Occasionally María would stop to point out one thing or another, and tell of some incident that had happened there.

Heather noticed a tall rock corral, quite close to the house. "A lot of work went into that. Why did it have to be built so strong? No animal is going to break out of it anyway."

"The Comanche might try to break in. When we know the Indians are close, we put the horses and mules in the rock corral. The gate is on the side by the house. When the Indians try to take the bars away and open it, we can stop them. Never have we lost an animal out of that corral."

"Do the Indians come often?"

"Not often. But when they come, they want horses."

The two women walked on up the slope and stopped finally at a small family cemetery where tall wooden markers stood stark against the blue sky. María crossed herself and pointed to the two tallest. "My mother and father. Next to them, a little brother who died of the fever at the same time."

On another cross Heather read the word. "Teresa."

"My sister," said María. "It was many years ago she died."

"The fever?"

"No, the Comanches. They found her on the road." She looked at the ground. "Do you know Joshua very well?"

"Not really. We came across him and your brother and Muley west of San Jacinto."

"Joshua was in love with Teresa. He wanted to marry her. That was a very long time ago."

Heather waited a little before she asked, "And now you want to marry *him?*" When María stared in surprise, Heather continued, "I saw the way you greeted him. It was plain to anyone with eyes that you were in love with him. Is he in love with you?"

María shook her head soberly. "I don't know. I don't think *he* knows. People all say I look like my sister. I know how he felt about *her.*"

"How long have you been in love with him?"

"Since I was a little girl. He came here, he taught us English while we taught him Spanish."

"You speak it very well."

"Even as a girl, I wanted to please him. I studied hard. I learned English better than anyone here, even Ramón, and he knew it before, from Bexar. But I was foolish. I was only a little girl. Teresa was a woman."

"You're a woman now."

"Perhaps it is still not enough. Perhaps another woman will come along and he will love her instead of me."

Heather got an uneasy feeling María meant her. "I am not your ri
val, María."

María managed a thin smile. "I meant nothing. But I could not
blame you if you wanted Josh. He has been wanted before."

"But no one ever got him."

"One day someone will. I hope it is me."

Down on the flat, Ocie Quitman rode alone, walking his horse,
studying the fields, looking over the scattering of Hernandez cattle.
María's eyes hardened with dislike as she watched him. "He is a
strange one, your Mister Quitman."

"*My* Mister Quitman?"

"Well, Mister Quitman, anyway. Ramón told us he would be so.
Before you came, a Mexican man and woman stopped here in an oxcart. They were in such a hurry they would not even let us cook for
them. They were afraid Mister Quitman would come."

Heather's eyes widened, for now she started putting odd bits of
fact together, and she thought she could figure the rest of the story.
She told María about Faustino and about Quitman's wife.

María's voice softened a little. "That, then, is why he dislikes us
all."

"It's more than just dislike. He's a good man in many ways, but
he's like one of your fighting roosters. He fights because it is in him
to do it. Give him room, María. He's been hurt, badly. He may hurt
a lot of others before he gets it burned out of his system."

CHAPTER

8

IT TOOK only a couple of days to catch up with what work the men needed to do around the Hernandez place, for the women and the youngsters had stayed busy while Ramón was off to the war.

Dent Sessum bent his back but little. Most of the time he walked around admiring the fields or riding one of his horses bareback over the grassland. The longer he looked at it, the better he liked it. While Ramón squatted with Joshua Buckalew beside Josh's coffee bucket one evening, Sessum strode up and made a blunt offer. "I'll buy this place from you, Hernandez. I'll pay you in American cash money."

Surprised, Ramón shook his head. "It is not to be sold."

"Better take my offer, *hombre*. Next time I won't likely bid as much."

"Next time I don't sell, either. This is my home."

"Home is where a man lays his head down to sleep. You can sleep comfortable someplace else, with American money in your pockets."

"I will sleep here."

"You can take and buy you some more land."

"Why? I do not want other land. Why would I sell?"

Sessum squinted one eye. "Because you're a foreigner livin' in a white man's country, that's why. The war's over. Goin' to be a lot of new people move in here now, people from the States. They ain't goin' to take well to havin' Mexicans livin' in their midst. Like as not they'd up and run you off and you wouldn't get paid a thing. Better you take my offer and go hunt you a place where you're welcome."

Ramón pointed up the slope. "See that cemetery? My father is there, and my mother. Some others too. This is Hernandez land, for always. I have fought for it against Santa Anna."

"Them new people movin' in, they ain't goin' to know that, or care. All they'll see is that you're a Mexican. Believe me, Hernandez, they'll move you. Or they'll bury you up in that cemetery with the rest of your folks."

Ramón set his cup aside and stood up straight. His leg had healed enough that he no longer walked with a stick. "Do you make a threat?"

"A prediction. And you can mark it down as the gospel."

Joshua Buckalew pushed to his feet and stepped in front of Sessum. "You heard him tell you he don't want to sell. Now you leave him alone."

"Let him fight his own battles."

"He did, at San Jacinto. If you'd seen him there, you wouldn't be so damned anxious to stir up a fight with him now."

Glaring, Sessum turned and walked away resentfully.

Ramón went back to Spanish. "Josh, do you really believe he has the money he talks about?"

Josh nodded. "I expect. I've had a feelin' for a long time that he and McAfee had somethin' hidden in that wagon."

"Where do you think they got it?"

"Not much tellin'. They didn't earn it. And wherever it was, you can bet they left there in the middle of the night."

IT WAS time for the men to go back and work their own farms in Hopeful Valley, to break their weed-grown fields and plant spring crops. They agreed to stay together for mutual protection as well as for the speed and efficiency they would gain by working as a team. They wanted to take Sessum's wagon, for it would be sitting idle and unneeded here.

Josh was sure that by now Sessum had gone off somewhere in the dark and had buried his money, so the wagon wasn't needed to store it. But Sessum argued that a wagon was a tremendously valuable piece of equipment these days, well-nigh impossible to replace. The trip would be a hazard to it that he felt no obligation to suffer, especially because he had no land yet and was, in his view, already contributing more than his share by the labor he was performing. That he worked at all was simply a demonstration of the goodness of his heart, Sessum declared.

The upshot was that they took Ocie Quitman's wagon. Heather Winslow said she could do without it. The men loaded Ramón's wooden plows and tied his work oxen behind the wagon. They loaded axes and shovels, seed corn and coffee. In the way of food, there was not much more they could take. For the most part they would live off of the land.

Muley watched the children at play, his eyes aglow. "Josh, how about me stayin' here and kind of helpin' tend to things? I could be a right smart of protection for the womenfolk."

Josh smiled. He knew Muley wouldn't be very watchful protection, for he would be playing games with the kids every minute the women didn't have him busy on some job or other. "Muley, we need you too bad ourselves. We've decided to leave Aaron's boy Daniel. He's not far from bein' a man, and he can shoot as good as any of us, just about. María can handle a rifle, and I expect Heather Winslow and Rebecca Provost could too, if the need come. They'll be all right, long as nobody strays far from the house."

Muley looked crestfallen. "Josh, I was helpin' them Provost boys learn to talk Mexican. They're startin' to do pretty good."

Josh's observation was that the boys had learned a lot more from the Hernandez brood than from Muley. Muley's Spanish was rudimentary and mostly wrong. "They won't forget what you've taught them. When we get back, you can take up where you left off."

Miranda Hernandez stood leaning against Ramón, and it was hard to tell which one was holding the baby, for each had an arm beneath it. Miranda wept silently, and Ramón tenderly assured her it wouldn't be long before they would be back.

Josh took María's hand. "If there's any sign of Indians, we'll come back in a hurry. Meantime, you-all stick close by. Don't let anybody get so far from the house that they could be cut off."

"You are the ones to be careful, Josh." Pain was in her eyes. "You will be a long way from help."

"We're takin' along our own. There's six of us."

Patrick Quitman was in his father's arms. "Now, son," Quitman was telling him, "you mind whatever Mrs. Winslow tells you, and don't you be causin' her no grief. I'll be back soon's I can."

"You goin' to take us home before long, Daddy?"

Quitman winced. "I don't know, son. We'll just have to see."

"I sure do wish we could go home."

Quitman looked away, and Josh could read the thought betrayed by the heavy furrows in the man's face. How could they go to a home that no longer existed, that could never exist again the way it had been?

Quitman warned, "You stay close to Mrs. Winslow. Don't you be runnin' off out of sight."

The boy hugged his father's neck. "All right, Daddy. *Vaya con Dios.*"

Quitman stiffened. "Where'd you learn that?"

"From Gregorio." Patrick pointed to the largest of the Hernandez boys. "Gregorio knows everything."

The brown-skinned lad shrank back in consternation from the hostility in Quitman's eyes. Quitman said, "Mrs. Winslow!"

Heather Winslow stepped forward. Quitman handed Patrick to her and said sternly, "Whatever teachin' is to be done for my boy, I want you to do it, or me. There's too many things he needs to learn a lot more than talkin' Mexican."

María Hernandez spoke, her voice edged with quick anger. "Gregorio has meant no harm, Mister Quitman."

Quitman stared at her a long moment. "And let's see that no harm is done, Miss Hernandez. If I decide I want him to learn Mexican, or to learn anything else you people can teach him, I'll let you know."

He climbed up onto the wagon seat and flipped the reins, the team quickly settling into the traces.

María watched him with eyes as hard as black shale. "Josh, will you do something for me?"

"Whatever you want."

"Run over him with his wagon, first time you have the chance. Don't kill him dead. Just kill him a little bit."

HOPEFUL VALLEY had no town, no store, no central settlement. It was simply a name some optimistic settler had hung on the whole general area which included the Provost place and Winslow's and Quitman's and a dozen others. Someday perhaps there would be a town, or at least a tiny crossroads settlement, when enough people came. It was a long way short of that yet.

The men halted first at the Provost place, hobbling the horses, staking the oxen, unloading the plows in Aaron's weedy field. The farmer took off his floppy hat and ran his huge hands through his graying hair, shaking his head as he gazed across the ragged, overgrown rows. "There's a heap of back strain ahead of us if we're to get any corn and cotton out of that mess this year."

Dent Sessum grunted. "Well, I'll stand guard and keep the Indians off of the rest of you, but I'll be damned if I see why I ought to break my back tryin' to make the other man a crop."

Josh flung a hard glance at him. At times, he wished it had been Sessum instead of his unlucky partner McAfee who had died under that Redlander's knife. "Don't you fret, Aaron. With all those kids you got, we have to see that you make a crop. Else it'll be up to the rest of us to feed you."

Aaron grinned. He called, "Hey, Muley, want to help me dig up a couple of graves?"

Muley looked stunned. "Well, Aaron, I was fixin' to help Ramón skin out this here deer we shot. We'll be needin' some supper."

"The deer can wait. Grab you a shovel, Muley."

Muley looked anxiously to Josh, but Josh jerked his thumb after Aaron in silent command. Muley put away his skinning knife, picked up a shovel, and went trailing with no enthusiasm. Josh winked at Ramón and followed the farmer.

Provost stopped where three crosses stood over a set of mounds beneath a huge old live oak tree. He wrapped his muscular arms around one of the crosses and pulled it up, dropping it to one side. Muley's gaze followed the cross, then cut back to Aaron, scandalized as the farmer said, "All right now, let's get to diggin'."

"Aaron!"

Grinning, the farmer rammed his shovel into the mud. "Go ahead, Muley. Anything that's down there ain't alive."

"No, sir, I wouldn't hardly think so."

Muley made a few perfunctory jabs with the shovel, his spirit not in it. Aaron had to do most of the digging. Presently his blade struck something. The sharp sound brought Muley's eyes wide open. Aaron knelt and cleared the wet earth from around a plowhandle. "Help me pull it up, Muley." Muley didn't move. Aaron finally had to tell him, "It's not nothin' like you think it is. Help me, Muley."

"It ain't nothin' dead?"

"No, Muley. I was funnin' you."

Muley stepped into the hole and helped tug. Josh reached down and took hold. They brought up a muddy plow.

Aaron said, "We buried everything we couldn't haul with us on the Scrape. We put the crosses up to fool the Mexicans."

Muley wiped his face. "Mexicans wasn't all you fooled, Aaron. That was a real funny joke." But he wasn't laughing.

In a little while they had dug up a considerable variety of tools from the first two "graves." Aaron said, "We'd best smooth these holes over and leave the third one like it is. Mostly it's got Rebecca's kitchen things in it. They'll be safer right where they're at."

The labor was hard and steady, for the weeds were rank and clung stubbornly to life. But the soil had dried enough on top that it worked without balling on the plows. The men used all the equipment they had, and all the animals, methodically turning up the fresh brown earth in rows straight as an arrow. They finished Aaron's fields, planting the corn and putting in the garden. Next they moved to the widow Winslow's place and did the same. That done, they went on to Ocie Quitman's.

Muley Dodd had a strong back, and work held no terror for him. But his was not a nature that could go indefinitely on hard labor without some relief. The third day at Quitman's, Josh noticed Muley's plow leaned idle in the row, the horse standing switching flies. Josh could see the rust color of Muley's holey shirt moving through the timber. Presently Muley came to the field in a trot, his face aglow with excitement.

"I seen some wild bees, Josh. I could find us some honey if you'd give me leave."

Josh looked across the field, surveying the large amount of work still to be done. But he knew Muley wouldn't be much help when his thoughts turned to bee-hunting. Muley's mind had a hard time keeping track of more than one thing at a time.

"I reckon it'd be all right if you had somebody to go with you for protection. Try Dent Sessum. He ain't been much help to us anyway." It would be a relief to get Sessum out of sight anyway. An idle man is always an irritant to the one who has to work. Besides, Josh knew the others were getting as tired of their straight venison diet as he was. They were low on coffee and cornmeal and hadn't had any sugar at all.

For days now, Muley had been watching for bees. He had already made his preparations, stripping a deerhide off without slitting it down the belly. He had turned it wrongside out, sewed up the bullethole and tied off the legs with buckskin strings. Then he had blown it up tight and let it dry in the sun. Now it was a tight case, big enough to hold all the honey a strong man could carry.

Muley slung the empty skin case over his shoulder. He carried an ax in one hand and a rifle in the other. Dent Sessum frowned, dubious about the whole adventure. He eased up to Josh and asked suspiciously, "You sure you ain't just sendin' me off on a fool's errand? Muley ain't smart enough to know a bee from a hummin' bird."

"Everybody's got his own talent. Bee-huntin' is Muley's."

Sessum snorted. "I'll wager he can't even find a wasp's nest. Tell you what, Buckalew: ever bit of honey he gits, I'll tote in on my own back."

Josh said to Muley, "You remember that now. He made you a promise." Muley grinned in excitement. Josh pointed a finger at him. "Don't you get so wrought up over your bees that you forget to watch out for Indian sign. You keep a sharp eye open, Muley."

"I will, Josh. You comin', Mister Sessum?"

When they were gone out of sight, Josh went back to his plow. They put in a long day of it and had the biggest part of the field turned by sundown. Josh stood stretching, both hands on his hips, and searched the landscape futilely for a sign of Muley and Sessum.

Aaron Provost climbed up from the creek where he had been washing the dirt and sweat from his face and hands. "You don't reckon somethin' went with them?"

Josh shook his head. "We'd of heard shootin'. Once Muley gets on a bee trail, he just don't know when to quit." He turned and watched Ramón Hernandez limp in from the field, walking his oxen.

Aaron followed Josh's gaze. "That leg's still gimpy."

"Mornin's, it looks like Ramón has healed up. You don't see much of a limp. Evenin's, time he's put in a hard day, it comes back."

"He's workin' too hard. You better talk to him, Josh."

"That's always been Ramón's nature. When he works, he works hard. When he plays, he plays like it's for the last time."

"You better talk to him anyway." Aaron turned his attention to Josh. "By the by, how's your arm?"

Josh blinked, and he rubbed the place where the saber had cut. He couldn't feel anything. In fact, he hadn't even thought about it. "I'd forgotten anything happened."

Ocie Quitman brought in the team he had been working to a heavy plow. He walked them over the steep creek bank, a way downstream from where Ramón was watering the oxen.

Aaron frowned. "Bank's almost flat where Ramón is. Plenty of room for all of them. Ocie don't have to go down the steep place."

"Just can't bring himself to get that close to Ramón."

"Think he'll ever come around?"

"He's been burned awful deep."

"You notice the way he's acted since we been here on his farm? Hasn't said three words in three days."

Josh nodded. "He told me he didn't think he could ever live here again. Too many ghosts. It'll be a good thing for him when we finish up and get off of this place."

Aaron kindled a campfire out of the banked coals. "It'll be better when he gets married again and has a soft, warm woman to smooth the rough edges off of him. I got an idea a woman like Heather Winslow could help make a man forget that one that died."

"He ain't said he figures to marry her. And I don't recall she's said anything about it, either."

"It'll happen. They need each other too bad." Aaron smiled tolerantly. "Besides, Rebecca has made up her mind to it. When that wife of mine decides a thing is goin' to be, you better take it for gospel."

Ramón turned the oxen loose to graze on the lush green grass along the creek. At dark the men would have to gather all the stock and pen them in a brush corral thrown together for protection against befeathered horse thieves. Finishing, Ramón picked up the empty water bucket. Aaron took it from him. "You set yourself down and rest. That leg must be givin' you fits. I'll tote the water."

"Leg's all right," Ramón protested. But he didn't argue much, so Josh took it that the leg was aching.

Slicing venison from a deer leg hanging suspended below a live oak branch, Josh said, "You got to go a little easier, Ramón. That leg is liable to cripple on you, permanent."

"The sooner we get all the fields plowed out and planted, the sooner I get home to Miranda and the baby."

"You don't want to go home on a bad leg. Tomorrow we'll find you somethin' easier to do. You won't be lookin' them oxen in the rear."

"I am not Dent Sessum."

"You're lame. He's just lazy. It's a religion with him."

Ramón sat up straight and pointed. "Then he is losing his religion."

Turning, Josh began to laugh. Muley Dodd came striding out of the timber, rifle in one hand, ax in the other. Behind him—way behind—Sessum struggled along, his back bent under the heavy load of the bulging deerskin.

Muley shouted long before he reached the camp. "Told you, Josh. Told you I could course me some bees. You ought to see what I found."

Josh waited until Muley came up to him. "I *do* see. If you'd of found any more, you'd of broken Sessum's back."

"That'd be a good idea," Aaron grumbled.

Muley glanced over his shoulder, then back to Josh. His voice dropped almost to a whisper. "Josh, I think I ought to tell you somethin'. That Mister Sessum, he ain't a nice feller."

Josh tried to act surprised. "What did he do?"

"He wanted to go back on his promise. He kept settin' the honey down and swearin' he wouldn't carry it another step. But a promise is a promise, ain't it, Josh? You always told me if I promised to do somethin' I got to do it. I told him that, and he wouldn't listen." Muley's voice reflected his disapproval. "But I foxed him, Josh. I told him I was fixin' to run off and leave him out in them woods all by hisself. He'd holler a little bit and then pick up the honey again. He'd carry it a ways, and then it was all to do over. He ain't very nice."

Dent Sessum struggled into camp and let the honey skin down.

His face and hands were swollen, for the bees hadn't taken the robbery without a fight. Muley showed not a wound. This one thing, at least, he knew how to do.

Aaron Provost ran his finger through some honey that had seeped out around the bullethole. "First honey I've tasted since I don't remember when. You fellers'll have to do this some more."

Sessum groaned. "Like hell. I'd rather follow a mule backwards and forwards over that field than follow this halfwit across all creation."

Angering, Josh said, "Tomorrow you remember you said that, because that's just what you're goin' to do."

Sessum flared. "I still ain't got no land of my own. I don't see as I need to do anything I don't want to."

Ocie Quitman had walked up, shoulders slumped in weariness, eyes bleak from the strain of being on this place that held so many memories. Somehow Sessum's complaint sparked a sudden blaze of anger. Quitman grabbed Sessum's collar and jerked. "You'd sure as hell better want to, or you'll sack your plunder and move out of here. Tomorrow you're goin' to sweat, Sessum, or I'm goin' to see you leave."

Sessum swallowed. He trembled a little after Quitman turned loose of his collar. He finally collected enough strength to declare, "All right, I been abused enough. First thing in the mornin' I'll head up to the Mexican's place and get my wagon and clear out. I got nothin' at stake with you people. You can just get along without me."

Quitman strode angrily away, past the other men. He grabbed the ax and began chopping firewood with a fury that couldn't have been caused by Sessum alone. Sessum had merely set off the fuse. Aaron rubbed his whiskery chin and stared through narrowed eyes. "He's got a terrible anger buildin' in him, Josh. He's takin' out a little of it on that ax. But it's goin' to be dangerous for the man that ever causes him to let all that steam out at once. You better keep Ramón clear of him."

Next morning, true to his word, Sessum saddled after a hasty breakfast and took off, riding north. In a way Josh hated to see him go. Little as Sessum had done, at least he had been an extra gun in case trouble came.

Before noon Sessum came riding back. Quietly he unsaddled and hobbled his horse. He carried his saddle and blanket and bridle up close to the camp fire and dropped them. He stared into the blaze a few moments before he could bring himself to look anybody in the eye. Finally he said in a subdued voice, "A man'd be a fool to ride across that country by hisself. It ain't nothin' you can see, but I swear you can almost smell the paint and feathers in every thicket. Bad as I hate it, I reckon we need each other."

JOSH AND Muley's corn crop was already well underway because Muley had planted it before he left with Ramón to join Sam Houston. It was overgrown now in weeds, so the main task was to hoe it without uprooting the corn. They turned in on the job with hands and hoes.

A day's work done, they huddled around the campfire, frying venison. Aaron pointed his square chin at Josh's field. "Josh, you're goin' to have you a corn crop laid by while the rest of us is still just thinkin' about it."

"There'll be enough here to feed everybody till the harvest comes in for the rest of you."

"Thanks, Josh. We knowed you'd feel that way. We'll pay you back when the time comes." His gaze drifted northward. "Sure am missin' Rebecca and the young'uns. Wisht we had our cabin up so we could all be closer home."

Josh said, "I been studyin' how'd be the best way to handle it, and whose cabin we ought to put up first. Way I see it, we ought to go ahead and build yours, Aaron, soon's we get my fields weeded."

Sessum spoke up, though it wasn't any of his business whose house was built first. "Why his? Why not somebody else's?"

"First place, Aaron's about as well located as anybody . . . in the center of things, I mean. Second place, he's got far and away the biggest family. Way I see it, we build Aaron's first. We build it big enough to take care of the extra folks awhile. By extra folks I mean Mrs. Winslow, and Quitman and his boy. And you too, Sessum, till you find a place for yourself. Muley and me, our place is closer to Ramón's than it is to Hopeful Valley. Anyway, we can camp on the creek bank all summer if we have to. We don't have to have a roof before winter." He glanced at Quitman. "How does that sound to you?"

Quitman nodded. "Makes sense."

"Way I see it," Aaron put in, "Mrs. Winslow is a special kind of case. Even if we was to go and build her a cabin, she couldn't hardly live there by herself. And she sure couldn't live with you, Ocie, 'less the minister come around first. It wouldn't look right. So what I'd figured was that Rebecca and me would make a place for her at our house. She can read and write good, so I figured she could teach all them young'uns of ours. Your boy too, Ocie. In return for her teachin', we'd give her a roof and take care of her till you two figure a proper time has passed and you marry each other."

Quitman poked a fresh chunk of wood into the fire. "You're takin' a right smart for granted, Aaron. Mrs. Winslow and me, we haven't talked about the idea of marriage."

"You will," Aaron said confidently. "Nature will get to you by and by. A man needs a woman, even if he *ain't* got a boy that's without a mother. And a woman needs a man, especially if she's ever had one and got used to it. You'll both get to thinkin' about it as cold weather comes on. Them two farms would make one nice big place, once you join them together."

Quitman's eyes narrowed. "I'm not ready to think about things like that."

Aaron nodded. "I know, so your friends have got to do that thinkin' for you, and have things prepared when you do get ready."

"Aaron, you meddle like an old woman."

"One of life's little pleasures. Costs nothin' and does a heap of good in the world."

After supper they lay on their blankets in the grass beside the log corral Josh and Muley and Thomas Buckalew had built years ago. Josh stared into the darkening sky, wishing the work were done, wishing he could get back and see María again. He thought of her much these long days, and these nights. He thought of the shining laughter in her dark eyes, like the laughter he remembered in the eyes of Teresa so awfully long ago. Sometimes, it was hard to be sure which sister he thought of, for they had looked alike, these two.

Time had slowly healed the pain of Teresa's death. He had almost forgotten what she looked like, though the emptiness remained. Then one day he had gazed into the eyes of María and had seen Teresa there. The love he had once felt for Teresa had been born again, this time for María. The loneliness of the years between had left him in the light of María's smile.

Muley's voice came in a shout. "Josh! There's somebody out yonder horseback. Josh!"

Josh was on his feet instantly, grabbing for his rifle. The men around him scrambled for their guns. The fire had burned down to coals, but everyone hurried to get away from it. If these were Indians, they would be looking for targets by the red glow.

A long call came from the edge of the timber. "Hello-o-o! Hello the house!"

Josh relaxed a little. It wasn't Indians. It occurred to him that was a hell of a poor choice for a call, because there was no house unless you counted the charred heap of rubble. He thought he detected something familiar about the voice. He shouted. "Who's out there?"

"Josh! Is that you, Joshua Buckalew?"

Josh gritted, "Damn!" for he knew the voice now. He shouted back, "Come on in. It's all right."

Ocie Quitman lowered his rifle. "I take it this is some friend of yours?"

"Don't know as I'd want to call him a friend. Acquaintance is more like it. He neighbors me to the north. Name is Alfred Noonan. He's a lazy old hound dog of a man who'd talk the bark off of a tree. Quarrelsome, got a tendency to be a little mean. Don't never lend him nothin'."

Alfred Noonan rode in the lead, his gray beard streaming a little in the breeze. A second man rode half a length behind him, and Josh couldn't see him well in the poor light.

"Josh, boy!" Old Noonan's gravelly voice rubbed like splintery wood. "I'd of swore you was killed in the big war. Didn't have no idea you'd come back till we seen your smoke awhile ago."

"Who's with you, Noonan?"

"See for yourself, Josh. It's Jacob Phipps, come back from the dead. Him that the Mexicans thought they'd killed way down below the Nueces. He come back, Josh, same as you did." Noonan quickly glanced over the faces. "I don't see Thomas. Was he . . ."

"He was killed."

Noonan nodded. "I'd of swore he was. Thought you was too. Thought everybody was but me. Then I come up on Jacob Phipps, and now you. The Lord's been bountiful in His mercy."

Jacob Phipps rode forward. He was thinner than Josh remembered him, and gray before his time, for Phipps was a young man yet, not even thirty. What Josh noticed most was the stiff left arm, hanging useless at Phipps' side. "Get down, Jacob. You had any supper?"

Phipps swung down and stretched out his right hand uncertainly. Josh gripped it. Phipps said, "I wasn't sure how you'd take it, me comin' here. We didn't always get along, me and you."

That was true, for Jacob Phipps and his brother Ezekiel, together with Noonan, had often been a thorn in Josh's side. From what Josh had heard, Ezekiel lay somewhere down near the Rio Grande, his head blown off by Mexican cavalry who had ambushed a foolhardy Texan patrol as Santa Anna's column started its march toward the Alamo.

Josh said, "Good to see you alive, Jacob. As for the rest, forget it. The past is gone." He pointed to the ruins of his cabin. "The future is all we got."

Phipps nodded sadly. "That's the truth if ever was. They didn't leave us nothin' but prospects. You say you got somethin' to eat?"

Josh introduced them around, though he found they'd met Aaron before, and there seemed a slight recognition of Ocie Quitman. They came finally to Ramón. Phipps shook hands with him, but Noonan stepped back, disapproving. "You mean, Josh, after all that's happened, you're still runnin' with *that* tribe?"

Regretfully Josh said, "I hoped the war would've changed you, Noonan."

"I hoped it'd change *you*. Your brother dead, and still you make friends with the likes of this?"

"Ramón fought on *our* side."

Noonan shrugged. "Knowed us Texans was bound to win, that's why. They're a shifty lot, them people. Always watch whichaway the wind blows, and they go with it. He knowed we'd come out on top of old Santy Anna."

Josh's voice took on a barb. "Last time I seen you, Noonan, *you* didn't think so. You had your tail between your legs, runnin' for the Sabine River just as hard as you could go."

Noonan's reddish face got even redder, but he made no direct reply. "You watch. Hernandez and his kind will turn against us first time they see a chance. You can't trust them a minute."

Ramón limped away, angry but carrying it with him rather than be the cause of trouble. Dent Sessum took old Noonan by the arm. "You look hungry, friend. Come on and we'll see what we can stir up for you. You sound like a man after my own heart."

Josh glanced at Jacob Phipps. "How about you, Jacob? Noonan speakin' for you, too?"

Phipps shook his head. "Me, I had all the fightin' I ever want. I'm ready to be friends with everybody, white, brown, black, or green. I stick with Noonan because I need him." He touched his dead arm. "But he don't do my talkin' for me, not anymore."

María Hernandez stopped in the edge of the garden and leaned on her hoe, gazing across the fields at the children, scattered up and down the long rows with hoes or bare hands, cutting or pulling the upstart young weeds that still tried to take hold among the cornstalks and the cotton. They had gone farther from the house than María had told them to. Squinting, she could see the oldest Provost boy Daniel, way down at the far end of the field, near his tied horse. Daniel held a rifle and was supposed to be keeping watch. But María noted that he was bending a lot, evidently pulling weeds with the rest of them.

"They have gone too far, Heather," María said. "We must speak to them about that."

Heather Winslow was on her knees, digging up onions. She pushed her bonnet back away from her eyes. "Children don't always listen. Do you see Patrick?"

"Way out yonder by Daniel."

"He's always tagging after one of the older boys, either Daniel or Gregorio. He's gotten awfully attached to that young brother of yours."

"I know. And your Mister Quitman will not like it."

Mrs. Winslow reddened. "I wish you wouldn't call him *my* Mister Quitman."

"Mrs. Provost talks as if it is all settled."

"It isn't. I wish people would stop trying to push us into something I'm not sure either one of us wants."

"He is not a bad man to look upon. I cannot say I like his temper."

"He is bitter. He suffered a terrible loss."

"So did you. You do not seem bitter."

"Some people accept things, and others don't. I've accepted what happened to Jim. It was part of the war. In a way I guess it was to be expected. But what happened to Mister Quitman's wife was not to be expected. It was too cruel even for war."

"He seems a hard man, but he is gentle with you, Mrs. Winslow. That means something, yes?"

"I think he must always have been gentle with *her*."

María frowned. "And so maybe you only remind him of her."

"Maybe."

María's eyes pinched. "I hope it is not so. One should be loved for oneself, not because one reminds a man of someone else. That would be a long and empty road, I think."

The corner of her eye caught a sudden flurry of movement, and she turned half around, staring out across the field. She saw the Provost boy running, leading the horse. The boy Patrick was racing alongside him. Near them, some of the girls had dropped their sticks and hoes and were running toward young Provost. Daniel lifted them up and put them on the horse one at a time until four girls were astride. María saw him wave his hat and start the horse running toward the house. Then Daniel was running again, keeping his pace slow enough that Patrick could stay up.

Daniel shouted, though María could make out nothing he said. Nearer the house, the other children had caught the importance of the sudden movement and seemed to be hearing what Daniel was shouting at them. They dropped everything and started to run.

Heather Winslow's face went pale. "María, what is it?" But she must already have known.

María was already running. "There is a rifle in the house. Come on!" She grabbed the rifle, a powderhorn, and a pouch of shot. She was out of the house again in seconds. She paused only long enough to prime the weapon. Then she was running for the field, racing toward the children. Heather hurried just behind her.

The four girls on the horse came galloping past the other running children. María threw her hands in the air as the horse approached her. The biggest girl reined to a stop, and María started helping the girls to the ground. "Run!" she shouted. "Run for the house!" Then she motioned for Heather. "Up! I'll give you a foot-lift."

Heather's long skirts got in her way, but she swung up, sliding the skirts far up her legs. She reached down and caught María's hand, helping María swing up too. María's bare heels thumped against the horse's ribs as she reined it around. The horse reluctantly went into a lope again. It had caught the excitement and wanted only to go to the house. María kept her heels drumming till she came up even with the second group of running children. She shouted, "Down, Heather. Take the rifle and get these children to the house. I'll go for the boys."

Heather pointed to a line of horsemen on the hill, riding down toward the field. "No, María, you can't. Look yonder."

"I think I can beat them to the boys."

Heather slid to the ground, falling to hands and knees and pushing herself up immediately. She reached for the rifle and horn and pouch. María said breathlessly, "You can reach the house before them, but keep the children moving fast. Use the gun if you have to."

María moved away from Heather in a lope, her heels drumming again. Heather began pushing the children. "Hurry. Run, girls. Boys, rush it up. You've got to run." For herself, she was running backward much of the time, watching María.

The horse galloped through the fresh green corn, trampling the stalks, almost losing his footing in the soft plowed ground. María was shouting first at the horse, then at the boys. "Run, run!"

The riders were coming down off of the hill, yipping and shouting. María's blood ran like ice, and her scalp prickled. Comanches, smelling blood. It mattered not to them whether they killed men or women or children, or whether they were American or Mexican.

I'm not going to get there in time. The terrible thought ran through her mind, and scalding tears burned her eyes. Neither boy was hers, or even of her blood, but the thought of seeing them slain like helpless deer brought an anguished "No!" from her tight throat. She drummed her heels harder. Another thought came. What if they did not kill the boys? What if they took them? The Comanches did that sometimes with children. She had known of many cases. The boys, if they survived the first hard days and weeks, might be treated first as slaves and later taken into the tribe. The girls might also be enslaved, and when they were old enough, taken for wife.

Better they die, she thought. *But better still if I reach them first. Then at least they'll have a chance.*

María held no illusions about what the Indians would do if they caught *her.* Years ago, they had caught her sister Teresa.

The boys were only fifty yards from her now . . . forty . . . thirty. She dared not look for the Indians, but some terrible curiosity forced her to do it anyway. She saw that they were not coming straight at her now. They were angling off.

The ravine. She remembered the ravine which cut across above the field. It was too deep, too steep. They were having to go around it. She remembered the many times Ramón had cursed that ravine for stealing runoff water the field needed, and now she thanked God for it.

She stopped the horse and reached down for Patrick's arm. The Provost boy gave the lad a boost. Then, almost in the same motion, Daniel swung up too, the rifle still unfired but ready.

Three on one horse, and the Indians all riding single. That made for a desperate risk, but there was no way to ease it, for which boy would she leave? She shouted, "Hold me, Patrick," and put her heels to work again. They quartered across the field, trying to get out of the plowed soil and onto the solid ground. She glanced back once, just long enough to see the Indians coming around the head of the ravine. They were close enough that she could hear their shouts, even over the hoofs and the little boy's sobs.

Ahead, Heather Winslow was almost out of the field with the other children. There remained a run of fifty yards to the house. They could make it. Heather turned and faced back across the field, the rifle coming up to her shoulder. María saw the fire and the smoke and saw Heather drop the rifle butt to the ground, preparing to ram down another load.

"She's trying to help us," María told the boys.

Daniel Provost's voice was frightened. "She can't hit them at that distance."

"She will worry them," María said.

Daniel looked back and gasped. "There's one of them way out in the lead. He's goin' to catch us, María."

She saw an arrow go by like the flash of a light, suddenly gone. "Can you shoot him?"

He tried to aim the rifle. "Not with us goin' thisaway."

"Then be ready. I'll stop. Shoot him."

She reined to a quick halt. The rifle boomed. Daniel shouted, "He's down. I got the horse."

María put the plowhorse back into a run. Ahead of her, Heather Winslow fired again and began to retreat, moving backward, watching, reloading as she moved. María shouted, "To the house, Heather. Run!"

Heather fired once more, then turned and ran. María allowed herself another glance over her shoulder. The Indians were coming, but now María was certain she would beat them to the house. She slid to a stop as Heather reached the arbor. Rebecca Provost held the door open. "You-all come a-runnin'! Come a'runnin', I say!"

María shoved both boys off of the horse. Patrick sprawled, sobbing. Heather grabbed him into her arms. María turned the horse into the stone corral and took time to shut the gate. Rebecca Provost shouted desperately at her, and at her oldest son. But Daniel stood his ground at the arbor, rifle to his shoulder, protecting María. She sprinted for the house. The Provost boy walked backward, keeping the rifle ready. The dogs scurried through the door ahead of María. The boy turned and ran. Rebecca Provost slammed the door shut behind them and dropped the heavy bar.

María's lungs ached. She had held her breath much of the time, taking it in gasps. She found herself trembling now, tears starting to flow. She looked fearfully around the room, counting. "The children . . ."

Rebecca Provost hugged Heather, then María. "They're all here, praise God. Hadn't been for you two girls, we'd of lost them all." The older woman let her tears stream without any effort to blink them away. María broke free, still struggling for breath. "Heather . . . you have the rifle . . . Will you use it . . . or you want me to?"

Hands shaking, Heather extended the rifle to arm's length. "If you can shoot straight, you'd better do it."

Miranda Hernandez sat on the floor, cradling her baby to her bosom and praying softly to her saint. Rebecca and Heather got all the whimpering children to lie flat around Miranda. María went to a shuttered window. Daniel Provost was at another, peering intently through the port.

Rebecca said, "Heather, you got more learnin' than me. Miranda's prayin' in her language. You pray in English. The good Lord ought to understand *one* of you."

Heather asked, "What're *you* going to do?"

Rebecca had brought the chopping ax in from the woodpile during the excitement. Now she picked it up. "I'm goin' to be holdin' this, just in case."

Hoofs pounded in the yard outside. An Indian made for the corral where María had penned the horse. Daniel's rifle roared. The bullet whined angrily off of the rock fence. "Didn't hit him," the boy shouted, "but he sure turned back." He began reloading.

An Indian galloped straight toward the house, lance poised. He hurled it, and the heavy wooden door trembled. María fired. The rider shrieked and flopped back, almost losing his leg-hold on the gotch-eared pony. As he whirled away, María glimpsed a blood-splotch on his side. She had creased his ribs, if she hadn't shattered them.

She took count of the Indians now. Six. Horse-stealing party, likely, but a party out for horses would not pass up any easy opportunity to bleed their enemies.

She saw two Indians riding one horse. One of them must have been the warrior Daniel had set afoot. For all practical purposes, then, they had put two Indians out of any real chance at action.

"Watch the corral!" she said to Daniel. "They'll try again for the horse. They have a man afoot."

One Indian got as far as the gate. His pony went down threshing, a slug in its belly. The Indian scuttled away.

The Comanches pulled back, shouting in anger. María knew none of the words, but the message was clear. Six men had only four horses between them now, and all the enemy were forted up in a strong rock house. Under normal circumstances the Indians would have left, for the Comanche was not one to throw his life away in a mad gamble. He killed when the odds were in his favor, and he melted with the whistling wind when the risk became too great. He was never ashamed to retreat, for retreat to him was not surrender. It was merely a realistic acceptance of a bad situation. He always intended to come back another time, when perhaps the spirits were smiling upon him.

For these men, retreat must be coming a little harder. They had seen nothing here but women and children. They probably were figuring accurately that if there had been any men here they would have come out to protect their families. It would be a galling thing for a Comanche warrior to go into camp and admit he had been set afoot and chased away by a few women and children.

"Be ready," said María. "I think they will try again."

She wished for more rifles. The Indians seemed to have none at all. They had used nothing but arrows and the lance, which she felt sure must still be stuck in the heavy door. "Can you see them, Daniel?"

"No. They're off to one side someplace. I can't see them through the porthole."

María moved across the room to watch the back of the house. She could see them out there milling around, uncertain, four men on horses, one standing, one sitting hunched on the ground, holding his side.

In the tightly closed room the dogs were barking and some of the children were whimpering. Their ears all rang from the roar of the rifles. Smoke hung thick and acrid. The children who weren't crying were coughing, choking on the smoke.

María saw one Indian come running, afoot. The horsemen gave him a few seconds, then came in a gallop, yipping and shouting.

"Two are coming your way, Daniel."

Two riders rushed toward the back of the house, but at such an oblique angle María could not take aim through the port. She held her fire and waited. An arrow thumped into the wooden shutters. Another struck the wood at the edge of the port and came flying in, its force blunted. It hit the rifle, glancing off. María's heart leaped with fright, but she forced herself to glance through the port. She saw the Indian afoot hurl his body against the shutters. The bar bulged and cracked. Almost in panic, María shoved the muzzle through the port and fired.

She realized instantly that had been a mistake, for now she had to take time to reload. The Indian threw his shoulder against the shutters again. The bar splintered, and the shutters swung open. For a second the Comanche paused there, blinking against the darkness of the interior while María fought to reload.

Mrs. Provost shouted, "You bloody heathen!" She ran at the Indian, the ax poised over her shoulder. The Indian tried to swing his bow into position to loose an arrow at her, but he was off balance. Just as the ax swung, he threw himself backward, out of the window. The blade split the bow and sank deep into the wooden sash. Mrs. Provost yanked it free, shouting in fury: "Hyahh-h-h, you red heathen! Git! Git, I say!"

Weaponless now, he got up. One of the dogs jumped through the window and raced after him, teeth bared.

María had her rifle reloaded. She stood back away from the window a little, trying not to make a target but ready to shoot when she had to.

Across the room, Daniel's rifle roared. "I got another horse!"

The Indians didn't try again. There were still six of them, and only three horses now. Even as it was, they would all have to ride double. They couldn't afford to lose another horse.

From her vantage point behind the broken shutters, María watched the Indians gather out of range. For a long time they milled, hands gesturing in argument. But cool heads prevailed, and presently the six Comanches melted away.

It was a long time before anyone ventured to open the door. When at last they worked up the nerve, Rebecca Provost slid the bar away, and Daniel pushed the door open. The lance bumped against a post supporting the arbor, and it clattered to the ground. Daniel moved out first, rifle poised. María and Heather went next, and finally Rebecca and Miranda.

Daniel picked up the lance, touching his thumb experimentally to the sharp metal point. "Filed out of a barrel hoop." He stepped into the yard. There two Indian horses lay, one dead, one slowly dying. Out at the field's edge lay another. There was no powder or lead to be wasted. He moved to the dying horse, slipped his Bowie knife from its sheath and cut the animal's throat. Walking back to the arbor, he said, "We didn't kill any Indians, looks like, but we sure played hell with their horses." He glanced at his mother, and his face reddened. "Mama, I hadn't ought to've said that."

Rebecca Provost threw her arms around him. "A boy ain't supposed to, but today you're a man. And a man can say anything he damn pleases."

Aaron Provost backed off and took a long look at the big new double cabin with its opening through the center, a loft over the dog-run for the boys to sleep in. "I swun, it's better even than what we had before. Rebecca'll be right proud."

The builders were gathering their tools and putting them in the dog-run to keep them dry. Josh leaned on his ax and admired the new structure with Aaron. "Still a right smart of finishin'-up work to be done, but I expect you and your boys can be doin' that along as you get to it."

Aaron grinned. "You fellers will all be my guests tonight. You can roll your blankets on the floor and sleep under my new roof. Once we bring the womenfolk, you ain't likely to have another chance." The grin slowly left him. "Been right concerned about the women, Josh."

"Aaron, we been back and forth over all these farms the last three-four weeks, and we ain't seen a sign."

"Sometimes the first sign you see of the Comanch is when he sends a dogwood arrow singin' at you."

"They're all right. María and the Hernandez family stayed there all by themselves while Ramón was gone to the war."

"Just the same, I'll be tickled to see Rebecca and them young'uns."

They left Quitman's wagon, for it would slow them down, and what few belongings Mrs. Winslow had could easily be carried in the Provost wagon anyway. They struck off southwestward, horseback. Homesick, Ramón held the lead. Once Josh felt compelled to catch up to him and slow him down.

"It could be dangerous, you gettin' so far out front by yourself."

Ramón said sheepishly, "I didn't notice. My mind was with Miranda and the baby. I hate to think of Miranda sleeping alone in that big, cold bed."

"You stay a little closer to the rest of us or she might sleep by herself for a long, long time."

They rode steadily through the morning, stopping at a creek to water the horses and to eat some jerked venison. Ramón was out front again as they topped the last hill and looked down on the Hernandez house. He waved his hat frantically. Josh and the others moved up in a hurry.

Ramón pointed to a blackened pile of charred timber and bones. "Josh, something has happened here."

Josh swung down and kicked at the remnants. A chill ran up his back as he counted three skulls. "Horses. Somebody's drug three dead horses up here and burned them."

Fright came into Ramón's voice. "We didn't have three horses here." Suddenly desperate, he set his mount into a hard lope.

Ramón was too far in the lead for anyone to catch him. Riding hard, Josh looked across the fields toward the house, hoping to see some sign of life. He saw none. He knew with a terrible certainty that something had gone wrong here. Then the door opened and the women hurried out under the brush arbor. The children spilled around them. Josh could see rifles in María's and Daniel's hands. *They thought we was Indians.*

Tiny Miranda ran forward to meet Ramón. Ramón slid to a stop and jumped down, grabbing her fiercely. Josh noted that Ramón's bad leg didn't seem to be bothering him much.

The dogs came running, barking. Patrick hurried out toward his father. "Daddy, Daddy, the Indians came!"

Ocie Quitman reached down and scooped the boy up into the saddle, crushing him in his arms. Quitman's voice quavered. "Son, what's that about Indians?"

"They came, Daddy, and they tried to get us."

Josh broke in, "Anybody hurt, Patrick?"

"Just Indians. María saved us, Daddy. Them old Indians was a-fixin' to get me and Daniel, but María came a-runnin'."

Quitman seemed to freeze. He stared into his son's face, dazed by the realization that he had come close to losing the boy.

Aaron Provost hugged first one of his children, then another. Rebecca waited patiently, and he squeezed her hardest of all. "Aaron, we been needin' you."

Josh dismounted slowly, his eyes on María. He reached for her hands. "María, I heard what Patrick said. Are you all right?"

She nodded, smiling. He opened his arms, drawing her to him violently. He whispered, "Thank God. If something had happened again . . ." He held her so tightly that she gasped for breath. "Sorry, María, I didn't go to hurt you. But all of a sudden I was rememberin' what happened to Teresa, a long time ago . . ."

She stiffened a little. "Nothing happened to me. Everything is fine." She dropped her head forward, against his chest. In a moment she said, "Teresa is still much on your mind, isn't she, Josh?"

He fumbled for an answer. "No, María, no. What happened here just brought it back, that's all."

The men gathered around and demanded a full account. Rebecca said, "You're the one to tell them, María." When María shook her head, Rebecca went on, "Then I'll tell it." She gave the whole story in rousing detail.

Ocie Quitman held his son tightly. Now and again, listening, he would glance covertly at María. Patrick would break in occasionally to say, "What you scared for, Daddy? It's over with."

When Rebecca had told it all, Aaron Provost took a long, thankful look at all his children. He reached out and clasped María's fingers in one of his big hands, Heather Winslow's in the other. "You little ladies, there ain't nothin' I can say that would be half enough."

Heather put in quietly, "María did most of it."

Aaron blinked. "It beats all nature, the way a woman can come through when she has to. Girls, I know you got no daddy—either one of you—but from now on you got the next thing to a real one. If ever there comes a time you need help—no matter what or how much of it—you don't have to go no farther than the Provost house." He glanced at Josh. "Boy, you hug that girl María and do it proper. If you don't, I swear *I* will."

Ramón and Miranda heard the baby crying—or said they did—and walked into the house, arms around each other. Muley led off his and Ramón's horses, the children following after him. Aaron moved toward his wagon, one hand on Rebecca's shoulder, the other on Daniel's. Dent Sessum tramped away to examine his own wagon, fearful the Indians might have done him some damage. Josh figured he would be looking after his money, too, wherever he had hidden it. Josh said to María, "I best see after the horses. But later I'll do what Aaron said, and I'll do it right."

Ocie Quitman stared at María, even as he clung to his son. She stared after Josh, but it was evident she knew Quitman was watching her. At length she turned toward the house. Quitman said, "Miss Hernandez . . ."

She stopped. He picked around for the words, and they came with difficulty. "I need to tell you . . ."

"It's not necessary."

"This boy's the only thing I got left in the world that means anything to me. They say you saved him."

María's voice was cool. She spoke in Spanish, throwing it in his face. "If I did, it was not because he was your son. It was in spite of that. Don't hurt yourself trying to say thank you."

Stung, Quitman watched her enter the house. Patrick stuck to him like a burr as he led his horse out and turned him loose. That done, he returned to the arbor and sat on a log bench, face furrowed, his hands absently running through his son's hair. He nodded while Patrick told him again about all that had happened, coloring it with a child's fears and fantasies. The Indians had all been nine feet tall, painted and feathered and riding horses big as a house. But María had come out for him and Daniel and hadn't been scared at all. Her pony had run like the wind. At length Quitman tried to switch the subject. "What else has happened, son? What all did you do before the Indians came?"

"We hoed the fields, and we played a lot. Gregorio's my favorite, Daddy. You know Gregorio?" Quitman only nodded. The boy said eagerly, "Gregorio's goin' to teach me how to twist a rabbit out of a hole. Did you ever twist a rabbit, Daddy?" When Quitman shook his head, the boy said, "He twisted one the other day. Got it up out of its hole and caught it."

Quitman frowned. "I hope you didn't eat it? That'd be like a bunch of Mexicans."

"No, sir, Gregorio turned it loose. Said no use killin' somethin' unless it's hurtin' you or you aim to eat it. I've learned lots of things from Gregorio. He's goin' to teach me a lot more."

Quitman's gaze ranged down around the sheds, where Muley and the Provost youngsters and the Hernandez children milled. "I don't reckon he'll have the chance, son. We're fixin' to leave here."

The boy's face fell. "Leave María, and Gregorio?"

Quitman nodded. "We've built a house on the Provost place. You'll live there awhile, Patrick. Mrs. Winslow will be there too. She'll look out for you when I can't be around. She's goin' to teach all you young'uns. You'll enjoy that."

"I'd rather we was stayin' here."

"We can't. This is too far from the valley. Anyway, you like Mrs. Winslow, don't you?"

"Sure, Daddy, but I wish María and Gregorio was goin' with us too. Couldn't we take them?"

"Their home is here, son. Everybody has to live where his land is."

"I wish our land was here."

Presently Patrick ran off to join the other children. Heather Winslow came out and took another bench, near Quitman. He was frowning in disapproval as he saw his son pair up with the dark-skinned Gregorio.

Heather Winslow said, "Don't worry about it, Mister Quitman. Gregorio is all right."

"I'd just rather see Patrick take up with the Provost boys more. Better he stays with his own kind."

"It won't matter long. Aaron says we're leaving here."

"Tomorrow. We've made a place for you to live at the Provosts'. Have they talked to you about givin' the young'uns some learnin'?"

"Yes. I said I'd be glad to, as much as I can do. It's a way to help earn my keep. Anyway, there doesn't seem to be anywhere else I can go. I can't live on my place alone."

Hesitantly Quitman said, "Teachin' ain't all they got in mind. They got other plans worked out for you. And for me."

Heather blushed. "I know."

"I hope you don't let it embarrass you. Far as I'm concerned, you needn't even think about it."

She looked away. "I'll confess, Mister Quitman, I have done some thinking about it."

He stared blankly. "Come to any conclusions?"

She shook her head. "No conclusions. It's still too soon after . . . I need more time."

Quitman looked relieved. "The same with me. I'm in no mood to be pushed into somethin' by other people, no matter how good their intentions are. Whatever I decide to do—and if I do *anything*—it'll be because I made up my own mind."

"They'll keep pushing us. Rebecca keeps saying your son needs a woman's care. She keeps saying *you* need a woman, and I owe you what a woman can give."

He looked at her in surprise. "It's hard on a man, once he's been married. But don't ever feel for a minute that you owe me anything like that. You don't. I wouldn't ask you to."

Her eyes were grateful. "I know you wouldn't, Mister Quitman. But let me tell you this: if I ever decided I wanted to, you wouldn't have to ask me."

María Hernandez walked outside. She glanced a moment at Heather and Quitman, then moved out to the garden. Heather's gaze followed her. "Mister Quitman, I don't mean to tell you what you ought to do, but it would be a bad thing if you left here without telling that girl you're sorry."

"Sorry about what?"

"I shouldn't have to tell you. In spite of everything, she went out there and brought Patrick back with those devils yapping at her heels. They would've killed her if they had caught her, or they would've carried her away. If it hadn't been for her, you wouldn't have a boy."

"What can I say to her?"

Heather smiled. "You're a straightforward man, Mister Quitman. The words will come to you." Heather arose from the bench and walked down toward the Provost wagon.

Reluctantly, feeling somehow trapped, Quitman stood up. He stared at the dark-haired girl, who was pulling beans and dropping them into a tightly woven willow basket. He took a few steps toward her, stopped, clenched his fists, and took a few steps more. He stood behind her, trying for words that didn't want to come. "Miss Hernandez . . ."

She turned to look at him over her shoulder. "Yes?" He stood in awkward silence. She said, "You were about to say something?"

He frowned, his fist balling up. "Yes, and I expect you know what."

"I think so. I can see the pain in your face. It hurts."

"Like pullin' out my own teeth."

"Then forget about it, Mister Quitman."

"No. I always been one to pay my debts."

"I am just a Mexican. You have said so. You owe me nothing."

A touch of anger came, and he wasn't sure whether it was at her or at himself. "Yes, you're a Mexican. I won't lie about it: that's what makes it so hard for me to say. But I *will* say it if it kills me. I oughtn't to've treated you the way I done. I reckon it ain't your fault bein' born what you was. And what you done for my boy leaves me a debt I can never pay you for."

Her eyes were hard. "I think you resent that it was me. You wish it had been anybody else—Heather Winslow, or Rebecca—anybody but this Mexican girl."

His face pinched. "You see right through a man, don't you?" He shrugged. "I reckon you got cause to hate me, but that's the way it is. I can't help the way I feel. I can't cover it up and act like it ain't there."

Some of the harsh dislike faded from her eyes. She looked at him strangely. "That is true, Mister Quitman. You can't, and you don't try. There are some who smile and talk nice but hate inside. You are not one of those." She looked down at the willow basket. "She must have been a good woman, your wife."

His voice tightened. "Yes, she was."

"I am sorry you lost her."

"It had nothin' to do with you. I got no reason to make you share the blame for it. It's just somethin' inside me I can't control. I can apologize for it, but I can't stop it."

"Then the best thing is for you to stay away . . . from all my people."

"That's what I been tryin' to do. Luck just keeps throwin' us to-gether. And now I'm owin' you . . ."

"I do not accept the debt. Some of my people did you a bad wrong. Whatever I did, take it as a payment on what my people owe to *you*."

She carried the basket back to the house. He watched till she passed through the door and out of view. He stopped to pick up a long string bean she had dropped, and he shifted his gaze down to the shed where Buckalew was.

He remembered then the talk of Buckalew marrying this girl. He thought, *Maybe Buckalew isn't as far wrong as I figured him.*

CHAPTER

11

IT WAS a busy summer, for there were not only the crops to be weeded and garden plots to be tended and stock to be worked, but there was also all the rebuilding to be done, the war scars to be rubbed away with muscle strain and sweat and determination. Josh's cattle had scattered. Many were completely gone, taken perhaps by beef-hungry Mexican troops. In the unsettled country to the west roamed wild cattle, descended in freedom from those which had strayed long ago out of the Spanish mission herds. These cattle were spotted and striped and every color a man had ever seen, their horns long and their legs longer. They fleshened well on grass and were far less gamey than the wild deer and turkey and bear which kept so many settlers' ribs from showing through the skin. Brought home, gentled enough to stay, they would be good for trading in the settlements. When they had time, Josh and Muley and Ramón and Gregorio rode west, picking up wild cattle where they could find them. Often they had to rope them with rawhide *reatas* and throw them down and tie up a leg to slow them and make them workable. Sometimes they necked them to gentler cattle brought along from home. Slowly through the summer they built their herds by going out and bringing in what Nature had provided. Some cattle they kept; some strayed right back where they had come from.

There was this about early Texas: if it *was* a big and untamed land, and if its people *were* poor and ragged and ever standing in the presence of danger, at least Nature herself was bountiful. No man went hungry if he had a horse and a rope, or if he had a rifle and powder and ball, or if he had the knowledge and material to build even a snare.

When they weren't after cattle, Josh and Muley and Ramón were sometimes out searching for the mustangs which roamed these hills and valleys in numbers beyond counting. They built wings and traps and hazed the horses into them, then caught them Mexican style with their heavy rawhide *reatas* and brought them to hand. These were grand days, these fleeting days of summer, and it pleased Josh that Ramón was once more learning to laugh. It was not the high, easy laughter of the old days, but that would never come back. That was killed forever. Even the little chuckle that followed a good ride on a mustang bronc was an improvement, though, and Josh was gratified.

They spent so much time gentling these captured horses that summer was far gone before Josh realized they had not made any preparations for building a cabin. They'd slept in the open through the warm weather, but he and Muley would need tight walls and a roof before the fall northers began moving in with the chilling bite of raw prairie wind.

After the corn crop was harvested, Josh and Muley started looking for cabin timber. They chopped down trees, stripped off the branches, and dragged in logs at the end of a *reata*. As he could, Josh measured off the size the structure was to be and started cutting and shaping the logs, notching the ends to fit together. He fashioned this cabin bigger than his old one had been, for in the back of his mind was the notion that one day he would bring María here to live. He would ask her someday, when he had the place fixed up the way he wanted it, the way it ought to be for a woman. A man could live in any kind of a house, so long as it kept the rain off of his head. But he couldn't expect a woman to live that way, not if he had any real feeling for her.

Because his crop was the earliest in, Josh had shared his corn. He hauled roasting ears to the neighbors. Later, as the ears hardened, he had carried grinding corn to the Provosts and Mrs. Winslow and Quitman, and Jacob Phipps. He had even given some to Dent Sessum and Alfred Noonan, living like a pair of boar hogs in the squalor of old Noonan's place. This, with the game they killed, saw the settlers through until their own crops could ripen.

In return, they owed Josh and Muley a cabin-raising. They would have done it debt or not—all, perhaps, but Sessum and Noonan. Those damned reprobates didn't seem to feel they owed anybody anything. Josh was surprised to see Sessum and Noonan ride in the morning everybody was to gather and start raising the cabin. He was not made joyful by their coming. Nevertheless, he tried to be civil.

"Didn't figure I'd see you-all." He might have added that the only time he *ever* saw them was when he took them something, like the roasting ears.

"Never miss a cabin-raisin'," Noonan enthused. "Been to many a one in my day. I do hope you got some drinkin'-whisky. Me and Sessum, we been whettin' our bills."

Josh hesitated to admit it. He and Muley had taken some cattle down into the settlements for trade and had come back with several jugs of whisky, among other things. It would be neighborly to furnish an occasional snort to friends helping bring up a cabin. He told the old man, "I expect we can dig up a swig or two when the time comes."

"It's always time," Noonan said. But Josh didn't offer.

Sessum said, "Buckalew, you got somethin' me and Noonan could be doin' to help you?" He didn't sound particularly eager, but maybe he thought it would help hurry the whisky. Josh decided to see how much work he might get out of them. He knew they would get plenty of his whisky.

"We'll need more clapboards for the roof. I got logs sawed for the job if you-all would like to rive them for me."

Normally one man could rive logs, but Sessum and Noonan made a two-man job of it. They would place the sharp edge of the froe on the upended short log and drive it down by pounding on its blunt upper edge with a wooden hammer, splitting off a board about an inch thick. The rate they started, Josh calculated they could spend a week. But it would keep them out from under foot.

"Where's Jacob Phipps?" he asked. "Surprised you didn't bring him."

Old Noonan grunted. "Tell you the truth, Josh, I been a mite disappointed in him. He ain't been none too friendly of late. You know one day he even had the gall to tell me and Sessum to git ourselves off of his place? And us old friends, the way we was. I swear, you can't put your faith in nobody anymore."

The war had cost Phipps an arm, Josh thought, but it seemed to have sharpened his judgment. He asked Sessum, "How about you? Still huntin' you a place to buy?"

Sessum shook his head. "I still got my eye on the place your Mexican friend has got, if he'd just talk business."

In Josh's view, the thing that had drawn Sessum's interest at Ramón's was the neatness of it, the way the fields were clean-worked and the crops coming along well. Sessum didn't recognize the work that had gone into it to get it that way, and the work it would take to maintain it in that condition. If a man like Sessum got hold of it, the place would look like a disaster had struck inside of six months. "Ramón won't sell. You'd just as well forget it."

Sessum shrugged. "Man never can tell what may happen. The Mexicans are liable to decide they want to leave, and I'll be in a position to buy."

"They been here longer than any of us. Nothin' is apt to change their minds. You leave them alone, Sessum. You'll likely find somebody else willin' to sell, if you'll look around."

"I been watchin' Jacob Phipps. He's havin' hell tryin' to work that place of his with just one good arm. I figure one of these days he'll give up and take an offer. Who knows? I might be able to buy his land and the Hernandez place both if they go cheap enough. You'd have me for a neighbor on both sides of you, Buckalew."

Josh turned away, scowling. He'd as soon have a Comanche village on one flank and the cannibalistic Karankawans on the other.

A couple of horses showed up to the west, and a high-wheeled Mexican cart drawn by mules. Ramón Hernandez led the way on a big, brown horse. He was bringing the whole family—Miranda, the baby, María, and all the brothers and sisters. Hickory loped out to greet them, barking all the way. From east came Aaron and Rebecca Provost in their wagon, bringing with them Mrs. Winslow and Patrick and all the young Provosts. Ocie Quitman rode alongside with lanky Daniel Provost. Their dogs bounced in front of them, setting up a barking contest with Hickory. The Provost children jumped out of their wagon and raced toward the Hernandez family. Patrick climbed down shouting, "Gregorio! Hey, Gregorio!" Quitman tried to stop him, but the boy was away like a deer.

It took a while for everybody to get through with the hugging and the howdying. Presently the women hauled out their cooking utensils and took a critical look at a side of beef which had been placed over the coals early in the morning. Josh and Muley squatted on their heels with Aaron and Ramón to swap talk. Pretty soon Muley became bored with it all and trailed off after the youngsters. Ocie Quitman listened, but his gaze absently followed the women.

Been a long time now since he lost his wife, Josh thought. *Nature's starting to work on him. He's probably gone to thinking more and more about Heather Winslow. And he ought to. She's a right handsome woman.*

Old Noonan came around and began wedging into the conversation. And once he started, he had a way of taking it over, asking the questions and giving the answers. One by one the men commenced getting up and looking for work to do. The foundation logs went down first. Then the builders started "rolling up" the side walls. By dusk, when Josh called a halt, they had the project well started. They were a long way from reaching the roofline, but the women would have a place to sleep tonight, "indoors."

Off and on during the day, as appetite hit them, the men had gone to the beef, slicing hot strips of barbecue from the carcass which had slow-cooked over the gentle heat of the coals. Now the women were preparing a regular supper. The smoke from their fire smelled good to Josh, for his stomach growled in complaint, and his muscles ached from straining with the heavy logs. He took a cup and walked to the fire, where Heather Winslow was stirring beans in a pot. He filled the cup with coffee and paused to visit a little.

"How's the school comin', Mrs. Winslow?"

"Not good, not bad. We just have to make do with what little we've got. Do you know we have only two books for the children to learn from? The Bible and *Pilgrim's Progress*. We have a copy of the United States Constitution, too, but we never got past the part about the pursuit of happiness. Daniel Provost said he's pursued deer, but he didn't know you had to pursue happiness. He'd never seen it run."

She smiled, but Josh didn't. It didn't strike him that way. He said, "Happiness is a hard thing to catch hold of, sometimes. Maybe it don't run, exactly, but it's got a habit of slippin' away from you."

"This ought to be a happy place you have here, Mister Buckalew. I like the way the creek lies, and all those trees. I like the view as you stand here and look off to the south and east. It will be a good place to bring a woman." She nodded toward the cabin. "It's going to be a big one. Of course you'll have to find a place to put Muley, once María comes here to live."

"I'll build him another cabin."

"You sound as if you already have your plans made."

"I done a lot of studyin'."

"Then maybe you ought to talk with María. I gather that she's not sure what your intentions are."

"I figured they've always been understood without me sayin'."

"By you, maybe, but not by her, Mister Buckalew. A woman doesn't like things taken for granted. She wants to hear them said out loud."

He grimaced. "Truth is, Mrs. Winslow, I never have been around women much. I had some sisters, but they was older, and I never did understand them anyway. They all cussed about men, then up and married the first ones that come along and asked them. María . . . she was not much more than a little girl first time I ever saw her. I reckon that's the way I've thought of her, till just lately."

"Till you realized all of a sudden that she was a grown woman, like her sister had been?"

He stared into the coffee. "I rode up to their house one day, and for a minute I would've sworn she was Teresa. It was like all the years had rolled away and Teresa had come back from the long ago. You've got no idea the way I felt."

Heather Winslow mused, "I can imagine. It would be as if Jim were to ride in here right now, come back to life." She frowned, "It could happen, you know . . . I mean, somebody could come along who looked like Jim, who talked like him. But it wouldn't *be* Jim. Nobody else could ever be him, no matter how much he looked like him, or how much I wanted him to be. Jim's dead. There's no use me looking for him."

Josh studied her over the cup. "Is the teacher tryin' to teach *me* somethin'?"

"Just this, Mister Buckalew: María is a woman with a love in her, and she'd be good for a man who really loved her. But a person who has room for so much love also has room for a lot of hurt. Don't you hurt her."

"I wouldn't for the world."

"You might, and not mean to. Be careful with her, Mister Buckalew."

AFTER SUPPER, María took a bucket and walked down toward the creek in the near darkness. Ocie Quitman sat on his heels by a small campfire, old Noonan's incessant rattling falling upon his ears but not penetrating the mental shield Quitman had raised. He watched the girl go out of sight over the creekbank. Quitman pushed to his feet, stretched, then began moving toward the line of trees, taking his time as if he had no place to go, nothing to do but exercise his legs. He walked down the creek bank and met María starting up, straining. "That looks heavy," he said. "I'll carry it for you."

She stood frozen in surprise, the bucket at arm's length.

He said again, "I'll take it."

"Why?"

"I told you. It's too heavy."

"I've been carrying buckets like this for years. I'll carry them the rest of my life."

"Well, I'll carry this one." He reached for it, and she gave it to him. He made no move to start up the bank, however. She stared, her eyes still showing surprise.

Finally she said experimentally, "How have you been, Mister Quitman?"

"All right. Been workin' awful hard."

"It seems to do you good. You look well."

"I look like a tired man older than I really am. But work's good for a man, especially if he's got heavy things on his mind. Keeps him too busy to worry much, or grieve. Work's a good healer."

"I suppose."

Frowning, he looked away from her. "Miss Hernandez, I followed you down here on purpose."

"For what reason?"

"To talk to you, to unload a little bit of guilt, maybe. I've said things I'm not proud of. I been wantin' you to know. I carried an awful anger, before. I've worked a lot of it off, I think."

"Have you changed your thinking, about . . . *things?*"

He shook his head. "I wouldn't lie to you. Some things burn so deep in a man that he can't root them out, no matter how much he'd like to. But I want you to know I'm sorry for the pain I've caused you. I had no right."

"I have no grudge against you, Mister Quitman."

"I didn't have the right. It was just in me to hurt you . . . to hurt *all* of you."

She shrugged. "That's all behind us. Anyway, you apologized before."

"The way I apologized was an insult in itself. I didn't mean it, and you could tell I didn't. Now I *do* mean it."

Her narrowed eyes held to his for a long time before a faint smile tugged at her mouth. He was hunched over, leaning strongly to the side where he held the bucket of water.

"That looks heavy, Mister Quitman. Maybe you should let me carry it."

He eased at the sight of her smile. A tiny hint of one crossed his face and disappeared, for smiling did not come easily to Ocie Quitman. "You've just taken a heavy load off of my shoulders, Miss Hernandez. I reckon I can carry the bucket."

JOSH KEPT the jugs hidden out and fetched them one at a time at a deliberate rate calculated to keep anyone from getting drunk. There was no stopping old man Noonan, though. For every swallow anyone else took, he took three. His Adam's apple bobbed up and down several times with each lifting of the jug. The more he drank, the wilder, louder, and more continuously he talked. It occurred to Josh finally that the old scoundrel probably had found his jug cache, so he had Muley slip out and move it. Surely enough, they were one jug shy. Old Noonan was hiding it out.

Against his protests Josh found the cabin getting completely out of hand. Aaron Provost virtually took over the project. What Josh had seen as a two-day job turned into quite a bit more, and his envisioned one-room cabin became a big double cabin with a liberal dog-run separating the two halves, one common roof over the whole structure. When the roof finally went up, it didn't lack much being as big as the one they had built for the Provosts.

To all of Josh's protests, Aaron waved his hand in dismissal. "One fine day you'll be bringin' María home to this place, and first thing you know there'll be some black-headed young'uns runnin' around and we'd all have to come back over and build it bigger anyway. Just as well do it now when we won't be in the way of nothin'.'"

So, up it went. The one armed Jacob Phipps mixed mortar and fitted stone and put up a fireplace in each section of the cabin, smiling in pride as he backed away to admire his handiwork. This was something he could do and do well despite the handicap war had thrust upon him.

Noonan and Sessum were out of sight half the time, sleeping on the creek bank. Noonan, in particular, had a lot to sleep off.

When the cabin was finished, Aaron Provost gathered the others around him and walked out a hundred feet, turning to look back in the dusk. He made a sweeping gesture with his hand. "What it lacks for purty, it sure makes up for stout. You can live to be a hundred and six, Josh, but you'll never have a better house."

Josh nodded his appreciation. "I don't know why I'd ever *want* a better one. All I can say is thank you."

"You're welcome. We owed it to you, and by johnny there can't nobody say a Texan don't pay his debts. It's all complete, Josh, floor to the roof. Got fireplaces, got tables and benches and a bed. All you lack now is a woman to put in it. That's somethin' you'll just have to take care of for yourself." Aaron squeezed María's shoulder. She looked down, her face reddening.

"There'll be time enough," Josh said.

"Not as much as you think, maybe," Aaron responded. "Winter's comin'. Fireplace ain't goin' to be enough to keep you warm."

Ocie Quitman watched María's face, and his eyebrows furrowed as he listened to Aaron's good-natured joking.

Aaron said, "Josh, you still got another jug hid out?"

"Just one more. That's all that's left."

"Let's get it, then. No house is finished proper till the builders have had them a chance to take a drink under its roof." Aaron put his arm around Josh's shoulder and pulled him toward the cabin. The others followed. Only María waited there, and Quitman. She stared at the new cabin, her dark eyes beginning to glisten.

Quitman's voice was quiet. "You oughtn't to be sheddin' tears, Miss Hernandez. It's a good house. From what I hear, it's goin' to be yours."

She shook her head. "That's what everybody says. Everybody but Josh."

"He hasn't asked you?"

"No."

"You want him to?"

She cut her gaze to him a moment. "For a long time I've wanted him to. Now I'm not sure anymore."

"I thought you were in love with him."

"I thought so too. I've thought so ever since I was a girl. But love has to come from two people . . . it can't be all with one."

"You don't think he loves you?"

"I think he thinks he does. But it isn't really me. It never was."

Quitman found himself walking slowly toward the cabin, beside her. Worriedly he asked, "So, what're you goin' to do about it?"

"What *can* I do? Wait till he asks me, then tell him we've both been wrong."

"It'll be a disappointment to him."

"At first, till he realizes I'm right."

"And this cabin, that's been built for you?"

"There will be another woman sometime, one who doesn't look like my sister Teresa . . . one he can love for herself and not for somebody else."

They were at the side of the cabin now. Quitman halted, hands flexing nervously. "María . . ." He broke off. Always before he had called her Miss Hernandez, if he had given her a name at all.

She turned. "Yes?"

"María, I lost somebody once. She didn't look anything like you." His chin dropped, and he groped for the right words. "I don't hardly know how to say it . . ."

Her face pinched. "I think I know what you're trying to say. Be careful . . ."

"María, I wronged you, and I worried over it. I couldn't figure out why it ought to bother me so much. The last few days here, seein' you all the time, I knew why."

"Mister Quitman, don't . . ."

"You got every cause to hate me; I got no right to expect anything else. And if I told you I'd lost all the feelin' I've had against your people, I'd be lyin' to you. But damn it, María, in spite of all that . . ."

She stared at him in painful silence.

He said, "The last few days I've fought it. My eyes have followed you everywhere you moved, and I've fought it. I didn't noway want it to happen, but it's happened anyhow. So, help me, María. Curse me . . . hit me. Do somethin' to make me stop bein' in love with you."

She said quietly, "I'm not sure I want to."

"It isn't any good. I oughtn't to've told you."

"You didn't have to. I've sensed it as long as you have."

"You must've been laughin' at me."

"No, it wasn't funny."

"Then you must've hated me."

Her fingers reached out and gently closed over his hand. "I don't hate you. I never did."

He took a step forward, close to her. He reached a hand behind her neck and pulled her toward him, bending. Her face turned upward, and her eyes closed as he found her lips. He kissed her with a cautious gentleness. Her arms went around him, and her mouth pressed tighter, and he cast away the caution, the gentleness. He let loose the pent-up anger and the hunger and the aching loneliness that had built so long. She gasped for breath.

A sharp voice jerked him back and brought him halfway around.

"María!"

Joshua Buckalew stood at the corner, face creased in surprise. "Quitman, what in the . . ."

Ocie Quitman turned loose of the girl and faced Josh. Josh seemed frozen in his tracks. Then he moved, fists clenched.

Quitman said, "Buckalew, it ain't like it looks . . ."

"Ain't it? María, you go in the cabin. He ain't goin' to bother you no more."

María didn't move. Her eyes were big and dark and frightened.

Josh swung his fist. It struck Quitman solidly on the chin and he staggered back into María. She tried to grab him, but he fell, almost tripping her when he went down. She cried out as Josh reached down to grab Quitman's shirt and haul him back to his feet. She grasped at Josh's hands. "Josh, don't do it . . . Don't . . ."

Josh wasn't listening to her. "Damn your soul, Quitman! After all the things you've said . . . and then you try to take her like this. I'll beat you to death."

María had hold of Josh's arm. "Josh, listen to me . . ."

Josh pulled away from her and struck Quitman again, sending him stumbling backward into the log wall. Quitman hunched there, shaking his head, clearing his eyes. Then the anger rushed into his face and he surged out swinging. The two men rammed into each other like a pair of bulls fighting. Arms muscled by hard work, hands toughened by rain and wind and sun, they swung and pounded and slashed and jabbed, one pushing awhile, the other giving ground, then reversing. They circled and fell and rolled and pushed to their feet and pounded again until their shirts hung in ribbons and blood streaked their faces like Indian war paint. They grunted and cursed and shouted in their anger. One went to his knees, and then the other. They fought until they were far out from the cabin, almost to the bank of the creek. At the end they were staggering, and each man almost fell every time he swung. Ocie Quitman finally stumbled and went to his knees and couldn't come up anymore. Josh teetered on the edge of the bank, trying to keep his footing, trying to focus his eyes, trying to find Quitman one more time.

Aaron Provost's strong voice broke through to him. "Josh, for God's sake, don't you think there's been enough?"

María Hernandez cried, "Josh, it's over."

Josh gritted stubbornly, "Where's he at?"

In fury María gave Josh a push that sent him stumbling backward over the bank and into the cold water of the creek. He splashed and floundered, sputtering. "There!" she cried. "Cool off a little!"

Weeping, she knelt to try to help Ocie Quitman to his feet. Bewildered, Ramón came to her aid. He got Quitman up, staggering. Aaron Provost strode over the bank and climbed down to extend a huge hand to Josh. "Boy, I got no idea what's happened between you two, but you sure have tore each other up. This is a hell of a way to celebrate a new cabin."

Jug in his hand, old Noonan was snickering to Dent Sessum. "It's that gal, Dent. They'll do it every time. I been knowin' Mexican gals for years and years, and that's the way they'll do you. Hug and kiss and sweet-do you while you're there, and the minute you're out of sight they're flashin' their eyes at somebody else."

Ramón Hernandez reached down for a handful of mud from the edge of an old rain puddle. Noonan's mouth was wide open when Ramón came up with his hand and plopped the mud in. The old man coughed and spluttered and cursed.

Aaron brought Josh up out of the creek. Ocie Quitman waited there, leaning on María's thin shoulder for strength. Their eyes met, anger still crackling in Josh's. But the anger had burned out of Quitman. The ashes held only a cold regret.

"I didn't mean it to happen, Buckalew. But God help me, I'm in love with your Mexican girl."

CHAPTER

12

THE FESTIVE mood which had lasted through the building of the cabin was gone like summer smoke. Even the children sensed the change and bedded down quietly, the play gone out of them. Ocie Quitman moved his bedroll out beyond anyone else's, and though he awakened with morning's first light and rolled up his blankets, he made no move toward the house. He sat out there alone, brooding, his gaze lost in the light fog which masked off the sunrise.

Old Alfred Noonan held his head in his hands as he raised up in his blankets beside the corral and watched Quitman, half hoping there might be another fight but knowing there wouldn't be. That was why Quitman was staying out there by himself.

"Damn," Noonan complained hoarsely, "looks like Buckalew could've got a better grade of drinkin'-whisky, us buildin' him a cabin and all."

Dent Sessum only groaned and turned over. Noonan pushed him with his foot. "Dent, stir yourself."

Sessum raised up irritably, blinking in a sleepy confusion. "What the hell's the matter?"

Noonan shook his head. "Ain't nothin' the matter. All of a sudden I got me a notion things is fixin' to get better." He could see

Ramón Hernandez up and moving around, loading his high-wheeled cart.

Sessum rubbed his forehead and whispered some choice words about how it felt like somebody was splitting his head with a chopping ax.

Noonan growled. "You ain't no worse off than me. I got an awful taste in my mouth this mornin'. Can't figure out whether it's like bad whisky or black mud."

"Mud, likely. You got the Mexican to thank for that."

Noonan scowled and cut a hard glance toward the distant Ramón. "And I do intend to thank him good and proper. Man can't go around lettin' them chili-eaters get away with insults, or first thing you know they'll think they own this country again."

Sessum's eyes were rimmed with red. "What you intend to do about it?"

Noonan looked around him furtively. "Dent, I think I've figured out somethin' that'll be good for both of us. Me, I got a grudge to settle with Ramón, and anyway, I just don't like Mexicans. You, you been wantin' to buy that piece of land from him but he won't listen. I bet his *widow* would listen."

"He ain't got no widow."

"He's fixin' to have. It could happen today . . . this very mornin'."

Sessum blinked, trying to absorb the meaning of it all, but it was too big for him.

Noonan said, "Everybody's had Indians on the brain since that raid over at the Hernandez place. Now, if somebody was to shoot Ramón, who do you reckon would catch the blame for it?"

"The Comanch."

"You're soberin' up, Dent. Now, the way I see it, them Mexicans'll eat breakfast pretty soon and start home. Way things went to hell here last night, they'll be wantin' to leave. We could do the same, only we could double back, ride in the creek aways to lose our tracks, then lay in wait where the brush comes up close to the trail. After it's done, we just follow the creek till we lose our tracks again, then we go on home with nobody the wiser, and Ramón Hernandez a hell of a lot deader."

"What'll Jacob Phipps think?"

"He don't need to know. We come here without him; we can leave without him."

Sessum rubbed his chin, his eyes gradually coming alive. "It's a pleasure to know you, Noonan. I'm proud to ride with a man who uses his head for somethin' besides a place to put his hat. You goin' to give me first shot?"

"Think you're sober enough to hit him?"

"I'll *be* sober enough, if there's one more drink left in that jug." Sessum pawed around beneath the blankets. Finding the jug, he tipped it up and shook it. But they'd been too diligent the night before. It was empty.

Sourly Noonan said, "Looks like a host would see to it he had enough whisky so a man didn't run out."

As a smuggler and a filibusterer in Texas even before the days of Stephen F. Austin, old Noonan had done his share of fighting against Mexican soldiers and customs officers as well as against Indians. When Dent Sessum started to tie his horse in the brush, the old man impatiently grabbed the reins. "Damn it, Dent, you're as green as a gourd vine. Your horse is liable to jerk loose when the shootin' starts and leave you afoot. Tie a rope to your reins and hang onto it. That way you always got hold of him."

Noonan showed Sessum how to tie a length of rawhide *reata* to his reins, then loop the end over his arm. "A horse is lots of things, but smart ain't one of them. He don't like a rifle goin' off in his face. This way you get far enough from him that he don't spook so bad. You got both arms free, and still you don't let him run loose."

A thin fog still clung to the ground and obscured the view of anything more than fifty yards away. They crouched a long time in the brush, till Dent Sessum's legs went stiff. His fingers played nervously up and down the stock of his long rifle. "Sure do wish I had me another jug."

"You'd be drinkin' out of it, and you couldn't shoot straight."

"Why don't they hurry up and come on? You sure we got out ahead of them, Noonan? They could've already passed this way."

Noonan gritted, "Calm down, Dent. You're gettin' the shakes, and that ain't goin' to help none. They'll be along directly."

Sessum hunched his shoulders. "I swear it's gettin' cold. Fall ain't far enough along for it to be this cold."

"It's just you. You got the trembles from that whisky wearin' off. Scared, Dent?"

"What I got to be scared of?"

"Nothin'. That's what I'm tryin' to tell you. A Mexican's easy to kill. Just send a bullet whistlin' by his ear and he'll die of fright."

"That ain't the way I heard tell about the war."

"Folks lie. There ain't nothin' to killin' a Mexican. You'll see. Square yourself up."

From east it came, out of the fog, the wailing of wooden wheels rubbing against a wooden axle. Noonan turned in triumph. "See what I told you, Dent? You can hear one of them Mexican carts a mile away. Now, you get ahold of yourself."

They crouched lower and waited. Sessum's hands still played nervously up and down the rifle stock and on the barrel. Cold sweat popped out on his forehead, and he rubbed his sleeved arm across his face.

Noonan turned and frowned at him. "Dent, you sure you still want the first shot? Maybe I better take it."

Sessum shook his head. "I've took a right smart off of him too. I've took it off *all* of them. I want my bullet in him first."

Noonan shrugged. "All right, but don't you miss."

The groaning of the wheels came louder. Both men squinted and tried to see into the fog. Sessum's tongue darted back and forth across dry lips, and again he rubbed his sleeve over his face.

Noonan pointed. "There they come. You can see them now."

Ramón Hernandez rode his brown horse a little in front of the cart. He held a rifle balanced across his lap. His head moved slowly from left to right as his gaze swept the patches of brush that lay on either side of the trail. It touched the thick oak where Noonan and Sessum crouched, but they were hidden by the heavy green foliage.

The two Mexican women and the children rode in the cart, all but the boy Gregorio. He trailed behind, a-horseback. In his hands was an old blunderbuss.

Noonan whispered, "Now, Dent, you just move slow, and don't be in no hurry. He'll be in your sights plenty long enough."

Sessum licked his lips nervously and leveled the rifle, resting its long barrel across a limb. He blinked hard, turned his cheek to wipe the sweat onto his shoulder, then returned to the sights. His hands trembled.

"Wait, Dent . . ." Noonan warned. "You're goin' to miss."

But Sessum jerked the trigger. The rifle belched.

Noonan spat in disgust. "See there, Dent, I told you; you missed him." Noonan brought his own rifle into line. The children were screaming, and Ramón reined around to lope back to the cart. In the swirling confusion Noonan took aim at what he thought was Ramón. After the roar of the rifle, he heard a high-pitched scream. Through the black smoke he saw a small figure lurch forward in the cart. "Hit one of the women," Noonan hissed. The horses danced in fright, jerking against the reins looped over Noonan's and Sessum's arms.

A ball tore through the leaves over their heads. Noonan gritted, "He'll be comin' in a minute, that Mexican. If he sees us, we'll have to kill them all."

"What'll we do?"

"We've spilt our chance. We better be gettin' the hell up and gone."

Rifles still empty, they swung onto the horses and moved out in a lope. Noonan looked back over his shoulder, thankful for the fog. "One good thing," he muttered, "he'll move cautious, thinkin' we was a passel of Indians. It'll give us time to clear out."

They rode in a hard run for a few hundred yards, then slowed to an easier lope to spare the horses. After a couple of miles they gradually came to a stop. Noonan turned his head so that his right ear was toward the direction from which they had come.

Sessum asked anxiously, "Hear anything?"

"Only you. My old ears ain't the best anyhow. Maybe you better listen for both of us."

Sessum stood in the stirrups, turning his head slowly. "Quiet as a grave."

Noonan nodded in satisfaction. "Didn't figure he'd come chasin' us and leave the women and kids. Especially, him not knowin' but what we was Indians."

Sessum frowned. "I seen that woman fall. You shot her instead of Ramón, didn't you?"

Noonan shrugged. "Ain't no way to tell. Never pleasured me none to kill a woman, but them Mexican women breed more little ones anyway, and little ones grow into big ones, and we'd just have to kill them someday."

They rode west until they struck a creek, then rode down the bank into the water. They rode in the water's edge for a couple of miles, glancing back occasionally for sign of pursuit. Noonan saw no reason there ought to be, and he found no evidence of any.

Finally he said "I reckon we been far enough. Let's get up out of this creek and head for home."

"Suits me," Sessum replied, and reined his horse around. He touched spurs to him and climbed up the steep bank, Noonan trailing. As he reached the top, Sessum suddenly jerked on the reins.

"Noonan!" he shouted in terror.

An arrow thumped into his chest and drove halfway through. Before he had time to fall, another arrow thudded between his ribs. His eyes rolled back and he slipped out of the saddle, tumbling, skidding, sliding down the muddy bank.

Sessum's horse lost its footing and slid back into Noonan's with an impact that jarred the old man loose from the saddle. Still gripping his rifle, he slammed against the muddy ground and pushed himself to his feet. He grabbed at the reins, but the horse broke away from him and ran. He shouted at Sessum's horse, which almost ran him down in its mad break to escape.

Mouth open, Noonan stood on wobbly legs and stared in helpless fear at the half dozen riders who suddenly towered above him on the creekbank. He got a glimpse of feathers and bare chests and bows, of gotch-eared ponies and bull-hide shields. He raised the rifle and remembered he never had taken time to reload it. Dropping it, he turned to run in the soft mud. A sharp pain stopped him in mid-stride. He grabbed at his side and felt his fingers clasp the shaft of an arrow, imbedded between his ribs. The numbness passed and the pain rushed on with the sudden intensity of hellfire. He tried again to run but found his legs would not bend, his feet would not move. He heard the thump of another arrow and felt it like the blow of a huge hammer against his back.

Twisting half around, Noonan stared in wordless horror at the warrior heeling his pony down the bank and coming at him in a run. He stared in deadly fascination at the heavy stone ax in the Indian's hand. He saw the strong brown arm come up. His eyes followed the downward arc of the stone as it swung savagely toward his head. The last sound he heard was his own terrified scream.

Heather Winslow came back into the cabin with a plate and an empty coffee cup. She was shaking her head. "Mister Quitman didn't eat much. Said he wasn't hungry. Drank the coffee, was about all."

Joshua Buckalew sat frowning down at his heavy cowhide boots. He said nothing.

Heather added, "He wants to know how long before we're ready to leave. He's impatient."

Aaron Provost grunted and turned to look sharply at Josh. "Ain't no use you two partin' with this thing hangin' over you. Sooner or later you both got to come to some understandin'. Why not start now and get done with it?"

Irritably Josh said, "What's there to talk about? We try to talk, like as not we'll end up fightin' again. He done what he done, and that's all there is to it."

Aaron argued, "He didn't go to. You ought to know him well enough to realize that of all the women on earth, María would be one of the last he'd want to fall in love with. Man just can't always help himself."

Josh arose and impatiently slapped a hand against his hip. "The whole subject pains me. I'd as soon not talk no more."

Aaron shrugged. He glanced around for his wife. "Rebecca, you got them kids about all ready to go? No use us wastin' any more time around here. It's a long ways."

"You and the boys can load the wagon," she said, her level gaze on Josh rather than on her husband. Josh couldn't tell whether she sympathized with him or blamed him. In the lingering of hurt and anger, he couldn't bring himself to care much.

He said, "I appreciate all you done, buildin' me this cabin. I'm sorry things went to hell at the last."

Aaron grimaced. "Life's thataway. 'Bout the time you figure you finally got everything on a downhill pull, somethin' comes along and stands you on your head." He walked out of the cabin, paused in the dog-run to frown at the lingering fog, then strode on out into the yard, hollering orders at the young ones. Most times Josh would have helped them tote their goods to the wagon, but this morning it wasn't in him. He leaned against the log wall and watched disconsolately. He hated to see them all leave; yet, he wanted to be alone awhile, to think things clear. A man couldn't study a problem out with people waiting around to hear what his decision was.

Josh cast a glance toward Ocie Quitman, who sat on his rolled blankets way out yonder. His fists knotted, and he found them painfully sore. *Dammit*, he thought with a surge of self-anger, *keep control of yourself. The world hasn't come to an end yet.*

It came to him that Aaron had been right about one thing. Feeling the way he did about Mexican people, Ocie Quitman wouldn't have wanted to let himself develop any feeling for María Hernandez . . . not even a passing physical desire, much less anything stronger or more lasting. Josh let his gaze follow Quitman as the man pushed to his feet and began to pace restlessly. *Bet he feels guilty about the whole thing. The kind of pride he's got, it probably torments his soul to find out just how human he really is.*

Under other circumstances, Josh might have found it in himself to pity Quitman, even. If it had been some other Mexican girl . . . But not María. *He's not good enough for her. After all the things he's said, he's not fit to walk the same ground where she's been.*

Daniel Provost brought up the horses and began to help Aaron harness the team. Ocie Quitman came near the cabin for the first time and saddled his own horse. He carefully avoided looking at Josh.

Heather Winslow stopped beside Joshua Buckalew and fidgeted, plainly wanting to say something but finding nothing that didn't sound hollow to her. "It's a good house, Mister Buckalew. And this thing with María . . . you'll get it straightened out. I never met a better girl."

"Thank you." He was surprised at the hoarseness of his voice. "I'm sorry you had to be around and see it. I expect you were disappointed with Ocie Quitman . . . and with me."

"I'll live over it, Mister Buckalew. And so will you."

She walked out to the wagon and helped Patrick Quitman up into the bed of it, with the Provost youngsters. Muley stood there, sadly telling them all goodbye. Aaron Provost gave each of the two women a lift up, then placed his foot on the right front wheel and swung his big frame onto the seat. "Come over when you can, Josh. We'll shoot a fat doe." He hollered at the team, and the wagon began to roll.

Ocie Quitman sat on his horse, waiting for the wagon to come even with him. When it did, he pulled in beside it, Daniel Provost a-horseback on the other side. Quitman looked back over his shoulder at Josh. He rode a few yards, pulled around, and came to the cabin.

"Buckalew . . ."

Josh watched him distrustfully. "Yes?"

"Buckalew, I . . ." Quitman broke off, his face twisting. He held silent a moment, then said bitterly, "Aw, hell, what can a man say?" He turned and started after the wagon.

The first shot came from somewhere out in the fog, a long way off. Josh stiffened. He heard another shot, and a third, in quick succession.

Three guns. Even counting the old blunderbuss, Ramón had left here with only two. The fog seemed to close in on Josh. A hard chill paralyzed him. "Quitman, they're in trouble."

Quitman's face was grave. "Get your horse."

Aaron Provost wheeled the wagon around and brought his team back in a long trot. He shouted, "Daniel, give me your horse. You women and kids . . . back into the cabin!"

Josh told Muley to help Daniel guard the cabin. Quitman was out forty yards in the lead when Josh and Aaron and Jacob Phipps swung into their saddles. Josh spurred hard to catch up. Aaron and Phipps never did catch up, quite.

The cart's tracks were easy to follow, the wheels having pressed the curing grass deep into the soft, wet ground. Riding in a run, Josh listened for other shots. He heard none. Why hadn't there been more? The question ran again and again through his brain. Maybe they'd been overrun. He could think of several reasons, and he didn't like any of them.

Once he glimpsed Quitman's face and found it as fearful as his own.

Through the fog he saw the dark shape that must be the cart. "Yonder, Quitman, ahead of us."

They slowed their horses to a trot, wary, and only then did Aaron and Phipps catch up. Rifle cradled high, ready for trouble, Josh squinted, trying to see. The fog drifted a little, and he could make out the huddle of figures around the cart.

"There! They look like they're all right."

Ramón whirled, the rifle in his hands. He lowered it as recognition came. "Careful," he called. "They may still be around here."

Josh heard some of the children sobbing. He tried to see through the tight group of frightened figures. "Ramón, is everybody all right?"

The Mexican's face answered him before his voice did. "Josh, María is shot."

Josh hit the ground and dropped the reins. The children pulled aside to make room for him, but they stayed close to the cart, crouched in fear. María lay still.

"María!" Josh dropped to one knee. Miranda Hernandez gave him a quick glance, and he could see dread in her eyes. She had torn open the neck of María's dress and was pressing a crimson-soaked handkerchief to a wound above María's breast. Tears streaked Miranda's face. "It is bad, Josh."

Josh lifted the handkerchief. He gasped as he saw the ragged hole which a rifleball had torn. He put the handkerchief back in place. "Did it go all the way through?"

Miranda shook her head. "The ball is still in there."

"Then we got to get her to the cabin, and quick."

He looked up, and his gaze stopped at Ocie Quitman. The man's face was drained of color.

Aaron Provost was asking, "Ramón, where was they shootin' from?"

Ramón pointed toward the brush. In his nervousness he made no effort at English. "There. Two shots. I fired back one time. I heard two horses run away."

"Reckon they're all gone?"

"I have not tried to go and see."

Quitman's voice was cold. "*I'll* go see." He started walking.

Aaron shouted, "Quitman, if they're there, they'll kill you!"

Quitman did not slow down or look back. He kept walking, the rifle up and ready. He moved stiffly, as if whittled from wood.

María groaned. Voice breaking, Josh could only whisper. "You'll be all right, María, I promise. You'll be all right." He bent down and placed his cheek against her forehead, his eyes afire.

From out in the brush, Quitman called, "They're gone."

Cautiously Aaron and Jacob Phipps followed him. Josh looked up and saw Ramón through a blur. "Ramón, let's put her into the cart." They rolled out blankets to make as soft a bed as possible. It would be a rough ride back to the cabin, for there was no kind of spring or leather sling on these Mexican carts to take up any of the shock. By the time they had placed María on the blankets, the other three men were back.

Ocie Quitman looked gravely at the girl. "How is she?"

Josh shook his head. "Bad."

Quitman's chin dropped. His eyes were hidden by the brim of his hat. When he looked up again, his face was dark with a fury Josh had never seen. His voice was quiet and deadly. "It wasn't Indians. We found boot-heel marks out there, and tobacco juice."

Jacob Phipps said regretfully, "It was Dent Sessum and old Noonan."

Aaron said, "They must've thought we'd never look at their tracks. They been drinkin'; maybe they didn't think at all."

Ramón's eyes filled with tears. "They must have been after me. They hit María instead."

Josh held the girl's shock-cold hand. "We'll settle with them later. Let's get María back where we can take care of her."

Quitman reached out. "You got a pistol in your belt, Buckalew. I want it."

"What for?"

"I'm not waitin'. I'm goin' after them now. I can't go up against two men with just a rifle. Whichever one I shot, the other would get me while I reloaded."

"We'll all go, Quitman, together. But first we got to think of María."

"I *am* thinkin' of her, and I'm thinkin' of them that shot her. You stay with her, Buckalew. It's your place; she's your girl. She always was." Quitman reached and took the pistol out of Josh's belt.

Josh could see murder in his eyes. "We could be wrong. It could've been somebody else. It's the government's place to pass judgment."

"We're not wrong. And we got no government, not out here. I'll see you when I get back. You take good care of that girl, Buckalew."

Jacob Phipps blocked Quitman's path. "You figurin' on shootin' them wherever you find them?"

"Like a pair of killer wolves."

"I'll go with you, Quitman."

"Old Noonan's a friend of yours, ain't he, Phipps?"

"He used to be."

"Then you stay here. I don't want to fight *three* men." He shoved Phipps aside. Phipps called, "Wait, Quitman."

Quitman turned, eyes narrowed. "Don't you give me no trouble, Phipps." He stood a moment, his terrible eyes boring into Phipps until Phipps' chin dropped. Quitman swung onto his horse, rode out to the brush, paused a moment, then moved into the fog, following the tracks.

Phipps looked after him, frowning. "Old Noonan's a big talker and all, but he *has* been a fighter in his time. He'd fight again if Quitman was to corner him."

Josh said, "If we get the bullet out, and if we can tell María is goin' to do all right, we'll go help Quitman."

"That may not be soon enough. I think I'd best trail after him."

"You worried about him, or about Noonan?"

Phipps shrugged. "Both, I reckon. There was a time I thought a right smart of that old man, even with all his faults. I'd rather see him take his chances with a court than have Quitman shoot him down like a mad dog."

"There's no stoppin' Quitman right now. He's after blood."

"Maybe he'll cool off before he catches them. Anyway, I'll trail along."

Phipps rode off into the fog.

JOSH RODE in the cart, holding María's cold hand, feeling tears burn his eyes each time she moaned. Every little bit he would take up the handkerchief to let the blood wash the wound clean, then put it back again. Without help, she would have bled to death before now. Times, when he felt he was going to break down, Miranda would reach across and grip his arm. For a little woman, Ramón's wife had a lot of strength. "Faith, Josh. Faith."

They carried María into the cabin, the white-faced Rebecca Provost and Heather Winslow rushing ahead to clear a place for her. "The table," Josh said breathlessly. "We got to put her on the table and get the bullet out. You-all get some hot water started."

Aaron had planed down some boards riven from logs and had built Josh a heavy table, held together with stout pegs. Josh and Ramón placed María there on blankets Heather had spread. Josh stood back, looking down on the still girl.

"We got to dig that bullet out. Who's goin' to do it?"

Everybody looked at somebody else. All eyes came back to Josh. He shook his head. "You women—you got skilled fingers."

Rebecca demurred. "It'll take a man to have the stomach for it."

Josh looked in vain to Ramón, for he could see Ramón beginning to weep. Aaron raised his own trembling hands. "A thing like this, Josh, I got ten thumbs. It's up to you."

María's eyes came partially open. She tried to speak, but the words were unclear. Josh leaned over anxiously. "Don't talk now, *querida*."

"Ocie . . ." she murmured. "Where is Ocie?"

Josh swallowed and looked away. Quietly he said, "He's around."

"I want him. I want him here."

A taste came to Josh's mouth, a taste like gall. But he whispered: "He'll be here, María. Don't you fret; he'll be here."

She lapsed back into unconsciousness. Cold sweat broke on Josh's face. "I don't know if I can do it."

"You operated on that bushwacker boy," Aaron said.

"And he died."

When the water was hot, he picked up a knife with a stiletto blade. He had to go by feel rather than sight because the blood kept welling up. Each time his hands started to tremble, he paused, taking a deep breath or two. And while he worked, he prayed. María stirred, the pain reaching her through her unconsciousness. Once Josh thought he would have to give up, for sickness rolled in his stomach. But from somewhere he took strength to keep on. And finally the ball came out. He dropped it, and it rolled against his boot on the dirt floor. He realized he'd held his breath a long, long time. He let out what had been compressed in his lungs and took a deep breath of fresh air. He let the wound bleed a moment to wash it clean, then called for a hot iron to sear it over. María lunged against him and cried out, then went limp.

Josh's tears flowed unchecked. "Jesus, don't let her die again!"

CHAPTER

14

Sitting in a rough chair beside the bed, he heard a horse running. He raised his head to listen. He blinked the haze from his burning eyes and saw that Aaron and Ramón were listening too. Aaron went to the door.

"Can't see him for the fog. Way he's ridin', there's somethin' wrong."

There's a lot wrong, Josh thought numbly. *There's an awful lot wrong.* He pushed stiffly to his feet and dragged himself across the dirt floor to stand beside Aaron. Ramón had stepped into the yard. Jacob Phipps broke out of the fog, splashing across the creek and up the steep bank.

"Quitman's in trouble!" he shouted. "Indians!"

Josh heard, but he was too numb to move. It took a moment for the message to soak in on him.

Phipps shouted, "They got him cornered up in the limestone bluffs. I don't know how long he can hold out."

Aaron grabbed his rifle and went out the door. "How many?"

"Couldn't tell for the fog, not for sure. Seven or eight, maybe ten. Too many, that's for certain."

Ramón came for his rifle. He paused. "Josh, you coming?"

Josh looked at the girl. She hadn't moved or moaned or anything since he had seared the wound. Her face was almost gray. "María . . ." He clenched his fist. "We can't leave her now." Resentment came in an angry rush. "Dammit, he got himself into this. We tried to tell him."

"Maybe you should stay, then. We'll go to Quitman."

Josh touched the girl's hand and found it cold as ever. But there was still a pulse. "I don't want to leave her, Ramón. But she'd want me to go. Wait, and I'll get my rifle."

He rode hunched, his mind and soul still in that cabin and only the shell of him out here on horseback, riding in the fall chill. He only half heard Jacob Phipps telling what had happened.

"I trailed along behind him aways, and he must've caught on. All of a sudden he rode out from behind a live oak tree with his rifle on me and told me to get away and stay away, or he was liable to put a rifle ball through my other arm. I tell you, I was sore tempted to come on back. But I decided maybe I still ought to be around, so I let him have a long start, and I trailed him again. He come to the creek. The tracks led off down into the water. I reckon he figured the same as I did, that they was tryin' to throw off anybody that might come after them. But bein' who they was, they'd head in the general direction of Noonan's cabin. Quitman's tracks led thataway, so I followed.

"It was the fog that saved me when the Indians jumped him. They was so interested in him that they didn't see me. He must've had a little warnin', because I heard his horse runnin' before they ever started to whoopin'. He took out across the creek and headed west toward the bluffs, them Indians after him like hounds after a rabbit. There was too many of them for me to help him. I trailed along till I knowed he made the bluffs. I heard him fire a shot or two. After that, I turned and came back here." Phipps was apologetic. "I'd of stayed if there'd of been anything I could do. But they had him hemmed, and I couldn't have got through to him."

Aaron said, "You done the right thing."

Phipps turned to Josh. "How's the girl?"

Josh shook his head. "I don't know. I just don't know."

They came to the creek, and Josh could see the tracks where the Indians had gone up the opposite bank. Ramón pointed. "They were coming down the creek. Quitman was going up the creek, following Sessum and Noonan."

That brought Josh up with a shudder. "Then the Indians must've run into Sessum and Noonan before they found Quitman."

Phipps shivered. "I thought of that awhile ago. I figure Quitman wasted his trip. Them Indians likely already done to Sessum and Noonan what *he* was intendin' to do. *More,* even."

Josh managed to collect his wits. Perhaps what brought him to reality was the brutal certainty of what must have happened to that hapless pair of scoundrels. He wondered if it had been quick, or if the Indians had taken their time. When they weren't in any hurry, the Comanches had their ways. It wasn't a thing Josh would wish on anybody. But thinking of María, the cold clay color of her face when he had left her, he didn't care whether death had come quickly or not for Sessum and Noonan. He found no sympathy.

A vagrant thought ran through his mind: that hidden money wouldn't do Sessum any good now. Or anybody else, either. Chances were it would never be found.

Josh knew the bluffs Phipps had spoken of. He had sought wild cattle here many times, and mustangs. This ground was almost as familiar to him as his own yard and fields that he had plowed and harvested and built his cabin upon. "It's not far anymore," he said cautiously. "We better spread out a little and keep a careful watch. We don't want them jumpin' us by surprise. We'd rather have it the other way."

It worried him, the fact that by Phipps' account the Indians had them somewhat outnumbered. Josh had long heard people brag that a white man was the equal of several Indians in a fight, but he had taken that as idle boasting. The few hostile Indians he'd met hadn't been anything to mess around with. If Quitman was still alive, the best chance they had to rescue him was by using their one bit of leverage—surprise.

Somewhere ahead of them, he heard a shot. He saw some of the anxiety lift from Aaron's face. The farmer edged over to Josh. "Quitman's rifle. I know the sound of it. They ain't got him yet."

Josh eased a little. "He's likely found him a good place with the bluff to his back. They can't get to him except straight on."

Aaron nodded. "The Comanch, he loves a good fight, long as he knows he's goin' to win it. But he don't fancy suicide. They're probably just laid up there, figurin' on wearin' him down."

"Quitman's got his rifle and my pistol," Josh reasoned. "Long's he don't let both of them get empty at the same time, they'll show him a lot of respect. They know that sooner or later he's either got to come out or starve. Time don't mean much to an Indian."

Phipps said nervously, "Right now we need old Sam Houston to general for us. I don't like suicide any more than the Comanches do."

Josh found all the men looking to him for leadership. He didn't want it. He wasn't sure he knew enough to give it to them. He had no plan. All he'd thought of was that Quitman was trapped, and it was up to them to get him out of trouble. How, he didn't know.

Finally he said, "Since we know he's still there, let's go easy; take our time and figure how we can do this right. Fog ought to let us get in pretty close."

They rode in silence, Josh watching for the outline of the bluffs to begin showing. Presently he heard another shot. Quitman's rifle. It occurred to him that the Indians probably had no guns, for he hadn't heard any. Only a scattered few rifles had fallen into Indian hands by trade, plus an occasional one stolen in a raid or taken from a murdered white man. Most Indians still didn't know how to load and fire a rifle even if they came into possession. But the bow could be as deadly as a rifle, within its range. Even more so, in one way, for a Comanche could unleash several arrows while a white man was reloading a rifle for just one more shot.

They were near the bluffs now. Josh knew, though he could not yet see them. He raised his hand for a halt. He leaned forward in the saddle, listening. He couldn't hear anything. He pushed on, slower now, watching where his horse stepped, keeping him away from rocks that he might kick and cause a noise. Josh's hand tightened on the stock of his rifle. He found himself breathing faster.

Then, from out in the fog, he heard the restless stamping of horses' hoofs. He held up his hand again and halted to listen. Somewhere up there, he reasoned, the Indians' horses were being held in a safe place away from fire. Josh swung down from the saddle and looked back. "Ramón," he whispered, "you want to go with me? Aaron, you and Jacob watch after our horses."

Ramón beside him, Josh walked carefully, watching his footing, peering cautiously through the fog. At length he saw something move, and he dropped to one knee, pointing. Ramón nodded.

There were the Indian horses. As the fog drifted, Josh glimpsed an Indian a-horseback, tending them. The brave's attention was not on the horses, however; he was looking westward, where the bluffs lay. After a few moments another rifle shot echoed against the unseen limestone walls, and the horses stirred restlessly.

Josh whispered, "He's not lookin' for any trouble from thisaway."

Ramón said, "You want to try to get him? I could use my knife."

Josh shook his head. "Not yet. If somethin' went wrong, he might raise an alarm before we're ready. Let's ease around him and see how the rest of them are spread out."

Crouching, they moved at a tangent from the Indian horses, carefully keeping to the live oak brush for cover, because now and again the fog drifted enough to leave them exposed for anyone who happened to be looking in their direction. In a little while the picture was clear to Josh. As he had expected, the warriors had spread themselves in a ragged line just back from Quitman's position at the base of the bluff. He was bottled up in there like whisky stoppered in a jug. Josh couldn't see him, though once he caught the flash of the rifle. He pointed, and Ramón nodded. He had seen too. Josh made a sign for retreat.

When they were back with Aaron and Phipps, Josh knelt and brushed away the mat of old live oak leaves and acorns so he could draw a rough map on the ground. "This here is the bluff. Right here is Quitman. The Comanches are scattered along like this . . . here, and here, and here. We couldn't see them all, but we took a count on their horses. There was ten, plus Quitman's." He glanced at Phipps. "Two of them horses belonged to Sessum and Noonan."

Phipps grimaced. "I figured that."

"If all the Indians was mounted to start with, and they picked up Sessum's and Noonan's horses extra, that comes out to eight men."

Aaron counted on his fingers. "Four of us. That's two to one."

"Quitman makes five. From where he's at, he can help."

Aaron frowned. "Never did go much for Indian-fightin', not even when the odds was in our favor."

"We got no choice, except to leave Quitman there. Likely these are braves out on a horse raid. If we don't stop them here they'll come on and hit one of us anyway . . . maybe all of us. We'll still have to fight."

Phipps asked, "You got a plan, Josh?"

Josh shrugged. "Not much. We just hit them and hope the surprise makes up for the difference in numbers."

Ramón said regretfully in Spanish, "Lately it seems all we've done is fight. The war, first. Then Mexican army stragglers, then that group of Redland renegades. Now the Indians."

Josh said, "It's a raw country. If we stay here there'll be more fightin' yet before we've won this land free and clear. And I intend to stay!"

Ramón replied, "If I fight now, perhaps my sons will never have to."

"Everybody has to fight, in his own way and in his own time. You're all ready to go, I hope."

They made a long arc to the left, walking their mounts slowly and watchfully. At length Josh put up his hand. "We've got them outflanked now. From here we can ride in on them and take them one at a time. The horses will be yonder." He pointed. "We'll rush the horses first and drive them right in on top of the Indians. If that don't confuse them, nothin' will."

He started to go on, but he hesitated. There was one more thing which needed to be said. His gaze moved from one man to another, and he spoke gravely. "Quitman's just one man. If he lives but one of us dies, we haven't gained anything. We've just swapped lives. I'm no hero and got no wish to ever be one. Let's just hit them hard and fast and make as little target as we can get by with."

They moved into a trot toward the horses. From up against the bluff, the rifle fired again. *Good,* thought Josh, *that'll hold their attention for a minute.* He leaned forward, straining to see the horses. When suddenly they showed through the fog, he saw that the Indian guarding them was still mounted, looking toward the cliff. Josh touched spurs to his horse and moved into a run.

Hearing him, the Indian turned, surprised. For a second or two he stared in disbelief. Then he brought up his bow with his left hand as his right hand reached back for an arrow from his quiver. Before the arrow touched the bowstring, Josh plowed into him. He drove the rifle butt into the warrior's ribs, then swung it up and jammed it against the chin. Grunting, the Indian slid over his horse's side, still clutching the bow, trying to bring the arrow to the string. Then Ramón was there, knife blade flashing. He leaned out of the saddle, the knife streaking down and coming up red.

The horses shied away, moving toward the Indians. Josh waved his hat and shouted. The other men started shouting, too. The horses broke into a run.

The first Indian jumped up from behind a scrub oak, consternation in his eyes. Not quite comprehending, he waved his arms and shouted, trying to turn the horses. They split around him. Josh's rifle butt slashed, and the Indian fell.

The racket stirred the others, who could not see clearly through the fog but knew instinctively that something had gone wrong. One by one the running horses sped past them or split around them. An arrow sang past Josh, and he saw an Indian whipping another arrow into place. Josh fired, knowing as he did so that for the rest of this run he was carrying an empty rifle. Well, by George, at least it would make a damn good club. He spurred and shouted and fell right in behind the running horses.

Another Indian arose, arrow fitted. Josh dropped down over his horse's off-shoulder. He felt the impact as it struck his saddle, and a sudden burn told him it had at least creased his thigh. Another shot sounded behind him. The Indian fell.

Two shots gone. Only two shots left among us.

His horse stumbled, almost fell, caught its footing, and ran again. But its movement was labored, and Josh saw the arrow driven into its shoulder.

I'll be lucky to finish this run before he falls.

In front of him, behind him, he could see the bewildered Indians, loosing arrows. The horse stumbled. Josh kicked free of the stirrups and hit the ground rolling, holding onto his rifle. He heard the rip of cloth and realized the arrow which grazed his thigh had pinned him to the saddle. He jumped to his feet, hopping, looking around desperately. He held the rifle in both hands, like a club.

Through the fog he had a clear view of the bluff now. He saw an Indian rise up and take aim at him, too far away for the clubbed rifle to help him. Partway up the bluff, fire flashed, and the Indian fell.

Then Phipps reined up beside him. "Up, Josh. Hurry!"

He offered Josh an empty stirrup, and Josh swung up behind him.

Ramón Hernandez spurred to the base of the cliff. Ocie Quitman clambored down to meet him. Ramón leaned over, extending his arm. Quitman caught it and swung up, landing on the horse's hips. An Indian came running to stop them. Ramón fired. The Indian dropped his bow and sank to his knees.

One shot left, Josh thought. *Wonder who has it?*

Aaron Provost slowed to wait for Ramón and Quitman. As a Comanche stepped from behind a live oak, Aaron squeezed off a shot. It missed, but it clipped leaves above the Comanche's head and showered them on him. His arrow went astray.

"Let's get out of here!" Josh shouted. Aaron came in a lope, waving his hat at the loose horses. Ramón and Quitman were just behind him. Looking back over his shoulder, Josh saw a couple of arrows in flight, but they would fall short.

We're out of their range.

They circled around the horses and brought them finally to a nervous, milling stop. Josh slid off, going to one knee and pushing back to his feet. He felt the thigh, and his hand came away with a small streak of blood. The arrow had not cut deep. "Anybody hit?" he asked anxiously.

No one else was except Ocie Quitman. Quitman's arm was bleeding. Stepping to the ground, Quitman slid up his sleeve and examined the wound. "Just enough to teach me humility," he said, "I'll live." His gaze lifted to Ramón, then went to Phipps and Aaron and Josh. "Men, I don't know what to say. I hope *thanks* will do."

Josh waited for someone to reply, but no one did. He said, "That's good enough. I expect you'd of done the same for any of us."

"They as good as had me. I was almost out of powder." He looked at Jacob Phipps. "You went and trailed me, even after I told you not to."

Phipps nodded. "Seemed like the thing to do."

Quitman turned to Ramón. "And you . . . you're the one who went in there and picked me up. You're the last one who had any reason to do it."

Ramón shrugged. "I had a reason. María."

A frown came over Ocie Quitman. He turned his face to Josh. "She's all right, isn't she? You wouldn't have left her if she wasn't all right, would you?"

Josh said tightly, "She looked bad when we left her."

"Then, you ought to've stayed."

"The women were there. They could do as much as I could."

Quitman stared at the ground. "Josh, I wonder why you came after me atall. I've caused you a right smart of trouble." He gripped his arm, where the stain was still spreading. "I think the best thing for me to do is take my son and go somewhere . . . to get away from here."

Josh said, "Let's talk about it later." He pointed to Quitman's horse, which stamped nervously among the Indian ponies, the saddle still on its back. "Right now you better catch that bay. I'll take Sessum's. I don't have the nerve to try to get my saddle . . . not right now."

Aaron gave him a boost up. Josh motioned. "Let's go see about María."

REBECCA PROVOST and Heather Winslow waited anxiously in the doorway as the men rode into view. Josh could see them counting fearfully, making sure no one was missing. Rebecca hurried out and threw her arms around Aaron as he stepped out of the saddle. Muley and the children came running, and Josh dropped his reins into the first pair of eager hands. Ocie Quitman grabbed up his son and gave him a fierce hug, then set him down. Together he and Josh walked to the door. Heather Winslow met them there. Tears stained her cheeks.

Josh asked with anxiety, "What about María?"

"She's conscious now. We tried to lie to her about where you'd all gone, but I think she knew."

Josh and Quitman stepped into the room and haltingly moved toward the bed where María lay. Her eyes opened, and she blinked, trying to recognize the men against the light of the open door. Her hand came up weakly, and she gave a sharp little cry. "Josh!"

"I'm right here, María."

"Did you find Ocie? Did you bring him?"

Josh halted. "We found him, María. He's here."

Quitman glanced at him in surprise. Josh gave him a nudge forward. "Go on. It's you she was callin' for when we took the bullet out. It's you she really wants, not me."

Quitman dropped his hat to the earthen floor and moved forward with slow, uncertain steps. He knelt beside the girl and said hoarsely, "I'm here. I'm here if you want me."

Her hand reached out, and he took it. "Yes, Ocie," she whispered. "I want you." He dropped himself down beside her, his cheek to her own. Josh could hear her sobbing quietly and thanking the saints.

Quitman was telling her, "I'm not a good man for you. You know me. I'm hard and I'm mean, and when I get an idea in my stubborn head, nobody can tell me I'm wrong."

"I am stubborn too."

"It won't be easy. You know how I've been. I'll be hard to change."

"But I want you, Ocie."

Throat tight, Josh turned and walked toward the door, where Heather waited. He tried to smile, but it was a poor attempt, and he gave it up. It hurt too much. "She'll live, Heather. She wants to, and she's a strong little woman, that María. Anything she wants bad enough, she'll get."

"And she wants Ocie Quitman."

Josh nodded.

Heather stared at him in wonder. "You'd give her up, just like that?"

Josh flinched. "What I'm givin' up is a dream, Heather, a mirage. María never was mine to give up, really. There was a time she thought she loved me, I guess, but she was just a girl. She hadn't met anybody else. I thought I loved her too, and in a way I did. I still do. But it was never right, not from the start."

He stepped outside and leaned against the wall, his gaze drifting aimlessly over the field, over the rolling prairie and the sun-cured grass. "She took me back, Heather; that's all it ever really was. When I was with María it was like she had come to me from somewhere out of the past, out of a time that was gone but that I never could quite turn loose of. She wasn't really María, not to me. She was always somebody else, somebody I had to say goodbye to years ago but never quite let go of. Deep inside me, I guess I've sensed it awhile now. That's why I never could bring myself to talk to her about marryin' me. While ago, when I took the bullet out, I found myself prayin' she wouldn't die again." His fist clenched. "Die *again*. It wasn't María I prayed for; it was her sister Teresa. It was *always* Teresa."

Heather waited a long time before she asked, "Do you think you can turn loose now?"

He nodded slowly. "It won't be easy, but I'll have to."

Heather took his hand. "Josh, I had to, once. Maybe, if you wanted me to, I could teach you how."

He turned and looked at her as if he had never seen her before. It occurred to him that he never really had. "Maybe you can, Heather. Maybe you can."

ABOUT THE AUTHOR

I WAS BORN at a place called Horse Camp on the Scharbauer Cattle
Company's Five Wells Ranch in Andrews County, Texas, in
1926. My father was a cowboy there, and my grandfather was the
ranch foreman. My great-grandfather had come out from East Texas
about 1878 with a wagon and a string of horses to become a ranch-
man, but he died young, leaving four small boys to grow up as cow-
punchers and bronc breakers. With all that heritage I should have
become a good cowboy myself, but somehow I never did, so I decided if I could not do it I would write about it.

I studied journalism at the University of Texas and became a livestock and farm reporter in San Angelo, Texas, writing fiction as a
sideline to newspaper work. I maintained the two careers in parallel
forty-two years. My fiction has been mostly about Texas, about areas
whose history and people I know from long study and long personal
acquaintance. I have always believed we can learn much about ourselves by studying our history, for we are the products of all that has
gone before us. All history is relevant today, because the way we
live—the values we believe in—are a result of molds prepared for us
by our forebears a long time ago.

I was an infantryman in World War II and married an Austrian
girl, Anna, I met there shortly after the war. We raised three children, all grown now and independent, proud of their mixed heritage
of the Old World on one hand and the Texas frontier on the other.